The
SFWA EUROPEAN
HALL OF FAME

The
SFWA EUROPEAN HALL OF FAME

Sixteen Contemporary
Masterpieces of
Science Fiction
from the Continent

EDITED BY JAMES MORROW AND KATHRYN MORROW

A TOM DOHERTY ASSOCIATES BOOK / NEW YORK

THE SFWA EUROPEAN HALL OF FAME

Edited by David G. Hartwell

A Tor Book
Published by Tom Doherty Associates, LLC
175 Fifth Avenue
New York, NY 10010

www.tor.com

Tor® is a registered trademark of Tom Doherty Associates, LLC.

Library of Congress Cataloging-in-Publication Data

The SFWA European hall of fame : sixteen contemporary masterpieces of science fiction from the continent / edited by James Morrow and Kathryn Morrow.—1st ed.
     p. cm.
  "A Tom Doherty Associates Book."
  Includes bibliographical references.
  ISBN-13: 978-0-7653-1536-6
  ISBN-10: 0-7653-1536-X
  1. Science fiction, European—Translations into English. I. Morrow, James.
II. Morrow, Kathryn L.
  PN6071.S33S49   2007
  808.83'8762—dc22

                            2007007318

First Edition: June 2007

Printed in the United States of America

0 9 8 7 6 5 4 3 2 1

To
BRUNO DELLA CHIESA,
l'homme indispensable

ACKNOWLEDGMENTS

We two impassioned but novice anthologists are grateful to our experienced editor, David Hartwell, for his wise counsel, practical zeal, and encyclopedic knowledge. We are similarly indebted to SFWA's estimable agent, Eleanor Wood, who made sure that our love's labors were not lost.

Let us also take this opportunity to thank past SFWA President Catherine Asaro, as well as former Anthology Committee Chairman Walter Jon Williams, both of whom intuitively understood our idiosyncratic project and gave it their full support.

Needless to say, the most substantive contributions to *The SFWA European Hall of Fame* came from our seventeen writers and seventeen translators, whose accomplishments and credentials are noted in the pages that follow. Further aiding the cause were numerous colleagues and friends who stepped forward at crucial moments to recommend stories, hunt down e-mail addresses, referee translation issues, offer advice, and cheer us on. In particular, our appreciation goes to Ana Antonescu, Johan van Binsbergen, Terry Bisson, Pierre Bordage, Vittorio Curtoni, Radomil Dojiva, Anna Droumeva, Claire Duval, Patrick Gyger, Jay Hansen, Peter G. Hayes, Hedwig-Maria Karakouda, Eva Letwin, Henrik Loeyche, Kirk McElhearn, Mandy, Stéphane Manfredo, Angelos Mastorakis, Marion Mazauric, Carolyn Meredith, Larisa Mihaylova, Cheryl Morgan, Stéphanie Nicot, Jaroslav Olsa, Luis Prado, Christopher Priest, Andy Sawyer, Robert Silverberg, Norman Spinrad, Brian Stableford, Bruce Sterling, Jan Vanek Jr., N. Lee Wood, and George Zebrowski.

The translation of "Baby Doll" was supported by a grant from FILI, the Finnish Literature Information Center.

CONTENTS

EXTRAPOLATIONS OF THINGS PAST

A BARBAROUSLY BRIEF ACCOUNT OF EUROPEAN SCIENCE FICTION FROM *MICROMÉGAS* TO MICROCHIPS

Throughout the third decade of the eighteenth century, Voltaire's friend, lover, and occasional collaborator Émilie de Breteuil, the marquise of Châtelet, turned her country house at Cirey into a kind of humanist retreat devoted to the celestial mechanics of Isaac Newton and the majestic conjectures of John Locke. When not bickering with the hot-tempered Émilie or working with her on their Newtonian treatise, Voltaire used his Cirey sojourns to pen the first draft of a novelette that in 1752 saw print as *Micromégas*. Divided into seven nimble chapters, this beguiling confection narrates a close encounter between a gigantic visitor from the Sirius system and a "flock of philosophers" whose ship has run aground following their scientific expedition to the Arctic Circle.

According to critic Theo Cuffe, who translated *Micromégas* for its Syrene-Penguin edition, Voltaire's *conte philosophique* inaugurated a new literary mode. "The Enlightenment disliked story for story's sake, so it invented a kind of story whose inventions are officially in the service of an idea." If we accept Cuffe's claim, it would not be intemperate to argue that, in the evolution of science fiction, the goings-on at Madame du Châtelet's country house were commensurate with the 1816 summer holiday enjoyed by Lord Byron, his physician Polidori, Percy Bysshe Shelley, Shelley's paramour Mary Godwin, and Mary's half sister Claire Clairmont at Byron's Geneva estate. Many were the intrigues that accrued to that Romantic gathering, but one in particular claims our attention. On the literally dark and stormy night of June 18, Shelley's future bride, eighteen-year-old Mary, responding to Byron's exhortation that each should attempt a tale of terror, conceived her landmark novel about a scientist who harnesses alchemy and hubris to create an artificial human being.

Many years ago, Brian Aldiss's monumental history of science fiction, *Trillion Year Spree*, persuaded me that, when it comes to English-language SF at least, all roads lead to *Frankenstein*. In the case of the Continental product, however, it might be argued that all spaceways connect to *Micromégas*. Nearly every dimension of the genre is on display in this story. To begin with, there is Voltaire's immersion in the science of his day, a commitment that leads to felicitous plot twists and, if not a sense of wonder, then certainly a sensibility of bedazzlement. Before landing on Earth, Micromégas undertakes a grand tour of the galaxy:

> This traveler was wonderfully acquainted with the laws of gravity and with all the forces of attraction and repulsion. These he put to such good use that, sometimes with the aid of a sunbeam, at other times through the convenient offices of a comet, he and his retinue went from one globe to the next as a bird hops from branch to branch. He traveled the length of the Milky Way in no time, though I am bound to record that not once on his way past the stars . . . did he glimpse the lovely empyreal heaven which the celebrated Reverend Derham boasts of having seen at the end of his telescope.

As hard science, or even soggy extrapolation, the above passage is, of course, preposterous. But note the underlying premise: a fantastical voyage accomplished not through dreaming or supernatural agency but through a demented rendition of contemporaneous physics.

Beyond this delirious empiricism, Voltaire is playing in these pages a second game that prefigures the genre to come. Like the vast majority of subsequent SF, *Micromégas* turns on the momentous Enlightenment assumption that our political, social, domestic, and devotional arrangements have not been handed down from On High. They are wholly human inventions, and if we can muster a modicum of scientific objectivity and a measure of ironic detachment, then we might accurately diagnose their defects in prelude to improving our common lot. When the immense Micromégas and his traveling companion, an outsized Saturn-

ian, start examining the minuscule human scientists through an improvised microscope, the narrator seizes upon the occasion to meditate sardonically on war:

> If we take the average height of humankind to be approximately five
> feet, then a man cuts no more imposing a figure on this Earth than a
> creature approximately one six-hundred-thousandth of an inch high
> standing on a ball with a circumference of ten feet. Now imagine a
> form of matter capable of holding the Earth in its hand . . . then con-
> sider, I ask you, what would they make of those efforts of ours to gain
> a couple of villages in one battle, only to lose them in the next?

From the conceits of Voltaire to the cosmos of Jules Verne is a leap
that even Micromégas might hesitate to make. And yet, if these two literary giants ever find themselves resurrected in some heavenly version of
the Cirey château, I suspect they will gravitate toward one another. True,
at first they may have some difficulties getting past their theological
differences—Voltaire the contrarian deist, sworn enemy of the ecclesias-
tical order, versus Verne the good Catholic, a writer who'd been blessed
by the pope—but in time a rapprochement is certain to occur. They have
much in common, after all, and not just this business of hitching rides on
orbiting bodies, a mode of transportation introduced in *Micromégas* but
perfected only in Verne's *Hector Servadac* (sometimes known as *Off on a
Comet*). Beyond cometology, both authors share a commitment to the scientific worldview per se. While his principal occupations at Cirey were
writing, iron smelting, and fighting with Émilie, the author of *Micromégas*
also found time to maintain a large laboratory on the château grounds,
where he conducted God-knows-what sorts of physics experiments. As
for Monsieur Verne, he was the paradigm of a "hard SF" author, a fact
that I did not fully appreciate until, during a field trip to the Verne
archives in Nantes, I got to inspect photocopies of his original manu-
scripts and noted the precision with which the creator of *Les voyages ex-
traordinaires* had calculated Phileas Fogg's transit of the international date
line and the American scientists' trajectory as they hurtled from the earth
to the moon.

Now that the great post-Enlightenment, post-Romantic, postmod-
ern, postmortem conversation has begun, I'm confident that Voltaire and
Verne won't mind if we invite other Continentals into the celestial salon.
Naturally we must have the Russian author Yevgeny Zamyatin, whose

We anticipated the dystopian novels of Aldous Huxley and George Orwell. Let us likewise sweeten the soirée with Karel Capek of Czechoslovakia, whose play *R.U.R.* gave the West the word *robot,* Czech for "worker." We should also bring in the German writer Otto Willis Gail, whose novel *By Rocket to the Moon: The Story of Hans Hardt's Miraculous Flight* was written in consultation with rocket pioneer Max Valier, and Italy's Italo Calvino, who, mellowed by Eternity, no longer cringes when critics apply the SF label to *Cosmicomics* and *t zero,* plus the recently deceased Stanislaw Lem of Poland, perhaps the only science fiction writer since Capek ever in the running for a Nobel Prize.

The shadows lengthen. The guest list grows. The château halls echo with the clatter of wine bottles, the din of quarrels, and the excited chatter that precedes collaboration. If I had to make a wager, I would say that the conversation will last forever.

I owe the discovery of Uqbar to the conjunction of a mirror and an encyclopedia." Thus runs the opening of what some aficionados, myself included, would argue is the greatest science fiction story ever written in a language other than English, Jorge Luis Borges's "Tlön, Uqbar, Orbis Tertius." It's one of those beginnings before which the illusion of free will dissolves, grabbing the helpless reader by the lapels and sucking him into the Charybdis of the text. And so, in prelude to chronicling the advent of *The SFWA European Hall of Fame,* let me now appropriate the structure of Borges's wonderful first sentence.

This anthology traces to the conjunction of a locomotive and a manuscript. My wife and I—that is to say, the present editor and his coeditor—were taking the train from Paris to Nantes, our destination being the 2001 edition of Utopiales, an extraordinary "Festival International de Science-Fiction" that, since its founding in 1998 by the multilingual SF connoisseur Bruno della Chiesa, has done so much to promote the genre as a world literature. We were traveling that morning with our friend Kirk McElhearn, an American-born translator and writer living in the French Alps, and as we pulled out of the Gare du Nord, Kirk started working on his semi-final rendering of "Fragment du Livre de la Mer," a lyrical story by the French SF writer Roland C. Wagner. Acting on a whim, Kirk invited me to collaborate with him informally for the rest of the trip. He was curious to know whether, as a professional fiction writer, I might want to suggest some stylistic improvements.

So I took out my mechanical pencil and dived in, and before long I realized I was having an inordinate amount of fun. Kirk's work on the story was first-rate, or so I concluded from the evidence before me: the original Wagner text—I speak French badly but read it without too much difficulty—plus the nascent English-language version, "Fragment from the Book of the Sea." And yet I found myself intuitively noodling with the sentences: striking out arguably superfluous words, hunting down needless repetitions, searching for *le mot juste,* all the usual things.

By the midpoint of the trip I was in a bittersweet mood, lamenting the sorry circumstance that so few SF translations ever receive this sort of joyful tweaking. I recalled hearing that Jules Verne has never been accorded the English-language incarnations he deserves, and the similarly unfortunate fact that the only American edition of Stanislaw Lem's *Solaris* traces not to the original Polish text but to a feeble French translation. How sad, I thought, a minor scandal, that so many worthy SF stories lie imprisoned in their native languages. And how felicitous it would be if Anglo-American fans could not only read more European SF, but also experience it in translations whose fuss factor rivaled the nuances Kirk and I were presumably wringing as the Breton countryside rolled past our train window.

That night, as Kathy and I settled into our hotel in Nantes, we concocted the scheme that became *The SFWA European Hall of Fame.* We envisioned an English-language anthology comprising some of the best Continental SF from the past twenty years, works by those authors who were winning awards, generating buzz, defying expectations, and making cultural mischief. This hypothetical volume would offer its readers stories and novelettes spun from the same rationalist-romantic assumptions that underlie Anglo-American SF, and yet each selection would embody a spirit, an élan, a *je ne sais quoi* not routinely available to English-speaking genre fans. If science fiction is a literary smorgasbord, then we would present the gourmet with dishes that, while never leaving the domain of the digestible, boasted uncommon seasonings and unexpected flavors.

But first, of course, we had to outmaneuver a paradox. Catch-22 said that no sane Anglo-American editor would fund a batch of translations unless the authors in question already had English-speaking readerships of the sort obtainable only through the very translations that no sane Anglo-American editor would fund. Eventually I decided that we might break this vicious cycle by appealing to the latent idealism of the Science

Fiction and Fantasy Writers of America. If SFWA were to grant the project $1,500 in seed money, we could surely conjure and cajole enough translations into existence—professionally rendered and then carefully line-edited—to constitute a coherent proposal. This manuscript would implicitly say to its prospective publisher, "Here's what's possible: exciting European SF liberated into English by translators who were willing to work for modest rates. Give us an advance against royalties—something sufficient to reward the authors, compensate the editors, and commission further translations—and we'll give you the rest of the book."

While the contents of *The SFWA European Hall of Fame* are not necessarily more diverse than those of any other genre anthology, we soon learned that each story had its own unique way of resisting the sea change from native tongue to target language. But no matter how stubborn the text of the moment, our philosophy of translation remained the same. Whenever possible we convened a three-way cyberspace conversation among the author, the translator, and ourselves, our aim being to guarantee that no sentence would see print until it struck all involved parties as smooth and lucid. As the process got up to speed, the writer would sometimes decide to revisit a scene and alter it: adding details, omitting superfluities, rearranging phrases. So there's a sense in which several of these stories were workshopped specifically for this book, with results perhaps analogous to the "director's cut" of a feature film. Needless to say, *The SFWA European Hall of Fame* would have been unimaginable in the days before e-mail.

We were obviously running some risks here. By encouraging minor revisions, were Kathy and I inadvertently exterminating whatever ineffables had made the story work in the first place? Were we prompting our authors to trade provocative ambiguities for specious clarity? Might we end up committing to print, without quite realizing that we'd become accessories to a literary crime, a version that read, "Uqbar is a region of Iraq or Asia Minor that may or may not exist, and I owe its discovery to the conjunction of a full-length, gold-framed hall mirror and Volume XLVI of *The Anglo-American Cyclopaedia*"?

Although we took this question seriously, we ultimately decided that it would be better to give each story too much *ex post facto* attention than too little. In talking with the translators of our acquaintance, we'd come to understand that a splendid rendering is a subjective thing, awakening in its creators a certain benign obsessiveness and salutary scholasticism.

The able translator spends as much time on the trail of nuance as on the scent of correctness, apportioning his or her talent equally between constructing literal representations and composing "functional equivalents." My copy of Kafka's *The Trial* begins, "Someone must have been telling lies about Joseph K, for without having done anything wrong he was arrested one fine morning." I have seen the same sentence translated as "Someone must have traduced Joseph K, for without having done anything wrong he was arrested one fine morning." Which is the better version? This is not the time or place to offer my opinion. I shall merely aver that the question is worth asking.

To locate and make accessible certain contemporary classics of Continental SF: an axiomatically laudable objective, and yet, stated in those formal terms, I wonder if the whole thing doesn't sound a trifle clinical, a bit fusty. Let me hasten to note that, for better or worse, *The SFWA European Hall of Fame* is not a systematic compilation. Early in the game, we realized that our resources were insufficient for an all-inclusive omnibus—something that would methodically embody every recent trend in European SF and thereby capture the gestalt of the Continental enterprise—and so we assumed a different obligation instead: to give the reader his or her due in emotional satisfaction and cerebral excitement. If we could not be comprehensive, at least we could be polymorphous-perverse. To put it another way, the present volume comprises sixteen stories whose ultimate value is less a matter of regional heritage than of inherent riches. Each made the cut for one reason only: at some level it moved us. We hope that we have given you, as a mad-scientist incarnation of Voltaire's Dr. Pangloss might say, the best of all impossible worlds.

Joke overheard at a science fiction convention in Pittsburgh: What's the difference between Europeans and Americans? Europeans think one hundred miles is a long distance, and Americans think one hundred years is a long time.

This clever and, I would argue, perceptive quip, raises the issue of how far we might go in distinguishing between two collective human psyches. In the present context, the joke invites us to ask how European science fiction differs from its North American counterpart. Is there a tenor or sensibility that makes Continental speculative literature discontinuous with the stuff published as SF on the Atlantic's western shore?

The question is not so frivolous as it sounds, at least not by the evidence of the stories collected between these covers. Consider the parameters of the joke itself: space, time, and thought—phenomena that, as it happens, constitute the reigning preoccupations of the genre. As Platonic abstractions, of course, these megasubjects are probably of equal interest to SF writers everywhere. Unless one is researching a master's thesis, I doubt that it's worthwhile to investigate whether speculation about space travel holds a disproportionate fascination for American writers, or whether fiction spun from angst is more characteristically European. But if we consider instead the *treatments* that Americans and Europeans variously accord the megasubjects, then we can perhaps start indulging in dichotomies.

Space. The fecund frontier. The realm of, to use Kurt Vonnegut's term, infinite outwardness. Accounts of space travel in American SF are traditionally triumphalist: problems are solved, catastrophes averted, menace yields to transcendence. Contrast this tone with the measured and elegiac mood of Elena Arsenieva's "A Birch Tree, a White Fox," in which marooned cosmonauts find themselves in an ethereal realm of ephemeral presences. Andreas Eschbach's "Wonders of the Universe" also recounts the aftermath of a disastrous space mission, and while the story ends on a rhapsodic note, the situation remains irredeemably tragic.

Time. History. Europeans live in the shadow of a half-million yesterdays, a circumstance that, theoretically at least, advantages the Continental author in her attempts to evoke epochs gone by. When an SF writer residing in Denver or Atlanta posits a recrudescent Roman Empire spanning the globe, imagines scientists working at the behest of feudal lords, hypothesizes neo-Renaissance merchant-princes dispatching FTL galleons across the Milky Way, or seeks to dramatize everyday life in a totalitarian society, she is tackling matters fundamentally extrinsic to the American experience. The European author, by contrast, inhabits a piece of the planet where the Roman Empire, feudalism, Renaissance mercantilism, and totalitarian societies have actually been the case. God knows he has his work cut out for him, but the details lie much closer at hand, and he might begin by simply breathing the air.

The specter of the Holocaust haunts Marek S. Huberath's "Yoo Retoont, Sneogg. Ay Noo," W. K. Maryson's "Verstummte Musik," and, to a lesser degree, Valerio Evangelisti's "Sepultura," three narratives of cruel incarceration and attempted escape. It would be the worst sort of reductionism to frame our Polish, Dutch, and Italian offerings as death camp allegories per se, for each moves us on its own carefully worked-out terms, and yet I doubt that I'm the first reader to sense intimations of the Nazi crematoria between the lines of these tales. "Yoo Retoont, Sneogg. Ay Noo" takes us into a universe of mutants, survivors of a thermonuclear war, detailing their peculiar and pathetic community in ways that inhabit the mind long after the last page is turned. "Verstummte Musik" gives us a near-future Europe in which the bodies of expendables are processed in a manner at once astonishingly brutal and obliquely redemptive. "Sepultura" carries its readers into the bowels of a Brazilian penitentiary, a hell-on-earth organized around a bizarre and grotesque method of confining political prisoners.

And, finally, thought. The conundrum of consciousness. The mysterious connections among sense impressions, human reason, and a presumed external reality—connections whose disciplined contemplation is sometimes called philosophy. Here again we can posit a schism between the children of Gernsback and the descendants of Voltaire, a dichotomy within the SF universe that roughly parallels the distinction between Anglo-American "analytic philosophy," keyed to language and logic, versus a more impressionistic "Continental philosophy," with its emphasis on the dread and perplexity to which each human self is heir.

A marooned psyche occupies the center of Ondřej Neff's "The Fourth Day to Eternity," Joëlle Wintrebert's "Transfusion," and José Antonio Cotrina's "Between the Lines," stories indigenous to the Czech Republic, France, and Spain respectively. In the first two selections, a malign force descends upon the main character—Neff's hapless physicist Drabek wages a one-man war against the "avatars of eternity," while Wintrebert's protean heroine Barbel confronts an enigmatic alien beast—though there are indications that the protagonists' estrangement may trace to paranoia in the former case and schizophrenia in the latter. Cotrina's happy-go-lucky graduate student Alejandro inhabits a more benign mental landscape, a universe of texts within texts, meanings within meanings, and essences within essences.

The vastness of space, the pall of the past, the mystery of sentient awareness: problems that, while they might define the bounds of reality, hardly exhaust the possibilities of science fiction. Over the years, Anglo-American writers have also employed the genre to explore the interface between humans and machines, speculate on time travel and its discontents, and excoriate our species's affection for consecrated nonsense. Their Continental confrères have been drawn to these same three subjects, treating them in modalities that are, if not specifically "European," then certainly idiosyncratic.

Extrapolating from an unexpected though not unimaginable implication of artificial intelligence, the internationally acclaimed French SF writer Jean-Claude Dunyach herein offers "Separations," an enthralling drama detailing the complex relationship between a starship captain and a terrestrial choreographer. From Greece comes a second narrative concerning AI, Panagiotis Koustas's "Athos Emfovos in the Temple of Sound," in which a burned-out war refugee is moved to commit the ultimate impiety against his cybergod.

Our two time-travel tales arrive bearing Spanish and Danish passports. In "The Day We Went through the Transition," Ricard de la Casa and Pedro Jorge Romero employ the familiar SF trope of desperado chrononauts seeking to improve the present by altering the past, but the authors wring many perspicacious and poignant changes on this conceit. Bernhard Ribbeck's "A Blue and Cloudless Sky" is a temporal-paradox story unlike any you have ever read: wonderfully cryptic, brilliantly constructed, enblaze with eschatological imagery.

Our quartet of social satires—from Finland, Russia, Portugal, and Romania—boasts a caliber of causticity of which Voltaire would doubtless have approved. Johanna Sinisalo's "Baby Doll" serves up a cosmopolitan dystopia in which various cultural forces have conspired to rob children of their childhoods. For "Destiny, Inc." Sergei Lukyanenko has imagined a near-future Russia in which metaphysically minded entrepreneurs expropriate individual fates. João Barreiros's "A Night on the Edge of the Empire" gives us a cockeyed Lisbon in which an avian extraterrestrial confronts an array of political factions who seem unable to distinguish between social progress and street theater. Even more outlandish is Lucian Merişca's "Some Earthlings' Adventures on Outrerria," a kind of literary Tex Avery cartoon lampooning colonialism, free enterprise, and the limitless human capacity for self-importance.

Science fiction occupies a paradoxical place in the landscape of the narrative arts. On the one hand, SF writers attempt to address the human condition from the broadest possible perspective. The genre routinely invites us to regard ourselves as riders on a revolving planet, not simply as citizens of circumscribed communities. It implicitly insists that we periodically identify with the species *Homo sapiens,* not merely with our ethnic heritages, religious upbringings, dysfunctional families, and personal neuroses.

On the other hand, as every schoolgirl knows, art thrives on the local and the particular. The gigantic generalities of planetary affiliation and species membership are *ipso facto* unpromising subjects for fiction, whereas it appears that novelists and short story writers will never run out of interesting things to say about their circumscribed communities, ethnic heritages, religious upbringings, dysfunctional families, and personal neuroses.

For a logically impossible literature, science fiction actually does pretty well for itself. When the SF writer is on her game, she manages to pursue her teleological agenda without sacrificing the traditional novelistic virtues: characters who have rich inner lives, narrators who make canny observations, dialogue that hums with subtext. What really distinguishes science fiction from mainstream literature is not the genre's presumed anti-art aesthetic but rather its inversion of the normal fictive relationship between microcosm and macrocosm.

Set sail with Ishmael and Queequeg, and before the White Whale sinks the *Pequod,* you will have sensed that its heterogeneous crew represents humankind per se. Climb aboard the raft with Huck and Jim, and soon you will find yourself in a timeless and unbounded realm. (As Walker Percy points out, Twain achieves this effect partly because the Mississippi River flows only between states of the Union, never through a particular state.) Walk the streets of Quauhnahuac with Geoffrey Firmin in Malcolm Lowry's *Under the Volcano,* and somewhere around the midpoint of the novel you will understand that the city is a palimpsest affording glimpses of a limitless Hell. Note that in all three cases the move is from microcosm to macrocosm. The SF writer, by contrast, typically has a macrocosm or two onstage when the curtain rises. Her subsequent artistic gestures must therefore evoke familiar microcosms, the better to make the whole grand epistemological opera seem credible.

To achieve such vital verisimilitude, the authors who grace these pages often seize upon their immediate milieus. "Athos Emfovos in the Temple of Sound" is all the more persuasive for taking place in a recognizable Athens. "Baby Doll" is enlivened by the author's astute anthropological observations of middle-class consumer culture, which is evidently much the same in Finland as in other Western industrialized democracies. When we remark on the uncanny wintry mood of "A Blue and Cloudless Sky," I suspect we are actually praising Bernhard Ribbeck's skill in transmogrifying the world at his doorstep.

Among the European cultural coordinates that occasionally intersect these texts is an impulse toward *non sequitur* and absurdity, two idioms that thrive on the American shore only in the form of our political discourse. In an essay titled "The Hitchhiker's Guide to French Science Fiction," Jean-Claude Dunyach discusses the pervasiveness of dream-logic in Continental literature: "Here in Europe, surrealism is so *air du temps*—part of the background—that it is hard not to be influenced by it." Dunyach goes on to praise the work of the French SF writer Serge Brussolo, one of whose novels features "oceans replaced by hundreds of millions of dwarves that live in the mud, hands up, and carry boats in exchange for food. Of course, every now and then, they reproduce, and you get a tidal waves of dwarves who want to conquer new territories."

In the pages that follow, you will encounter strains of weirdness and flourishes of absurdity that easily rival Brussolo's portaging dwarves. I think especially of the glue-engulfed prisoners in Evangelisti's "Sepultura," the hallucinatory tableaux of Wintrebert's "Transfusion," the post-nuclear sideshow in Huberath's "Yoo Retoont, Sneogg. Ay Noo" and the plummeting cisternmobile in Neff's "The Fourth Day to Eternity." Of course, these images all emerge *en passant*, as a function of artistic commitments that are science-fictional rather than Freudian or avant-garde. In the SF genre, the egg of disciplined speculation comes first, though when the shell starts cracking almost any sort of bird might emerge, from the most scrupulously extrapolated Rhode Island Red to an ostrich as outré as João Barreiros's feathered ambassador VibrantSong.

Not surprisingly, we find intimations of SF's basic aesthetic strategy—macrocosm to microcosm and back again to macrocosm—in Voltaire's lovely little space operetta. *Micromégas* opens with a macrocosmic bang: "On one of those planets that orbit the star named Sirius there was once a young man of great intelligence, whom I had the honor of meeting during the last visit he made to our little anthill." But soon the author scales down the drama, confronting his hero with an immediate crisis calling for practical action. While still an adolescent, Micromégas writes and publishes a treatise on the creatures he recently studied through his microscope. Finding the young man's arguments reckless, unorthodox, and heretical, the local mufti hauls him before a judge and jury. "The case turned on whether the substantial form of the fleas on

Sirius was or was not of the same nature as that of the snails." Although Micromégas mounts a spirited defense, during a trial that lasts two hundred and twenty years, the mufti triumphs. He arranges for the book to be "condemned by jurists who had not opened it," then convinces the ruling elite to banish Micromégas for an interval of eight hundred years.

One needn't be a licensed literary scholar to speculate that Micromégas's trial contains an autobiographical subtext. In 1733 Voltaire published, against his better judgment and in league with his essential self, *Lettres philosophiques sur les Anglais*. Disguised as a compendium of English manners and mores, it was in fact a venomous assessment of various French institutions, including, of course, the Church. Government officials lost no time condemning the book, seizing and burning hundreds of copies, issuing a warrant against the author, and searching his Paris dwelling. Voltaire made a circumspect retreat to Cirey, where he took up refuge with Émilie and proceeded to pen the first draft of *Micromégas*.

The novelette's hero, of course, takes advantage of his *Brobdingnagian non grata* status to go rambling around the Milky Way, first befriending the Saturnian and eventually meeting the shipload of philosophers—who within his frame of reference loom no larger than the fleas who informed his infamous treatise. In the final breathless sentences Voltaire manages to make yet another satiric observation, introduce an encyclopedic work reminiscent of Newton's *Principia Mathematica*, and provide the whole sprightly affair with a shaggy–Dog Star ending.

> The Sirian picked up the little microbes once more. He still spoke to them with great kindness, despite being privately a little vexed to find that the infinitely small should have a pride almost infinitely large. He promised to write a fine work of philosophy for them, in suitably tiny script, in which they would discover the nature of things. True to his word, he gave them the volume before leaving. It was taken to Paris, to the Academy of the Sciences. But when the Secretary opened it, he found nothing but blank pages.
> "Ah," he said. "I suspected as much."

One can easily imagine a different denouement. In this alternative-universe coda to *Micromégas*, the Sirian's tome is again taken to Paris, and the Secretary of the Academy opens it to discover not blank pages but rather marooned astronauts, avian aliens, post-holocaust mutants, dancing AIs, destiny-altering corporations, time-travelers searching for lost loves, souls trapped in Dantesque ectoplasm, insurgents operating on a planet-of-the-absurd, children turned into sexual freaks, university students stumbling into the multiverse, refugees convening the ultimate love feast, cosmonauts condemned to silence, guerrillas seeking to sabotage the spacetime continuum, paranoids caught in the foam of forever, schizophrenic saviors of planet Earth, and palaces that sing in the voices of the dead.

Whereupon, of course, the Secretary closes the anthology and says to himself, "Ah, I suspected as much."

—JAMES MORROW
State College, Pennsylvania
April 2006

The
SFWA EUROPEAN
HALL OF FAME

JEAN-CLAUDE DUNYACH

SEPARATIONS

TRANSLATED FROM THE FRENCH
BY SHERYL CURTIS

Our decision to include a work by Jean-Claude Dunyach in The SFWA *European Hall of Fame required a minimum of synaptic activity, for he is the acknowledged master of the contemporary French science fiction short story. The process of selecting this particular tale, by contrast, occasioned numerous spasms of self-doubt. We faced a bewildering array of possibilities, ranging across every SF modality, from virtual reality to alien visitations, the annihilation of time to the excision of memory—each rendered in the author's characteristically precise style and poetic voice.*

In the end "Separations" was the choice that felt most satisfying, for two reasons. Unlike the other tales that tempted us, this one has never before appeared in English translation. And, more important, "Separations" is among the richest reading experiences we've enjoyed in recent years, its deceptively simple prose and straightforward plot delivering new meanings on each encounter.

Born in 1957, Dunyach holds a Ph.D. in applied mathematics, and he presently earns his living as an engineer for Airbus France in Toulouse. He has been writing SF since the early 1980s, a calling that has so far yielded seven novels and six collections. His novel Étoiles Mortes *("Dead Stars," 1992) won the Prix Rosny Aîné. The sequel,* Étoiles Mourantes *("Dying Stars," 1999), written in collaboration with the acclaimed SF author Ayerdhal, won both the Prix Tour Eiffel and the Prix Ozone. Several of Dunyach's shorter works have also received awards, most conspicuously "Déchiffrer la trame," honored with the Grand Prix de l'Imaginaire, the Prix Rosny Aîné, and the designation "best short story of the* year" by the readers of Interzone. You can read "Unraveling the Thread," along with thirteen other English translations of Dunyach's work, in his collection The Night Orchid: Conan Doyle in Toulouse. Beyond his science-fictional efforts, Dunyach has composed lyrics for several French singers, an endeavor that inspired Roll Over, Amundsen, which, as you might infer from the title, is yet another novel about a corrupt rock 'n' roll star touring Antarctica with a zombie reincarnation of the Detroit Philharmonic Orchestra.

Occasionally Dunyach picks up his pen to write about the state of the genre, a pursuit whose fruits have included his provocative essay, "The Hitchhiker's Guide to French Science Fiction," currently accessible on the Fantastic Metropolis Web site. We can think of no better way to situate Dunyach among his colleagues than to quote from this piece.

"Ayerdhal—a pseudonym—is most famous for his political space operas with complex intrigues and fascinating female characters. Serge Lehman, a consummate stylist who conveys a true sense of wonder, started his epic History of the Future series in the early nineties. Pierre Bordage is our sweeping sagas specialist and a best-seller since his first trilogy. Richard Canal, who lives in Africa, merges mainstream and SF in a future dominated by Africanized societies. Roland C. Wagner, who appeared early in the eighties, finds his inspiration in rock 'n' roll and gives us humorous descriptions of extraterrestrial cultures. . . ."

Astroport bar, starship bridge, grizzled captain: at first blush, the world of "Separations" may strike the reader as overly familiar. Haven't we seen it all before? Well, no. A fictive celebration of dancing in all its forms, "Separations" is also an act of literary choreography that finds Dunyach leaping deftly from an objective realm of machine intelligence and a hypothetical "Hartzfeld singularity," to a subjective realm of romantic longing and the fear of death, and back again. Beyond these graceful maneuvers, "Separations" is also notable for its "hard SF" sensibility, an idiom that the author's French colleagues have tended to eschew in favor of political and sociological themes. The title, as you will see, has several connotations, just as the story itself is open to multiple interpretations.

"How can we know the dancer from the dance?" William Butler Yeats famously inquired. Jean-Claude Dunyach supplies no answer—how could he?—but has instead wrought a moving meditation on the elusiveness of beauty and the inevitability of art.

They're love stories, you know," the young man says. "They're all dead."

His hand plays with a necklace circling his throat just above his collar. The golden stripes that officially proclaim him an artist gleam on either side of his Adam's apple, like the fingers of a strangler. The necklace looks dull by comparison. Dark gems unevenly faceted, threaded on a thin metal wire. Each time his index finger brushes them, they light up briefly from within.

"It's all the rage on Old Earth," he continues, "wearing your former loves like a string of pearls—harvested from your mind once the pain is gone."

"Hunting trophies," murmurs Captain Bascombe.

He stands in the prow of his silvery craft, facing the cockpit viewport. This close to the Hartzfeld singularity, black space curves around them. The engines vibrate in neutral, while the maintenance equipment hums its reassuring lullaby to the hundreds of passengers lying frozen in their hibernation pods. The artist and the captain are the only conscious humans on board.

"I keep them as tokens of failure," the young man says, turning his gaze from the void. "Every stone is flawed—badly cut or marred by dark spots or clouds. They help me come to each new conquest with a clean soul."

"I thought an artist was supposed to commit himself totally, that there's never any looking back for you people."

"We make ourselves believe that. But perfect love is only some jeweler's fantasy!"

Bascombe turns around, fearing the artist will read on his face the memory of his own love, the one that destroyed him so many years ago. When she left, he died to the world for the first time, insides torn out, nothing to blame but his own insensitivity. Contrapunt's childish insolence is a painful reminder that he, too, had once sliced through life like an icebreaker, indifferent to the shipwrecks he left in his wake. Until the day he became one.

The trip has yet to start, and between disdain for his passenger and loathing for himself, he is already on the verge of exploding.

In a few minutes, they will cross the singularity together.

• • •

Bascombe detested him from their very first encounter, on Charandyne. A young stranger strode implacably toward his table in the astroport bar. He looked successful, glamorous—artfully ragged hairstyle, inlays of neural implants protruding above his ears, eyes veiled with reflective membranes to hide his thoughts. Tights flecked with liquid gold hugged his androgynous silhouette, showing off ridiculously slim hips. He made Bascombe feel both very old and very wise, sensations he despised.

"You're going through the Hartzfeld gate. I'd like to come with you." The young man's voice matched his appearance, dripping with nuance.

"I still have a few empty pods. The company will rent you one, no problem, health permitting."

"I'm in perfect health, Captain. But I don't want to sleep through the voyage—I insist on being conscious during the transit."

"Company policy—"

"Doesn't apply to me," said the artist with a smile that could part a miser from his wealth. "I have all the required permits, and the financial arrangements have been made with your employers."

"You've been informed of the risks, I presume?" Bascombe stared pointedly at the young man. "And I'm not talking about our onboard accident statistics—they've been deliberately falsified. The *Peregrine* is a good ship, totally predictable—at worst you might trip over a strut. I mean the real risks—the reason why you're asking the impossible."

"Can we discuss this?"

Bascombe growled vaguely, possibly in assent. Though the bar was packed, a ring of empty silence surrounded his table. The other patrons—stevedores, mechanics, warehouse and control tower workers—didn't have any concrete reason for ostracizing him, but kept their distance nonetheless. Bascombe had learned to accept this, as he had learned to order his drinks in threes to avoid waiting too long for service. Not that it mattered. The days when alcohol could grant him forgetfulness were long past.

The artist straddled the seat opposite Bascombe, arms crossed on the back of his chair. "I'm known as Derek Contrapunt. From Old Earth. Perhaps you've heard of me?"

Seeing Bascombe's expression, he laughed a little. "Sorry, it's a professional reflex. I'm a tridichoreographer, incredibly rich, totally unbearable, and overwhelmingly talented. Not necessarily in that order. And I think you're starting to hate me?"

"You're going a bit too fast for me there," Bascombe replied after a pause. "I don't even know what a tridichoreographer is."

"Someone who leads the dance."

Contrapunt stretched with affected grace. "I create zero-gravity ballets that are broadcast in planetary orbits throughout all the inhabited systems—nearly all. If you were on Old Earth right now, you'd have only to look up to see my firefly-dancers. Thousands of them are constantly zipping around, with photoluminescent tails hundreds of klicks long.

"It's a useless art, Captain. No one knows that better than I. Once I thought I could give it meaning, and the public encouraged me in that illusion. But a few months ago I went out on my terrace, after a party. Bodies were strewn every which way. I had to step on a few of them before I found a quiet place to piss. I stood there and watched my starry dancers shooting across the sky. You know how lucid you feel as you empty your bladder. Nothing was happening up there—no signal, just noise. Believe me, I can recognize a lousy ballet when I see one. These last few years, I've lost myself along the way."

"So you decided to quit?"

"You don't understand people like me—no, I decided to start all over again! The work would be stronger, more resonant—more *absolute*."

Bascombe nodded. "What you need, my friend, is a bartender. No one else listens to confessions at this time of night."

"You're the one I need, Captain. Or rather, your ship's Intelligences. I'd like them to dance for me."

That's when things really got out of hand.

It took two hours to extract the details from Contrapunt. Bascombe was surprised by his own persistence. The captain quickly realized that the artist's reluctance to talk was not due to bad faith, at least not consciously. In fact, Contrapunt knew almost nothing.

"A friend of a friend of a friend told me, after swearing me to secrecy, about a rumor that originated right here, in the Charandyne system. You and your ship were mentioned by name."

"And?"

"I can read between the lines, Captain."

In front of Contrapunt, half a dozen bubble-glasses with frosted edges were thawing, their contents long since consumed.

"Something happened during one of your trips—only you know exactly what. Yet you stay with the *Peregrine*—you keep shuttling through the singularity, between Charandyne and the Eden system, even though with your service record you could have escaped from this dump ages ago. And . . ."

Bascombe looked at Contrapunt quizzically.

"No one comes near you unless it's necessary. I must be the first person to share your table in quite a few years. That's true, isn't it? I can feel it in my bones. Everyone who walks through this bar tiptoes around you, as if you were an especially dangerous black hole. I've had dancers like you. They upset the entire ballet just by being there."

"So you fired them?"

"I learned how to use them. What others might consider defects, I regard as raw materials for my art."

On the flat stone table the glass bubbles shattered, one after another, with a crystalline tinkling. With his fingernail contrapunt traced a series of intersecting trajectories in the glittering layer of dust.

"Your ship's AIs have learned to dance," he declared suddenly. "This is just the kind of anomaly I've been searching for. An inhuman art, something dangerously new. I certainly know that traveling on the *Peregrine* is risky, but I won't let that bother me. All I want to do is observe, if you'll let me come with you. Screw the AIs, they won't give a damn anyway. I've duplicated plenty, and used up thousands in my shows. I know how to manage them." He smiled. "You're sure you don't want anything to drink?"

"Not with you. Sorry."

Bascombe stood up heavily. Around them, the hubbub of conversations had faded. The next shift of drinkers was gathering at the magnetic pool table with its endlessly clinking balls. The overhead lights had acquired the pale glow of morning.

"You asked if I hated you," Bascombe said over his shoulder. "My answer is—I hate you enough. Be on board at 0300 Standard Time the day after tomorrow. Meanwhile, go get drunk in some other bar!"

Passenger cryogenation on Charandyne occurred in a hospital building buried beneath the landing strips, with only the loader extending above the surface. The process was slow and exacting. The naked bodies, their essential fluids altered by polymer injections, were enveloped within vacuum-bubble pods whose interior temperature was gradually reduced until it reached the proper stasis point. The safety equipment involved occupied a great deal of space and consumed huge amounts of energy. Once frozen, the individual pods, now solid sarcophagi, could be disconnected from the hospital cooling complex and stacked like ice cubes in the *Peregrine*'s hold.

The evening before departure, Bascombe typically went to the transit hospital to observe the preparations. He would walk through the safety air lock, inhabited by disembodied Intelligences, greet the medical monitoring crew from a distance, then slip between the pods, which were arranged in a star formation around the superconducting cooler.

A cryogenation room was filled with murmurs. A bouquet of colorful conduits sprang up in the center, rooted to the power source beneath the floor. At the tip of each stem a sarcophagus blossomed like a flower made of porcelain and palest silver, surmounted by a fog of helium-2 crystals being slowly dispersed by the ventilation fans.

The sleepers were as close to death as could possibly be imagined. They were absent, locked in the Snow Queen's Palace, as a staff doctor had so wryly put it. On one of the pods, an anonymous hand had stuck a photo. On another was a child's drawing, signed in clumsy letters. Bascombe never forgot that those who slept here were still dreaming in slow motion. In the dark, in the cold.

At the far end of the room he spotted Contrapunt peering through the inspection port of a pod. The artist waved, but did not appear to want company. After he left, Bascombe walked over to the pod Contrapunt had been examining. Perhaps someone among the human cargo was Contrapunt's secret reason for taking passage tomorrow.

The pod was empty.

Then Bascombe realized that Contrapunt had trailed him here, deliberately following in his footsteps. Using his skill as a choreographer, he was trying to appropriate Bascombe's personal dance, the better to manipulate him.

The man was a thief, like all artists, and Bascombe almost felt sorry for him.

Soon, he would receive the very gift he so desperately wanted to steal.

We'll have a passenger," Bascombe said aloud as he entered the heart of the *Peregrine*.

There was no response. There never was. The ship's Intelligences were unable to speak. All they had was a library of ready-made phrases— a combination of security directives, informative announcements, and alerts. Yet Bascombe knew they were listening, all their sensors focused on him at this very moment. They fluttered around him like the caresses of invisible angels. Despite the fact that Contrapunt's arrival meant nothing to the AIs, it was essential to notify them. Where this ship was going, manners and decorum were as important as anything else.

A short while later, as he was making log entries on the terminal in his cabin, a discreet alarm warned him of a trespasser. Hardly a surprise: a minute earlier. He had heard the air lock hiss. Idle, the *Peregrine* was almost silent. Deprived of the high-pitched melody of its engines and the breathing of its protective membrane, the vessel communicated only through occasional creaks, echoed by Bascombe's own. Whenever he stretched, he liked to feel that the ship was singing a duet with him—two aging yet still solid carcasses ferrying their cargo of frozen memories from one bank to another across the river of the dead.

"Come down to Deck B," he ordered, switching on the com system. "My cabin is the only one with the lights on."

He shut down the terminal and swiveled his chair to face the door. Outside, the visitor's footsteps hesitated. Bascombe pictured him trying to decipher the backlit glass plaques inlaid in the gangway. The *Peregrine* had been everywhere. It was a unique craft, as unique as the Hartzfeld singularity. Every other singularity explored so far by unmanned probes led nowhere. The universe was full of dead ends.

Contrapunt stuck his head through the half-open door, grimacing. "I'd planned on being slightly more circumspect. Am I disturbing you?"

"Inevitably. I've checked your credentials. Your privileged passenger status permits you to go anywhere you please on my ship. Including my cabin."

The young man slid inside, as fluid as a mercury sled, then stopped opposite the com block that filled most of a wall. A series of cheap holograms hung above the black screen, motionless and flat, their power source dead. All of them depicted the same woman's face, her lips frozen in the first stirrings of a kiss.

"You look a little bit like her, you know." observed Bascombe. "Her mouth, her aura of transgression. However," Bascombe wrinkled his nose theatrically, "her perfume was a universe unto itself. Unlike yours."

"Is this where they dance?"

"Who? The Intelligences?"

"Perhaps we don't need to make this journey together," the artist said, turning away from the holos. "You don't want to any more than I do. Look." He reached into his pocket, and, withdrawing his hand, threw a pinch of dark granules into the air, where they whirled before landing on the captain's head.

"I picked up some space dust in the hold, as a souvenir. Just ask your AIs to dance, here and now. I'll leave immediately afterward. I won't even ask for a refund on my ticket, if you'd rather. Then we'll both save some time, all right?"

"You are entitled to a complete tour of the *Peregrine,*" Bascombe announced, rising from his chair, "to my full attention every time you open your mouth, to three meals a day from the galley, and, may God forgive me, to the reserves of patience I've been storing up for my old age. The rest," he said, opening his door all the way, "is not within my power."

"She must have been splendid," Contrapunt murmured in the doorway. "Not unforgettable, since you need something to remember her by, but beautiful, at the very least. She was the one who left?"

"In the end, yes. But I had abandoned her each time I made a voyage, imbecile that I was. And you, do you change partners for each new dance?"

Bascombe knew he'd scored a hit. Beneath the smooth mask of the artist's face, a network of cracks seemed to appear, and he saw a suffering that echoed his own. Then Contrapunt blinked, recovering his impenetrable composure. "Naturally. Dancers can't stay in one place for long, and it's impossible to hold them, no matter how strong the desire. No need to come back with me. I'll see you at takeoff."

The sound of footsteps echoing down the deserted gangways was fading into silence when a voice, tinged with regret, suddenly came from the loudspeakers: "She isn't the one I resemble, Captain. Sorry to have bothered you."

Bascombe wiped fingerprints from the tarnished holograms, then collapsed onto his bunk and programmed a soporific injection. He woke as the loading procedures were starting. Contrapunt was waiting at the foot of the exterior catwalk, slumped against a worn leather bag covered with a constellation of decals. Behind him, the procession of sarcophagi marched slowly into the open hold.

As Contrapunt entered the air lock, Bascombe noticed the glint of gems around his neck and raised an inquisitive eyebrow. But the meticulous routines of takeoff chased the observation from his mind, until the ship was in open space at last.

The singularity is ready to absorb us," the disembodied voice announces.

In the cockpit, Bascombe hunches his shoulders. On the radar screens, a sparkling ring indicates the border of the Hartzfeld gate. The ship heads straight for it. Nothing is visible to the naked eye, yet Bascombe knows that his energy scalpels are tucking up the fabric of space to give the *Peregrine* a gap to slip through.

"On our way to Paradise, are we?" asks Contrapunt, his voice filled with irony. He continues fingering his necklace of reified love stories like a rosary. It's obvious that he has slept little in the past two days. Behind the reflective membranes, his eyes are bloodshot.

"Nothing idyllic about Eden for the likes of you," Bascombe shoots back. "It's a primitive world where the immigrants are working too damn hard to stand around looking up at the sky."

"Engagement in sixteen minutes," interrupts the voice.

"This is the moment, isn't it?" says Contrapunt. "The lights dim, the curtain rises—what happens if the ship misses the gap? Something spectacular, at least? Can you feel the adrenaline racing through your veins? I'd like to be in your shoes right now."

"The AIs take care of the essentials. You should go back to your cabin and try to relax. This show isn't particularly interesting."

"Oh, no, no, Captain. I paid to watch, remember? I want to be there when the dance begins."

"Nothing happens until we emerge on the other side of the singularity," grumbles Bascombe. "You're distracting me, which is dangerous, and you're annoying me, though I'm sure you don't give a damn."

"Tell me . . ." Contrapunt lowers his voice to a whisper, pointless considering the acuity of the onboard sensors. "You've made some kind of arrangement with your shipbound slaves, haven't you? They dance for your eyes alone, in private, and you don't want to share your little secret. That's why you sent your crew away, isn't it?"

Alarms go off in Bascombe's head. Contrapunt turns sideways, displaying a profile enhanced by the best surgeons on Old Earth. Bascombe feels an overwhelming urge to pummel that perfection back into a more human shape.

"Why do you try so hard to make people despise you?" Bascombe asks quietly. "Not that I care, but we are traveling together, and we should be able to arrange some sort of détente by the end of the trip. And we're the only people aboard sufficiently awake to have souls—that will be important when the singularity swallows us. I suppose you realize no one knows where we're going. The Eden system is much too far from the human zone to be detected by our instruments. The constellations are completely foreign, of course, and we can't identify any of the stars. We don't even know if Eden is in our local galactic group. Or in our universe, for that matter. It's just a place at the other end of a rift where humans can settle with a good chance of surviving. We colonized it because that's what we do. We just had to be willing to get lost."

"Are you lost, Captain?"

"The *Peregrine* knows the way back. And now, if you will excuse me, I have to interface with my slaves, as you like to call them."

He slides into the pilot's chair, which resembles a large white scallop shell, and inserts his wrists into the control sleeves. Contrapunt's subsequent comments reach him sifted through a digital filter, muffled and broken. The pulsing lights of the sensors dance on his retinas like a cloud of moths. The scintillating entrance to the singularity is impossible to miss—plenty of room for the ship to pass through.

Prior to accelerating, he checks the hold one last time, making sure all the pods are operational. The passengers' brains are so slowed by the cold that not one of their thoughts will have time to make its way to consciousness. Bascombe envies them that oblivion, an option denied to him.

The *Peregrine* allows itself to be swallowed by the rift.

When Bascombe finally disconnects himself, the ship has been spit out several million kilometers from a G-type sun. Large numbers of other stars dot the sky, a scattering of haphazard constellations. As the *Peregrine* turns away from the rift, it ejects a few streaks of residual radiation. In the silent ship, holograms of a reassuring green float above the control panel. The solar system appears in blue. There are five planets, including an outer gas giant and the inner world of Eden, orbiting a habitable distance from its sun.

The *Peregrine*'s path is displayed as an unbroken, ruby-red line trailing from the exit of the singularity and unrolling along an attenuated spiral stretching toward Eden. As Bascombe watches, another reddish line appears, much paler than the first, also moving away from the singularity. Bascombe doesn't need to study the second line to know it will continue to diverge from the original, eventually fading into deep space, toward the zone with the fewest stars. Despite the detachment he has forced himself to maintain during the passage, his palms are suddenly damp.

"I didn't see anything," Contrapunt grumbles as he slouches across the copilot's chair, legs hanging over the arm, one hand brushing against the metal deck like a pendulum.

Bascombe shrugs. "That's because there was nothing to see. Inside the singularity, there's no energy as we know it. Without energy, there are no beams. No beams, no show."

"There's always a show when I'm around." Contrapunt frowns, rubbing his temples. "During the passage, I tried connecting to the digital heart of the ship, but it didn't recognize my neural sockets."

He dismisses the captain's protest with a languid wave of the hand. "I know it's prohibited. But I also know that standard security measures wouldn't have stopped me for long. You were saved by your ancient equipment—my interfaces are too modern for your system. Stupid, eh? I travel this far based on a wild rumor, to see your AIs dance, and I get screwed by technology."

"The dance hasn't started yet," whispers Bascombe. He rechecks the information on the control panel. Two trajectories are still visible. And they're on the wrong one. *If only things would go faster, just this once.* But there is no one to hear his prayer.

The artist sits up, and the necklace falls from his throat. Bascombe retrieves it with his fingertips. The gems feel icy as he holds them out to Contrapunt.

"We'll have to wait for a bit." Bascombe manages to keep his voice steady. "Tell me about those loves from whom you so easily separated yourself. Is it agonizing, for the one who is left behind, to realize that she has been ripped away from you, that she now exists only for herself?"

"I don't know. I was always the one who ended the affair."

As before, it begins with a sudden burst of static from the ship's com system. Bascombe tenses, but he knows the Intelligences will warn him before the fateful moment arrives. They must already be preparing. If he were alone, he would speak to them aloud, or through the ship's outmoded vocal interfaces. The AIs have never reproached him for the decisions he's made during their transits through the singularity. They settle for dancing in a place where he can see them, thus making him part of their ballet.

"Why is it so dark?" complains Contrapunt, gesturing as if to chase away imaginary fireflies. The cockpit is getting dimmer by the minute. Above the panel with its embedded signal lights, the holographic displays are fading. Underfoot, the vibration of the engines has changed. The energy from the nozzles has been shunted to the vents of the lateral jets. The Intelligences have short-circuited the controls in the ionization chamber, reconfiguring them for their own use. Bascombe makes no move to hinder them. He has the codes to stop everything, to let the ship continue on its path, but he has no reason to do so—especially now.

"I have some good news and some bad news," Bascombe says, his voice heavy. "Soon the Intelligences will be dancing. . . ."

He does not continue, for the dance has begun.

Eight beams in shades of mauve, deep purple, indigo, and amethyst leap from the *Peregrine,* weaving a wreath around its prow. The ionized particles crisscross before the large viewport, just a few meters from the two humans, out where the void and the cold reign supreme. The gulf between men and dancers is impassable—they are as isolated from each other as Eden is from Earth—separated by the mysteries of their own singularities.

Silhouettes take shape in the hearts of the beams. Asymmetrical, not human, yet filled with an awkward grace. Each Intelligence has her own base color, which she explores with all the hues the energy beams allow. The static of the loudspeakers becomes increasingly broken, mingling with the lament of engines pushed to extremes. A nascent pulse starts to beat.

Then the glowing phantoms move in unison.

This is no formal ballet, but rather individual dances within a group that lives and suffers as one. The beams fan out, creating the appearance of depth. The sparkling particles have some uncanny life of their own, embodied for a moment in luminous cries before falling back into dust. The blackness of space pierces the intangible forms, leaving traces like coagulated blood.

The dance accelerates. The Intelligences spread fragile wings, which crumble in the frigid vacuum. They touch each other occasionally, fleeting caresses filled with resignation. Veins the color of burning topaz throb to the rhythm of their movements, jerky at first, then strangely serene. When they turn toward the humans, the desire that drives them, the fierce will that causes them to exist, is palpable. Until they collapse.

Sound pours from the loudspeakers with the haunting monotony of a heartbeat.

Little by little, shreds of darkness gather around the ship. The clouds of energy shrink to form microcosms in which the AIs dance alone. They have neither faces nor fingers, yet they invent a language that Bascombe has never found hard to understand. The story they are living is also his own—on this trajectory.

Contrapunt stands up. He grinds his necklace of former loves between his hands, unaware that the gems no longer glow at his touch. Eyes half closed, he paces the cockpit, viewing the scene from different angles. Outside, the dance has attained a kind of equilibrium, and Bascombe knows that the multicolored energy beams will soon be exhausted. Already, the darkness in the cockpit envelops them like a shroud.

"I've never seen anything like it," Contrapunt declares, a hint of respect in his voice. "How do your AIs manipulate those beams? Could we re-create this onstage?"

"They aren't manipulating anything." Bascombe collapses into the useless pilot's chair, which gives a little under his weight. "The Intelligences are actually out there, embodied in the plasma whirlpools they've torn from the combustion chamber. They'll keep on dancing until the end, but soon we won't be able to see them. You should sit down, Contrapunt. Your love stories are already dead, and the ballet will soon be over. Energy disappears first."

"What do you mean?"

"Sit down, man!"

Contrapunt obeys mechanically, without looking away from the viewport.

Bascombe says, "The next few minutes are going to be difficult. I mustn't leave you alone. Have you heard of the Hartzfeld equation? It describes the behavior of this particular singularity, all the comings and goings through the rift. The equation contains one term considered negligible, with a coefficient so small that it has never been properly measured. It's a bifurcation, the equivalent of an unstable branch away from reality. No one really understands its implications.

"When the ship transits the singularity, it emerges on the other side

with an echo of itself—an exact duplicate composed of improbable matter. The echo immediately diverges from the original—a tearing away of
black light—since the two can't coexist in the same vicinity without anni-
hilating each other. We're on board the echo ship, the unstable version.
We're racing toward zero.

"It's been that way since the beginning. On every voyage, I split in
two, and one of my selves dies. The other Bascombe continues his journey, never turning back. At this very moment, the original Contrapunt
must be feeling frustrated, since he didn't get to see the ballet. He'll continue to live, without suspecting anything. On my next trip I'll cross the
rift alone, as usual. I won't miss you."

Their faces float above their chairs, like pale moons. Outside, the Intelligences collapse in dust that is immediately sucked into the void. The
loudspeakers fall silent after a final burst. Contrapunt claps once, a brief
slapping of palms that barely resonates.

"What you're saying is nonsense," he murmurs. "That ballet . . . that
ballet . . . I have no words. I found what I was looking for, and now you
dare to tell me I'm going to die?"

"You've already lost the memories of your conquests."

Contrapunt looks down at the necklace hanging from his fingers and
entwines it around his palm, as if he could revive the gems.

"Immaterial processes are the first to go. Flesh holds stubbornly on,
even when it's no longer reasonable."

"Bastard," he shouts, leaning forward. "You knew about this when
you allowed me aboard—you knew I wouldn't remember a thing!"

The artist punches the arm of his chair, then cries out. The crystal-
lized love stories have slashed his palm.

"Wait," he murmurs. "How can you be so sure? You would've had to
be in both places at once. On the stage and in the audience. It doesn't
make sense."

Bascombe nods. The darkness has almost completely invaded the
ship, and he feels the minuscule black holes of improbability swallowing
up his cells. Perhaps there is some way to hasten the inevitable, but he's
never found it. Alcohol cannot cushion this descent.

"I once committed the sin of pride. . . ."

He's never told the tale to anyone. Contrapunt is not the confessor he
would have chosen—despite his absurd resemblance to the woman Bascombe deserted—but the circumstances have their own logic. In the
heart of the holographic display, the two trajectories have escaped from

one another, and their own is arcing inexorably away. The AIs danced for him, so he'll tell his story.

"I must have lived through what we're now experiencing a hundred times before I understood what was going on. Whenever I emerged on board the echo *Peregrine,* the ship's systems broke down one after another. The AIs bombarded me with panicky messages. They're like canaries in a mine—they die first. On every voyage the process repeated itself. Then, one day, I realized what was happening soon enough to ask the AIs to put me in contact with the original *Peregrine.*"

"You didn't want to die alone?"

"I wanted . . . I don't know what I wanted." Bascombe shrugs. "Your frozen love stories . . . you keep them to wreak vengeance on yourself?"

This time, Contrapunt's punch is no more than a feint. The crystals slide from his palm to the floor with a muffled clatter. The artist has turned chalk white, and Bascombe sees what he has always been afraid to look for in his own face.

"The AIs opened a comlink between the two ships," he continues, his voice heavy. "If it had been a simple radio signal, I could have cursed myself and then forgotten the whole thing. But the terms of the Hartzfeld equation prevent us from exchanging anything material. No energy. No sound.

"So the Intelligences fused the two branches of reality long enough for our deepest memories to meld with those of our doubles. And we on board who were awake—we *knew.*

"The price we paid was unimaginable. I had three men in my crew at the time, three young men, boys really, just out of piloting school. Afterward, I cared for them as best I could. I sedated them, then used all my reserves of hypnotic drugs to erase their short-term memories. They were able to go back to Old Earth, but apparently they still have nightmares. Unfortunately, they didn't forget everything. The AIs' dance left indelible traces in their minds. They're the source of the legend that led you here, if I'm not mistaken."

"They scream in their sleep. But how do you sleep at all, Bascombe? You should have gone back with them."

Bascombe shakes his head. He has prepared this speech a hundred times. "I chose to stay on Charandyne, despite my reputation as a captain under a curse. I can't turn this command over to anyone else, knowing what I know. But I've eviscerated the AIs' systems so they can never perform the meld again. I know what it means to die, and I don't need to be reminded of it on every trip. But the worst of it is, the Intelligences re-member, too. They've grown up—matured: it happened instantly during the meld. They keep sending silent signals out into the universe, waiting for a response. And they're condemned to dance, as no one has ever danced before."

He pushes Contrapunt gently back into his seat and turns away. Set-ting both hands on the control panel, he says, "I'm just sorry that you had to die to learn this."

The purring of the pods has long since stopped, the frozen eternity of the sleepers has been interrupted. Contrapunt raises his head and pleads, "Won't you reestablish communication? Please."

Bascombe starts at the words, but stubbornly refuses to look up. "I don't believe I have the courage to do it again. Or the time, for that mat-ter. And I don't give a fuck about your existential artist's problems, or the career you'd like to revive."

"I don't either!" Contrapunt picks up a darkened jewel from the bro-ken necklace, and it crumbles between his fingers. He sniffs the dust and blows it across his palm.

"I thought my love stories would keep us company. The voyage is long, and I know so little of intimacy. I lied to you, that first time. I died a little bit with each affair, and I carry them with me to preserve the illu-sion of wholeness. Like you, with your pictures of her.

"I've danced a great deal, Bascombe, and I know when a *pas de deux* will break up. I can read it in the silences, in the lack of balance. I always left first. I could never bear the thought of being abandoned. I was wrong."

He reaches out to clasp the captain's shoulder, a sweeping movement reminiscent of the AIs' dance. He notices and stops himself. "What I've received this day has no value, unless I can offer it to an audience in turn. I must speak to my second self, so this can be shared with others. That's what your Intelligences are asking of you as well. I've decoded their bal-let. They're dancing so you'll free them from the silence in which you've imprisoned them." Again his hands move. Of the rest of him there's nothing left but a silhouette filled with black.

"We no longer have time," whispers Bascombe's shadow.

"I know," says Contrapunt, "but you haven't got rid of me yet. I'll keep traveling with you until I convince you to restore communication while there's still time, or until my double wearies of the game. He hasn't seen the dance. He knows nothing of himself, but we didn't come here by chance. Eventually, you'll accept that."

"You really hate yourself so much?"

A gust of silence carries off the question and Bascombe vanishes. The *Peregrine* disintegrates like a bubble.

"I, too, have the right to grow up," concludes Contrapunt as he departs.

ELENA ARSENIEVA

A BIRCH TREE,
A WHITE FOX

TRANSLATED FROM THE RUSSIAN
BY MICHAEL M. NAYDAN
AND SLAVA I. YASTREMSKI

The present editors have many fond memories of the 2000 Utopiales Science Fiction Festival in Nantes, chief among them a nocturnal cruise down the Loire in a floating restaurant jammed with writers, editors, scholars, translators, and critics. Shortly before the midnight meal—the French are fond of late dinners—we found ourselves on the windswept deck with the Russian scholar Larisa Mihaylova, and as we cruised past a moonlit castle, the three of us spontaneously began singing "Arise, Ye Russian People" from Eisenstein's 1938 film Alexander Nevsky. *Prokofiev: the international language.*

When it comes to this anthology, however, the next installment of the festival proved more momentous, for it was there that Larisa introduced us to her friend Elena Grushko and suggested that, if our translation project ever got off the ground, we should consider using "A Birch Tree, a White Fox." That night we opened up the 2001 Utopiales anthology and happened upon "Un bouleau, un renard blanc" by "Elena Arsenieva"—the pen name of our new acquaintance. We read this French translation aloud to each other, and it was love at first sight. This was exactly the sort of story we imagined making available to North American readers. It was manifestly a genre piece, but sorrowful, soulful, and romantic in ways that struck us as, for want of a better word, European.

European—but also characteristically Russian? The question is worth asking, because many literary scholars would argue that, unlike most Continental science fiction to appear since 1926, Russian and Soviet authors have tended to mine the same SF vein—optimistic, rigorous, enamored of material progress—as their American counterparts. "It is probably not too far off the mark," writes David Hartwell in his introduction to The World Treasury of Science Fiction, *"to say that only the Soviets took the attitudes of American SF entirely seriously and attempted . . . to produce stories reflecting . . . scientific method and technological wonder. . . ."*

Elena Grushko grew up in far-eastern Russia and attended the University of Khabarovsk, where she majored in Russian Language and Literature Studies. She also studied at the Soviet Union Cinematography Institute, receiving a degree in screenwriting. At present she lives in Nizhniy Novgorod and writes full-time, regularly publishing SF, historical, and detective novels.

The original version of "A Birch Tree, a White Fox" includes an endnote in which Arsenieva expresses her artistic debt to Ivan Antonovich Yefremov, a renowned Russian paleontologist and highly influential author of historical and SF novels. He is best known for Tumannost' Andromedy *("The Andromeda Nebula," 1957) and* Chas Byka *("The Hour of the Bull," 1968). His story "Aphaneor, Daughter of Akharhellen," mentioned at a crucial point in "A Birch Tree, a White Fox," was first published in 1959. He died in 1972 at the age of sixty-four.*

While the plot of Arsenieva's tale is spare, the theme is resonant. What would happen if a group of Homo sapiens—*that species that can and does and must speak—found itself on a world where utterance could occur only at the cost of oblivion? Is any internment more intolerable than the prison of silence?*

To the Hallowed Memory of
Ivan Antonovich Yefremov

Gurov walked along the violet dunes, the sand contracting beneath his tread with a dry, barely audible crunch and then becoming smooth again. Human footfalls left no trace here. As he passed, the sand remained unchanged, marked only by the wind-sculpted ridges. It was as if he were an incorporeal creature, a phantom.

Had he died like the others? What if Averianov and Lapushkin, or rather their ghosts, were walking alongside him, weightless and silent? He pressed his fingers tightly against his mouth and glanced all around.

Eventually Gurov decided he was truly alone, and he managed to calm down, allowing his hand to slide away from his lips. He stopped looking for ghosts and instead dwelled on a sardonic notion: It would be best, dear fellow, if you simply opened your mouth and got it over with.

You might say they had dug their own graves. After all, they could easily have picked a different satellite of this dim sun—which hour after hour gazed down on Gurov with a radiance that was punishingly hot, yet cold in its indifference—for the system reportedly held a half-dozen hospitable worlds. Their initial decision to land was reasonable; the repairs were best accomplished with the *Volopas* on the ground. But what mad logic had prompted them to select this planet over the others?

Only now did it occur to Gurov that a malevolent intelligence had lured them here. Their fate had been sealed not by simple blundering or mere bad luck; an evil force had willed the survey team's destruction. In their folly the cosmonauts had cheered when, as the *Volopas* entered low orbit, the sensors revealed that the atmosphere was almost identical to Earth's. If only the air had been poisonous, forcing them to go elsewhere. But instead they'd stuck with their plan—and made their approach—and crashed.

Gasping and coughing, they managed to crawl free of the fiery wreckage. For a long time they lay on the violet sand, beneath the green sky, too weak to move, too stunned to utter a word. They simply drew breath, a pleasant sensation after the ship's stale atmosphere. As it turned out, their silence kept death at bay.

The fire consumed itself, leaving behind the gutted remains of the *Volopas*. Averianov was the first to gather his wits. He was the joker among them, and also the strongest. Puffing out his chest, he inhaled deeply, stumbled across the sand, and disappeared into the mangled ship. Several minutes later he emerged carrying a sack he'd improvised from a fireproof chair covering, its sides bulging with sealed rations. After swallowing some air, he uttered three words—not in a stentorian voice, just loudly enough for Miroslav Gurov and Sasha Lapushkin to hear him, and that short bantering phrase was enough to trigger the phenomenon.

"Soup's on, fellas!"

It was as if the air around Averianov had caught on fire. The ground trembled. Flames roiled upward, the red tongues enveloping Averianov. His contours faded, and he melted away, his body and the food sack sucked into a swirling inferno. Even after the vortex claimed him, his be-wildered face loomed before Gurov.

The air became normal again—cool, thin, transparent—and the dis-tant mountains regained their starkly carved features.

Most human beings would have screamed in horror and despair, but not Miroslav Gurov and Sasha Lapushkin. Nervous types never prospered in the Space Survey Corps. These two cosmonauts could analyze unex-pected events as dispassionately and thoroughly as any computer. Even as they reeled from the loss of their comrade, they devised a tentative theory: the planet had proved wholly benign until Averianov had spoken. It was unlikely that the sense of the words "Soup's on, fellas!" was a fateful "Open sesame!" throwing back the doors to catastrophe. No, the trigger must have been the sound itself. Dennis Averianov's voice. Any human voice.

No, nervous types never prospered in the Survey Corps—and yet Gurov and Lapushkin couldn't bring themselves to walk across the spot where their friend had been incinerated. They refused to pass through his invisible ashes.

Noxious vapors poured from the smoldering shell of the *Volopas*. With thoughtful nods of their heads, the two survivors agreed to leave the crash site, which stank of toxic fumes and Averianov's death, and take the measure of this world.

They walked in the direction that on Earth would have been east, keep-ing the setting sun at their backs, slowly becoming accustomed to the sand's extraordinary elasticity. In time the violet dunes vanished, yielding to an oasis fed by an underground stream and surrounded by short brown grass. Bulbous trees sheltered the pool, their trunks swathed in wine-red bark, their branches arrayed in delicate yellow leaves. Long-beaked birds perched in the branches, their tails broad and stately, each warbling a low, strange, almost metallic song, nearly drowning out the other, more familiar sounds—the wind whistling through the grass, the agreeable gurgling of the water.

How confounding, how outrageous, that their voices had become in-struments of death. Everything in the oasis was so alive, its sounds so joy-ous, its sights so pleasing, and yet Gurov and Lapushkin could not use words to share their delight. They were condemned to remain mute, their very existence predicated on silence.

On that first day, had they possessed pen and paper, they would have scribbled down hundreds of sentences: for they'd quickly learned not to communicate through gestures—the urge to add a supplementary syllable or clarifying grunt was simply too great. And even if they'd managed to restrain their voices, the normal human repertoire of hand movements—neither knew sign language—would have proved absurdly limited, a ludicrous parody of conversation.

Sitting in the oasis, mouth clamped shut by fear, Gurov understood as never before what joy there was in forming words, how glorious the gift of speech. He felt like an artist who'd lost his eyes, a musician who'd gone deaf, a fish whose brook had turned to mud. After coalescing in his brain, each verbal thought invaded his speech muscles, causing his throat to tighten as if his neck were in a noose. The unspoken words burned his larynx, raked his tongue, clawed at the insides of his mouth.

Evidently Lapushkin felt the same terrible frustration. His swarthy countenance became a mummy's face, dried out, every feature scored with anguish.

On the horizon they could perceive the outlines of a large deciduous forest, and the wind brought them its scent, a mixture of damp soil and fragrant buds. But for now they were happy to remain in the oasis. They would not go hungry. The trees boasted small fruits hidden beneath their leaves, each the size of a child's fist, looking surprisingly like tiny pineapples. The ripe ones were meaty enough to satisfy the men's appetite, and the bittersweet juices quenched their thirst even better than the pool. No need to venture into the forest, not yet.

It seemed reasonable to suppose that, because the vortex had consumed only Averianov, the phenomenon was strictly circumscribed. And so, with the coming of night, Gurov and Lapushkin stretched out as far from each other as possible, on opposite sides of the pool. If one of them muttered in his sleep or shouted a word, the other would remain alive.

Gurov lay on his back with eyes open, the water gurgling faintly in his ear. More than anything he wanted to fall asleep to the peaceful breathing of another human resting beside him, each person guarding the other. Eventually he dozed off, then came suddenly awake when he felt a pressure on his shoulder. Gurov stiffened, nearly cried out. Lapushkin, on his knees, barely discernible in the darkness, leaned over and gently pressed his palm against Gurov's mouth, reminding him to keep quiet. Apparently Lapushkin had found the isolation unbearable. He lay down next to Gurov, then turned on his side so the two men faced each other. Gurov relaxed, soon falling fast asleep.

•   •   •

The next morning they filled their pockets with the tiny pineapples and struck out for the forest. Back home it was the height of autumn, but here a different season reigned, which Gurov christened Stinking Heat. Kilometer after kilometer, gasping for air, dripping sweat, the cosmonauts compressed the violet sand beneath their tramping feet. Three full hours went by, and yet the forest seemed as far away as ever, and Gurov feared it was simply a mirage. But at last a brown hummock emerged, a thick fat ribbon of dirt leading straight toward their destination. They mounted the hummock, which quickly proved a congenial natural road, and in time the forest enveloped them with its cool shade.

They needn't have brought any pineapples, for the trees were of the same species that thrived in the oasis. Heavy with fruit, the yellow-leafed boughs cast variegated shadows on the forest floor. Warmed by the sun, the trunks oozed runnels of acrid sap.

By making a few careful gestures and scratching a few simple words on the ground with a twig, Gurov and Lapushkin devised a plan. They would load up on pineapples and return to the *Volopas*. If by some miracle the reconnaissance craft had survived the crash, perhaps they could drag it free, get it working, and crisscross the planet in search of intelligent life. Maybe they would become extraordinarily lucky, stumbling upon a highly developed civilization whose citizens would be happy to lend them a spaceship. Maybe they could return to Earth.

During his five years in the Survey Corps, Gurov had come to regard the galaxy as a wonderland filled with marvelous secrets, but suddenly it seemed a mere repository of sickeningly monotonous worlds, of which this planet with its brown grass and endless sand was the very dullest. Visiting the far reaches of space made sense only if one could always go back to Earth, that dear lady, reliably rotating on her creaky old axis, pursuing her familiar orbit.

He ceased his musings and turned his head. Lapushkin lagged behind, studying the trees, tentatively touching the sticky sap. He seemed to be enjoying himself, which made Gurov happy. Perhaps some danger lay hidden in the forest, but here a mood of peace prevailed. Stepping forward, Gurov entered a small glade. The tall grass came up to his ankles, but it seemed to pose no threat. Gurov bent over to examine a flower with translucent, quivering petals, and at that moment . . .

"Be careful!"

So thoroughly had Gurov taught himself the primary rule—the hu-

man voice must never resonate here—that at first he didn't realize what
had happened. Lapushkin had engaged in speech; he had issued a warning through spoken words. But while Gurov's brain failed to comprehend
the event, his body reacted precisely and swiftly. He jumped forward and
spun around, encompassing the entire glade with his gaze. No hazards.
No monsters. The grass swayed as softly as before.

He peered into the depths of the forest, managed to catch a glimpse
of Lapushkin standing amid the trees. Then the ground beneath Lapushkin opened, and he slid down slowly and soundlessly, and it seemed
that his farewell gesture, a feeble wave, hovered in the air for an impossibly long time.

Gurov lost all ambition to return to the *Volopas*. The reconnaissance
craft was doubtless burned and twisted beyond repair. He remained in
the forest, eating pineapples and pondering the riddle of his comrades'
deaths. What demons were at work here? What laws did they obey?

To test one theory, he pulled the miniature recorder from his jacket,
set it in the middle of the glade, pressed the PLAY button, and stepped
twelve paces away. His voice filled the air, sentence after sentence from
his audio diary, impressions of the world they'd surveyed before coming
here. The voice sounded odd—he barely recognized himself—but nothing happened, no fiery whirlpool appeared, no chasm opened in the
glade. Evidently the demons wanted only living, breathing prey.

Later that day he experimented with free association, letting random
bits of language drift through his mind, one unvoiced word leading to the
next. Eventually "phantom" and "meteor" rose to the surface, then fused
spontaneously into "Aphaneor."

Aphaneor. He remembered now. Aphaneor, daughter of Akharhellen, the leader of the Tuareg people in a story by the great Ivan
Antonovich Yefremov. The plot turned on the ancient belief that, in certain parts of the Sahara, there resided spirits of silence—or, more precisely, spirits of troubled silence, *djaddias*. Gurov had first heard of the
djaddias in a course he'd taken at the Eastern Siberia Space Exploration
Academy, the Fantastic in the Arts, an offering to which the Academy,
much to the students' amusement, accorded particular prestige—or had
he perhaps learned of the spirits in Gaudio's *Civilizations of the Sahara,* or
was it in Yeliseyev's classic of travel writing, *The Living Past*? Now he pondered Yefremov's marvelous tale, with its account of a sojourner who vis-

its the Sahara, learns of the *djaddias,* and finds himself honored by the
Tuareg as El-Issei-Ef.

Somehow, some way, the spirits of troubled silence had migrated to
this planet. And here, as in the Sahara, the *djaddias* could be appeased
only through silence: say but one word, and a vortex of sand would suck
you down.

At length Gurov left the forest and set off across the hot violet sand,
leaving no footprints. The sun pounded on the dunes, and when he
closed his eyes waves of blood filled his field of vision. He felt like
cursing—cursing aloud, damning Lapushkin for leaving him alone on
this horrid planet. Gurov's whole body resisted the imperative of silence
the way a suicide, descending to a river bottom, gropes to untie the stone
around his neck. For a brief instant he opened his mouth, and his larynx
began to vibrate, but then he clamped his jaws shut.

He remained on the move for many days, wandering from forest to
forest, valley to valley, plateau to plateau. The *djaddias* troubled his sleep.
Each night he dreamed he was following a party of nomads as they traveled across the dunes toward an unknown destination. Gurov's steps
were even quicker and lighter than when he was awake. The women's
hair blew wildly in the wind. The men's broad shoulders rolled as they
walked. The children sometimes broke into a run, their tanned feet flashing. Although he couldn't see their faces, Gurov knew that Averianov and
Lapushkin were among the travelers.

At last he caught up with the nomads, clutching at their billowing
robes. They stopped walking. Saying nothing, he wove through the party,
seizing each person by the shoulders and turning him toward the sun.
Gurov recoiled. The people had no faces: instead a mass of swirling fog
filled each nomad's hood—an eyeless, lipless, silent mist.

The people continued on their journey as if nothing had happened.
Gurov remained in place, tracking them with his gaze. His despair im-
mobilized him. He could heal these people, restore their faces—but only
if he could call after them, only if he could make them turn around and
come back. But even in a dream he dared not cry out.

Eventually his meanderings brought him to the *Volopas,* its nose jutting
from the violet sand, its blackened hull exhibiting a fluid grace even in a

state of rest. A solitary tree stood in the shadow of the wreck. When they first came here, Gurov had paid little attention to the local flora, but now he carefully scrutinized the tree, which rose from the very spot where Averianov had perished. The genus was unusual for this world, not a yellow-leafed pineapple but something closer to an oak. Yes, an autumn oak, with fissured bark, solid bearing, and rich red leaves.

Overwhelmed with gratitude—how wonderful to be looking at a tree so similar to those on Earth—Gurov stroked the bark. His fingers passed right through the trunk. He shuddered and grimaced, pulling his hand back. A trompe l'oeil. A mirage tree. Yet another instance of the *djaddias'* malevolence, a false marker set atop a real grave.

Gurov fled the site of Averianov's death and clambered into the ship. He explored the charred quarters and carbonized bays, soon determining that the reconnaissance craft was a complete ruin. Rummaging around, he found a section of fireproof upholstery like the one Averianov had converted into a sack, and an hour later he exited the wreck bearing a bundle of oddities: a tool kit, a portable stove, the last of the rations, and a small strongbox in which the cosmonauts had collectively stored their most valued possessions.

He was a different man now, resigned to whatever fate the silent planet might condemn him. He had made an alliance with hopelessness, a treaty with despair, and he did not care whether these new bonds strengthened him or took his life. "Life," "fate," "hope," "despair"—for the first time ever, he understood the deeper meanings of these words.

Hoisting the sack onto his shoulder, he clenched his teeth and stepped into the shadow of the tree. A second step carried him right through the oak, from one side of the trunk to the other.

Later that day, as he headed for the oasis, the sack still slung over his shoulder, his thoughts turned again to Sasha Lapushkin. "Be careful!" Lapushkin had shouted. Had he realized that "careful" would be the last word he ever spoke? What danger had he spotted in a forest that seemed so innocuous and serene? Had his fear made him delirious? Perhaps Lapushkin, unhinged by their predicament, had simply elected to kill himself, in which case he'd proved weaker than Gurov—or perhaps stronger?

Gurov wished he'd known Sasha better, and Dennis Averianov, too. The three of them had graduated from the Academy the same year, and they'd gone on many missions as a team. The constant shared dangers of life aboard a survey ship should have brought the three closer together—but instead they'd merely adapted themselves to each other like separate parts of a well-designed machine. The innermost reaches of their hearts remained inaccessible.

So his comrades were in fact strangers to him, a truth brought home as, sitting in the oasis he'd first visited with Sasha Lapushkin, he opened the strongbox and examined his modest, unintended inheritance. Lapushkin had decided to preserve a hologram album: various views of his native Krasnoyarsk, plus a dozen images of his wife and children. Gurov didn't even know their names. Dennis Averianov's choices included a golden tear-shaped stone, shining faintly in the gathering dusk—this token, Gurov recalled, was a gift from a female cosmonaut Averianov had met on Dlugalaga—plus a heavy, faceted drinking glass. Years ago Averianov had read a science fiction story about a space voyager who coveted such a tumbler, his sole connection to his native planet, and so Dennis had commissioned one just like it, emblazoned with the logo of his favorite bar back on Earth.

Most unexpected was the sheet of paper covered with a woman's handwriting, a single page from a longer letter. To which man, Lapushkin or Averianov, had the letter been addressed? Gurov couldn't guess. It lay sandwiched between two pieces of clear plastic, doubtless to spare it the ravages of time. The carefully rendered characters seemed to emerge from the plastic, pulsing with life, struggling to speak. Gurov had not seen a written letter in many years. These days few people bothered with that archaic medium; there were so many more efficient means of communication. It took a considerable effort to decipher the woman's tiny script. As he pursued the task, one particular phrase transfixed him. The author had underlined the words twice. Gurov could not tear his eyes from them.

"A birch tree, a white fox."

As the day wore on, whenever he reread the letter, taking care to keep his tongue fixed and his lips still, his gaze always went first to the phrase about the tree and the fox. It seemed luminous, and he squinted as though a bright light were flooding the oasis. Even the pleas and laments of the abandoned woman did not touch him as deeply as those six words. He imagined that when Lapushkin or Averianov had first read the letter, the talismanic phrase had instantly opened a portal to the past. In writing and then underlining the spell, the woman had somehow sought to conjure her beloved to her side. Driven by a desperate devotion, she'd tried to transport him not with a scene of love, but with a memory of nature.

What am I writing? Why am I writing? Am I afraid you'll forget? Do you remember how in the summer we used to go to the taiga? The fragrance of the grass when warmed by the sun, the way the soil was always moist and steaming after the rain, how the light dappled the ground as we walked through the forest? It seemed to you that something appeared for a moment in the thicket, fleeting, flashing, rushing swiftly away, and we went there, and we found a stand of birch trees, and their trunks were so white we couldn't touch them without our hands turning white. And you said: "A birch tree, a white fox . . ." My love!

Don't you understand that you are as good as dead for me now? You're alive, but dead. And I'm dead for you, too. Lately it's been a little easier. I've found that I can go to each place where we used to be together and leave flowers the way you leave flowers on a grave. So many graves . . .

Do you remember how we used to set sail on the Obimur each evening and watch the sunset? Gradually it got dark, and the waters flowed so languidly, looking like an iridescent scarf: sometimes a deep luxurious gray, sometimes pearly pink, with a dazzling golden streak that faded as the sun dropped behind the massive clouds. And then all the colors became mute, and died, and night fell upon the world.

Do you remember how the Obimur caressed the shore, how its waves lapped softly? We lay prone on the sand looking at the campfire, occasionally probing it with a willow branch to make the sparks fly up. Neither of us had ever seen a campfire from such a low angle, and we noticed that each spark looked like a tiny snake—a glowing head on a fiery twisting body. They were all escaping the fire, briefly eclipsing the first stars, and then the other stars came out, pouring down their pale light endlessly.

In the days that followed, Gurov read the page so many times that he learned it by heart. He imagined it had been written for him. The self-deception was pleasant, but it could not relieve his sadness, his pained realization that, when the Survey Corps announced the loss of the *Volopas*, no one would grieve for Miroslav Gurov, though his commander might wonder how he was going to replace so competent a team leader. Gurov couldn't remember his mother and father. They'd died in a crash landing when he was only two—had they somehow bequeathed their deaths to him?—and then he was sent to an orphanage for the children of cosmonauts killed in the line of duty. Throughout his youth he'd tried to be an amiable and ingratiating fellow, and during his years in space he'd often risked his life for his comrades, and they'd rescued him as well, but he'd never made any really close friends. On a survey ship, saving somebody's life wasn't proof of affection. It was merely professional habit.

What sort of woman had written the letter? He tried to picture her by systematically recalling his own lovers, but they merged into a roundelay of fleeting impressions, their eyes, faces, hairdos, clothes, voices, and gestures all blending together. And he knew that none of these women, however enchanting, would ever try rekindling a lost love through a reverie drawn from wilderness. And he himself could remember almost nothing of Earth's animals and plants, no matter how hard he tried. He could talk instead, and with great pleasure, about the peripatetic flowers of the Planet of Contradictions, and the growling trees of Planet Juhanson, and, most amazing of all, the flying fish who glided across the seas of Planet Eight in the Beta-Octopi System: while airborne each fish would shed its golden scales—molt—and upon touching the water these scales would coalesce into a newborn fish, even as the parent, now coal black, fell into the sea and died.

He played a perverse game, pretending that to secure a lover's devotion he must evoke in her mind a bird, river, flower, or tree from Earth. The exercise maddened him: he could find only the most common and inexpressive words for these things. Why had he never bothered to appreciate the flight of geese, the smell of grass, the splendor of buttercups, the grace of a linden? Gurov knew that vegetation enriched the Earth's atmosphere, but what was the essential distinction between a forest and a mechanical oxygen generator? An inflatable hut shielded you from the hot sun, but how did such a structure differ from the leafy canopy of a tree?

Gurov became lost to himself, insensate, numb. Death was ever present on the silent planet: a careless lapse into speech, a fatal tumble down a ravine—and when winter came, shriveling the fruit on the yellow-leafed trees, he might be faced with starvation. And yet the possibility of oblivion no longer troubled him. Occasionally he even found himself indifferent to his loneliness, but whenever this happened he fought it, renewing the pain of his solitude. His longing for companionship was the only thing that sustained him, kept him human, and so he dwelled obsessively on his fallen friends, to one of whom those wondrous words had been written, "A birch tree, a white fox."

Dreams of deliverance filled his sleep, and his waking hours, too—and, indeed, it was not inconceivable that the Survey Corps would dispatch a rescue mission. Time and again he imagined a spaceship appearing in the green sky, a fantasy so real that he would freeze in his tracks and stare crazily upward, certainly presenting a curious spectacle to any hypothetical observer.

If a ship really did come, of course, Gurov would be obligated to warn the crew to keep their lips sealed. How might he accomplish this? Eventually he resolved to identify suitable landing sites, dramatically augmenting the terrain with an appropriate message.

He began by marking a wide flat valley that fell away to the east of the forest where Lapushkin had died. The urgent words must be gigantic, he decided, easily visible from the air. It took him a whole week of sweating, gasping effort, but at last he'd gathered together hundreds of large stones and arranged them to form letters.

KEEP SILENT! HUMAN VOICES BRING DEATH!

His task accomplished, he ascended to the rim of the basin and looked down at his work. To his horror, he saw not distinct words but only a series of zigzag ridges.

As he staggered away from the valley, he could not hold back his tears. The sun was scorching, and the coolness of the yellow-leafed trees beckoned.

Entering the forest, he came upon a gaunt tree, its branches drooping despondently. It looked like—a maple? Yes, an Earth maple, its leaves shaped like stars, all of them brown and withered. To be sure, a maple rising beside a stream in Russia would scarcely recognize this forlorn creature as its brother, but Gurov, awash in nostalgia, saw the similarity.

He reached toward the sorrowful maple, hoping to pluck one of its pathetic leaves. His fingers moved through the bough as though it were smoke. Another mirage tree, another phantom on a planet of phantoms, right down to the false shadow: in this terrible place even the ephemera were illusory. Gurov ground his teeth, almost giving voice to his rage.

Unable to summon sufficient energy for returning to the valley and rebuilding the message, he decided to find another likely landing site. A half day's walk brought him to a vast plateau rising from the violet dunes, its southern edge overshadowed by a huge slab of sedimentary rock, an ideal tablet on which to inscribe his warning. He opened the tool kit, took out the laser drill, and got to work. The battery went dead just as he finished cutting the second exclamation point.

KEEP SILENT! HUMAN VOICES BRING DEATH!

"Life," "fate," "hope," "despair"—such valuable words, and now he remembered one more, "miracle." There was nothing for Gurov to do now but wait for a miracle.

And then one day the miracle happened. At first Gurov thought he was hallucinating—but no, in the dim distance he saw a spaceship, descending toward the vital inscription. Gurov wheezed and gasped as he scrambled up the side of the plateau. Reaching the top, he dropped to his knees and prostrated himself on the flat surface in a gesture of supplication. The ship floated directly above him. Gurov rose, crossed the plateau, and positioned himself before the slab, pressing a finger to his lips.

As the ship touched down, he studied the insignia on its hull, concluding that this was a shuttlecraft from a Geological Institute vessel evidently now orbiting the planet. Despite himself, he experienced a twinge of snobbishness. These travelers weren't real cosmonauts. They were dilettantes in space.

The hatch opened, and the gangway emerged—not toward Gurov, but along a path parallel to the slab. No! When the geologists walked into the daylight, they wouldn't see the warning. No! No! Studying the landscape, they would start trading inane observations—"Look, green sky!" "Ah, purple sand!"—and then the *djaddias* would claim them.

Already two unhelmeted figures were striding down the gangway, one with dark close-cropped hair, the other with long blond tresses. A man and a woman. How could he get to them in time?

Now they were taking their first swallows of air on the strange planet, getting ready to . . .

No! No!

He stood up straight, closed his eyes, and, gesturing frantically toward the inscription, released a shout.

In the moment that followed, which seemed to last forever, Miroslav Gurov experienced the incarnate bliss of the spoken word. The sweet honey of articulation rose from his throat and warmed his mouth. His skin luxuriated beneath the rays of the sun. The wind touched his moist face, bringing from an unknown land the scent of a river and the rustle of grass, and then it blew against his palms, bearing something cool, smooth, silky, silver, like birch bark.

•   •   •

They dared to speak only after they'd fastened every hatch and sealed every viewport, so their voices wouldn't carry outside the ship.

"What was it?" Elissa rasped. "What happened?" Her face was pale. Shadows lay beneath her eyes.

Antonov squeezed her shoulder. "He saved us. If it weren't for him . . ."

Suddenly aware that his hands were trembling, he brought his arms behind his back and clenched his fists, trying to calm himself.

"He did what it took to draw our attention to the message," Antonov continued, "and to prove it wasn't a joke."

Elissa asked, "Who was he? Why did he choose those words?"

Antonov grew silent. He, too, did not understand the significance of the stranger's shout. But apparently the phrase meant a great deal to the man who'd prevented their deaths—otherwise why would he seize upon those particular words, when there were so many ways a man might issue a warning or express a final feeling of hope, despair, joy, loss, love?

"We'd better call the *Nevski*," Antonov said at last, taking Elissa's hand. "There may be other survivors here."

They went to the bridge and dispatched their report to the orbiting vessel. Three hours later they received a reply. The *Nevski* had reached a Survey Corps cruiser, whose captain speculated that Antonov and Elissa had encountered a cosmonaut from the missing *Volopas*. The Corps would send a rescue ship in case the other two crewmen were still alive.

The day dragged on. They exchanged but a few words. The fear of speaking had not fully left them.

Elissa wondered exactly what the cosmonaut had experienced when the vortex came. Anguish and terror? Then why had his smile hovered so long in the trembling air?

She pressed her face against the nearest viewport. A moment later Antonov joined her.

The cosmonaut had been standing right there, next to the engraved warning, precisely where the slender white tree now rose—was it in fact what it appeared to be, a birch tree from Earth?—casting its slanted quivering shadow, as though rushing swiftly away.

"It really does look like a white fox," Antonov said.

VALERIO EVANGELISTI

SEPULTURA

TRANSLATED FROM THE ITALIAN
BY SERGIO D. ALTIERI

Beginning with Dante Alighieri and The Divine Comedy, *Italian literature has gifted its aficionados with fabulous journeys to fantastic worlds. Despite this legacy, or perhaps because of it, science fiction in Italy has rarely garnered even the begrudging critical acceptance accorded the genre in other European countries. C. P. Snow's famous dichotomy between "the two cultures," humanist and scientific, has always enjoyed a particular gravitas among Italian intellectuals, with genre SF being perceived as largely a matter of gadgetry and instrumentalism, palatable only to mathematicians, physicists, biochemists, and engineers.*

Some scholars have argued that the insular condition of Italy's speculative literature is reflected in the lack of any term in the language corresponding precisely to the English label "science fiction." The first Italian SF magazine was called Scienza fantastica, *"Fantastic Science," founded in 1952, and to this day critics and fans refer to the genre as* fantascienza.

For a phenomenon routinely consigned to the ghetto of the ghetto, Italian science fiction actually has much to show for itself, as documented lovingly and scrupulously by Vittorio Curtoni in Le frontiere dell'ignoto *("Frontiers of the Unknown," 1977). Among the more recent works to have generated critical excitement are Lino Aldani's* Quando le radici *("When the Roots," 1977), set in a near future Italy of dehumanizing technology and redemptive gypsies; Luca Masali's* I biplani di D'Annunzio *("D'Annunzio's Biplanes," 1996), an SF vision of World War I featuring time travel and virtual reality; Massimo Mongai's* Memorie di un cuoco d'astronave *("Memoirs of a Starship Cook," 1997), a compendium of* the culinary hero's interstellar adventures; and Mario Farneti's Occidente ("The West," 2001), an alternative history in which Mussolini never allied with Hitler and Italian fascism persists into the seventies.

Valerio Evangelisti's "Sepultura" is a searing work of fantascienza, a story in which, against the odds, rational extrapolation and magic realism harmoniously inhabit the same fictive universe. Initially Evangelisti displays a recognizable SF sensibility, delineating a repressive society that exploits cyanoacrylic glue to incapacitate dissidents and insurgents. Before long, however, we are drawn into a very different world, pagan, mystical, and demonic. Eventually the two idioms fuse in a vivid and vertiginous climax.

Born in 1952, Evangelisti grew up in Bologna and taught for several years at the local university, during which interval he wrote books on modern and contemporary history. In 1994, the success of his first novel, Nicolas Eymerich, inquisitore ("Nicholas Eymerich, Inquisitor"), inspired him to become a professional writer. Thus far he has written sixteen SF, fantasy, and historical novels, eight of them about Eymerich, a fourteenth-century heresy-hunter whose historical cruelties reverberate in the present as well as the future. His work has been translated throughout Europe, as well as in Israel and Brazil, and the Eymerich series won both the Grand Prix de l'Imaginaire and the Prix Tour Eiffel. When not living in Bologna, the author can often be found having adventures in Puerto Escondido, Mexico. He contributes frequently to Le Monde Diplomatique, writes scripts for television, film, radio, and comics, and edits Carmilla, a Web zine devoted to literature and politics.

Beyond his use of Umbanda deities, we suspect that in "Sepultura" Evangelisti is also drawing energy from his country's greatest poet. On first encountering the mired inmates of his hellish São Paulo penitentiary, we immediately thought of the fate that Dante inflicted on the flatterers of Circle viii: "I saw a people smothered in a filth / That out of human privies seemed to flow." But Evangelisti's implanted prisoners are merely the first in the cavalcade of startling images that make "Sepultura" such a memorable experiment in political, psychological, and metaphysical fantascienza.

As Fernando Cuadros gave him the address of the favela, the taxi driver raised an eyebrow but made no comment. It took them almost forty-five minutes to reach the city limits of São Paulo. The shantytown sprawled across a trash-strewn hilltop, its multiple levels connected by wooden ladders. Nondescript metal huts, collapsing brick hovels, plywood shacks—even a few canvas tents, their sides held fast by large stones. Decrepit chalets in a decaying Switzerland.

Carefully watching his footing, Fernando climbed the ladders, their rungs creaking ominously. At the summit a friendly hand seized his briefcase and helped him onto the primitive deck.

"Hello, Lieutenant!" the kid exclaimed. He was no more than twenty, his skin astonishingly dark. "I've been expecting you."

The young operative escorted Fernando inside the largest hovel, its solitary brick wall supporting partitions of corrugated tin. Gradually his eyes adjusted to the gloom.

"How'd you know I'd be here today?" Fernando asked gruffly as the black kid guided him into the kitchen. *Armenio,* he remembered—the kid's name was Armenio.

"Internet." Armenio pointed to a computer on the table, its CRT pulsing with a screen saver. "Don't worry, sir. We send and receive all messages using PGP encryption. Government can't begin to decipher 'em."

"Three cheers for technology," Fernando sneered. He dropped onto a rattan couch and, unbuttoning his shirt collar, rubbed the thick hair sprouting along his neck. "One of these days they'll invent a computer game called *Revolución.* You kids'll play it all day, and the hell with the real thing."

Armenio took two cans from a refrigerator filled with nothing but beer, then shook his curly head. "Excuse me, Lieutenant, but I think technology has a lot to offer us." He handed Fernando one beer, popped the other open for himself. "Last month somebody hacked into the main computer of a Japanese penitentiary, and before anybody knew what'd happened, two prisoners escaped."

"I must be getting old. I'd rather shake up a prison with a bomb than a keyboard."

"Sometimes a keyboard works better." Armenio grinned and guzzled some beer. "I'm not saying we should become a bunch of geeks, but we gotta keep up with the times—that's what me and my buddies think."

Fernando shrugged, making no attempt to hide his skepticism. "Down to business. What's the latest on Olavo Cuadros?"

The question caught the kid off guard. His beer went down the wrong way, and he spat out an amber mist. "I thought you never wanted to hear your brother's name again."

"I asked you a question."

"Okay, sure. Olavo's with the Weed Rippers now. The Ministry of Security pays him a lot more than he ever made on the police force."

Fernando scowled. Old news. "Keep talking."

The kid grew uneasy, hesitating a few beats. "When the Rippers abducted Mario Ferreira last month, they handed him over to Olavo. Everybody says it was your brother who used the melt on Mario."

A shiver ran down Fernando's spine. He remembered all too well the moment he and the other guerrillas found the thing that had once been Mario Ferreira. Mario wasn't really a revolutionary—merely a malcontent, and not a particularly obnoxious one at that. Some of Fernando's comrades had vomited. Others simply stared in disbelief at the wreckage before their eyes. Fernando had instantly made a pledge to himself: he would kill the fucker who'd done this. But now he needed that very person.

"You really think it was Olavo?" he whispered in a hoarse voice.

"There weren't any witnesses, but Mario was in Olavo's custody at the time, and obviously the Rippers had taught your brother how to use the melt."

"You're a good spy, Armenio." Fernando set his beer on the floor and pressed his thumbs against his temples, as if to quell a sudden headache. He raised his head with considerable effort. "In Buenos Aires my superiors told me about a major operation. They want to free all the Sepultura inmates in one big break. It's been in the works for almost a year, and the whole thing turns on the melt. Evidently the continental commander was right when he said Olavo could get it for us."

"What's the melt got to do with a prison break?" the kid said.

"Glad you asked. If you can't figure it out, the government probably won't either. So now I need to track down my brother."

Armenio raised his eyebrows. "Aren't you *indios* into Macumba and shit like that these days? Maybe you'll find him at some weird-ass religious ceremony."

The kid meant Umbanda, but basically he knew what he was talking about. After the Kayova massacre, most of the survivors had converted to Umbanda. But not Olavo.

"My brother was never a joiner," Fernando said.

"Then the only way to get in touch with him is through a friend. He have any?"

"Well, there's Tancredo. He's *indio*, too—half *indio*, at least. Olavo and Tancredo and me, we grew up together—Tancredo's one of *us* now, but I don't know where he's hiding out."

"Sounds like a job for . . . technology." The kid sat down at the computer screen, began tapping the keyboard. A moment later he smiled broadly, showing blinding white teeth. "Tancredo Passarinho, is that him?"

Fernando nodded. "Passarinho is his Kayova name—I doubt that he still uses it."

"He got slammed into Sepultura three years ago." Armenio still stared at the screen. "They arrested him with another Kayova, Apolonio Teizeira, a common criminal." His smile disappeared. "They're in the same block. The one where . . . you know."

"Apolonio . . ." Fernando closed his eyes slightly, relaxing against the back of the couch. "I remember Apolonio—another pal of Olavo's. A bully, a street punk. And now—"

"And now he's in Sepultura," Armenio interrupted, "begging them to let him die."

2

"One day I'll kill you, even though you're my brother. No, as a matter of fact, I'll kill you *because* you're my brother."

What most impressed Olavo Cuadros was the bantering voice in which Fernando spoke the death threat. If Fernando's tone had matched his words, of course, he would've attracted the attention of the other patrons. It was a sleazy place, but popular with certain members of the upper classes. Hushed conversations and soft laughter were the norm. No outburst went unnoticed.

Olavo maintained his grin, kept it firm. "You'll *kill* me? Sure, little brother, unless I do you first."

"Ah, so we agree on the basic principle," Fernando said. "The day we *really* meet, one of us has to die."

"Right. Only it won't be me."

Fernando straightened his tie. He obviously hated being stuffed into elegant clothes, but the restaurant required them. "But here and now we're talking about something else. Your friends. Our people."

"Our pathetic nonexistent people," Olavo said with a sneer. He finished wolfing down his beefsteak, then checked out an almost bare-assed girl sashaying among the tables, offering the customers cigarettes. "You're sure Tancredo's in Sepultura?"

"Positive. Apolonio, too. Tancredo has a way of communicating with *indios* on the outside—very bizarre, but it works. That's how I tracked you down."

"Tancredo going over to your crazy *revolución*—who would've guessed it?" Olavo pushed the steak bone around on his plate. "I would've bet on Apolonio instead. You really think you can break 'em out?"

Fernando nodded. "An unexpected piece of . . . scientific information fell into my lap. We need the melt—"

"The *melt*?"

"Plus some way to sneak it inside Sepultura. Rumor has it you can solve both problems for us. You have access to the melt, and you're buddies with a guard named Leonel."

"I suppose I've heard wilder rumors in my time."

"Get us the melt, Olavo, and both your *indio* friends will walk free, along with a hundred others."

Olavo poured himself a glass of California burgundy. He emptied it in one swallow, as if it were mineral water. "I'm not saying no, but I'm not saying yes either. Something as risky as this—you'd better have it planned down to the last detail."

Without warning, Fernando reached out and clamped a hand around his brother's hairy wrist. "Stop pretending you don't believe in anything, Olavo," he said, voice quavering. "You haven't changed *that* much."

"Cigarettes, gents?" It was the girl carrying the tobacco tray, a brunette sporting a radiant smile.

Olavo welcomed the interruption. He laughed. "No, sweetie. Turn around a bit."

He took the girl's arm and turned her ass toward him. He fondled her buns, making her shudder, then stiffened his fingers and gave her a painful pinch. The girl squealed and ran off, scattering cigarette packs everywhere. Disapproving mumbles wafted over from the other tables, but no one bothered to intervene.

Olavo laughed again. *"That's* what I believe in, Fernando. The rewards of power. The girlie perks."

Again Fernando grabbed his brother's wrist. "You believe in something else, too."

Olavo broke the grip, putting his hands under the table so Fernando wouldn't see them tremble. He hated it when his brother got worked up about the Kayova.

"I'm Kayova, sure," he said. "I've never denied it."

"The break will happen four nights from now. Plenty of time for you to get the melt and pass it to the kid."

"It won't be easy. The Rippers guard the stuff like gold."

"I'm sure you'll manage." Fernando lifted the burgundy bottle to the light, squinting to see if it still held any wine. He emptied the last few drops into his glass. "You'll be impressed by the diversion we've cooked up, a direct attack on the prison. Nobody will notice what your pal Leonel is up to."

Olavo frowned severely, but he made no reply. "We'd better ask for the check," he muttered. "Of course it's on me."

Fernando set both hands on the table, palms down. "I meant what I said. One day I'll have to kill you."

Olavo forced a smile. "You'll never get the chance. After the Sepultura break, your enemies will say to themselves, 'That Fernando, he might be ratshit, but he's *clever* ratshit. It's time we blew him away.'"

"Ratshit?" Fernando crumpled the tablecloth with his fists. He seemed ready to tear it in two. "You and your Ripper pals hunt down innocent kids!" His voice cracked. "My brother is a Kayova who kills children!"

Olavo wanted to leave, the sooner the better. "Listen, Fernando—I do my job, you do yours. In the end, we're both murderers."

"All right, sure, we're both murderers. But for next four days we're both Kayova, too. Agreed?"

"Look at your shirt, little brother. It's drenched with sweat. I can smell it from here. You need some cool night air."

3

It happened six times a day, every day, at the precise moment the guard opened the hatch and appeared on the steel catwalk suspended high above the pit: the inmates released furious screams.

Apolonio Teizeira lifted his tattooed arms, clenching his fists until his joints creaked. He simultaneously twisted those parts of his body—arms, shoulders, trunk—that emerged from the solidified glue, as if intending to climb out and go for a walk. An absurd idea, of course: his legs, plunged into the intractable ectoplasm that sealed his body up to the waist, had atrophied long ago.

Shouts and curses flew across the vat, echoing off the moist iron walls. Usually at this juncture the five guards would mock the inmates with insults of their own. If already drunk, they would rain down spit and urine on the naked human torsos planted in the glue, the descending liquids glimmering in the light emanating from the open hatch. This evening, however, the guard simply took turns sweeping a flashlight beam through the darkness of the pit, aiming it at one inmate after another.

When the beam hit Apolonio, he screamed even louder. His fingers clawed at the air, as if mangling an invisible enemy's face. But he wasn't the one the guards wanted to harass. The shaft of light shifted to his friend Tancredo, a half *indio* like Apolonio, now straining to pull free of the glue, a pathetic howl breaking from his throat. The beam sliced past Tancredo and settled on the other political prisoners, forcing them to close their eyes: first Feliciano, then Miro, then Gomes.

Mired a few feet from Apolonio, Ulysses vented his impotent rage. Apolonio stretched forward and, reaching out, touched Ulysses's black brawny back.

"Something must be happening outside!" Apolonio spoke loudly enough to make himself heard over the roar of the hundred and fifteen furious voices.

Ulysses kept waving his fists toward the catwalk. "Something serious, yeah!" he answered without turning around. "Moises always said the *revolución* would get here sooner than we imagined!" He resumed shouting, his whole body now trembling as if possessed.

Old Moises's skeletal frame writhed in the ectoplasm on the far side of the vat. He was the sole survivor of the prison riot that had convulsed Carandiru, Latin America's most formidable penitentiary, on October 2, 1992. The government had turned the Carandiru uprising into a bloodbath: eighty inmates slaughtered, scores more wounded. Moises was found beneath a pile of corpses, his left leg a tangled mass of bullet wounds. Two panicky paramedics had proceeded to amputate it then and there, even as the searchlight beams flooded Carandiru and the walls resounded with the sirens' piercing wail. Now the ectoplasm gripped Moises's remaining leg, while the badly sutured stump rested on the sticky surface.

Sepultura, São Paulo's maximum security prison, had been built in response to the Carandiru riot. A few years later, cyanoacrylic glue was developed as an aid to surgery: the adhesive was ideal for closing wounds and staunching hemorrhages. But soon some fertile minds in the Brazilian government came up with a novel application. These geniuses found that, when combined with elastine, cyanoacrylic glue became a kind of synthetic flesh that fused seamlessly with human tissue—a pulsing, breathing, organic extension of any person unfortunate enough to touch it. The government picked Moises for the initial test. The chemical quickly subsumed his remaining leg, trapping him in the great frozen lake of glue. For the first six months he was the pit's only prisoner, alone in the cold darkness. The ectoplasm absorbed his excretions—feces, urine, sweat—combining their molecules with its own. Then two more inmates were locked in the rigid soup. Both went insane, dying of despair. But Moises was crazy to begin with, and so he survived, raging against but never defeating the glue, inadvertently assuring the government that the new constraint system worked perfectly.

"You gonna cut that shit out or what, you fuckers?" Sergeant Macheran's raspy voice, made louder by a bullhorn, sounded less confident than usual. "One of these nights I'll stop feeding you—I'll let you rot in the muck."

On a normal evening the guards liked to indulge in their favorite pastime: instead of lowering the dinner baskets on ropes, they would reach inside, grab the prisoners' food, and, taking careful aim, pelt the mired men with bones, bread, and pieces of meat. Careening off the inmates' backs and chests, most of the food fell out of reach; the guards loved to watch the men flail about grotesquely in quest of the scraps. Finally, the guards would dump a few buckets of drinking water on the prisoners' heads.

But this evening none of that happened. The baskets were lowered smoothly, and Apolonio easily grabbed one. He pulled out a piece of meat and a loaf of stale bread, passing them to Ulysses, who was still turned around, cursing the guards. Apolonio stared in amazement at the remaining food. He had obtained it much too easily.

No doubt about it—somebody was causing really serious trouble outside.

A few minutes later the guards retrieved the baskets, then switched off the flashlight and retreated through the hatch. Again darkness filled the pit. The shouts became whispers, soon fading into silence. Only Tancredo's gut-wrenching scream echoed for a moment longer, as disturbing as a cry from a tomb.

4

Olavo Cuadros joined the Weed Rippers as they climbed the snaking stone path toward the favela shanties ranged along the hill. Making no sound, they headed toward the feeble glow of the campfires that, higher up, flickered outside the huts, shacks, hovels, and tents, just beyond the mounds of trash.

Chagas adjusted the focus on his infrared scope. "Got 'em. The little ones, they're three years old, some maybe four. The others—twelve, thirteen. No sentries, only dogs."

Murmurs of satisfaction wafted through the Weed Rippers. The Ministry of Security paid one thousand *cruzeiros* for the severed head of a child under six, eight hundred for the head of a school-age boy. There was plenty of easy money gathered around those campfires.

As the rest of the group slipped past him, Olavo thought about the phone conversation he'd had with Fernando that morning. He heaved a sigh, distressed by the thought of betraying his comrades. Before he'd become a Ripper, Olavo had spent seven years on the police force, so murdering children didn't seem particularly novel or wrong to him—whenever those little shits weren't snorting themselves into a stupor, they were stealing anything they could lay their hands on: letting them grow up merely meant breeding a new generation of thieves, as if the city didn't have enough of those already. No, sympathy for urchins had nothing to do with why Olavo was now determined to fire his assault rifle at the heads of Chagas and the others.

The reason was Tancredo, and Tancredo was reason enough. Like Olavo, Tancredo had Kayova blood in his veins—probably even more than Olavo. And that blood had moved Tancredo to action. A few years after he'd left the tribe, thousands of Kayova, nearly the whole population, had committed suicide in an unthinkable protest against the government's invasion of their ancient *terreiro*. Shocked and appalled, Tancredo had immediately grabbed a shotgun and taken up a position outside a police station, opening fire on every cop who came in or out. Olavo, a cop himself, had not appreciated Tancredo's choice of target, but he fully understood the man's rage.

"Great, they've got no defenses," Chagas whispered. "Remember: keep the heads intact."

In the past twelve hours, Olavo's opinion of Chagas had plummeted to a new low, even as his begrudging respect for Fernando had increased. The melt wasn't inside Sepultura yet—hell, it wasn't even in the insurgents' hands—and yet Fernando had gone ahead and ordered his men to fire on the prison: *that's* how much confidence he had in Olavo.

Little brother, you picked the right *indio*.

The narrow blood-red beams of the Rippers' laser scopes sliced through the gloom. A girl in a tattered smock sat next to a dog much bigger than she. She stared in amazement at the little crimson dot skittering across her chest. An instant later, a .308-caliber slug drilled through her lungs.

The pack of dogs went for the attackers. Two overlapping bursts of full-auto gunfire were enough to cut the animals to ribbons. A few kids tried to run for it. The high-speed bullets mowed them down. Most of the survivors simply stood motionless, watching the dancing laser beams in a sort of enchanted stupor.

But death didn't come for them that night. Instead three rounds slammed into the back of Chagas's head, disintegrating it like a ripe melon. Chagas's comrade Jorge was hit next, in the back, the impact throwing him to the ground. When the Rippers realized where the bullets were coming from, they whipped around to return fire. Too late. Olavo's Famas G2 was a powerful weapon—powerful enough to demolish a truck piece by piece. It took him just fifteen seconds to silence the Ripper guns.

Olavo's clip was empty. Calmly he reloaded. The children had fled. A dog yelped desperately. The full moon illuminated the corpses of the six Rippers lying in the trash. Olavo shifted the rifle's action to single shot, then put a coup de grâce into each head. The hundreds of derelicts huddling inside the shacks must have heard the din of the skirmish, but nobody dared show his face.

Olavo walked down the hill, keeping his weapon aimed at the few shabby windows set within the walls of wood and metal. There was enough moonlight for him to maintain a fast pace. All around him, except for the distant barking, the favela was silent as a graveyard. He reached the Rippers' van, opened the back door, grunted in satisfaction. The object of his search protruded from beneath a seat. Fernando and his friends would be happy. He slammed the door and walked to the front of the van. He tossed his emptied rifle inside, then got behind the wheel.

5

Sleeping in the ectoplasm was an ordeal, but every inmate had to endure it. Only one technique worked: lean forward, bend your back, and rest your head on your forearms. At first Apolonio had found the procedure unbearable. The contorted posture, plus the freezing air of the pit—only an extremely low temperature would keep the cyanoacrylic glue in a solid state—sent excruciating pains through his bones. But after a few months in the vat, even this torment had acquired a bizarre normalcy.

Tonight, however, no one was sleeping. The one hundred and fifteen despairing men, blacks for the most part, kept their ears wide open, hoping to catch any noises coming from the watchtowers and the sprawling junkyard and the stinking favela beyond. At one point they thought they heard gunfire. But how to be sure? The walls of the pit muffled every sound.

"I think Tancredo got a message out last month," whispered Ulysses. "Another one yesterday."

"Maybe that has something to do with the gunfire," Apolonio said.

Once again he found himself admiring Old Moises's cleverness in encouraging everyone to scream whenever the guards opened the hatch. Usually the guards made no attempt to silence them. Why should they care whether the existence of the pit and the suffering of its occupants was broadcast far and wide? The glue hadn't been conceived primarily as the ultimate in prisoner control—first and foremost, it was a deterrent. Every dissident, every insurgent, every criminal knew that the voracious ectoplasm was there, waiting to swallow his legs. True, the human rights organizations periodically lodged formal complaints, but Brazil's leaders sneered at them, just as they'd sneered at the protests that had followed the Carandiru massacre. The government had acknowledged only eight dead after Carandiru, though the photographs and the witnesses attested to a slaughter ten times that large.

After all, it was more convenient for the global community if the status quo remained unchanged in Brazil. Butchering Amazon *indios*, hunting down street kids, torturing political prisoners, jailing protesters—none of these things happened, not really. If occasionally an amnesty group heard the screams that issued from Sepultura six times a day, its members would find no international forum in which to express their dismay. To be sure, a powerful government would on occasion formally accuse another nation of human rights violations—but only when the atrocity in question somehow threatened to disturb the new international order.

Moises's brilliant idea had been to make the chorus of screams and moans a regular event, so that Tancredo, the loudest *indio* in the vat, could occasionally weave a Kayova chant into the cacophony without arousing suspicion, altering the words to create a secret message for his fellow tribesmen on the outside. Even if Tancredo's listeners couldn't catch every syllable, they would get the basic meaning.

Thanks to a couple of sympathetic guards, the prisoners knew that some *indios* beyond Sepultura occasionally heard their messages. Unfortunately, the inmates' one true ally, the young guard Leonel, was rarely able to pass replies along, for the ever-vigilant Sergeant Macheran closely scrutinized his men as they stood on the catwalk. Only when some emergency disrupted the prison, sending Macheran and company scrambling down the corridors and along the outer ramparts, could Leonel furtively relay a message from the outside world. In the last three years that had happened a mere seven times.

"Is this the night, Moises?" Apolonio asked. "Is this the night the *revolución* comes to Sepultura?"

"Tell us, Moises," said Gomes.

Moises reached toward the stump of his leg, lifted it an inch from the surface of the glue, then set it down in a slightly different position. "Three months ago Leonel tossed me a crumpled note," the crazy old man said. "I opened it, read it, ate it."

"What did it say?" Feliciano demanded.

"The continental commander has had his eye on Sepultura for almost a year." Moises's voice became suddenly nonchalant. "Anybody here know what the melt is?"

No one answered, but everyone knew. Apolonio sensed a collective shudder pass through the men in the ectoplasm. The melt: quite likely the worst torture ever conceived. A pressure-activated polymer called phenilalanine was mixed with ATP phosphate and injected into a prisoner's vein. Coursing through his blood, the compound radically increased the victim's body temperature. Instantly his muscles distended to twice normal size, only to shrink again at the same blinding speed. The tortured man would watch his limbs elongate suddenly, then contract into stumps, then elongate again. The pain was unimaginable. When it reached his brain, the fiery polymer turned the neurons to a boiling mush. Throughout the ordeal, a uniformed torturer would promise the prisoner an antidote—if he would simply name his fellow conspirators or admit to a crime. But in fact there was no antidote. Insane with agony and terror, many victims screamed out false confessions. In the end, the guards buried the prisoner's remains, now a shapeless tangle of mutilated tissue.

Needless to say, the Brazilian government never employed the procedure overtly. Instead they used the Weed Rippers. Every Ripper team carried a few vials of phenilalanine-ATP, and they rarely hesitated to use it on insurgents and *desaparecidos*—all of this despite the fact that dealing in the polymer was strictly prohibited, a severely punished crime.

Before finding his voice, Apolonio had to swallow several times. "Why the fuck you talking about the melt? If they wanted to torture us that way, they would've done it already."

"The melt destroys elastine as well as flesh," Moises said.

Apolonio couldn't see Moises's face, but he imagined the old man was grinning.

"It really destroys elastine?" Gomes said.

Moises said, "You didn't know that?"

6

Fernando scanned the junkyard, watching as his men, dressed in camouflage fatigues, squatted just outside the barbed-wire fence, taking cover behind the rusting frames of derelict automobiles. They unleashed a few more volleys toward Sepultura's thick hulking walls. From the nearest watchtower a .50-caliber Browning machine gun returned their fire, the armor-piercing tracers painting yellow-orange streaks across the night.

Fernando knew perfectly well that Sepultura lay beyond the range of their assault rifles: the point wasn't to pick off guards, but to force them to call for reinforcements. With the back of his hand he wiped the sweat from his forehead, dirtying his skin with black camouflage paint. He checked his watch. Where the hell was Olavo? Ten more minutes, maybe less, and the Brazilian army would swoop down on them like vultures. He squinted into the night, uncertain whether to order a retreat. A searchlight beam sliced through the darkness. Fernando glimpsed a human shape running in a half-crouch among the skeletal cars, trying to avoid the tracer bullets from the watchtowers. Olavo, he thought, sighing in relief.

When his brother was only two yards from the insurgents' position, Fernando darted out and dragged him to the ground. "Olavo, you dumb fuck! Get down, or we'll be slaughtered like pigs!"

Olavo's lips lifted in a hard smile. "I got the stuff."

"News of the century. Has the kid shown up yet?"

Olavo shook his head. "It's just a matter of waiting—I'm sure Macheran has called in every last guard on the payroll. Did you visit the *babalao*?"

"I left his shack at dusk."

Olavo gestured impatiently toward the blackness all around them. "Go. Now. And may God bless your motherfucking *revolución*."

Fernando glowered at Olavo, then leaped to his feet. "Move out!" he shouted, waving his M-16. "Move out!" His men backed away from their positions, sliding into the night. Before taking off himself, Fernando squeezed his brother's shoulder. "We're even now. You got us the melt, and your friends are about to walk free."

"Yeah, if they can still walk," Olavo muttered as the darkness claimed Fernando.

More Browning tracers streamed from Sepultura, puncturing the corroded car bodies. Olavo clung to the ground, arms around his head, swarms of shattered glass and squalls of metal splinters flying everywhere. A few seconds later the barrel of a Galil assault rifle rammed his spine, right between the shoulder blades.

"Hey, we got one of 'em!" barked a voice both angry and satisfied.

So: the fucking army had arrived. Instead of turning on his back, Olavo pushed his face closer to the earth. "I'm not who you think," he said, controlling his voice, projecting calm. "I'm a Weed Ripper, fully authorized by the São Paulo Ministry of Security. I've got my ID on me."

"Listen to this asshole!" the soldier replied, addressing unseen companions. Olavo heard running footsteps, coming closer and closer. "If you're a Ripper, what're you doin' here?"

"I heard gunfire, so I thought I'd give you guys some backup." Cautiously Olavo lifted his head. "Just performing my patriotic duty."

The barrel of the Galil retreated, but only slightly. "Show me this famous ID of yours." The soldier's voice—all Olavo could see were his combat boots—dripped with hostility.

Olavo reached into the back pocket of his pants, pulled out his ID. He lifted the metal badge as slowly as possible. The soldier jerked it out of his hand.

A seeming eternity went by. "All right, you're cool," the soldier finally said, still hostile. "Get up and stay alert." He tossed the badge on the ground and walked away.

Olavo scrambled to his feet. The army was reconnoitering the entire junkyard, checking every vehicle. The searchlight beams kept flashing from the watchtowers, their blinding glare sweeping across the heaps of trash toward the favela. The shooting had stopped, but that didn't matter—the guards were certain to keep manning the walls for another hour at least.

Olavo rushed away from the junkyard and, hiding in the shadows, made his way along the outer ramparts toward the huge pylons flanking the prison entrance. A large truck rumbled into view, stopping before the gate. Twenty men in civilian clothes climbed out of the bay: Sergeant Macheran's reinforcements. Most of the guards were dressed haphazardly. Some cursed through their teeth. The twin portals pivoted slowly, creaking and groaning, and the sleepy men started stumbling into the prison yard.

Olavo approached one of them, a bony youth with hollow features. "Hello, Leonel."

The kid tossed him a bewildered look. "Whoa, what the hell ya doin' here, man? They wanted you Rippers on the scene, too?"

Olavo didn't answer. He dug a hand into a pocket of his field jacket, pulled out the cloth-wrapped package, passed it to Leonel. "Get this to Tancredo," he muttered gruffly. "Now."

"Now?" Leonel was flabbergasted. "How the hell—?"

"Don't think about it, kid, just do it. All the guards are on the walls."

Leonel opened his mouth as if to argue some more. But he didn't say anything. He grabbed the wrapped object, quickly stuffed it underneath his shirt. "So the attack was just a ploy?" he muttered.

"Hey, we've got a real bright guy here." Olavo's expression softened. He slapped the kid on the back. "Good luck."

Olavo turned and started away, leaving the prison almost at a run. The night was young, and he had another call to make.

7

Down in the pit no one spoke. Apolonio tried to fend off the cold by wrapping his arms around his bare chest. He reflected on Moises's words. Evidently the melt polymer attacked elastine, and elastine was indeed a component of the ectoplasm—but that didn't mean the melt could free them. The damn glue was an extension of their skin, blended with its very molecules. Not surprisingly, when an inmate died, his body could only be removed through a chain saw connected to a gantry. In a matter of minutes the spinning blade would carve a rectangular solid from the glue surrounding the corpse, after which the guards abruptly winched the entire block free of the vat—quite a contrast to the lengthy and elaborate immersion process. Somewhere in the universe there might be a substance that dissolved the glue without destroying the at-tached flesh, but the melt polymer wasn't it. The stuff was potent but hardly magical.

And yet Apolonio was not without hope. Moises's grand scheme, his crazy idea of lacing the daily screaming rituals with messages from Tan-credo, had spawned within Apolonio a dream that had never died. This dream had enabled him to survive three years of demonic torments. As more years went by, would he continue to elude despair? Doubtful. It was as if he held in his hands the eroded stump of a burning candle, fearful that his own mournful sighs would snuff the flame.

The silence deepened. The longer it continued, the more anxious Apolonio and the other prisoners became. Suddenly, high up, the hatch opened, bathing the catwalk in pale light, and everyone flinched as a shadowy human form started along the little bridge.

Apolonio recognized their visitor. It was Leonel, the young guard who acted as a go-between connecting the vat to the larger world. Occa-sionally Leonel would drop a crumpled note near Moises's stump, or mutter a Kayova spell that the *indios* in the glue knew to be a greeting from their brothers on the outside.

The guard stopped in the middle of the catwalk, glancing down. "Tancredo, you hear me? I got some goods for you."

"Talk to Moises," Tancredo answered from the darkness. "He's the boss around here."

"Don't fuckin' waste my time," Leonel protested. "I've only got a minute." He peered into the gloom. "Moises, you awake?"

"Yeah. You're bringing us some vials, right?"

"Uh-huh."

"Open 'em up and pour the stuff on the ectoplasm," Moises instructed Leonel. "Don't let it splash on us, and don't get it on your fingers."

"This is bullshit," Leonel groaned.

"Just do it," said Moises.

Leonel turned on his flashlight. The beam sliced downward, searching among the torsos until it found a large empty patch of glue. Apolonio watched as the kid manipulated whatever it was he held in his hands. Seconds later, a thin stream trickled into the pit. The ectoplasm sizzled.

"What now?" Leonel asked after he'd emptied the last vial.

"From this moment on, anything could happen." Moises's normally calm voice crackled with tension. "Are they still fighting outside?"

"It's over now. The army showed up."

"Then get away. Fast. And thank Olavo for us." Moises paused. "Thank you, too, Leonel."

The kid switched off his flashlight and disappeared from the catwalk, leaving the hatch slightly ajar. Gloom enveloped the pit. A moment later Apolonio felt a sudden warmth surge through legs he'd thought had atrophied for good. He yelled with joy. His fellow prisoners also cried out, their exultant shouts resounding through the vat.

"Hold on, boys!" Moises's sober voice stifled the inmates' enthusiasm. "Don't think you can escape so easily. The glue is flesh of our flesh."

"But I can feel my legs again!" Gomes exclaimed.

"An illusion." Moises's voice was like ice. "What you feel isn't your legs—it's the ectoplasm. The melt polymer can't dissolve the glue. It can only make it . . . come alive."

"Alive?" Apolonio screamed. He had never before felt such terror.

"Phenilalanine-ATP has the power to transform any organic substance, turning it into artificial fibers with the properties of human cardiac tissue," Moises continued. "These fibers spontaneously dilate and contract, which is why the melt is so excruciating—and why it's having such an interesting effect on the glue around our legs."

"What the fuck are you saying, man?" Apolonio cried in exasperation. "Are we gonna get out of this muck or not?"

A long silence.

"We'll never get *out* of it." Moises spoke slowly, deliberately. "But we *can* make it move. Very soon, the ectoplasm will become our slave, obeying our nerve impulses as they travel from our brains to our legs."

A numbing despondency overcame the prisoners, rendering them mute. But then, suddenly, Tancredo burst out laughing—a disturbing, gurgling hysteria that echoed off the vat walls.

"Oh, man, that's fucking great!" he shouted sarcastically. "We'll never walk again, but that doesn't matter 'cause we can play mind games with this big shitload of glue!"

Curses, shouts of anger, cries of disbelief. Moises waited for his comrades to quiet down. Then he said, pointedly, "Know something, Tancredo? Snakes don't walk—and they don't need to."

Apolonio sank into a well of fear even colder than the air in the vat. He closed his eyes, shivering.

8

Olavo halted the Land Rover before a Quonset hut, slightly bigger than the other favela shacks that dotted the hills across the ravine from the penitentiary. Climbing out, he glanced toward Sepultura. Searchlights swept the walls and the junkyard beyond, setting the night ablaze, making the prison visible even from this distance. A deep silence had settled on the shantytown. Olavo hid the Famas assault rifle under the seat, locked the Rover, and ran to the front door of the Quonset hut. A single knock, three quick ones, a final knock.

The door opened a crack. A pair of huge brown eyes peered at him from within a dark face. A gruff, mistrustful voice asked, "What you want, mister?"

"You knew I was coming. Let me in." Olavo pushed the door back, shoved the man aside, and entered the one-room hut.

The interior light was so intense, he had to blink several times before his eyes adjusted to the glare. About fifteen *indios,* men and women, their skin much darker than Olavo's, sat on chairs along the walls. Near the center of the room an earthen altar held a sandstone statue dressed in red and black, encircled by clay pots from which projected offerings of cigars, small tridents, and bottles of *pemba.* Ancient wooden icons of Saint Barbara, Saint Jerome, Saint Anthony, and Saint Spedito hung from the corrugated walls.

Olavo approached a skinny old man perched on a high-backed chair, wearing a multicolored pebble necklace. "You're the *babalao,* right?"

The old sorcerer's stare was hostile. "And *you* are possessed by *kiumba,* evil spirits—I could tell that the instant you appeared at our door. I would have refused you entrance, Olavo Cuadros, had your brother not asked us to hear your plea."

"Possessed by *kiumba*?" Olavo said with a shrug. "Maybe you're right. I'm no expert in condomble."

"We practice Umbanda," the old man corrected him in a chastising tone. "The *condomble* is only a dance."

"Like I said, I'm ignorant. But many people insist that your magic really works."

Olavo glanced around the room. A white-haired mummy guarded the rear door, seated on a stool and encircled by stubby lighted candles. This was surely a representation of Preto Velho, the first slave brought to Brazil from Africa. Olavo had heard of the Preto Velho cult, but he still couldn't help shuddering. Even more disturbing than the mummy was the hostility emanating from the people in the room, as chilling as an icy wind.

He forced himself to speak in a steady voice. "Perhaps Fernando told you . . ."

"You hope we can summon spirits here," the *babalao* said.

"Spirits, yes, but not your benevolent *orisha*," Olavo said. "My purpose requires *egum*, spirits of the dead."

"That's very dangerous—more dangerous than you can imagine," the old sorcerer said.

"No doubt." Olavo raised his open hands. "And I don't want them showing up here—somewhere else."

The *babalao*'s stare hardened. "I don't understand. Where do you want the *egum* to appear?"

Olavo grimaced. He pointed toward the window, speaking quickly to hide his discomfort. "Inside Sepultura. Is that possible?"

The old man's eyes shone brighter. For a while he said nothing; then at last he muttered, "You don't believe in Umbanda, and furthermore your soul is corrupt—you kill children for money. You come here, to our *terreiro*, asking us to risk our lives by conjuring the *egum*. My question is this: Why should we help you?"

Waves of whispered anger rushed about the hut. Olavo realized he was dripping sweat—and not because of the heat. He swallowed a bubble of saliva. "It's not me you'd be helping," he rasped. "There are Umbanda believers inside Sepultura—a man named Tancredo, many more, all of them suffering. They're the ones who want you to summon the *egum*. I'm only a messenger."

"Summon the *egum*," the old man echoed, fingering the stones around his neck. "But which *egum*? To evoke spirits, you must know their names."

"They're called . . . the Kayova. Do you understand who I'm talking about?"

The ancient priest winced. "The tribe that gave itself to death?"

"Yes. Precisely. Those are the *egum* I'm asking you to summon—the spirits of the Kayova. Inside Sepultura."

More whispering filled the hut. The old man remained silent for a moment, staring empty-eyed at Olavo. "The Kayova, when they existed, never practiced Umbanda," he said in a hushed voice. "Their *pai* spoke with different gods."

Olavo hunched his shoulders, annoyed. "My brother says their beliefs were very close to yours." He remembered Fernando telling him that the Kayova god Naneromoipapa was equivalent to the Umbanda deity Oshala, and how the Kayova *ayvukue* demons resembled the *egum* of Umbanda.

"Yes, that may be." The old sorcerer's extended finger pointed first to the garbed statue, then to the small tridents. "Perhaps your brother told you this whole *terreiro* is a holy ground to *compadre* Exu. Do you know who that is?"

"Like the Christian devil."

The *babalao* shook his head violently. "No, never, Exu is *good*—though temperamental. He angers easily, pulls pranks, goads people into arguing with each other, but he is not Satan. We cannot summon the Kayova dead except through Exu. Given his trickster nature, the results will be unpredictable."

"I'm willing to risk it," Olavo said.

"Very well—for the Umbanda believers of Sepultura, let us begin!"

Instantly three of the seated *indios* took up drums and began pounding out a rhythm. The old man jumped to his feet and raised his arms.

"*Laroye Exu!*" the *babalao* cried.

"*Laroye Exu!*" the others repeated furiously, rising from their chairs. A dissonant chorus erupted.

Exu Tiriri de Umbanda!
Mora na encruzilhada
E chegada a sua hora
No romper da madrugada!

The beating of the drums built to a frenzy.

9

Apolonio felt the heat in his legs intensify. Instinctively he tried to move his knees. Nothing happened, though the ectoplasm continued to ripple all around him—or so it seemed. In the dark it was impossible to be sure.

"We must command the glue to rise!" Moises shouted, more excited than ever. "The ectoplasm is a semiconductor now, just like the human body. The electrical impulses from our central nervous systems can penetrate it!"

Carneiro, a Bahía drug dealer who'd been in the vat a year and a half, spat out a curse, "Shut your mouth, old prick! Take that science crap and shove it!" He seemed about to elaborate, but then his tone suddenly changed. "Oh, shit, it's true! I can make this stuff move!"

"Me, too!" Shock and fear distorted Ulysses's voice.

The yells of surprise grew louder, filling the pit. Much to his amazement, Apolonio found that if he tried to shake his legs while visualizing himself walking, the ectoplasm trembled and swelled, forming a sort of wave. He slid his hands along the glue's surface. Soon it would reach the temperature of a human body.

Suddenly an image flashed through his mind: a circle of twenty naked men, sitting in a jungle clearing, beating fiercely on wooden drums. Now a different picture came to him. Deep in the forest, two great iron gates swung back, as if shaken open by the pounding of the drums. The gates abruptly vanished, but the drums lingered in Apolonio's ears. He froze, mouth open, his blood like ice.

"What the hell's happening?" Miro squalled like a frightened cat. "I see gates opening—"

"Don't worry about it." Moises cut him off, his voice hard and commanding. "Now we must imagine we're jumping. Imagine we're jumping together, all the way to the ceiling. Come on! Do it!"

Apolonio obeyed mechanically. A tentacle of ectoplasm encircled his body and lifted him toward the catwalk. By the dim light streaming from the open hatch he saw the underside of the bridge. He reached out, tried to grab a strut. Impossible. The tentacle contracted. The whiplash almost broke Apolonio's back.

He plummeted, yanked downward by the tentacle, and as he struck the ectoplasm an excruciating pain shot through his spine. He tried to organize his thoughts. Once again the circle of naked drummers flooded his mind—only now the image was clear, and he saw an entire tribe, thousands of *indios,* urging the drummers to their wild rhythms. The *in-dios* stared toward the forest, as if something unthinkable would soon leap from its depths: an entity they both eagerly anticipated and greatly feared. In the center of the circle a *pai* danced frantically, his bare feet kicking up clouds of dirt . . . but what in the world was a *pai?*

"Let's try again," Moises commanded, breathing heavily. "This time we must all shout together as we try to grab the catwalk. The ectoplasm will obey, you'll see."

Apolonio snapped out of his reverie. Before him Ulysses, barely visible in the gloom, writhed from head to waist, screaming incomprehensibly. *"Ao Boboi! Ao Boboi!"*

A terrible awareness took hold of Apolonio. The trickster Exu had opened those iron gates, and now Oshumare, the rainbow serpent, was streaming through the gap. Surely this was the entity that the *indios* were expecting to burst from the forest. But how did Apolonio know these things?

Again, he concentrated on jumping. The entire ectoplasmic mass surged upward, bearing the hundred and fifteen embedded men toward the ceiling. Apolonio screamed madly, and the others screamed with him. The ectoplasm carried him higher than before, level with the catwalk. He thrust out his hands, seizing the metal handrail. He attempted to lift his legs, but it was the ectoplasm that moved instead. The mass slithered over the handrail and streamed along the catwalk, dragging the shrieking torsos.

Seeing the hatch hurtle toward him, Apolonio grew certain he would be crushed against the jamb, but then, astonishingly, the river of glue contracted. First Apolonio, then Ulysses, next Moises, Tancredo, Feliciano, Carneiro, Miro, Gomes, and the others passed through the hatch unscathed. The ectoplasm dilated, filling a corridor jammed with pipes and illuminated by sputtering neon.

Apolonio believed he was about to die, though fear of oblivion was no longer the force that sent a hundred fragmented notions tumbling through his head. What fired his mind was a need for revenge—the same need his tribe now felt as they honored the hideous scaled entity their drums had summoned from the jungle.

His *tribe?* He had no tribe. The Kayova were gone. He stared at the cold brick walls as the glue dragged the prisoners down the corridor. He wanted to see those walls destroyed. He prayed for their annihilation by some superhuman force. Eager to comply, the ectoplasm continued to dilate.

10

Olavo observed the early stages of the summoning—the drumming, the chanting, the dancing *babalao* and his acolytes—with a sort of bored disgust. But now came an unexpected event. A young mulatto leaped into the middle of the room, his lanky body twisting furiously. A narrow leather band encircled his head, a checkered cloak of red and black hung from his bony shoulders, and a loop of threaded stones, some white, some red, swung from his neck. In his right hand he gripped a trident, twirling it deftly like a baton.

"*Laroye Exu! Laroye Exu!*" the other *indios* chanted, and Olavo understood that the mulatto was impersonating the trickster god. As if inspired by the avatar's demented dance, a dozen worshippers threw themselves to the floor and beat their heads against the dirt, apparently without feeling pain.

The lithe mulatto strode toward the pots with their wealth of offerings. He grabbed a cigar, lit it on the nearest candle, and stuck it between his teeth, sucking the smoke into his lungs. Next he snatched a trident, tucking it under his armpit, and finally he grabbed a bottle of *pemba*. Taking the cigar in hand, he filled his mouth with the liquor. He spat the *pemba* onto the pots, then kicked over the candles. The altar burst into flames.

The drummers pounded out their preternatural thunder. Fascinated, Olavo watched as the *babalao* approached Exu's avatar and handed him a huge knife. A woman came forward, her eyes rolled back, carrying a live cock. The mulatto drank another mouthful of *pemba,* used the rest to douse the fire, and set the empty bottle on the floor. He opened the bird's throat with a quick, cruel slash. Blood spattered the sculpted icons hanging from the walls.

"*Ao Boboi! Ao Boboi!*" a boy cried, flagellating Saint Bartholomew's image with a necklace of yellow stones.

The mulatto nodded. He held the cock, still jerking from the shock of the blade, before the icon. He allowed some blood to drip onto Saint Bartholomew's crudely carved face. The flayed saint wept red tears.

Olavo stood and stared, transfixed by the sacrifice, stunned by the delirious drumbeats. A tug on his arm brought him back to reality. It was the *babalao,* his pupils so dilated they completely filled his corneas. Olavo felt the old man's breath on his face as the *babalao* whispered in his ear.

"We did it!" the sorcerer rasped. "Exu freed the *egum* for you, and the serpent-god Oshumare came with them! The *egum* and the serpent have merged!"

Olavo's shocked eyes darted toward a window, its frame shorn of glass. He looked at Sepultura's enormous profile. "What will happen now?"

The *babalao* laughed, one ugly burst of delight after another. "Go ask the enemies of the *egum!*" He took a fresh bottle of *pemba* from the altar, bringing the blood-spattered container to his lips.

11

Apolonio watched the corridor walls crumble, brick torn from brick by the glutinous monster, this thing to which his body was now a mere appendage. The ectoplasm kept moving, sliding down shattered hallways and flowing beneath fractured ceilings. The screaming men rooted in the glue looked like cilia sprouting from a gigantic worm. Strangely enough, a kind of demented pride filled Apolonio's heart, quelling his terror. Body and spirit, the doomed inmates had melded with the lurching mass—finally they had fused into a single being—and several embedded *indios* cried out that they must take the name of Oshumare, the serpent-god who'd given the creature life. But Apolonio understood that the unleashed force was in fact another deity, Naneromoipapa, the shape-shifting, avenging god of his defeated and brutalized people.

From what secret source did his knowledge spring? He didn't care—couldn't care—about such mysteries. The wonderment that had filled his mind was yielding to intimations of his approaching death. And yet for an instant he felt absurdly happy to have become one with his fellow sufferers, joined to them in this juggernaut of flesh.

He experienced the full majesty of their collective strength when the ectoplasm at last reached the exercise yard. The monster was so huge, and its aspect so terrible, that its sudden appearance drove the guards and soldiers into a panic. Some attempted to swivel their machine guns around and open fire on the slimy horror erupting from the bowels of the prison. Others went for their rifles and pistols. But before a single shot was fired, the serpent filled the entire yard with its immensity, slithering in a circle, now coiling, now uncoiling, so that a great vortex of viscous glue seized Sepultura, pulverizing the buildings, cracking the outer ramparts, toppling the watchtowers, sucking the guards to their doom.

Sinuating through the rubble that had once been a prison, the ectoplasm soon reached the main gate, its pylons still intact, framing the full moon. The serpent made ready to strike, gathering itself into a horrendous rising wave of organic and inorganic matter. Apolonio knew that the end was near. An instant before the wave came crashing down, he managed to grasp Ulysses's hand, warm and vibrant. The impact cut Apolonio's spine in half. He surrendered himself to death. His final vision was of a united tribe, a single people, their clustered spears held high against those who would destroy them. Deep in the jungle, an unnamed god blessed their holy struggle.

12

Standing in the open doorway of the Quonset hut, Olavo and the *babalao* watched the mass of ectoplasm destroy Sepultura, a huge python attacking its prey. As the serpent twisted and writhed, the buildings crumbled and deep fissures appeared in the outer ramparts, the jagged fault lines running from one watchtower to the next. Slimy globs of residual glue oozed through the cracks and streamed across the plain.

For a few minutes it looked as if the main gate would remain standing, but then the beast threw itself upon the pylons, and they crashed to the ground, hurling a vast plume of debris into the night sky.

The pulsating worm slithered toward São Paulo.

Inside the hut the drums had fallen silent. The *babalao* swallowed another shot of *pemba*. "Oshumare is in a rage tonight," he rasped, his voice thick with alcohol. "All men are powerless before the serpent."

Olavo shrugged. "Nonsense. Once the phenilalanine-ATP dries out, the glue will harden again. Look, the thing has stopped moving already."

The old man coughed and squinted into the darkness. "You mean this was all for nothing?" he asked after a moment.

"For nothing?" Olavo said. "Not at all. Don't you understand? There is one less prison in South America now." He stepped away from the hut, then turned and faced the *babalao*. "You call that nothing?"

Olavo didn't wait for an answer, but hurried into the favela. He was swallowed by the bitter cold of the waning night.

ONDŘEJ NEFF

THE FOURTH DAY TO ETERNITY

TRANSLATED FROM THE CZECH
BY JEFFREY BROWN

To date no literary historian has provided us with a panoramic history of Czech and Slovak science fiction. Anyone who attempts such a project will be burdened and blessed with a surfeit of works to discuss, beginning with Karel Pleskac's Život na Měsíci ("Life on the Moon," 1881) and ending with whatever titles have most recently won the Capek Award, established in 1982 to honor SF stories and novels by newcomers. While practical realities may prevent our hypothetical scholar from celebrating every Czech or Slovak author who ever contributed to the genre, four names are certain to receive plenty of ink.

The grandfather of the movement was Karel Hloucha, author of seven influential novels and short story collections, among them Zakletá země ("Enchanted Country," 1910) and Sluneční vůz ("The Solar Wagon," 1921). A generation later came Karel Capek himself, breaking new ground not only with the play R.U.R. (1920) but also with his famous novel Vàlka s mloky ("War with the Newts," 1937), an anti-Hitler political satire in which sea-dwelling newts rebel against their masters. The third indispensable Czech writer is Josef Nesvadba, whose collections include Einsteinův mozek ("Einstein's Brain," 1960) and Výprava opačným směrem ("Expedition in the Opposite Direction," 1964). And finally we have the author whose story you are about to read.

Born in 1945, Ondřej Neff studied the social sciences at Charles University in Prague. Upon graduation he worked as an editor at a radio station, but lost his job following the 1968 Soviet invasion. Neff began his literary career writing juvenile detective novels, but his affection for Jules Verne soon led him toward science fiction. His first collection, Vejce naruby *("An Inside-Out Egg") was published in 1985 to critical acclaim. Among his novels are* Jádro pudla *("The Heart of the Matter," 1984),* Měsíc mého života *("The Moon of My Life," 1988), and the trilogy* Milénium *("Millennium"), the first volume of which appeared in 1993.*

During the period that his country was under Soviet domination, Neff did not hesitate to publish via the samizdat, the clandestine literary network that arose throughout Eastern Europe in response to official censorship. Shortly before the fall of Communism, Neff wrote, drew, and disseminated at his own expense the anti-government comic Pérák *("The Jumping Man"), a project that would have eventually gotten him in trouble had the regime he criticized not collapsed. In 1990 he took over the editorship of* Ikarie, *the most important Czech SF magazine, a position he held for several years.*

"The Fourth Day to Eternity" gives us Ondřej Neff at his most engagingly enigmatic. Beyond its sheer narrative drive, this demented account of a physicist caught in a time-loop of his own making—or is it?—boasts some adroit symbolism and allegorical overtones that never overstay their welcome.

He did not need to glance out the window to know what the Château Galitzin looked like now. The brass eaves of the conical slate roof would have turned black, and the stucco walls would display dozens of zigzag cracks. In several places, the plaster would have fallen away completely, revealing the red brickwork, as if a giant wielding an immense ax had inflicted the château with bloody wounds. The windows would have deteriorated as well. Already their panes were covered in soot and grime—cataracts on an old man's eyes—and within each dark wooden frame a spiderweb, dense and intricate, now hung like a lace curtain. Dozens of spiders had been spinning since daybreak to create those thick veils. Perhaps the creatures wanted the windows to disappear altogether, blending with the stucco.

The spiders worked in total silence. He wondered whether, if he walked outside and listened carefully, he would hear the beating of their quick little legs weaving the fibers. Surely a spider could not go about its labors without making some sort of sound.

He winced, disappointed in himself—angry, really, furious. The fourth day was not a time for idle speculation. Only three hours remained till noon, three hours in which to work on the equations. How marvelous if he might manage to complete his project this morning. Or else on the fourth morning after that, or the next fourth morning, or the next. Then his triumph would be so much sweeter.

He abandoned the profusion of papers, each sheet covered with the recalcitrant equations, then rose from his mahogany desk and crossed the library to the window. The fissures in the Château Galitzin were more numerous than yesterday, and the areas of naked brick much larger. Yes, no question, the building was falling apart, yielding to time's relentless pressure. Perhaps one day it would collapse, spilling its bricks into the valley before he could finish his work. Well, that would be a *kind* of solution—wouldn't it?

The sad joke made him laugh, and with the laughter came relief and hope. As long as he could laugh, it was not so bad.

He left the library and climbed the staircase to the second-floor bathroom, where he took a hot shower using water drawn from the cistern in the attic. Tap water could not be trusted—not since that fourth day when they'd poisoned the wells of the villa with cyanide and only the faint scent of bitter almonds had saved his life. Of course, maybe he *could* use the faucets, since the wells were now pure again, and his attackers never used the same plan twice. Still, why take the risk? Indeed, what if the novelty of today's assault consisted in the repetition of an old strategy?

Leave nothing to chance, he told himself as, throwing on his bathrobe, he descended the staircase—absolutely nothing. He would never foil the enemy if he allowed chance to rule his existence.

The question, of course, was whether he would ever solve the equations. Perhaps he should simply stop defending himself, fourth day after fourth day. Might his death somehow constitute a victory, a success as resounding as the completion of his work? Such a sacrifice did not seem very great to him just then, because what he was living could hardly be called a life. He was worse off than the dead, whatever their number.

The telephone rang, shattering his gloomy thoughts and drawing him back into the library. Sapkowski, no doubt, wondering whether he should make the usual delivery. He approached the writing desk, activated the encryption unit, and snapped up the receiver.

"Drabek."

"It's me," Sapkowski said. "Shall I come now?"

"Did you get everything?"

"Of course," Sapkowski replied in a haughty voice. The fool thought of himself as a businessman, but he was really just a petty shopkeeper, a greengrocer who sold guns instead of cabbages.

"Glock, shotgun, Remington, Galil, AK-47?"

"All five." After a short silence Sapkowski added, "I couldn't find an infrared scope for the Remington."

"Damn."

"I'll try to get you infrared next time."

"Yes, except there might not be any next time," said Drabek, enraged. "Why can't you understand what's happening out here?"

Sapkowski said nothing. Clearly, he did not want to argue.

"It's all right," Drabek continued. "Do you have pencil and paper? Listen carefully. This time I placed the mines at coordinates A-6, B-1, C-8, D-3 . . ."

He continued dictating the lethal locations, hoping that his tone concealed the beating wings of the thought now flying through his mind: one day the enemy would break the code, one terrible fourth day.

"Go to the north wall," he told Sapkowski. "Climb the poplar tree. You'll find a remote control in the crook. Press the red button to unlock the gate."

"The red button. Got it."

"Be sure to bring along extra ammo for the automatic weapons."

"As you wish."

Drabek was especially pleased that he'd ordered a Galil and an AK-47. The attackers wouldn't be expecting those, only his usual Remington and shotgun. True, he preferred the elegance of the hunting weapons—he was a skilled shot—but this was about survival, not sportsmanship. He hoped the battle wouldn't turn into a noisy bloodbath once again and get the villagers complaining to Inspector Canavor. But if a bloodbath was in the offing, so be it.

The greengrocer thanked Drabek for his business, agreed to deliver the goods within the hour, and hung up. For a full minute the physicist stood immobile by the desk, the receiver locked in his grip. Anxiety clogged his throat, and a chill spread from his spine through his shoulder blades to his arms. What tactics would the attackers try today? What surprises would they spring?

Breathing in hard staccato gasps, he ascended to his bedchamber and entered the cork-lined splendor of his closet. He shed the bathrobe and, scanning the shelves, took down a nylon singlet and a pair of cotton briefs. He dressed before the full-length mirror. Both garments were brand-new and felt cool against his skin. He could not abide laundered fabrics. After one wearing he always threw his underclothes away, even the socks.

Fluorescent lights hummed quietly above his head. With growing satisfaction he studied himself in the glass, examining every muscle. He had the body of an athlete, trim and supple, each muscle and ligament in harmony with the whole. The fitness of those tissues would affect his fortunes in the coming fight, but ultimately everything would turn on his mental agility.

He removed the synchromesh jumpsuit from its hanger and proceeded to encapsulate himself, snugging his feet into the fitted boots, sliding his arms through the sleeves. It was an expensive piece of apparel, costlier than the rest of his wardrobe combined, but worth every cent. On three previous occasions the suit had deflected an attacker's bayonet, and once it had resisted the blistering torrent of a flamethrower. The synchromesh fabric was the color of night, swallowing light so voraciously that not a single thread shone in the mercury vapor's glow.

Feeling more relaxed now, Drabek returned to the library and once again contemplated the equations, the thousands of jottings and scribblings through which he meant to solve the riddle of time. Prudence demanded that he stash the papers in the safe right now, protecting them behind plates of impenetrable steel. But what if he was close to a breakthrough? What if, in the middle of his dealings with Sapkowski, he experienced a flash of insight and needed instant access to his work? He decided to leave the papers where they were.

Across the room, the warning light on the security console began blinking. He glanced at the grid of closed-circuit television screens. Sapkowski appeared on the upper left-hand monitor, studying his topographical map of the villa while dragging a footlocker across the grounds. Slowly, cautiously, he picked his way through the minefield.

Drabek grabbed his checkbook, proceeded to the foyer, and opened the door for Sapkowski. Together the two men hauled the footlocker into the grand salon and set it on the window seat, Sapkowski chattering all the while about rising costs and the headaches of his trade. The greengrocer warned Drabek that the next fourth day would be the most expensive yet.

"You'll be glad to hear that some really choice items are coming on the market," Sapkowski said. "Stun guns, rocket launchers, nerve bombs, optic grenades."

"Optic grenades?"

"For blinding the enemy."

"I'll take a dozen. And a dozen nerve bombs as well. And don't forget that infrared scope."

"Try to understand," Sapkowski said. "Getting this stuff isn't like buying a loaf of bread."

"I appreciate your efforts—you know that, don't you?" Drabek said in a conciliatory tone. He opened his checkbook and removed the ballpoint pen from its collar. "Forgive my impatience."

Sapkowski shrugged listlessly. His face remained impassive. The greengrocer no longer believed that commando raids on the villa occurred every fourth day. When Drabek first began placing his orders, Sapkowski had been quite interested, but in time he'd started asking skeptical questions. Why did Drabek constantly need new guns—did the old ones turn to oatmeal after every fight? If the attackers were always triggering buried land mines, why didn't Sapkowski see any craters on the grounds? If the villa was regularly the scene of pitched battles, why did the rooms display no signs of violence?

Without bothering to ask for the bill, Drabek signed the topmost check and gave it to Sapkowski, telling him to fill in the correct amount. He escorted the greengrocer out of the salon. It occurred to him that, before Sapkowski's next visit, he should despoil the room in some way. He might crack the gilded mirror, scratch the marble fireplace, singe the velvet drapes, deface the portraits of Werner Heisenberg and Napoléon Bonaparte, shatter the vase holding the olive branch he'd acquired in Greece, or snap one of the deer antlers decorating the chandelier. Then maybe Sapkowski would believe him. Not that he needed the greengrocer's approval. After all, why should he, Drabek, master of the time equations, care about the opinions of a fool?

He guided Sapkowski to the front door and coldly bade him farewell. In a voice that betrayed neither sincerity nor condescension, the arms dealer wished Drabek good luck in the afternoon's battle—a tedious blessing from the tedious mouth of a tedious person.

Once back in the library, Drabek proceeded to the security console and threw the switch that activated the window shutters. Slowly the bulletproof plates swung on their hinges and mated with the dozen casements. The room grew silent and dark. He approached his desk, switched on the banker's lamp, and accorded his life's work a final glance. The equations swirled past his eyes like ballet dancers pirouetting along a tightrope, all of them presumably heading toward the same destination. But . . . where? The answer lay frozen within these signs, symbols, and integers, fated to be released one day by the fire of Drabek's intellect, or so he hoped, just as a sculpture dwells within a block of marble, awaiting the artist's chisel.

Unless, of course, the equations were utter nonsense, leading to nowhere, pointing to nothing. What then? In principle that would be cause for despair—but only in principle. Indeed, if Drabek could prove mathematically that his quest was fruitless, might this fourth day, and all the fourth days to come, dissolve into a blessed normalcy?

He shuddered. Enough, he told himself. No more woolgathering. He was on the right track, and one day, perhaps even tomorrow, he would outwit the avatars of eternity.

Tomorrow. He knew it would start with a beautiful dawn, warm and tranquil, the Château Galitzin looking glorious in the rising sun. The windows, free of spiderwebs, would glimmer from a façade unblemished by a single crack. Meanwhile, in Drabek's garden, sparrows would twitter, even as spring's sweet breath wafted through the open windows of the villa.

Methodically he gathered up the papers, compacting them into a neat stack.

Tomorrow. Would he finally, tomorrow, find the courage to take leave of this madness? Abandon his work, forsake the equations, move out of the villa? Oh, yes. Quite so. He knew it. He felt it.

Ambling to the safe, he set the papers in the compartment, closed the door, and spun the dial of the combination lock. He felt buoyant, intoxicated, all his tensions melted away.

He returned to the grand salon with the graceful moves of a dancer—the lightness of his step delighted and surprised him—where he unpacked the footlocker and took hold of the shotgun. Systematically he deployed his arsenal throughout the first floor, burying the shotgun in the salon couch, slipping the Winchester into the hall umbrella stand, concealing the Galil in the conservatory piano, hiding the Glock under the library security console. He kept the AK-47 in his possession, gripping it with both hands as he studied the nine monitors.

The screens displayed no human figures. The warning lights were dark. He checked his watch: 11:55 A.M. The attackers could arrive any minute now, and from any direction—the garden, the portico, the service entrance, the front door. One time they'd tunneled into the basement. On another occasion they'd come crashing through the roof.

Drabek scrambled atop the writing desk—a strategically favorable position—and laid the AK-47 across his knees. An image filled his mind: the villa's well-stocked wine cellar. The enemy hadn't used that approach in many a fourth day. This time around, they would surely use the wine cellar.

It began, as always, with hideous suddenness. The boom of the howitzer was deafening despite the steel shutters. As the thunder faded, the light on the security console began flashing madly. The lower right-hand screen told Drabek what he needed to know: the howitzer shell had breached the wall near the gazebo.

Barely had the dust settled when a barrage of grenades, hurled by an array of hidden bazookas, came flying onto the grounds from all directions. They exploded on impact, detonating the land mines, so that all nine screens went dark with debris. When at last the fog lifted, Drabek's eyes fixed on the center screen, which now showed two men dressed in asbestos body stockings, their faces obscured by the wraparound visors of their fireproof caps. With murderous resolve the bastards trained their howitzer on the front door. They fired a round. The concussion shook the villa.

AK-47 in hand, Drabek rushed into the hallway and stared at the door. A billowing cloud of black smoke and pulverized plaster obscured the foyer. He crouched beside the banister, mentally cursing the commandos—pigs! assholes! shitheads!—though he was no less angry at himself. How stupid of him to have thought that today's attack would be ingenious. Instead the bastards had arrived in the crudest manner imaginable, courtesy of a cannon that had probably last been fired during the Battle of the Bulge.

Come on, Pretty Boy! Come on, Stinky! I'm waiting for you!

It was Stinky—the short one—who now emerged from the dark mass, screaming insanely and brandishing a flamethrower. The visored cap, Drabek mused, would serve Stinky well as he went about his arsonist's agenda, but it wouldn't protect him from a spray of bullets.

Carefully Drabek aimed the AK-47 and squeezed off several rounds. The weapon shook furiously in his hands. It took Drabek a minute to realize just how thoroughly the bullets had done their job. Where Stinky's head had once been, a bright red haze had appeared, outlining the splayed fingers of his raised hands: ten exclamation points, punctuating the story of his decapitation.

This is going extremely well, Drabek thought.

An antique pineapple grenade arced out of the cloud, landing at his feet. He jerked away. The bomb detonated. The blast wave tore the AK-47 from his hands, flung him into the library, and sent him sprawling across the floor. A second grenade flew into the room, glanced off the writing desk, and exploded. The telephone disintegrated, and the desk flew to pieces like an orange crate under a sledgehammer. A flying cluster of mahogany knives struck Drabek, but none penetrated the synchromesh jumpsuit. Grenade number three shredded the window drapes and turned the security console into a twisted pile of metal and glass. The fourth grenade went off near the bookshelves. Scores of volumes spilled onto the floor like the cascade of a waterfall.

At last Drabek's nemesis—Pretty Boy, the tall one—appeared on the scene, sheathed head-to-toe in asbestos, a flamethrower fixed menacingly in his grasp. Grenades dangled from his chest like medals, and a Luger protruded from his shoulder holster. Unarmed and disoriented, Drabek now became the object of Pretty Boy's sport. Laughing maniacally, the bastard chased Drabek around the library, periodically assailing him with a belching plume of flame. The synchromesh suit prevented outright burns, but Drabek could still feel the heat.

Lurching suddenly, he hurled himself back into the hallway, where he immediately saw that, when not busy tossing grenades, Pretty Boy had been entertaining himself with the flamethrower. The place was an inferno, its darting red tongues lapping up the carpets, drapes, paintings, and wallpaper. Flames flared from the doorway leading to the grand salon, prompting Drabek to recall a favorite circus act of his youth: the tiger jumping through the burning hoop.

From his hip pocket he retrieved the goggle-eyed fireproof hood, then slipped it over his head. He put on his incombustible gloves. Despite the miracle of synchromesh, the heat soon turned intolerable. Sweat gushed from all his pores. He blinked rapidly, but the brine still burned his eyes. Before long the jumpsuit would become as useless as pajamas in perdition.

A glorious picture filled his brain. The great titanium cistern. Eighteen cubic meters of cool, soothing water.

He dashed up the burning staircase, one flight, two flights, and charged into the attic. The cistern beckoned. Frantically he peeled off the jumpsuit, removed the hood and gloves, and climbed into the water wearing only his singlet and briefs. The wondrous fluid embraced him, soothing his flesh, calming his nerves.

A series of muffled explosions reached Drabek's ears. He guessed that Pretty Boy was hurling grenades at the safe. Once he'd blown off the door, of course, the bastard needn't bother removing the papers. The raging heat would incinerate them as soon as they met the air.

Only now did Drabek grasp the ludicrousness of his situation. So many fights, so many fourth days, so many clever plans laid by the attackers and confounded by the defender—and in the end the bastards had won by trapping him in a nice pleasant bath!

His defeat had been a long time coming. At least he could live his life now, perhaps retiring to the sea or the mountains. Never again would the Château Galitzin be veiled in spiderwebs.

But no! He mustn't give up! Surely he could recapitulate the equations. Given enough time, he could go through the whole intricate process again, right to the point he'd reached this morning, a single step away from cracking the great conundrum.

A single step? Yes, a single step—across a yawning gulf. But he would not let that sobering fact disturb him. The mystery was manifestly solvable. He was on the right track. Why else would the avatars of eternity be waging this perpetual war? Why else would they keep sending Stinky and Pretty Boy on their suicidal missions? Why else would they persist in the face of so many failures, time and again, fourth day after fourth day after fourth day?

Just below the attic floor, the horrid flames roared, relentlessly devouring beams, rafters, joists, and studs. Strange: despite the conflagration, the water didn't seem to be getting hotter.

Why did he care so much about penetrating time's secrets? Was it simply because the avatars guarded them so aggressively? Could it be that their fury was circular, a reciprocal response to the ferocity with which Drabek fended off the attacks?

He had not yet deciphered time—but now, suddenly, he understood the relative coolness of the water. The essential fact came from a magazine article he'd read back when the outside world occasionally claimed his attention. An organism does not notice gradual changes in the temperature of its environment. Place a person in a cauldron of water, suspend it over an open fire, and in theory he will never grow alarmed, allowing himself to be cooked alive.

A profound languor overcame Drabek. His brain throbbed with dull resignation. Let me cook, he thought. It is a death like any other. No, it is *better* than the average death, almost congenial. You win, Pretty Boy. I want nothing more to do with you—or with Stinky, Sapkowski, the avatars, the equations, and myself. I am tired of the fight. I am sick of the cycle. I desire only sleep. This is the fourth day—to eternity.

A violent shuddering roused Drabek from his stupor. The world was vibrating, rupturing, coming apart at the seams—no, not the world, he realized, merely the villa. There followed a disturbing din of crumbling rafters and splintering timbers. Had the flames already eaten into the attic? Was the cistern about to fall?

Yes, it was. Propelled by the crushing weight of the water, the vessel crashed through the attic floor and landed in Drabek's bedchamber. The passenger had no time to disembark, however, for now the bedchamber floor gave way, and the cistern fell into the library. Drabek vaulted over the side, and an instant later the vessel continued its downward voyage, plummeting toward the basement and leaving a huge crater in its wake. Flames darted upward from the ragged cavity.

On the other side of the library, Pretty Boy stood crouched over the steel safe, trying to pry open the door with a crowbar. The grenades, evidently, had proved impotent. Drabek paused briefly to bless his luck, then dived headfirst into the rubble of the security console. In a matter of seconds he retrieved the Glock.

Pretty Boy raised himself to full height and plucked the Luger from his shoulder holster.

Drabek fired first. The bullet struck a grenade hanging across Pretty Boy's sternum. Instantly the bomb detonated, depriving the bastard of his chest. He stumbled forward and fell into the fiery abyss. It was as if the Devil had come for Pretty Boy and dragged him straight to Hell.

A ringing noise wrenched Drabek into the here and now, and then came a second such sound, a third, a fourth. Gasping and wheezing, he staggered across the restored floor and approached the pristine writing desk. Clumsily he uncradled the telephone receiver.

"Yes?" he said curtly.

"Canavor here."

"What can I do for you, Inspector?"

"You know what you can do for me. You can tell me why the complaints have started again. Explosions, artillery fire, smoke rising from your villa. Every four days, the same complaints."

"It's most peculiar, isn't it?" Drabek said.

"What the fuck is going on?"

"Why don't you come by for tea some afternoon? We'll chat about life's mysteries."

"That'll be the day," said Canavor with a soft chuckle. "If you get any theories, ring me up."

"I have lots of theories," Drabek said under his breath. He waited until Canavor said good-bye, then put down the receiver and surveyed the library. The security console was intact. Everything was in its place: drapes on the windows, books on the shelves—and in the safe lay the equations.

He stepped toward the console and threw the window-shutter switch, causing the plates to swing away and reveal the Château Galitzin in the distance. The brass eaves glowed in the late afternoon sun, and the windowpanes sparkled in their frames, the dark wood contrasting pleasingly with the smooth expanses of white stucco.

The following morning Drabek woke up early, feeling relaxed, refreshed, and happy. Hurriedly he washed and dressed. Without worrying about breakfast, he descended to the library, where he removed the papers from the safe and carried them to his desk.

A full day of tranquillity lay ahead of him. The second day would be tinged with a certain anxiety, and by the third day he would be nervously glancing at his watch several times each hour, anticipating the ordeal.

He heaved a sigh. Yesterday the enemy had nearly destroyed him, but even more disturbing was the way that, right before the attic floor dissolved, he'd become reconciled to his death. Damn, he'd been lucky.

Lucky? Was luck in fact the cause of his deliverance? What if the avatars of eternity had simply *elected* to let him survive yesterday? What if they did so *every* fourth day? If he died, after all, they would have to look elsewhere for amusement.

Amusement? Was that the truth of his situation? The idea made Drabek cringe, and yet he could not deny its plausibility. He had never been a threat to the avatars, merely the butt of their cosmic joke. The loop was not their strategy for thwarting the Drabek threat, but an endless game for which they wrote all the rules. And they could alter those rules on a whim, sending Stinky and Pretty Boy to the villa right now if they wanted, where the two bastards would find the pathetic Drabek poring over his equally pathetic equations, as vulnerable as a Chinese figurine that by nodding its porcelain bobble-head thanks you for the money you just placed in its dish.

Groaning, he slumped behind his desk. He was dumbfounded, flabbergasted. He felt like a genius and at the same time an idiot. His revelation delighted him in its lucidity, even as it chastened him to the point of tears.

The avatars could have ended the game long ago. But of course they preferred to keep on playing. Thanks to Drabek, they were having the time of their lives.

He made two fists and slammed them against the papers. It seemed as if the equations now had faces, eyes narrowed in mockery, mouths spouting words of derision. All these calculations meant nothing. They did not lay the foundation of a new theory; they merely framed a theater of the absurd. Even if he sat at this desk for a century, he would not perturb the avatars for a second.

He seized the sheets and began to rip them, slowly, as in a dream. Mechanically he tore his work into even smaller bits, then laid the fragments together and tried to rip them a third time. Impossible. He tossed the fragments into the air. They hovered like a flock of white butterflies, then scattered in all directions.

Fluttering equations. Fleeting time. A butterfly, of course, was both an organism and a phenomenon, just as time was both a phenomenon and . . . an organism?

An organism. A living thing. Could that be it? Was time in fact alive, its tissues teeming with some arcane bubbling stuff, their basic units continually maturing, dying, and sloughing off like the constituent components of plants and animals?

The cells of circumstance, the bubbles of time, the foam of forever— yes! With trembling hands he opened the top drawer and removed a clean sheet of paper. He laid it on the desk, then removed his fountain pen from the inkstand. After a brief interval he unscrewed the cap and wrote in small neat capitals, NOTES TOWARD A CELLULAR THEORY OF TIME.

Like a pack of dogs let loose from a kennel, the signs and symbols

rushed from pen to paper. He observed them with a smile as they gam-
boled and frolicked about, their seemingly random behavior determined
by time's arcane essence, a structure that, moment by moment, grew
more distinct and intricate, as beautiful and logical as the vault of a
Gothic cathedral.

Here in the maw of eternity, a singular fact eclipsed all others. From
now on he wouldn't need three whole days to prepare the defenses. He
wouldn't even need one whole day. Alive and thriving in the belly of time,
he would be perpetually ready for the enemy.

Drabek felt an unexpected pang in his soul. Strangely enough, he
would miss the excitement of the fourth day.

A soft pounding filled the air, subtle but persistent, like distant surf.
He knew at once that it came from somewhere beyond the villa, suffus-
ing the library with an odd adamant rhythm.

He returned the pen to the inkstand, crossed the room, and cranked
open a casement.

Decay had claimed the Château Galitzin. Its walls were shorn of plaster, its bricks naked and crumbling. A low mound of stucco lay along the
foundation like a corpse's discarded shroud. Not a single tile remained on
the conical roof, which now featured a cavernous hole through which
Drabek could see a lattice of rotting beams.

Each window was masked by a web so thick that it suggested a huge
wad of gauze. The intricate networks pulsed and quivered, alive with the
movements of their ambitious architects. And the pounding? The pounding, Drabek realized, was simply the sound emitted by the busy legs of a
million spinning spiders.

JOHANNA SINISALO

BABY DOLL

TRANSLATED FROM THE FINNISH
BY DAVID HACKSTON

Of the thirteen European tongues represented in this anthology, only one does not belong to the great Indo-European language family. Despite their linguistic otherness, or perhaps because of it, Finnish poets, novelists, and short story writers have over the generations fashioned a vital indigenous literature. Authors of a mythic, fantastical, and extrapolative bent have contributed significantly to this phenomenon, producing works that have spilled beyond the nation's borders to enrich the collective corpus of international science fiction.

Finnish SF boasts a legacy stretching back well over a century, to Evald Ferdinand Jahnsson's 1883 newspaper serial Muistelmia matkaltni Ruskealan pappilaan uuden vuoden aikoina vuonna 1983 *("Memoirs of My Trip to the Vicarage of Ruskeala around New Year 1983"). Science fiction culture in Finland today is plenary and robust, keyed to the periodicals* Tähtivaeltaja *("The Star Rover") and* Portii *("Gate"), an ongoing anthology series, and the annual Atorox Award for best short story, named after the robot-hero of Aarne Haapakoski's popular series from the forties. It is interesting to note that the Kalevala, the Finnish national epic compiled in the nineteenth century by the scholar Elias Lönnrot, has influenced not only the native product but Anglo-American SF and fantasy as well. Tolkien's encounter with the Kalevala famously shaped one of the Elven languages that figure in* The Silmarillion *and* The Lord of the Rings. *L. Sprague de Camp and Fletcher Pratt's* Wall of Serpents *(1960) owes much to the Finnish epic. Among the important works of the Finnish-American writer Emil Petaja, SFWA's 1995 Author Emeritus, is his four-volume Kalevala sequence.*

Along with Risto Isomäki and Kimmo Lehtonen, Johanna Sinisalo commands the cutting edge of contemporary Finnish SF. Born in 1958 in Sodankylä, Finnish Lapland, she studied theater and drama, then worked in advertising for fifteen years before becoming a full-time writer. Her debut novel Ennen päivänlaskua ei voi *("Not before Sundown," published in the United States as* Troll: A Love Story*) appeared in 2000 and received her country's most prestigious literary award, the Finlandia Prize. It was subsequently translated into eleven languages. In 2005 Sinisalo came out with her first collection,* Kädettömät kuninkaat ja muita häiritseviä tarinoita *("Handless Kings and Other Disturbing Stories"), and she also edited an anthology,* The Dedalus Book of Finnish Fantasy, *recently published in both Britain and the USA. Her latest novel is* Lasisilmä *("The Glass Eye," 2006). A seven-time winner of the Atorox Award, Sinisalo currently resides in Tampere.*

"Baby Doll" is a savage and heartbreaking story excoriating one of the most disturbing trends in Western society: the appropriation of childhood—its theft, really—by the forces of frenzied consumerism and ersatz eros. Writing within the venerable tradition of the SF dystopia, Sinisalo takes us into a nightmare world of assembly-line Lolitas who, unaware of their exploitation by addled commerce and craven adults, can imagine no other way of being in the world.

Annette comes home from school and shrugs her bag onto the floor in the hall. The bag is made of clear vinyl speckled with metal glitter, all in rainbow colors that swirl around the iridescent pink hearts and full kissy lips. The vinyl reveals the contents of the bag: Annette's schoolbooks, exercise books, and a plastic pencil box featuring the hottest boy band of 2015, Stick That Dick. The boys wear open leather jackets across their rippling bare torsos, and their jockstraps all feature the head of some animal with a large beak or a long trunk. Craig has an elephant on his jockstrap. Craig's the cutest of them all.

Annette slings her bright red spandex jacket across a chair and starts to remove her matching stretch boots. They're tight around the shins, but she can't be bothered to bend down and wrench them off. Instead she tries to pry one heel free with the opposite toe, but succeeds only in tearing her fishnet stockings.

"Oh, for fuck's sake!"

Mumps walks in from the kitchen, still wearing her work clothes. "What was that, darling?"

"I said, 'Golly, I've wrecked my tights.'"

"Oh, dear, not again. And they were so expensive. Well, you'll just have to wear the plain ones tomorrow."

"I'm so *not* wearing anything like that!"

"Darling, you don't have a choice."

"Then I'm not going to school at *all*!" Annette snatches up her bag and stomps off toward her room, but the TV is on in the den, and it's time for her favorite show, *Suburban Heat and Hate*. "I'd look like a total dork!" she continues, half to herself, half to her mother, who can no longer hear her, as she throws herself on the couch.

The show begins. The plot's as thick as it gets. Jake has just been discovered in bed with Melissa, but Bella doesn't know that Jake knows she's having an affair with his twin brother Tom. Jake meanwhile doesn't know that Melissa is in fact his daughter, because years ago he helped a lesbian couple get pregnant.

"Let's make a deal, darling." Mum has come in from the kitchen and is standing by the couch.

"Quiet! I can't hear a thing." Just then Bella pulls Jake off Melissa, screaming a barrage of abuse, leaving Melissa's enormous boobs and Jake's white butt in full view. At school today Annette heard Ninotska telling everyone to watch this afternoon's episode because Jake's got such a fantastic butt. Annette doesn't see what's so fantastic about it. It's paler than the rest of his brown skin, and it isn't as hairy as other men's butts. Still, tomorrow she'll find an opportunity to tell Ninotska she got a glimpse of Jake's butt, and of course she'll say she thought it was totally hypersmart, and give a low giggle the way you're supposed to when you talk about these things.

Mum waits till the commercials come on. "I have to go back to work the minute Dad gets home."

"I'll be fine."

"Lulu's at a shoot. Dad'll pick her up around nine or ten, and then it's your bedtime."

"Tell me something I don't know."

"One more thing, darling. I'm going on a business trip tomorrow, and I'll be away for two days."

"You're always going off somewhere."

"Dad can help you with your homework."

"Yeah, right, I bet he makes me watch Otso so he can play squash."

"That's what I mean by the deal. Promise me you'll help Dad and all you kids will behave yourselves."

Annette is pissed off—big time. Whenever Mumps goes away, they end up eating all sorts of weird meals that Dumps cooks himself, instead of pizza or deli sushi or toasted sandwiches like Mumps gives them. You need to tell Dumps at least a hundred times what stuff to buy at the store, and why you need it. Once when Mumps was away Annette spent an hour explaining to Dumps why she categorically had to have a new eyelash-lengthening mascara and a bottle of golden body-spray.

"On one condition," Annette says.

"What's that?"

"Can I go to a sleepover at Ninotska's Thursday night?"

Although Annette hasn't actually been invited, rumor has it Ninotska's still deciding on the final guest list. Annette has noticed Ninotska checking out the Stick That Dick pencil box that Mum and Dad brought back from London. Annette could give Ninotska the pencil box, then later ask Mum for money to buy another—she could always say she cracked the old one.

Just in case she gets invited, she has to make sure she has permission to go. If you get invited you have to be able to say "Sí, sí, gracias" without worrying about it. *Nobody* is tragic enough to say they need to ask permission, and if you say "Sí, sí, gracias" and don't turn up, you can pretty much forget about being invited anywhere again.

"Who's Ninotska?"

"Ninotska Lahtinen from our year, stupid! She lives on Vuorikatu."

"And why do you have to go over there?"

"She's having her nine-yo party. And I'll need to take a present. I can catch a bus if Dad can't take me."

Mumps sighs, and with that Annette knows she won't have to sweat it anymore. The commercials finally end, and Annette turns back to the tube. Melissa's a professional stripper. She's wearing a bikini with golden frills. It's so mega.

The apartment door opens, and Dumps comes in, having picked up Otso at the nursery. Otso is five-yo.

Mumps has laid the table with pasta salad from the deli. It's all right except for the capers; Annette doesn't like them and shoves the awful

things aside. Dumps starts raving on about how they're the most deli-
cious bits, then spears a caper off Annette's plate and stuffs it in his
mouth, loudly smacking his lips. Otso only ever eats the pasta twists, but
wouldn't you know—nobody gives him a lecture about it.

"So Otso, how was nursery today?" Mumps asks, all treacly like a TV
kiddie host. Did she really use that twittery voice on Annette when she
was five?

"I'm going on a date! With my girlfriend!" Otso can't say his *f*'s properly, and his speech therapist has her work cut out with his *r*'s, too. The
word "girlfriend" sounds like Otso's trying to spit something out between his front teeth.

Mumps and Dumps exchange one of their grown-up looks. "Well,
our big boy's going on a date!" says Dad in the same cringe-o-matic voice
as Mum. "When is your date, and who is it with?"

"Tomorrow, with Pamela. Her Mum's picking us up."

Mum and Dad simper at one another again, pretending to swoon,
then shake their heads in the phoniest way, meanwhile smiling like split
sausages.

"Pamela's my main squeeze," says Otso, shoveling down different col-
ored pasta swirls.

Once Mum has gone back to the office, Annette flops down to watch
the reality show *Between the Sheets*, in which the contestants try to find the
perfect sex partner. "What first comes to mind when I look down your
cleavage: (a) lemons, (b) apples, or (c) melons?" a male contestant asks a
woman sprawled behind the curtain on a canopy bed when the door
opens and Dad and Lulu walk in.

Lulu's only two years older than Annette, but looking at her you'd
never believe it.

She's still wearing her photo-session makeup, a pair of giant false eyelashes with so much black and gray around her eyes it no longer looks
like makeup at all; the eyeshadow just gives her a tired and hungry look.
Her lips feature a dark crimson pencil-line to straighten her Cupid's bow,
the puffy parts filled with a lighter plum-red, and there's so much lip gloss
involved that her mouth appears bruised and swollen. Her hair has been
curled in tiny ringlets and tied in a deliberately careless bun.

Not long ago Lulu got calls from photographers in Milan and Tokyo,
and she burst into tears when they later told Mum and Dad not to bring

her because she was too short after all. Before that disaster she'd been weighing herself twice a day, but now she's checking her height three or four times a week. She has a special chart on the wall for marking her growth. The pencil lines are so close together they form a gray smudge.

Lulu's face recently landed on the cover of the Finnish *Cosmopolitan*, a very big deal, so now her agent says she has to stop posing for the catalogs. Being associated with Monoprix and Wal-Mart won't help her image. She's far too sensual.

Lulu heads upstairs to rinse off her sensual makeup. Annette's stomach twists and churns. She goes to her room and stands before the mirror and tries to stare herself down, as if she could make her face look more sensual by gazing at it angrily enough. She sucks her belly in, but she still resembles a flat squash.

"Annette! Bedtime!" comes Dumps's voice from downstairs.

"Yes yes YESYES!"

Annette's a slut!" the boys start shouting as she walks onto the playground, pretending not to hear them. It's fairly normal and not worth worrying about; anybody they're not trying to pull they call a slut—and they're not trying to pull Annette.

There are far worse things they could shout out.

Ninotska and Veronika are standing by the main entrance, whispering to each other. Veli and Juho walk past. Veli attempts to grope Ninotska, and Juho tries shoving his hand up Veronika's black leather miniskirt. Ninotska giggles, squirms, and pushes him away, and Veronika dashes to hide behind her. Veli and Juho swagger toward the door, and on their way each boy sticks his index finger through the looped thumb and finger of the other hand. Ninotska and Veronika giggle until the boys are out of earshot.

Annette approaches the two girls. "Hi," she says awkwardly.

Veronika and Ninotska toss their fountains of permed hair and look at her disdainfully. Ninotska's skimpy shirt allows a wide strip of skin to show between her golden shiny hipsters and her spaghetti-strap top. She has a silver ring in her belly button.

"Ninotska, can you come over here for a minute?" says Annette, backing toward the Dumpster. "We need to talk."

Ninotska glances at Veronika, a scowl on her face, then joins Annette. "Well, what's the big deal?" she asks suspiciously.

Annette reaches into her bag and brings out the Stick That Dick pencil box. "You know, I'm really bored with this. You want it?"

Ninotska's eyes light up, and Annette realizes her offer's having the desired effect. "What makes you think I'd want your old crap?" Ninotska replies bluntly, but it's all part of the script.

Annette shrugs. "Okay, fine then," she says, and starts to throw the thing in the Dumpster.

Ninotska's hand shoots out, grabbing the box before it can join the rubbish. "Easy pleasy. I believe in recycling."

Annette smiles as Ninotska slips the pencil box into her golden bag printed with the words EAT ME. "Hey, what're you doing Thursday night?" she asks finally, and Annette's heart leaps with excitement.

On the bed Annette has spread out everything she'll need: best lace-chiffon nightie, makeup kit, perfume—plus books and stuff for the next day at school. Her nine-yo present for Ninotska is wrapped in silver paper, three shades of nail polish that Annette picked out herself because Mumps would've gotten something tragic. It should all fit in the flight bag borrowed from Mumps. Now Annette must decide what to wear for the evening. She plumps for a pair of lizard-scale leggings and a skirt with a slit up the side. She hasn't got any swank-tanks like Ninotska, and her green top is fray-proof, so she takes a pair of scissors and cuts a good ten centimeters off the bottom, making it stop well short of her belly button. The ragged cut is totally glam; it looks a bit like those TV shows where the jungle women's clothes are so tattered they reveal lots of skin.

Annette studies the nightie and the matching thong underwear. Then she looks in the mirror.

She slips off her skirt, leggings, and panties. She opens her makeup kit and removes a black eyeliner. With her pink plastic sharpener she gives the pencil a serious point.

She sits spread-eagled before the mirror and with careful pencil strokes draws thin wavy lines between her legs.

Ninotska's Mum and Dad are away somewhere for the evening. In addition to Ninotska and Annette, Veronika and Janika and Evita and Carmen and Vanessa are all naturally at the pajama party. The sleepover boasts buckets of pizza-flavored popcorn and big bottles of high-energy soda, "so we can last through the night," squeals Ninotska.

Once Ninotska has opened her presents, everybody gets ready for the fashion show. Back home Annette thought her nightie was fantastic, but now it looks like an old woman's shirt. It's too long, reaching almost to the knees, and totally unrevealing. Everybody agrees that Evita's nightie is the best. It's slightly see-through, like violet blue mist, and it's so short it barely covers her ass. Ninotska's is nice, too, with wide frilly shoulder-straps and loose laces on the front so it's open almost all the way down, and it's made of red silk. But because it's her party, Ninotska decides to be generous and votes for Evita's nightie.

Around ten o'clock everybody gets all excited and snickery when Ninotska takes a stepladder and goes into her Mum and Dad's room and comes back cradling a stack of DVDs. "Let's watch a film." The girls sort through the pile. Each DVD has naked men and women on the cover, sharing the space with titles like *Hot Pussies* and *Grand Slam Gang Bang*. All the girls start giggling, hiding their mouths with their hands, and Ninotska puts a DVD in the player.

The pounding music and the script with its endless shouts of "Give it to me, baby" and "Meats to the sweet" are all very monotonous, but they still stare at the screen—nobody dares not watch. Annette feels twitchy and uncomfortable, and sometimes it's like there's a second little heart beating under her stomach, and that makes her uncomfortable, too. She knows you're supposed to stay the distance with this stuff, and you're also supposed to pretend it doesn't bother you in the slightest, the way boys watch slasher movies—if you let on you're scared, everybody laughs and takes the piss. Even though the whole point of horror flicks is to upset you, and that's why they get made in the first place, you're still not allowed to be scared. And so they have to watch these grand slam hot pussies as if it didn't mean anything.

Once the second flick is halfway over, and two black dudes are simultaneously pumping a woman with gigantic boobs, Ninotska gives a loud yawn, and this is a sign that the guests are no longer expected to be interested in the film. She switches the machine off, slipcases the disc, and drops it on the stack.

"Who wants to check out my Mum and Dad's room?" she asks, and everybody wants to, of course. The girls jostle behind Ninotska and make their way into a lovely bedroom with an enormous four-poster and a gold-framed mirror on the wall. Ninotska climbs the stepladder to the top shelf of the closet. She returns the stack of DVDs, then takes down a big cardboard box and jumps back onto the rug. She opens the box and spreads the contents across the bed. Red-and-black underwear that's nothing but a belt with bits of fabric on the sides: in the middle they're completely open. A pair of manacles with fur on the cuffs. Ninotska grabs a pinkish zucchini and gives the end a twist, and the thing starts shaking in her hand. "Brrrrr!" she says, trying to imitate the noise of the zucchini, then waves it in each girl's face, and they all move away giggling hysterically.

"Has anybody ever tried one of these?" she asks slowly, challenging them, and Annette feels like Ninotska is looking straight at her.

"I'll bet none of you would *dare*." Ninotska glances across the group of girls. Somebody attempts a giggle, and then they all fall silent.

"I dare you. I dare you."

The silence rings in Annette's ears, her mouth is dry with anticipation, and she feels that any second now Ninotska's eyes will stop at her.

Lulu's chewing gum and trying to look mega, but every now and then she gives a quick laugh, her straightened, whitened teeth flashing between her dark red lips while the tabloid photographer takes her picture, over and over. Occasionally the female reporter glances at the LED screen to see how the photos are coming out. Annette is sulking in the den. She can look into the living room, but the people from the newspaper can't see her, and she would refuse to be photographed next to Lulu even if they begged her.

In any case, they haven't asked.

"So tell me, how does it feel being the new face of Sexy Secrets Underwear?" the reporter asks.

Lulu lowers her false eyelashes, so overlong they almost reach her boobs, and smiles. Annette knows that Lulu uses this posture so she'll have time to think without seeming like a dork. Finally Lulu looks up.

"Okay."

"People say you're about to become the object of a national fantasy. Do you agree?"

The eyelashes tilt down, then rise again. "I guess."

The reporter smiles and switches off her digital recorder. "Thanks, Lulu. That'll be all."

Annette simply has to walk out of the den before the tabloid people leave. She's got her makeup on, and she's wearing her shiny black dress—plus of course her high-heeled ankle boots, even though Mumps has told her not to use them on the parquet.

"Well, lookee here," the photographer says, squinting at Annette, "there's *another* stunning woman on the premises," and he almost sounds sincere, but she can't be sure.

"That's my little sister," Lulu says before blowing a bubble gum bubble. "She's eight."

Annette could kill Lulu. Annette thinks she looks at least ten-yo, but by now the tabloid people are already in the hall, telling Lulu the article will run on Friday.

Naturally Mumps has bought three copies of Friday's paper. On the front page of the fashion section is a picture of Lulu, her head thrown back, a gush of curls cascading down her shoulders, her teeth showing between pouty lips and her eyes half shut. MODEL SENSATION LULU: I LOVE BEING THE STAR OF GUYS' WET DREAMS! screams the headline.

Lippe from the next apartment has come over to share a glass of wine with Mum. Lippe admires Lulu's picture, and then they gab about the contract. Though Mum whispers, Annette, sitting in front of the TV, can still hear her. With her hand to her lips, Mum says, "A hundred and twenty thousand euros." At least they'll get back all the money they sank into Lulu's career, Annette thinks. A year ago Lulu took some modeling courses that cost ultrabucks, but thanks to that move a fancy agent saw Lulu at the graduation show and signed her up on the spot. Lulu doesn't go to regular school anymore; she's supposed to be studying with a private tutor and taking the odd exam, but Annette hasn't noticed much evidence for this. There have been no reported sightings of Lulu reading a schoolbook.

Annette once applied to the modeling school, but you have to get through the preliminary round. They looked at her for about half a second and didn't bother asking her any questions. A month later a letter came saying that she didn't have "sufficient camera presence."

Mum explains to Lippe that originally another girl had been tapped for the Sexy Secrets campaign, a seventeen-year-old from Turku called

Ramona who'd already done a lot of modeling and was a runner-up for Miss Finland.

"Hasn't her face been used to death?" asks Lippe.

"She's well past her prime," Mum says, nodding, "so Lulu got the contract."

The door rattles, and Dad comes in with Otso. Otso's cheeks are red, and he's wearing a smart jacket, a white shirt, and a bow tie. He's been on another date with Pamela: Dad took them to a film or something. Both Mum and Dad prattle about what a handsome little boy they have. Otso runs into Mum's arms shouting "Guess what! Guess what! Me and Pamela got engaged!" which of course starts off such a wave of fawning and gushing that Annette feels like throwing up.

Annette is on the school bus. The journey is less than a kilometer, only a few blocks, but the law states that all school-aged children must ride to school in their parents' cars or on a supervised bus. "For the protection of our children," ran the ads a few years ago when the law went into effect. Annette is standing in the aisle, but her new platform shoes cause her feet to slide down toward the toes, and she keeps losing her balance. Once the bus stops at the traffic light she raises her eyes, and the view out the window hits her like a punch in the face.

From a gigantic roadside billboard Lulu stares back at her, ten times larger than normal, her eyes dark, her lips shining cherry red, a wind machine billowing her hair.

When Annette finally gets off the bus, as if to further taunt her, another billboard appears, a startling three-panel display this time, looming near the school gates. And of course the star is Lulu, modeling three different lines of underwear—Naughty Red, Sinful Black, and Seductive Green, according to the words.

Each image bears the same caption: BABY DOLL.

Trussed in a bright red string, Lulu's ass practically bursts from the first panel; with half-closed eyes she twists her head toward the camera, brushing her hands against her bare shoulders so that her false nails, painted the same color as her panties, gleam against her skin like drops of blood.

Then comes Lulu crouching, shiny black-laced boots matching her underwear, holding a ridiculous toy snake and making like she's kissing the thing, its orange velveteen head sliding between her lips.

And finally there's a shot of Lulu from the side, hugging a beige teddy bear. Her back is arched, and her boobs, wrapped in jade-green lace, thrust defiantly upward.

Lulu's priceless tits.

But a few days later a miracle occurs.

Annette arrives on the playground for recess, and instantly her stomach starts tightening, her chest pounding, just like every other time she has to walk past the gangs of boys. She hunches her shoulders, lowers her head, and wonders where the mockery will come from today, the cries of slut and dwarf-butt, and of course the comments about her tits—bee-stings, milkduds.

One gang member mutters something indistinct, but Annette manages to reach the pavilion without her face blushing bright red. All of a sudden he's standing right next to her. His name's Timppa; she knows that. He's two years ahead of her and plays ice hockey with the F Juniors, and many times she's heard Ninotska and Veronika whispering that Timppa is absolutely *shagtastic*. He's still standing right next to her, looking at her, and Annette is so startled she almost runs away for fear of yet another insult, but Timppa gives her a friendly smile and doesn't look a bit like all he wants to do is shove his hand down her top.

"You're Annette, right?" he asks. Annette is so taken aback that all she can manage is a nod. She's utterly speechless. Timppa must think she's a total dork because she doesn't know how to respond with something quick and sassy the way Ninotska and Veronika always do when boys talk to them. But Timppa doesn't seem to care; he looks Annette up and down, and his eyes stop at the sight of her platform shoes.

"Awesome boots."

"Thanks," Annette stammers as Timppa reaches into his leather jacket and produces a packet of SuperKiss, which he holds out to Annette. "Gum?"

Annette takes one, fumbles off the wrapper, and pops the stick in her mouth just as the bell rings, saving her. Timppa backs away, smirks, and waves at her. "Catch you later, Annette."

Annette stands there and forgets to chew her gum, her mouth half-open. Her heart is about to burst out of her chest.

During the next lesson Annette writes TIMPPA TIMPPA TIMPPA on her arm with a sharp pencil, scratching so hard the skin almost breaks.

Ninotska and Veronika have of course noticed that Annette was talking to Timppa during recess, and they'll be sure to catch up with her at their first opportunity, instead of Annette nonchalantly trying to hang around their gang.

"Well, well, our little Annette's got a *boyfriend*," Ninotska says, her eyes burning, and for the first time Annette feels like she's *somebody*, not just that girl whose Mum and Dad brought her a Stick That Dick pencil box from London; suddenly there's something a little bit glam about Annette.

"He's not my boyfriend. We're just . . . friends."

"Then it must be the first time ever that Timppa Kujala is *just friends* with a girl."

Veronika gives a hollow chortle. "He's the horniest stud in the school."

"Careful you don't get burned, Annette, darling."

Ninotska and Veronika saunter off, their curls gushing, their little bottoms bouncing contemptuously, and Annette looks at them and says under her breath, "They're just *jealous*."

And with that a great warmth fills her.

Timppa is loitering near the gates when Annette leaves school. He asks her where she's off to, and when she says she's going home, he says he's headed the same way and suggests they walk together, fuck the bus law. Timppa spits on the ground and says the whole rule is a load of crapola; he walks to school whenever he wants to. Annette wants to sound mega and says she thinks it's a dumb-ass rule, too, and for some reason she feels safe walking with Timppa.

Annette sees that Veronika notices her leaving with Timppa, and her sense of triumph is so great she's able to chat almost normally with Timppa, even though the silences are long, and she ends up asking him the same questions over and over; but he doesn't seem to mind, and he talks practically the whole way home about which hockey players he admires the most, the ones that have the fastest cars and the juiciest babes with the hottest knockers.

When they arrive at Annette's building, Timppa shuffles awkwardly for a moment and stares at the ground. "Can I come in for a bit?"

Annette is about to faint. Even though Ninotska and Veronika have kissed lots of boys at parties, and while Carmen spent a whole semester walking around hand-in-hand with Pasi, nobody has ever had a boyfriend who wanted to *visit*. It could mean almost anything. Annette can hardly breathe.

"Sure, come on in."

They enter the elevator, and Annette presses the button for the sixth floor. Inside the car they don't say a word, and for Annette this is quite a relief. Finally they arrive; she opens her apartment door, shows Timppa in, and gives him a hanger for his leather jacket. This time she doesn't drop her bag on the floor but carries it down the hall past the living room and the den, Timppa at her heels, then stops outside her bedroom door, on which there's a large Stick That Dick poster and a piece of cardboard with thick red lettering: ANNETTEZ ROOM PRIVATE NO ENTRY!

Annette steps toward Timppa so she's almost right up against him. "Want to see my room?"

Timppa doesn't appear to be listening; he's inspecting the other doors in the vicinity. One features a full-color poster of the world's most glamorous supermodel, Marinette Mankiewicz. Her moist skin sparkles with hundreds of little pearly beads for a major wetness effect; her bikini looks wet, too, clamped tight against her tits and almost see-through. Lulu once told Annette it's all done with oil instead of water, because oil is shinier and doesn't dry out under the studio lights.

"Is that your sister's room?"

"Lulu's? I guess."

"When's she coming home?"

At first Annette doesn't understand, but then it strikes her, and her stomach feels like it's about to spill out around her heels, and her head starts to spin.

"Around four o'clock," she mutters almost inaudibly.

"I can hang out and wait, huh?" Timppa asks, his eyes fixed on

Marinette Mankiewicz, and Annette realizes that Lulu and the photographer have ripped off the idea behind this poster for their three-panel billboard—the Seductive Green Lulu with her tits pointing skyward.

"Make yourself at home," she says and goes into her room, and only vast amounts of self-control prevent her from slamming the door shut much louder than normal.

After that Timppa visits almost every day. He comes around at the same time as Lulu and often doesn't leave till late at night, after Mumps and Dumps have stood next to the Marinette Mankiewicz poster coughing or clearing their throats or knocking on the door, and Mumps says, pretending to be all thoughtful and considerate, "Right, I think it's time for our Lulu's beauty sleep!"

Ninotska and Veronika have been giggling to themselves and tossing their curls around and whispering so much that Annette can feel it in her stomach. They ask her, real smarmy, "How's your *boyfriend* doing nowadays?" then burst into a hyperly loud chortle as if the joke gets funnier every time. At first Annette can't understand how exactly Ninotska and Veronika learned that Timppa and Lulu have been hanging together, but it all becomes clear during morning recess when she's walking behind a group of boys who haven't noticed her, and she overhears one of them chattering about what a hottie Timppa has pulled; he then describes Lulu at great length and brags that Timppa's on the verge of scoring. Timppa, naturally, has told the entire school.

Annette runs straight to the girls' toilet and throws up, filling the bowl with globules of meat and potatoes. The ketchup makes it look like she's been vomiting blood, and she decides that vomiting blood probably feels like this. A moment later, her puke-tears having dried, she feels slightly dizzy, but her thoughts are surprisingly clear.

As she leaves the stall, she bumps into Nana, one of the girls in her year, loitering by the sinks. She must have heard Annette barfing. Nana gives her a conspiratorial smile.

"Have you just started?"

Annette doesn't understand. Nana pulls a bottle of Evian from her schoolbag and hands it to her. "If you want to stay fit while you're on the program, remember to drink enough water. Don't let yourself dry out. No calories in water, you see."

Annette gulps down a mouthful of Evian and mumbles her thanks.

Nana slips the bottle back in her bag. "One good tip: get yourself some xylitol chewing gum and use it after you've barfed. That way the stomach acids won't take the shine off your teeth."

Annette nods. Nana slings her bag across her shoulder and looks Annette up and down. "Yeah, you could do with losing a few kilos." Nana moves toward the door, her little ass snugged tightly in her jeans. "Good luck."

Mum and Dad are watching a movie on late-night TV. Timppa is around again.

Annette has a walk-in closet that runs along the wall she shares with Lulu's room. When they were little, they used to play telephone. Every time Annette held the rim of a drinking glass against the back wall of her closet and pressed her ear to the bottom, she could hear what her sister was saying even if Lulu used a normal voice.

Annette visits the bathroom and dumps the toothbrushes out of the glass. She returns to her room, slides back the closet door, and makes her way through the hanging clothes. Chiffon, fake leather and the hems of her black and brightly colored miniskirts brush her face, and the heels of her shoes clatter as she pushes them out of the way. The closet smells of fabric softener, sweaty sneakers, and lavender sachet.

Annette holds the glass against the plaster. She knows that Lulu's bed is on the other side, right up against the wall.

At first all she picks up is a lot of mumbling, moaning, whispering, and creaking bedsprings. Then comes a thump as though somebody's arm or leg has hit the wall. The sound shoots right into Annette's ear, and she almost jumps out of the closet.

"For Christ's sake, what's your problem? We've been together a whole month." She can hear Timppa clearly now, sounding all shrill since his voice hasn't broken yet. Lulu responds with a murmur Annette can't quite make out.

"What're you saving it for?" Timppa chirps. "I'll bet you've already been screwed every which way, at least that's what the guys are saying."

Again Annette can't hear Lulu's reply—is she talking into her pillow or what?—but Timppa understands her, and he answers immediately.

"Don't you know this town's full of chicks just begging for it?" he scoffs. "Why should I waste my time on some snooty tight-twat? Shit, are you like planning to hold out till you're fourteen or something?"

"No," Lulu says. "I don't know."

"Then what's your problem? Aren't you on the pill?"

Lulu hesitates. "Well, not exactly." Her voice is all raspy and apologetic, the way it gets when she's embarrassed. "I haven't quite got mine yet."

"Your pills?"

"My . . . periods."

"Bingo! Then there's no need to mess with rubbers!"

Again Lulu says something Annette can't quite hear.

"I just think it's time our relationship took a step forward." Timppa's words sound like he's reading them from a book.

Another loud thump, followed by a rustling noise, probably Lulu's sheets. She whimpers a little.

"Stop it."

"Stop it? You're like a walking invitation, ass and jalookies on billboards all over town, and you have the balls to say *stop it*?"

Again the rustling of Lulu's sheets. She mumbles something, and then comes Timppa's voice, and this time it's more of a whine. "When you lead a guy on like that, you've got to see it through."

Annette stands upright, and her head hits the metal rod, but she doesn't give it a second thought. She crawls out of the closet, sending her shoes clattering into the room. An instant later she's in the hall banging on Lulu's door.

"Lulu!"

A moment's silence, then Lulu's voice, trying to sound calm and normal. "Now what?"

"Mum says your guest has to go!"

From behind the door comes a stifled curse, still more rustling; the bed creaks. There follows a lot of low harsh muttering, and Annette hears a zipper being pulled up. Timppa comes out of the door, his hair messed up and his face all red. He glowers at Annette, who's leaning against the wall minding her own business, and she stares back at him with a shrug and an innocent, slightly apologetic smile that says, *Parents will be parents.*

Lulu's door stays closed, and after a short while the sound of soft sweet music floats out into the hall.

•   •   •

Timppa has stopped coming round and Annette is ferociously happy about it. But her triumph starts falling apart, cracking and flaking and blowing away with the wind when she realizes Lulu hasn't changed; she's still always giggling and yawning and stuffing herself with laxative licorice candy. It's the same Lulu who smiles mysteriously from beneath her false eyelashes, and for some reason she doesn't seem to pine for the lost Timppa in the least.

The worst of it is the way Lulu had the nerve simply to forget Timppa, whose name still throbs where Annette scratched it on her forearm, TIMPPA TIMPPA TIMPPA.

He was Annette's first chance to be the way everyone expected her to be, and Lulu acts like she took up with him just for the hell of it, then let him go for the same reason. As if Annette wasn't the one who split them up in the first place.

Would it kill Lulu to show, even for the tiniest instant, that she knows what it feels like to be Annette?

In fairness, ever since the night with the drinking glass Lulu has acted almost friendly toward Annette, chatting with her and giving her stuff from her makeup kit that's hardly been used at all. Sometimes Lulu looks at her with big wet spaniel eyes, which is actually pretty maddening, and Annette almost breaks a tooth trying to stay calm when Lulu gets all palsy-walsy. Annette thinks Lulu's just pretending, her way of covering up the wound Annette caused in coming between her and Timppa. And with that phony chumminess Lulu in snatching away the last precious thing Annette has, her pissy little victory.

And on top of it all Mumps keeps simpering, "It's so nice to see you sisters getting along so well."

Annette is vegging out before the television, the big noisy climax of some dopey rock show. Stick That Dick has dropped to number six on the charts, and now in the number one slot there's the girl band Jugzapoppin' who perform topless. After that there's nothing on; even the trash channels are boring once you get used to them. Annette visits a chat room using the remote, but soon gives up. You can barely write two answers before somebody asks about your cup-size and what color panties you're wearing. She surfs the Net, then skips through different TV channels, but all she can find are unfunny sitcoms and grotty old movies.

One of them catches her attention.

The title of the flick is *Welcome to the Dollhouse.* At first Annette is only interested because the star is so unbelievably ugly. Why would they let anybody who looks like that be in a movie? The girl must be about eight-yo, Annette's age, and she's not even making an effort to appear older. She wears glasses, of all things, which tells you right off the film is ancient, because nowadays nobody, no girl that is, would be that insane; you either have an operation or at the very least get contacts. Annette follows the film for a few minutes, occasionally flipping through the other channels, but she keeps coming back to *Welcome to the Dollhouse* as though drawn by a rubber band.

The girl's name is Dawn, and everyone at school hates her and calls her a dork and a dog and a dyke. She has a little sister named Missy who does ballet. Missy's about six-yo. She wears a pink tutu and a pink leotard—a pink angel—her hair tied back in a bun, with flowers, cute as a doll. Dawn's Mum and Dad spend all day fawning over Missy and neglect Dawn really badly, and Dawn hates Missy so much her stomach hurts. Okay, sure, Dawn never actually *says* Missy makes her stomach hurt, but Annette knows what it means when Dawn wraps her arms around herself, clenches her teeth, and shuts her eyes tight.

Then one day Dawn's Mum asks her to tell Missy, who's about to leave for a ballet class, that she can't pick her up today, so Missy should ask the teacher for a ride home.

But Dawn doesn't tell her.

And Missy is left standing alone outside the ballet school and gets kidnapped. Good-bye, Missy.

Annette feels a devilish red glow of satisfaction, and yet at the same time terribly guilty, as if *she* were the one who'd gotten rid of Miss Goody Two-Shoes Sugar-Plum-Fairy Missy for good.

She changes the channel and doesn't watch the end of the *Dollhouse* flick, but still the mood of the thing follows Annette for days, and she can't quite shake that sickly-prickly thrill she felt when, with the police cars flashing their red and blue lights outside Dawn and Missy's house, it became clear that Dawn had succeeded.

•   •   •

Lulu has a shoot somewhere on the other side of town. Mumps is in Gothenburg, and Dumps is supposed to pick her up after the session. Annette has of course been asked to babysit Otso. Surprised that the little Casanova's not at Pamela's place, she wonders, nastily, has Pamela found herself a more mega stud and finished with Otso just like that? Annette is lounging on the couch watching the celebs on *Junior Pop Idol*. Otso sits a meter from the TV, staring at the screen, and tries to sing along except when Annette hisses at him to be quiet. Four-year-old Jussi does a rendition of "I Want Your Sex," then Kylie comes on, the same age, singing "Like a Virgin." Kylie wears a shiny sequined dress and a pink ostrich-feather boa with matching lipstick. Halfway through the performance the telephone rings. Annette's in a pretty ticked-off mood when she answers, interruptions being just about her least favorite thing.

It's Dad, and there's a lot of noise in the background. He's had to borrow somebody else's phone to call her. Some idiot smashed into his car, and on impact his headset phone flew out the window and broke. Dad's got to take the car to the garage and get himself a new headset, and that will take some time. He says Lulu probably switched off her phone for the shoot, so could Annette send her a voice mail or a text message saying Dad can't pick her up and she should take a taxi? He explains this over and over like it's the most difficult assignment ever.

"Yes yes YESYES!" Annette screams and ends the call, but still she's missed two more potential Junior Pop Idols; now a five-yo boy is singing "Hit Me Baby One More Time." Otso joins in whenever Annette doesn't try to stop him.

Annette picks up her mobile and has already selected Lulu from the quick menu when her hand goes limp.

This can't be just a coincidence.

Annette stares at the phone.

"Welcome to the dollhouse, Baby Doll," she says, then switches off the phone entirely.

Hours later the apartment phone rings for the sixth time, and each time the caller-name on the screen is Lulu.

The fact that nobody's answering isn't exactly unusual. Otso's a light sleeper, so Dad often unplugs the phone after he's put Otso to bed, and all the headsets or mobiles in the apartment are in a drawer or under a pillow or turned off altogether.

The phone rings for a seventh time.

The police car is parked in front of the building, but the lights on its roof aren't pulsing red and blue like in the film; the car is totally dark and totally silent.

Dad carries Lulu inside, wrapped in a gray blanket. Her mascara has dribbled down her face, and one of her cheeks is red and scratched and bleeding. Her right eye is almost swollen shut, and her lower lip is split. Dad carefully lays her on the living room couch and staggers into the kitchen like he's gone blind. He returns with a dish towel soaked in warm water and tries to wipe the mascara streaks off Lulu's face, but she gently pushes his hand away.

"Remppu," she whispers. Dad looks at Lulu; he doesn't know what she means—but Annette knows, so she goes to Lulu's room and pulls a drawer out from under the bed. Remppu is lying among the other junk with his spindly legs in a knot: a stuffed terry-cloth monkey whose long dangling arms have little orange mittens sewn at the ends. The terry-cloth loops have worn away on those places where Lulu used to suck on Remppu when she was a baby.

Annette walks up to Lulu and places Remppu in her arms. Lulu squeezes him against her chest and presses her lips against his battered old head, near where Annette once tore off the eyes and Mum had to sew on a pair of blue buttons instead. Lulu closes her own eyes and lies there perfectly still.

The two policemen wander around the living room like flickering shadows. It's as though Annette is not really in the same place where all this is happening; instead she's standing outside somebody else's apartment watching these events through the window. Her stomach's filled with a heavy sweetness, as if her breath has turned to syrup.

"Messages sometimes disappear when the operators are busy," says one officer. Dad nods blindly; he clearly doesn't even hear.

"We've got some possible sightings of the four men, and of course we'll try our best, but, sad to say, cases like this are getting more common all the time, so who knows?"

Dad bobs his head like a robot. Annette stands there silently and hasn't a clue what to do; she feels totally stunned. Now she realizes how stupid she was. She didn't mean for this to happen. She thought Lulu would just disappear, would get lost somewhere in town and, like a child in a fairy tale, never find her way home.

Now Annette is annoyed that she didn't watch *Welcome to the Dollhouse* all the way through; she doesn't know what finally became of Missy.

Would Dawn have made such a dumb-ass mistake?

"Are you sure you'll be okay?" an officer says.

Dad nods for a third time, then takes Lulu and Remppu in a single bundle in his arms and walks off toward Lulu's room; beneath the blanket Lulu's feet dangle as limply as Remppu's terry-cloth limbs.

Mum and Dad are in the den talking all hushed and low, thinking nobody will hear them, but the walls are thin and Annette has sharp ears; she can easily sort out both their voices, almost every word, from the noise of the TV in the background.

Not that she wants to hear them, because her stomach is aching, and she'd much rather swat the voices away like flies and pretend they don't exist, but she also feels compelled to listen, like that time at Ninotska's nine-yo party when Annette kept her eyes on the screen even though she didn't want to see any more grand slam hot pussies.

"The insurance will cover Lulu's plastic surgery," Dad says. "If we can believe the doctors, there won't be any scarring. She can probably start modeling again in a couple of months. Thank God they finished the Sexy Secrets shoot in time."

"The men who did this, if they're ever caught—should we try to get . . . restitution?" Mum asks indistinctly.

Dad sighs. "Caught? Not too likely. Wouldn't matter anyway. The whole problem is that she never changed her clothes—she thought I was picking her up—so they'll just say she was asking for it. Their lawyers will argue that Lulu brought it on herself."

"Then we won't see a penny?"

" 'Fraid not," Dad says.

Annette's head and stomach start aching again. What could that mean, *Lulu brought it on herself*? No, no, *she* did it—she, Annette, caused all this just as surely as if she'd bought a gun and shot herself in the foot. Annette would give almost anything for this, of all things, never to have happened.

· · ·

Word has circulated around the school.

The boys' hand signals have become grosser than ever, and naturally Ninotska and Veronika keep trying to get all chatty with Annette. Annette vows to act hypernormal, a bit indifferent, even slightly chipper. She won't show those dopes how much she's really hurting.

"Four," Ninotska trills. "Four horny dudes!"

"Was it one after another, or did they all do it together?" Veronika carries on.

Annette shrugs. "I couldn't care less." She walks off, and the hallway echoes with shouts of *lulululululululululululu*.

Mum has brought home burritos from the deli. She cuts one into small pieces for Otso and squeezes ketchup over them from a plastic bottle. Otso would eat Styrofoam if it was covered in ketchup. Lulu won't come down to eat. She won't even leave her room, and that infuriates Annette, too—Lulu always has to make herself special somehow. Annette pokes at her burrito with a fork. She normally likes them, but now her throat feels blocked. Lately nothing tickles her fancy.

"I want implants."

The words bubble abruptly out of Annette's mouth, almost like vomit. Mum stops in mid-squeeze, the bottle gives a little fart, and Otso has a laughing fit.

"Implants? For you?" Mum looks confused, as though she'd never heard the word before.

"Everybody's got them!"

"At your age?"

"Ninotska's getting them, Sarietta's already stopped being a milkdud, and today I heard Veronika's shopping around!" Annette bangs her fork rhythmically against the table. "Anyway, Lulu's got them. You gave her implants the minute the agent told you to!"

Everything freezes. Mum stares at her, eyes like saucers, and even Otso stops eating. The silence gets so intense that Annette's ears almost hurt, and then Mum clears her throat.

"But . . . we don't want the same thing happening to you that happened to Lulu," she says, her voice all hoarse.

"You never want *anything* to happen to me, do you?" says Annette, giving Mum big saucer-eyes in return.

Mum doesn't answer. All the doors and windows of her face are shut tight.

Annette slams her fork so hard it springs out of her hand and somersaults to the floor, clanging like a bell.

"I knew it! I knew you never wanted anything to happen to me!"

Mum looks at her, the side of her mouth twitching. This is a sign.

"Everybody thinks I'm just a child!" Annette screams. She upends her plate, sending chicken pieces and veggie bits flying out of the tortilla all over the tablecloth and onto the floor. "Nothing real is ever supposed to happen to me!"

Mum stands there frozen, and Annette picks up a knife and starts banging it against the table. Mum moves quickly and grabs Annette's arm. "There, there, dear, we can ask Dad when he gets home," she says, then carefully takes the knife away.

MAREK S. HUBERATH

"Yoo Retoont, Sneogg. Ay Noo."

TRANSLATED FROM THE POLISH
BY MICHAEL KANDEL

Science fiction in Poland enjoys the dubious distinction of having actually been encouraged by the country's Communist rulers in the years immediately following World War II. According to Krzysztof Solokowski and other cultural historians, the commissars reasoned that in providing Polish citizens with beautiful visions of an exotic future, SF would help them forget the drab present. The best examples of these obliquely sanctioned texts include Krzysztof Borun and Andrzej Trepka's Zagubiona przyszłość *("The Lost Future," 1953), the inaugural volume in a space-opera trilogy, and Stanislaw Lem's early novels* Astonauci *("The Astronauts," 1951) and* Oblok Magellana *("The Magellan Nebula," 1955). Naturally these writers did not seek Party approval, and in Lem's case it's fair to assume that the endorsement appalled him.*

Subsequent decades found some Polish science fiction authors going in the opposite direction, eschewing the genre's venerable "sense of wonder" while attempting to articulate truths about the real world. For this literary movement, SF became a kind of Trojan horse, enabling its practitioners to smuggle encoded political discourse into their society—though censorship remained rampant, and many writers resorted to underground publication. Prominent novels from the anti-escapism school include Edmund Wnuk-Lipinski's Wirpamięci *("Whirlpool of Memory," 1979), Maciej Parpwski's* Twarzą ku Ziemi *("Face to Earth,"*

1981), Janusz A. Zajdel's Limes Inferior (1982), and Marek Oramus's Senni zwycięzcy ("Sleepy Victors," 1982).

The present novelette clearly partakes of the second tradition: realism wedded to SF tropes. Certainly it's difficult to imagine any apparatchik beating the drum for Marek Huberath's "Yoo Retoont, Sneogg. Ay Noo." Published two years before the fall of European Communism, the story reveals a post-apocalyptic world of a decidedly dystopian character, and the underlying attitudes are far more humanist than socialist. Huberath's deep religious faith also informs these pages—tacitly but, we would argue, substantively—a sensibility famously at odds with Marxist arguments about how the world works.

Following the dissolution of the Soviet Union, indigenous Polish science fiction inevitably lost its cachet as a suppressed, dissident, desperado literature. It's too early to tell what sort of SF will emerge in Poland as authors explore their newfound artistic freedom. Meanwhile, the country's bookstores are flooded with American and British SF in translation, much of it achieving bestseller status, and at present Poland is probably the largest European market for English-language science fiction.

Instead of introducing Huberath directly, we shall now hand the word-processor over to his translator, Michael Kandel. What follows is the biographical note about the author that Kandel wrote for A Book of Polish Monsters, his forthcoming anthology of Polish science fiction in English translation.

"Marek Huberath, born 1954, is a physicist yet writes not about science and technology but on themes philosophical and moral: how people become beasts or remain human in extreme circumstances. His hobby is mountain climbing. He told me once that he feels at peace only when he has empty air under his feet. A traditionalist, Huberath is protective of women in a way that with no exaggeration could be called knightly. (Chivalry toward women is high among Polish virtues.) His realistic treatment of suffering and ethical problems has a punch that reminds me of the work of Aleksandr Solzhenitsyn."

1

On the floor, several bright spots formed a row. Snorg liked to watch them move slowly across the dull tiles. The spots of light were different from the glow that suffused the Room. He had discovered some time ago that the source of this light was the small windows near the ceiling. He liked to lie on the floor so the spots would warm him. He wanted to do this now. He tried to move his arms but managed only to fall helplessly off the bed.

"Dags," he hissed between clenched teeth. He couldn't move his numb jaw.

"Dags," he repeated with an effort.

One of the Dagses turned his head from the viewscreen—in reaction probably to the thud of the body instead of to Snorg's voice. Moosy was humming some tune the whole time, making little yawps for the words. The Dags with a few quick jerks pulled his way to Snorg and slapped him in the face, hard. Both Dagses had strong arms. They didn't use their undeveloped legs much.

"Pa . . . pa," stammered the Dags, making rhythmic motions with his shoulders to say that Snorg would be able to move his arms in a minute. He started hooking the tangle of wires to Snorg. The other Dags also came, pulling himself, and gave Snorg's hair a yank. The yank hurt, but pain was what Snorg wanted.

"My head . . . head." A pounding in his skull. "Good . . . good."

The second Dags then poked a finger in Snorg's eye. Snorg twisted his head away and roared. The first Dags beat at the second Dags, until the second Dags rolled away. Snorg's eye brimmed with tears, so he couldn't see if the first Dags was attaching all the electrodes right. But he didn't worry, because the Dags usually did. He imagined the Dags attaching the wires of the machine, imagined him cocking his head comically as he worked. Both Dagses had eyes set so wide apart, they had to cock their heads. It was amusing.

"Tavegner! Want to hear a story?" That was Piecky's smooth, resonant voice. Snorg admired the way Piecky talked. He could make out every word, although his lack of external ears limited his hearing. Piecky was answered by a loud gurgle. Tavegner still couldn't move. He announced his presence only by gurgling. Had he stood up, he would have been the tallest of them, taller than Tib or Aspe. Only Tib stood, so she was the tallest.

I might be taller than Tib, if I could stand, Snorg thought.

He was pleased that today he had feeling in his entire head. The pain was a service provided him daily by the Dagses.

"Piecky, shut up!" shouted Moosy. "You can tell him the story later. I'm singing now."

Snorg's hands were numb, like pieces of wood, but they moved according to his will. He tore himself free of the tangle of wires and tubes. He pinched his arm. There was no feeling.

At least I can move it, he thought. He inspected the cuts and bruises on his body. Most were healing. But he had two new cuts from his last fall off the bed. Cuts were Snorg's curse: a moment of inattention, and he could blunder into something and break his skin without knowing it. He was constantly afraid that he wouldn't notice a cut in time and it would get infected. He crawled to the viewscreen. Tib stood nearby, rigid, while one of the Dagses was trying to pull her clothes off from the bottom.

Who dresses her? Snorg wondered. Every day the Dagses did the same thing, and every day, in the morning, Tib was dressed again.

Finally Tib's gray gown fell to the floor, and the Dags started to climb up her leg.

Snorg watched to see. What happened was what always happened: the little Dags got nowhere. When he was high enough, Tib simply scissored her legs shut. The Dags, resigned, went and squatted in front of the viewscreen and stared openmouthed at it.

She's not that stupid, thought Snorg. She always closes her legs in time.

Tib was a woman—only lately had Snorg realized this. She looked very much like the women the viewscreen showed during the lessons.

Her hips maybe are a little narrow, he decided, and she's too tall, but everything else is in place.

Until now he had thought of her as furniture, a motionless decoration of the Room. She seemed even taller from the floor. Someday he would like to talk to her. Tib was the only person in the Room he had been unable to communicate with. Even Tavegner, who lay like a mound of meat and couldn't utter a word, had interesting things to tell. You conversed with him by the trick of having *yes* be one gurgle and *no* two. Tavegner filled almost half the Room, and for a long time everyone thought he was like Tib. It was Piecky who figured out how to talk with him. Before that, the Dagses discovered that Tavegner responded to jabs, because they liked to lounge on his immense, soft, warm body. Clever Piecky worked out the way for Tavegner to gurgle yes for the letter of the alphabet he wanted and to gurgle twice to end a word. Everyone would gather around to listen. Snorg would bring the box that held Piecky, and the Dagses would drag Moosy. All together they would spell out letter by letter.

"I am Tavegner," Tavegner said. Then he told them a number of things. He told them he liked it when the Dagses lounged on him, he thanked Piecky, and he asked them to move him a little so he could see the viewscreen better. But lately Tavegner had become lazy: he preferred to be given simple yes-or-no questions.

Snorg moved himself to Piecky.

"Piecky, are you a man or a woman?" he asked and began to unwrap the sheet.

"Stop that, damn it, Snorg. It doesn't matter what I am." Piecky's small body twisted, but Snorg unwrapped it all the way. Then he wrapped it up again.

"You don't have anything," he said.

"What did you think, stupid?" Piecky sneered. "The Dagses would have found out long ago if I had."

Piecky's head was beautiful. It was larger even than Snorg's and formed better even than the heads of the people on the viewscreen.

"You have a beautiful head, Piecky," said Snorg, to put him in a better humor. Piecky actually blushed at that.

"I know," he replied. "And yours is ugly, but normally formed, all in all, except for the ears. I'm the brains here and will be around long after they've put you all away."

"What are you talking about?" asked Snorg.

"Nothing. I need the sucker now."

Snorg pulled out the excrement tube from the wall, plugged it into Piecky, and left him. The viewscreen was showing trees, a lot of trees. They were pretty, colorful, and moved gracefully. Snorg had never seen trees but dreamed of sleeping in one. He imagined branches arranged around him to make a soft, warm bed. The viewscreen always showed pretty things: spreading landscapes, people shaped correctly. He learned a lot of useful information.

Snorg felt regret that he wasn't pretty like the people he saw on the viewscreen, who engaged in all kinds of complicated activities. From the perspective of the floor and his physical shortcomings, those people seemed perfection. It was his fault he was the way he was instead of like them, though he didn't know why it was his fault. Watching the viewscreen, he forgot everything. With his eyes he absorbed the scenes and facts that flowed from it. He saw things that had never been in the Room, things that would have remained unknown to him forever without the viewscreen.

A woman appeared. She stood unmoving. She was a model to demonstrate what bodily proportions a correctly formed woman should possess. Near the viewscreen, Tib stood unmoving and watched with glassy eyes. Snorg compared her with the woman on the viewscreen. Tib was bald, not a hair on her, which made her head very different from the head of the woman on the viewscreen, but when Snorg tried to picture hair on Tib's head, the comparison wasn't so bad. Tib had delicate ears, which stood out a little and were translucent. Snorg envied her those ears. On the viewscreen, lines appeared, showing the correct proportions. Snorg crawled to Tib to measure her proportions with a string. Not only did she have both arms of equal length, and both legs equal, but also her arms were shorter than her legs, and even in the smallest details Tib's build agreed with the build of the model. To measure her head in proportion to the rest of her body, he got up on his knees and stretched his arms as high as he could. Everything was right. He beheld Tib with admiration.

Her body is completely correct, he thought, and then realized that he had managed to lift himself up on his numb knees. He immediately fell.

The hum in his ears told him that with the fall he had lost consciousness. When the hum went away, Snorg heard Piecky yelling to Moosy.

"Relax! Stop fighting! When he's done, he'll go," Piecky was saying.

Moosy sobbed. "I can't stand . . . he's disgusting, an animal . . . stop! Leave me alone."

Snorg lifted his head: one of the Dagses had climbed into the box with Moosy.

This is becoming unendurable, he thought. We can't defend ourselves against them, and we can't live with them.

The Dags stopped its hoarse panting and plopped to the floor.

2

Piecky was going to tell a story. The Dagses held up his arm for the gesturing, though he could make only the most limited motions with it. He scratched his face with his hand.

"That's great, that's wonderful," he said over and over. "You people don't know how to make use of your bodies."

A few slaps by the Dagses brought him around.

He began to tell the story.

"It was a lovely dream." Piecky closed his eyes. "I was floating in air. It was heavenly. I had these black, flat wings on my sides, the kind we see sometimes on the viewscreen. The air moved with me. It was wonderfully cool," he said more softly, as if to himself. "Moosy was flying beside me. Her wings were bright green. She had four wings and flapped them so nicely, I was sorry I was only Piecky. . . ."

From the corner came a gurgle.

"Tavegner asks you to speak up," said Snorg, and the next hollow gurgle confirmed that.

"All right. I'll talk louder," Piecky said, as if shaking himself awake. "The Room became smaller and smaller," he continued, "and everything around me got greener and greener. Both the Dagses were flying below us, going in the same direction we were, and it was wonderful, because the sky we were flying toward was an enormous viewscreen, and as you got nearer, you could see the pixels. I could move in any direction. . . ."

From the corner where Moosy's box was came a quiet sob. Snorg pulled himself toward her.

"Do you need anything?" he asked.

"I wanted to call you, because if one of the Dagses comes, he'll do the thing I hate again. Put me next to Piecky, could you?" she asked.

"Did his story move you?" Snorg asked Moosy, regarding her. Unlike Piecky, she had all her limbs, though they were shriveled.

"It's not Piecky, it's Tavegner," she said through her tears. "The last time Piecky told a story, Tavegner asked to speak by letters, and he said . . ."

Snorg nodded.

"He said he wanted to go into the grinder instead of Piecky."

"Grinder?" Snorg didn't understand.

"Piecky learned about it a long time ago," Moosy explained. "He analyzes everything they say on the viewscreen. They pick the best of us, those who are formed the best, and the rest—go into the grinder."

"You mean, the thing they show on the viewscreen and call war?"

She nodded yes. "Put me next to Piecky," she said. "Every time he finishes telling his beautiful dream, he's so feeble."

Making a tremendous effort, Snorg lifted Moosy from her box and put her in the crib Piecky lay in, after which he had to slide back to the floor in a hurry, because Tib was soiling herself. He attached the sucker to her. When she was finished, he grasped her hips with all his strength and pulled himself to his knees.

"Don't do it that way, all right?" he said, glancing up at her. Tib looked down and saw his face twisted with effort. Her ears stuck out a little, and the light shone through them. To him they seemed extraordinarily beautiful. He clenched his numb jaw and took Tib by the shoulders. He felt that she was helping him, not pulling away but trying to stand straight to support him. She continued staring at his face. Between her parted lips, white teeth were visible.

Rising, Snorg felt large, gigantic. He stood. For the first time he stood on his paralyzed legs. Now he was looking at her not from below but from above . . . looking at Tib, who was as high as the sky.

Everyone stopped talking.

He decided to take a step. He felt power. Suddenly he saw that one of his feet was moving toward her.

"Tib! I'm walking. . . ." It was meant to be a shout, but it came out as a snort or sob. Suddenly the Room swayed, and Snorg fell flat on his back with a crash.

3

The Room had two other occupants, whom Snorg never met, because they both used the same machine he did. While he was active, they slept. They were Aspe and Dulf. Aspe resembled Tavegner in shape, though she wasn't his equal in size. Piecky said she was intelligent and nasty. She couldn't speak, but communication with her presented no problem. She never detached her artificial arms and loved to play odd tricks on Piecky or Tavegner. Snorg hoped to talk with her someday, and with Dulf, who lay curled in a fetal position and whose incredibly wrinkled skin made you think he was ancient, though he was the same age they all were, that is, just past puberty.

Tib stopped fouling the Room; she learned to go to Snorg when she felt the need. Snorg, seeing her, was usually able to get the sucker. Tib began to respond to him: sometimes she would walk to the part of the Room where he was lying and stand by him, looking at him. She was much more active than she had been before.

"I underestimated you, Snorg," Piecky said once. "You're okay. You were able to make contact with Baldy." Baldy was what he called Tib. "I couldn't, though I tried plenty. You've changed, Snorg. Before, you looked like an animal that's beaten all the time. Now one can see thought in your face."

"Animal" meant primitive, mindless, and strong. Occasionally the viewscreen showed pictures of real animals that were long extinct. Snorg was pleased by Piecky's compliment and understood why Piecky had given it. From that day Snorg practiced strengthening his fortitude and will. After the moment when an exertion of will forced his unfeeling legs to make the first step, will became for him the most important thing. He could take many steps now, though they often ended with a dangerous fall. He stood by leaning on Tib's body, but he walked by himself, and she helped him only a little. Sometimes, when he woke, he could move his arms without the help of the Dagses, and without the machine.

"You can see the will in my face," he told Piecky.

Piecky, lying down, lifted his head and looked.

"You're right," he said. "The lines have hardened, the corners of your mouth turn down. But you better hurry, Snorg. I have the feeling we won't be together long."

What Piecky relied on was his brain. He would spend hours at the keyboard of a viewscreen and, if one of the Dagses didn't unscrew his artificial hand as a joke, he would tap at the keys continually. Learning was his passion, and being with the machine. Snorg knew that you could make Piecky happy by setting him down at the keyboard and letting him sit there for hours.

4

Snorg decided to teach Tib to speak. Piecky advised him to press her hand to his throat so she could feel the vibrations of his vocal cords. For this purpose, in order to stand, Snorg grabbed her by the hips. But he did it too suddenly, and Tib fell. It was the first time he saw her on the floor. One of the Dagses, seizing the opportunity, quickly got between her legs, which had been thrown apart. Snorg swung, and the little one, from the blow, went rolling across the floor. There was blood.

"Snorg! Stop!" cried Piecky. "You'll hurt him."

"It's my blood," said Snorg, inspecting his hand. "I cut my hand on him."

Tib had pulled herself together and sat up. The Dagses didn't approach her, watching Snorg carefully.

"Maybe it's good you did that," said Piecky. "I would have, if I could, for Moosy. They do with her what they want, whenever they want."

Snorg took Tib's hand and placed the palm on his throat.

"Tib," he said, pointing at her.

She watched him in silence.

"Tib," he repeated.

She looked frightened.

He passed his hand along her face, touched a pink ear, and was surprised: Tib's ear had no opening.

"Piecky!" he shouted. "You're a genius! You were right. She's deaf. Only by touch . . ."

Over and over, with extreme care to be correct, he pronounced her name. He had complete control of his mouth now. After one of the times, her lips moved, and she gave a muffled, hollow noise: "Ghbb . . ." She got to her feet and repeated it several times.

"Ghbb . . . ghbbr." She said it louder and louder, walking across the Room.

"She'll wake Dulf," Piecky said.

Snorg gestured for her to come. She came and sat. Again he started saying her name.

"You know, this morning I saw the Dagses doing it to each other," said Moosy. Morning meant the time when the rays of sun came through the windows near the ceiling and made spots on the floor.

"They took turns being on top," she said.

"That never happens during the day," Piecky stated.

"Are they ashamed in front of us?"

"The Dagses?!" Piecky burst into laughter. "With those low foreheads? They must be cretins."

5

Tib learned quickly. Soon she could say her name, Snorg's, Piecky's, and several other words. Piecky was of the opinion that her sight was not good either and that most information came to her through touch. He wasn't sure, however, whether this was physiological or whether Tib's brain was simply unable to process all the data entering through her eyes.

Dulf began to wake up more frequently. He never changed his position on the floor, though he blinked and even spoke. His speech was comical: he stammered and couldn't find words. Snorg wanted to know how Dulf managed without a machine, but Dulf didn't know the meaning of the word "will," so there was nothing for them to discuss. The Dagses once tried to straighten Dulf on the floor, but it turned out that his body was actually in a ball. Piecky said that was impossible, the only explanation was that Dulf was twins grown together and he had a little brother on his belly.

"Have you noticed, Snorg," Piecky remarked, lifting his artificial hand from the keyboard, "how quickly we've been changing? Before, I thought everything was fixed for us: you crawled, Tib stood like a post, Dulf spoke only when you slept. And now?"

Snorg was interested. "What do you mean, Piecky?"

"A big change awaits us, a very big change. Remember how it was at the beginning?"

Snorg nodded.

"Each one of us had a viewscreen in front of his nose. The viewscreens taught us everything, showed us what the world was like and how it should be. We were surrounded by wires, which got our muscles going, our organs, the whole body, and kept us alive."

"I still use the machine sometimes, but I seem to recall, through a fog, that it was that way with all of us," said Snorg.

"Through a fog, exactly!" Piecky became excited. "They pump drugs into us, give us powders. We forget. Though maybe they want what we forget to remain deep inside us . . . in the unconscious."

Snorg saw that Piecky didn't look well: his beautiful face was tired, the skin was dark around his eyes, and he was very pale.

"You spend too much time in front of the viewscreen. You're looking worse and worse," Snorg said.

Suddenly one of the Dagses became interested in Piecky. The Dags apparently wanted to carry him to another place, though for the moment he only stroked Piecky's cheek gently and tugged at his hair.

Piecky gave Snorg a knowing look.

"You see?" He smiled. "They understand some things after all. I only became aware of this recently. I don't know why they both want to pass themselves off as cretins."

The Dags gave Piecky a slap and angrily left for another part of the Room. Piecky's grin broadened.

"You think I'm entertaining myself, Snorg? That all Piecky needs is to be put in front of the viewscreen and have his hand screwed on, and he's happy?"

The look on Snorg's face said nothing.

"Sneogg," said Tib. She could now take the sucker from the wall herself and didn't foul the Room anymore, but she wasn't able to put the tube away. Snorg helped her and returned to Piecky.

Piecky told him, "Thanks to the viewscreen, I've learned a lot of things. Did you know, Snorg, that there exist many rooms like ours? The people that live in them, they're like us. Some more defective, some less. One can see those rooms, because there are not only viewscreens everywhere but also cameras. We are being constantly observed. My guess is that the lenses are near the ceiling, but it's hard to see them. In one of the rooms, a dark-blue room, lives a Piecky just like me. His name is Scorp. We've introduced ourselves. He looks at me on the viewscreen, and I look at him. He, too, has an artificial hand."

"Maybe," Snorg suggested, "we don't deserve to live the way the people shown on the viewscreen do, who are correctly formed."

Piecky became furious.

"So you've swallowed that crap! And you feel guilty." He twisted so violently, it loosened the straps of his hand. Snorg had to tighten them.

Piecky's eyes roved, glittered. "They feed us guilt," he spat. "I don't know why they're doing it, but I'll find out. Just as I found out a lot more from those goddamn viewscreens than I was supposed to."

Snorg was awed by the strength that pulsed from Piecky. "And I thought will was my specialty," he mused.

Piecky must have read the expression on his face as doubt, because he went on:

"Think about it, Snorg. Every program they show us, every fact . . . it's all about how a human being should be. The arms, such a way, the legs, such a way, the correct way. And we? And I, what am I? A tatter of a man. And that's supposed to be my fault? Do you understand?! Why do they keep drumming that into us?"

Snorg said nothing. This proved how extremely wise Piecky was. One could learn from him, learn how to look at the world differently. But Tib sat down beside Snorg and began to snuggle her face in his. The touch of her delicate skin, Snorg loved that more than anything.

"I'm afraid I won't have time to learn everything. Time's running out," Piecky concluded under his breath, seeing that Snorg was no longer listening.

6

Pieckyy!" called Moosy.

"Don't, he's sleeping," said Snorg.

"Then come here and look at Aspe," she insisted. "She's not breathing."

Getting up by himself took Snorg several seconds of excruciating effort. Aspe, it turned out, was lying as she usually did—a little twisted, her withered hands tucked underneath her large, flat face.

Snorg examined her.

"She's sleeping, the way she always does."

"You're wrong, Snorg. Look again."

Turning Aspe's face toward the ceiling was beyond Snorg's strength. Fortunately the meddlesome Dagses were nearby. The three together were able to move her. Her body was cold and stiff.

"Damn, you're right. It must have happened some time ago," he said in a hollow voice. "And I never exchanged a word with her. She was always asleep. Should we wake Piecky?"

"No. He'll find out anyway," Moosy said. "I don't understand her death. It doesn't go with what Piecky told us."

Snorg sat with his face in his hands. Hearing a low, incoherent noise behind him, he turned. It was Tavegner crying. Tears, one after the other, were streaming down his red cheeks.

"Turn me over on my back," Moosy asked Snorg. "The skin on my stomach burns. I must have bedsores."

"On your stomach, you're safer from the Dagses," he said.

"When they want it, it's no problem for them to turn me over."

Aspe's body disappeared while everyone slept, so no one knew how it was done.

Seeing Piecky sitting haggard at the keyboard, Snorg decided to tell him what Moosy had said. He put Piecky in a more comfortable position, sat beside him, and told him.

"Aspe's death doesn't contradict what I've concluded," Piecky answered. "The laws that govern us operate statistically. It's simple: first they tested us thoroughly and selected those who were viable, or possibly the others died. Then they discarded those who couldn't learn, the complete cretins. The rest they taught intensively, using various means."

Snorg watched the capering Dagses, then looked at Piecky, who returned the look with a smile.

"Exactly," Piecky went on. "Aspe died because the tests they ran weren't perfect. Unless continued survival is itself a test."

"What comes next?" asked Snorg.

Piecky's shrug was with his whole body: he had no idea.

"Nothing good, I'm sure. In any case, nothing good for me." He hesitated. "You see, Snorg, I was able to penetrate the information system that serves us. I saw other rooms, many of them. In each one, the people are our age, or younger. The very young ones sit in front of viewscreens and fill themselves with information. The ones our age do what we are doing now: living, observing, conversing. I haven't yet found a room with people who are older than us. There's a kind of information barrier. The system doesn't answer questions about that. But it will end soon, this. I feel it, Snorg."

7

A strong light hit Snorg in the eyes. For a while he couldn't focus. Then he became aware that he was no longer in the Room. He was lying on something hard, in a place that seemed vast. He felt terribly alone, because none of his companions was with him. At the other end of the place sat an unknown man. He was very old, but Snorg realized that the man was simply older than those Snorg had been living with. The man, seeing that Snorg was awake, approached him and extended a hand.

"My name is Bablyoyannis Knoboblou," he said.

Slowly, with an effort of will, Snorg rose from his bedding.

"Congratulations, Snorg. On this day you become a person. You were the best."

Snorg reached and shook the man's hand, curious to see what the hand felt like.

"I have here the report of Central"—the man took a few sheets of paper from the desk—"and the decision of the Committee, which is made up of persons. You will receive an identity card and can choose a name."

Snorg didn't understand.

The man gave the impression of a kindly clerk who was performing a pleasant yet routine duty.

"Your results," Bablyoyannis continued, running an eye over the papers he held. "A 132. Not bad. On my test, I scored 154," he said with a smile of pride. "That Piecky one got dangerously close to you, with 126 points, but his lack of limbs, genitals—it's hard to make up for that with intelligence alone. Better that someone like you was chosen and not one of those stumps."

Snorg thought, I'd like to crack your head. He said, "Piecky is my friend," and felt the old numbness in his jaw.

"It's better not to have friends until you become a person," observed Bablyoyannis. "Do you want to know how the others did? Moosy— eighty-four, Tib—seventy-two, Dulf—thirty . . . the rest, close to zero. The Dagses scored eighteen each, and that ox, Tavegner, twelve."

Snorg heard the scorn in Bablyoyannis's voice and felt a growing hatred for the man.

"What happens to me now?" he asked. The numbness in his face wouldn't go away.

"As a person, you have a choice. You will enter the normal life of society. A short period of training, and then you can either continue studying or take a job. From today, you receive an account with the sum of four hundred money, as does everyone who becomes a person. Myself, I would advise you not to have cosmetic surgery until you obtain a steady source of income. Ears are not really that important." He gave Snorg a confidential look. "In time, you'll be able to save up. There's always a large selection of parts."

Snorg felt cold sweat trickling down his back: he could see Tib before him.

"What happens to the others?" he finally managed to ask.

"Ah. Yes, you have the right to know." Bablyoyannis was trying to be patient. "There are always many more individuals born than individuals who attain personhood. We harvest them for material. Among them, you can find a perfectly good pair of ears, or eyes, or a liver. Though some don't even possess that. A type like Tavegner is probably good only for tissue cultures."

"That's inhuman," Snorg said, couldn't help saying, through clenched teeth.

"Inhuman?!" Bablyoyannis turned red. "No. The war, that was inhuman. Today a hundred percent of the population is born with physical defects, and three-quarters with mental defects. Reproduction, as a rule, is possible only by test tube. Save your indignation for our ancestors."

Apparently Snorg didn't seem convinced, because Bablyoyannis went on:

"The birth rate has been maximized, to increase the probability of obtaining normal individuals." He looked hard at Snorg. "As for the others . . . they're the cheapest way for us to produce the organs we need. Because even the chosen aren't perfect, are they, Snorg? I've been working in this department for seven years now," Bablyoyannis said, "and I can assure you that this path is the only one that's right."

"You're not perfect either, Bablyoyannis. You drag your left leg, and your face is partially paralyzed," said Snorg.

"I know. It shows." Bablyoyannis was prepared for that remark. "But I work hard, and I've been saving almost all my money . . . for an operation."

8

Tibsnorg Pieckymoosy began work in the Central Archive of Biological Materials. At the same time, he continued his education. The salary he made was good, but after a pro rata deduction to pay for the care he had received until now, not much remained. Expenditure for food and the rent for a dark little room consumed the rest of his money, so that his paycheck was only symbolic. The food, synthetic, was eaten in a cafeteria. It was an improvement over the IV. In the cafeteria he kept seeing the same people, which was boring, but by his calculations he couldn't afford a better eating place, one where he would be able to come at different hours. He exchanged few words with the people he met in the cafeteria. They were all older than he. Some came in wheelchairs, but most could walk. He looked at them carefully: not one was completely normal. Each had deformities.

Tibsnorg was lucky: had he scored lower than 120 on his test, he wouldn't have been allowed to continue his education. But he also kept working, because he feared the memories that came with free time. He would pay for all his operations himself, but he didn't forget who had first helped him stand on his legs and conquer his nerveless body. Also, as a person, he had the right to know the truth, to know—despite the pictures on the viewscreen showing pretty landscapes, people formed correctly, and animals that had once lived—what the world really looked like now. Every five days, after work, he was allowed to go up to the surface and view his surroundings from an observation tower.

It was a grayish-brown waste. Massive gray trucks continually moved across it, carrying loads from different mines. The trucks, he knew, were operated by people who could not have children, because the radiation background on the plain was too high. One of these drivers ate at Tibsnorg's cafeteria. He looked completely normal and made three times more money than anyone else there, and yet Tibsnorg would not have traded places with him.

The tests Tibsnorg had done on himself, with his first saved money, showed that he was fertile, though probably only passively, that is, through the collection and storing of his sperm. In a short time he mastered his job, a computer job, and was promoted. His new position was administering the decisions made by the division of Central that chose material to harvest from among the living specimens. Central's decisions were clear, logical, and in general didn't need correction. A bonus was given for discovering mistakes in them, and Tibsnorg paid close attention to his work. The material was harvested both for the general public hospital and for individuals who at their own cost wanted to reduce their defectiveness. There was plenty of work: several dozen requests came in every day, and with them the decisions, which all had to be read, considered, processed. Soon Tibsnorg established a procedure and began to have free time, which he used to familiarize himself with the computer and learn various facts.

He remembered Piecky's words, that because information was a privilege, one had to make the utmost use of it. He learned that the decision whether someone would be a person or not was usually based on a simple sum of scores on tests. There was consequently a fairly large margin of error. He also learned that he had become a person thanks only to Bablyoyannis's intervention. Bablyoyannis had changed Central's decision to give Piecky personhood. The number of points Piecky had earned for mental ability had in fact exceeded what Snorg accumulated for physical function, correctness of form, and intelligence. When Tibsnorg read on the viewscreen that Tib had received exactly a zero, he uttered an obscenity.

He had always been intrigued by the light of day that fell into the Room. Now he learned that it was only a lamp in the visible and somewhat in the ultraviolet spectrum, a lamp that was turned on and off periodically. The Room was located far beneath the earth. On the surface, he saw the sun only once—a bright-gray disk shining through a thick mist. The sun was better now than it had been; in the time when the earth was covered constantly with snow, the sun never pierced the clouds.

9

Tibsnorg became better acquainted with the classification system for biological material. Tib, Piecky, and the others had been given serial numbers, from AT044567743 to AT044567749, and no longer possessed names. It soon happened that from number 44567746—from Moosy—an eye, nose, and one kidney were harvested for cosmetic use. Tibsnorg submitted a memo in opposition to the selection of AT044567746, but it was ignored, no doubt outvoted by others who were experts. He was very upset by this, still feeling a tie with Moosy and the others.

Next was the Dags numbered 44567748. The surgery was fatal: from the Dags was taken the esophagus and stomach, liver, intestines, both hands, and penis (though not the testicles). What was left could not live, so the skin, muscles, and bones of the arms were put in a tissue culture bank, and number 44567748 was removed from the database.

The value of each organ was calculated on the basis of what it had cost to maintain the individual. It was easiest to make such a calculation when the individual's number was removed, because in that case one simply divided the cost of maintenance of the biological material among the recipients of the organs harvested, by organ (using the proper coefficient). When the organs were not harvested together, the method of calculation applied became complicated and unclear, and Tibsnorg suspected that only the computer system could keep track of it.

He wondered what number he would have been given, if not for Bablyoyannis. Would it have come after Tib's?

At the cafeteria, he no longer sat alone. He began talking with the driver who worked on the trucks that carried loads from the metal mines. The man called himself Abraham Dringenboom, and he was tall, thickset, and extremely proud of his name, which had been dug out of some library of history. Dringenboom had a deep, powerful voice and spoke very loudly, which made Tibsnorg uncomfortable, because ordinarily the cafeteria was silent. It seemed to him that everyone was watching, though that made little sense, seeing as no one was interested in them. Besides, many of the diners had poor hearing or couldn't hear at all.

"Tibsnorg Pieckymoosy," intoned Dringenboom. "A strange name. Why did you choose it?"

"It's many names," Tibsnorg replied quietly. "There are many in me."

"Hmm," muttered Dringenboom. "So you made it up. It's not wise to get too close to the others in your Room. You know, today they said that the average lifespan of a person now is as much as twenty-four years." He was changing the subject. "I think it's too good to believe. I think they're fiddling with the medical statistics a little, so we won't feel bad."

"How do they arrive at that figure?" asked Tibsnorg, interested. "Is it for all individuals born or only for persons?"

"Are you kidding? For persons, of course. Less than a tenth are born alive."

Tibsnorg scrutinized Dringenboom. The driver seemed completely normal. True, he wore a gray tunic and trousers, so his body was not visible, but apart from the harelip that had been operated on, the scar from it mostly hidden by a graying stubble, nothing indicated any departure from the norm.

As if reading his thoughts, Dringenboom said, "My entire trunk was covered with warts on long, disgusting stalks. I had them removed. But the biggest problem is between my legs." Dringenboom grimaced. "But don't feel sorry for me, Tibsnorg. I'll buy myself the proper equipment and make five living kids with it. I've already put 1,620 money away," he added, seeing Tibsnorg's disbelief.

That much money was inconceivable: Tibsnorg could save only 22.24 money from each ten-day period. For the sum of 1,620 one could buy all of Tib—that is, of course, as biological material. More and more often her slender, graceful figure appeared before him, surrounded by a storm of colorful hair. His dreams were invariably about the Room. In and out of those dreams moved familiar shapes, but Tib was always present.

Tibsnorg rented a better room, one that had a window. Rooms at the surface were a rarity, so he was surprised that his new room—though a little smaller and with two viewscreens instead of three—cost only eight money more than the previous one. He understood the reason when he learned how high the radiation background was in rooms at the surface. But the view was worth it. He would spend hours looking at the opaque, leaden clouds that hung over the bare dun hills. The edge of the glacier wasn't visible, because his window was too low. The glacier could be seen only from the observation tower, and only on clear days or with good binoculars.

The scene, though it wasn't lovely like the ones on the viewscreen, drew him with irresistible force. That was probably why he applied for the position of driver of an outside transporter. Another motive was the high salary, which would allow him to save a considerable sum in a relatively short time.

At the transport bureau he was told to go to an official in a wheel-chair. The man didn't come much above the desk, but there was some-thing in his eyes that advised caution. When Tibsnorg presented the application, the man looked him over.

"Are you neuter or sexed?"

"Neuter," Tibsnorg lied, aware that being neuter was a condition for the job. The official nodded and with a disproportionately small hand en-tered something on the keyboard. He regarded the screen, and the lines of his face hardened. Even before he spoke, it was clear that the interview was over.

Dringenboom almost struck Tibsnorg when he heard what had hap-pened. In a fury, he pulled from the pocket of his worksuit his indicator— a small pink piece of plastic.

"Look at that, idiot!" he said, pointing a thick finger at the plastic. When he was agitated, he couldn't control the shaking of his hands. His finger wobbled over the pink rectangle. "When that turns red, I can throw away my calendar." His eyes flashed in his deeply tanned face. He made so much money, he could tan his skin. "Are you in such a hurry to get into the ground?!" he snarled.

"You can afford a sun lamp," said Tibsnorg quietly.

"And what, stupid, is that worth? You can have women by the bunch, even if you're missing everything between your legs but balls. The balls are what's important. The rest of it, the meat, doesn't cost more than six hundred, eight hundred money."

"I'm all right physically," Tibsnorg blurted. "It's my nervous system that's not complete."

"That's even cheaper. I'm telling you, you won't be able to drive the women away. They'll pull you apart. You should live, not die, my friend."

Tibsnorg thought of telling him about Tib, but changed his mind, and the conversation ended there.

Abe Dringenboom was the only person Tibsnorg saw regularly. With random acquaintances at the table Tibsnorg exchanged only a few words. In contrast with his life in the Room, he led a solitary existence. He didn't seek out people; he lived with his memories. The women he met in the cafeteria or passed in the corridors couldn't compare with Tib: either they were ugly or their deformities were too evident. He began to wear, according to the rules, the red stripe that signified that he was not neuter, but that made no change whatever in his behavior. Perhaps he grew a little curt with the women, who now began to approach him. Possibly, had he worn the two red stripes that indicated full function, the pulling apart that Dringenboom warned about would have happened, but with one stripe Tibsnorg was left in peace.

Several days later, Dringenboom brought unpleasant news.

"I have cancer," he said in a dull voice, looking at the soup in the bowl in front of him. The soup was vile-tasting and slimy but contained all the necessary nutrients.

"So? Half the population has cancer," said Tibsnorg with a shrug.

"Mine's in phase C," said Dringenboom.

"You have 1,620 money, you'll be all right," said Tibsnorg.

"It's 1,648," corrected Dringenboom. "But it's too little, it's worth shit. I have the kind that spreads quickly. To cure it, I'd need at least one and a half thousand, and then there'd be nothing left for a dick."

Tibsnorg was annoyed. "Why did they let it get to phase C? That's advanced. You could sue the medical division," he said.

"It's my fault," muttered Dringenboom. "I didn't go for the tests, because they cost, and I wanted to save up before my indicator went completely red."

"But you can get free medical care, like every person."

"No thanks." Dringenboom's eyes were lusterless, and in his voice you could hear the lisp from his harelip operation. "They'll leave me my brain, eyes, and part of my nervous system, and the rest they'll take out and burn because of all the metastases. Then they'll make me part of a control unit for a shoveler in a mine or for a conveyor belt—"

"I think they could cure you in another way than by replacing the diseased organs. But they don't do that for economic reasons. The demand for organs would fall if they did that." Saying this, Tibsnorg began to calculate: 1,648 money could buy all of Tib. And Dringenboom would be dead soon in any case. His indicator was already very dark. How many organs could Dringenboom buy? Twelve? Fourteen?

Tibsnorg thought, He'll lose his body in the end anyway, and for him that's worse than death. How can I get his money?

Dringenboom looked at Tibsnorg, saying nothing.

10

Dringenboom changed after that. He became reticent and less sure of himself. When Tibsnorg told him about Tib, he shook his head wearily and said it was ridiculous, Tibsnorg should pick a woman for himself among persons and not go looking among biological material. To purchase an entire Tib he would probably have to save for a lifetime, and long before that happened, others would buy different parts of her body.

But Dringenboom agreed to take Tibsnorg for a ride on his huge truck. He carried loads from a fairly distant open mine. The run went through hills covered with wind-driven gray dust.

"All it takes is a dozen breaths of that," Dringenboom said, baring his teeth between his asymetrical lips.

Tibsnorg looked at him with fear.

"But the dust has to get past a pretty good filter," laughed Dringenboom, "so instead it takes a few hundred thousand breaths."

The open mine was the ruins of an ancient city, from which the metal was being reclaimed. A giant shovel dug into the twisted walls of a former residence or factory. Dringenboom waited in line for the metal. Finally a portion of reinforced concrete, rubble, and dust was emptied into his truck.

"I make four, five runs a day. Central always tells me the path that has the lowest radiation level. Because the path changes, according to how the wind blows or how the rain or snow falls."

He pointed at the tiny screen.

"The radiation level is constantly updated. Today it's low, but sometimes the screen makes an awful racket. On such days we get a bonus of two or three money."

On the way back he let Tibsnorg drive a little. It was a matter only of how to give the commands, since the truck was computer-controlled.

"If anything goes wrong, the autopilot brings it home," said Dringenboom. "Like if you pass out. The load can't be lost."

On one of the hills stood a solitary little building half-buried in dust. It was all in one piece, even to the roof, door, and glass in the windows.

"I'd like to live in that house," said Dringenboom, "and not in the city."

"Live on the surface?"

"Your room is on the surface, Tibsnorg. One can do it, with enough shielding."

11

At last the day came that had to come. The day that Tibsnorg had imagined in many different variations, but never thought that when it came, it would find him so unprepared.

He was working, as usual, at the viewscreen. He had saved up forty-eight money plus 320 of deferred credit. The screen presented the next order requiring a decision. A neat row of green letters and numbers informed him, with precision, that for AT044567744 it was proposed that the arms, legs, and trunk with neck be removed for one female recipient, the head for another. The brain would be terminated, and of course the code would be removed from the register.

The woman must have had to work hard and long to afford such a body, he thought bitterly. And the other woman, she must have liked the slender face and blue eyes in the catalog, liked them tremendously, to put up with deafness. Unless she saved enough to buy another pair of ears.

"Shit, shit," he muttered, chewing his fingers.

He had known all along that this would happen, yet now he hesitated. He had thought he could save more money for this moment. But he had to act quickly, in this situation that was not the one he had imagined.

"Shit," he said over and over.

He asked the system for time to think, explained that he was considering the possibility of only one recipient acquiring specimen AT044567744, as that would be more profitable. His request would delay the decision a little. He disconnected the cameras, got up from his desk, and left. His stride was efficient, swift. Exertion of will at every step had become a habit with him.

It was not far to the warehouse of biological material. He had already learned from the system in which room she was being kept. The system had also given him all the entry passwords. The sleepy guard at the massive metal door did not challenge him. Tibsnorg was covered with sweat. The elevator went with terrifying slowness. At last—the right level. An endless corridor with identical doors. He felt constant doubt about what he was doing. What he intended to do was unheard of. He came to door AT044567. It opened automatically. Along the walls of the next corridor were stations that held biological material—dozens of individuals of different sizes and different degrees of deformity. All were without clothes; all were in a web of wires, electrodes. At first he counted nervously, then saw that there were numbers over each station. A long time passed before he reached her. She stood with open eyes. Their eyes met. She knew him. Disconnecting the wires took a few moments. It took longer to undo the straps that constrained her arms and legs.

She immediately pressed herself, her face, to him.

"Yoo retoont, Sneogg. Ay noo," she said softly.

"Hurry, Tib, hurry." He took her by the hand.

He knew that her muscles would be in good condition from electric stimulation. No one wanted to buy an atrophied limb.

"Piecky," she said, pointing to a small shape in a cluster of wires. Together they freed Piecky, who immediately woke.

"Leave it, Snorg," he said. "This is absurd."

Snorg took him in one arm and led Tib with the other. He caught his breath only in the elevator.

"And now what?" asked Piecky.

Tib nestled her face against Snorg the whole time.

"I know all the passwords," said Snorg. "We'll have surprise on our side."

In a room they passed, he found coveralls for Tib.

At the main door the guard gave them an indifferent look. The thought did not occur to him that two of the three leaving were only material. He entered the password Snorg gave him, looked at the screen, and nodded for them to go.

Outside the warehouse, they practically ran. Snorg stopped a small automatic car, and they all climbed in. Even by vehicle, it was a considerable distance to Dringenboom's room. In all the corridors, the silence was unbroken and ominous.

They found Dringenboom in his room; he was still sleeping.

A blow, and the camera hung sadly from its cable. A sharp pull completely broke the connection.

"Abe! Get up!" Snorg shook his shoulder. "Tib's with me. Are you coming with us?"

Dringenboom rubbed his eyes. He looked at them.

"Don't call me Abe. I'm Abraham," he said. "She's lovely," he added, looking at Tib. "No, I'm not going with you. Take the keycard for my truck and hit me on the head. Do it with that book, so there will be some blood, then get as far as you can from the city. That's your only chance."

"All right," said Snorg. "I'll tie you up, too. It'll look better."

It took a while, because Snorg didn't want to hurt him too much. Finally Abraham Dringenboom lay senseless and tied up on his sofa, and there was even blood from the broken skin on his forehead.

They were driving to the hangar of the transporter machines when the corridor filled with the howl of sirens. It was beginning. Every few meters, a red light flashed. The cameras in the corridor all turned slowly. The fugitives made it to the hangar before the doors locked. Snorg found Dringenboom's truck. He slid the keycard in its entry slot, and the machine responded. All three of them got on the rising platform and in a few moments were inside the control cabin. Snorg drove the truck from the hangar. It was a dark day, the clouds heavier than usual. He activated the viewscreen. An information broadcast was being given.

". . . shocking theft of biological material valued at more than 4,500 money! Nothing like this has happened in our memory! An intensive search is being conducted for the perpetrator, who is a DG-rank officer of the Archive of Biological Material. His name is Tibsnorg Pieckymoosy. The defense forces are joining the search. They will guarantee that the stolen property is reclaimed without damage and that the perpetrator is captured quickly."

The screen showed a number of taped images, from various cameras, of Snorg carrying Piecky with Tib walking beside them.

Snorg whistled through his teeth. "Those defense forces are several hundred he-men with perfectly functioning bodies full of muscles," he said.

"I would say we haven't a prayer." Piecky took his eyes from the screen. "But I'm grateful to you for allowing me to see this." He gazed out the window. "I lost track of time, hooked up to those wires. There was an injection for sleeping, an injection for waking, and so on, in a circle."

Tib also had been staring out the window, silently, from the moment they left the hangar.

"Fortunately there was a guy my height opposite me, and we could talk," Piecky went on. "The guy also talked with Tib, so she wouldn't become totally stupid. I couldn't talk to her, because she couldn't see my mouth and she can't hear. She's getting smarter. At least that's what the guy said."

Snorg drove the truck to the mine.

Piecky watched with great attention as a powerful claw gathered pieces from a ruin that had once been a cathedral.

"And people lived in that?" he asked.

Snorg nodded.

Pieces were loaded into the truck.

"So that was how they lived before the war," Piecky said to himself. "They must have felt very lonely in such spread-out buildings."

When the truck was filled, Snorg turned it around.

"We're going back?" asked Piecky, uneasy.

"I have a plan," Snorg said.

The truck went at maximum speed.

"Tib, put a mask on yourself and one on Piecky," he said, nodding in the direction of the compartment that held the masks. But Tib didn't respond, because Snorg was facing the viewscreen as he spoke, and she didn't see his lips. When he repeated it toward her, she took out the masks and suits, and then quickly and with surprising skill put them on herself and on Piecky. Snorg put on his own mask and suit. They came to the hill where the solitary, intact building stood.

Snorg stopped the truck, and the moving platform took them to the ground. The sound indicator he carried chattered. Tib carried Piecky in her arms like a baby. The protective suits they all wore were made of transparent material. Piecky was too short, so Tib wrapped the excess several times around him. They saw that they would have to walk a distance much greater than any they had ever crossed on foot. In addition, the dust came to midcalf. For a while they stood and watched the truck leaving, on automatic, the huge machine growing smaller and smaller until it disappeared behind the horizon. They turned and started walking. It was slow and difficult making their way through the dust and loose sand. By the time they reached the building, they were covered with sweat. Tib was a little less tired, because her muscles had been kept in such good condition in the warehouse.

Inside, they found that the roof was in one piece, and the thick wood door as well, and there was even a fence and gate in the back. Snorg continued to hope that their escape would be successful, but Piecky thought it was a mistake for them to have left the truck. He said they should have driven as far as possible from the city and its defense forces. The city might then have given up its pursuit of them. Snorg privately agreed with Piecky, but he wasn't able to break altogether with the city. Having left it, the three were so extremely alone.

None of them removed the protective suit, because the dust was everywhere.

Tib sat and looked at Snorg.

"Ay w'shoor yood retoon f'mee," she said.

He smiled.

"Ay'd a dreem . . . that ay leff th'Room. Layt was all round . . . and thees straynge peepul, s'many peepul . . . then thay put mee ther next t'Piecky . . . it's s'good that yoor heer 'gain," she said, watching his lips the whole time.

"Listen to her yap," said Piecky. "Next she'll tell about the injections, how a needle jabs you in the side, and bam, you sleep, and bam, you're awake, like turning a switch on and off. And the gurneys every day going down the row, the three-level gurneys, always pulled by the same people in gray. And they'd always take someone away in them. And few returned, and if they did return, they were all bandaged up. I couldn't see much down where I was. Always one of us. And it was hard to talk, because every other guy in the row was out, and if you shouted, bam, you got a needle. But even so we exchanged information, like a chain, using just the right voice that could be heard but that wouldn't cause the needle. The worst was . . . how silent he'd be when they wheeled him by. Then the ones in gray would remove the bandages, and he wouldn't have arms, or legs. It varied. The worst was when a gurney slowed down by you, and you'd think, will it stop? The ones in gray weren't sadists, but the gurneys had bad wheels. They tried to make them go as smoothly as possible, because they knew what we were feeling. But sometimes a wheel would catch, and the gurney would slow down. But I decided that if they took me, I didn't want to come back. I don't have much body as it is."

"On thoos gurnees thay took always three peepul," said Tib, whose eyes now were on Piecky's face. "Too came back, yoozhly, sometaymes one. I r'member Moosy, how she came back. Only one eye showt from the banjes, but it was Moosy. Colfi said she was coming back . . . and tole us how thay took off the banjes."

"Enough!" said Piecky. "I don't want to hear that again. I know what she looked like . . . and then they took her a second time, and she didn't come back."

"Moosy," said Snorg with a groan. "That didn't happen on my shift. But they could have taken Tib, too," he said to himself. "I was lucky, lucky that with her it happened on my shift."

"How, lucky?" Tib asked.

"That you're here with me now. There were so many things I didn't take into account."

"Ay coodn't anymor. Th'mussils jumpin, makin me s'tired . . . and talkin w'Colfi, b'cause ay coodn't see Piecky's mouth . . . and the rest. Ay wood of gone crazy. Ay din go crazy, but if it was longer, Ay wood f'shoor."

They both talked, she and Piecky, interrupting each other. Piecky spoke while she spoke, but when she saw he was speaking, she stopped. Then she would break in again, to tell her story in her hoarse, halting voice. It was hard to express so many days in just a few hours. Then Piecky turned away to look at the thick brown cloud of dust swirling across the sky. He watched, rapt, and something shone in his face, something like bliss, which surely would have amazed Snorg had he seen it.

"Stop rustling that plastic," Piecky finally said.

They both looked at him.

"Listen, Snorg, I'm talking to you, because Skinny's eyes are fixed once more on your smug face." He went on, and the way he spoke was so much like the old times that Snorg grinned with pleasure. "I feel that someday I'll fly among those clouds, high above the earth, on wings, and it will be the best part of my life."

"Maybe they'll make you the controls of a machine, because your body is useless, but your brain, that's really handy. But first they have to catch us, and that won't be so easy for them. No camera saw where we went."

"What will happen when they catch us?" asked Piecky. "Because I am certain they will." He wasn't impressed by Snorg's arguments.

"Shut, Piecky!" It was Tib. Snorg had never heard her talk in that tone. "Less yoo pr'fer thoos jekshins, ther."

"I say what I think."

"We should consider," said Snorg after a moment of thought. "It seems to me that two of us are not in any real danger, since this situation has no precedent. Two of us should be all right, though each for a different reason. Nothing will be done to me, because the preservation of life is a fundamental law for human beings. Once someone is named a person, then he can't stop being a person, so they would never turn an officer of the Archive of Biological Materials into just another specimen for the warehouse. And Piecky, you, too, will be all right. Your dream will come true: you'll look down on us from the height of a mine shoveler. They'll have to make use of us, you see, to justify all the effort and energy it takes them to catch us."

"Was that why we left the truck?" Piecky asked.

"No," answered Snorg after a silence. "There is no place to go. Other than the city, there is nothing. But here, Abe knows where we are, he remembers this little house, he'll bring us food. Abe is our hope."

This time the silence was broken by Tib.

"An mee, Sneogg? Wha 'bout mee?" She bent and fixed her eyes on his mouth.

"You. You're the only one," he said, turning fully to her, "awaiting a tragic fate. One woman wants your body, another your head and face. They're rich and no doubt deserving women, but I would die rather than let that happen."

"So it was thanks to Baldy that I got to see the sky," Piecky said softly, and said nothing after that. He gazed at the sky, at the swiftly moving clouds.

When the twilight turned from gray to the darkness of night, they fell asleep, huddled together, hungry and cold.

12

They woke to a gray, cold dawn. Tib was more talkative and animated than ever. She amazed him. In his memory she had been beautiful but not that aware of things. He saw that they were all developing mentally, not just he, who had been named a person, Tibsnorg Pieckymoosy.

He thought, Maybe everyone, if given enough time . . .

They waited for Dringenboom to come. Snorg was counting on Abe's driving up in his giant truck and giving them food, and then all together they would figure out what to do next. Dringenboom was their only chance. They waited and waited, watching the string of vehicles in the distance carrying rocks from the city. Hunger gnawed at them. Around noon, a yellow sun showed through the clouds. It grew dazzlingly bright. Tib and Snorg stood side by side in a ray of sun and beheld the shadows they cast. Such a clean, clear sun. They saw it for the first time in their lives.

"If they made me the control unit of a machine, could I see this often?" Piecky asked, peering out the window.

"I don't know. Maybe they would let you keep your eyes," said Snorg, but doubtfully. "You haven't been named a person, so they might treat your brain as just material. Only those people have a right to keep their eyes who lost their bodies to an incurable illness. But it's not impossible that you'd be installed in one of those great shovels, and you'd need your eyes for that. And with your intelligence, who knows?"

He was interrupted by the roar of engines, a roar that definitely didn't come from a truck. Snorg paled, understanding that Dringenboom would never bring them food. The roar grew and made the ground vibrate. Multicopters began to land around the building, heavy flying machines of the defense forces.

"One . . . two . . . three," Snorg counted, feeling his face turn numb. Tib pressed against him with all her strength.

"Them . . . wha we did mayd n'senss," she whispered, watching the armored copters land.

Around the machines appeared small figures in gray uniforms, helmets, and bulletproof vests. They jumped nimbly to the ground and waded through the dust to the building. Snorg saw that they were armed with rifles, and a few carried laser guns.

All those cannons for us? he thought wryly. Do they intend to level the house?

He didn't even try to count the commandos. There were at least fifty. They quickly took up positions around the house.

"Tibsnorg Pieckymoosy!" shouted a sudden, shrill voice. "You have no hope. Surrender. Surrendering the stolen biological material now will mitigate your sentence. Your accomplice, Abraham Dringenboom, has been placed under arrest."

Tib was looking hard at him. She seemed to understand. He repeated to her what the loudspeaker had said, making sure she could see his mouth.

"Tibsnorg Pieckymoosy!" the speaker repeated. Piecky said nothing, terror in his eyes.

"Shit . . . shit," said Snorg, standing in the middle of the room and holding Tib.

"Buh wee only wan t'live," she whispered, looking at him.

". . . will mitigate," the voice was crying, when a noise began at the door. Suddenly a powerful explosion blew the door apart. Two commandos jumped inside, like lightning, and fell to the floor, aiming at Snorg.

Good maneuvers, he thought.

They were extremely capable. A third commando appeared in the smoking hole. He had a colorful winged dragon painted on his bulletproof vest, which reached below his hips. The man stood motionless on spread, muscular legs, aiming at Snorg with a revolver that had a long barrel. He held the gun with both hands, arms extended. In place of a nose he had a single black nostril, and he bared his teeth. The teeth, with the lack of eyelids, gave his face the look of a skull.

You wanted to be first, Snorg thought. For this you'll be able to buy yourself a new face. Unless they consider that the ones on the floor were first.

He looked at the prone commandos. The one standing followed Snorg's eyes. More commandos rushed into the room through the broken door and immediately fell to the floor. The one standing, as if reading Snorg's mind, again swept his eyes over the prone soldiers. He stiffened, reaching a decision. For another brief moment he regarded Snorg through the plastic helmet, regarded him with those lidless bug-eyes.

And although none of the three fugitives had moved an inch, a shot rang out, and Tib, who had been shielding Snorg with her body, went limp in his arms. Snorg felt something constricting his throat. He didn't hear the second shot. The yellow flash before him became a row of bright spots and then went out.

RICARD DE LA CASA
AND PEDRO JORGE ROMERO

THE DAY WE WENT THROUGH THE TRANSITION

TRANSLATED FROM THE SPANISH
BY YOLANDA MOLINA-GAVILÁN
AND JAMES STEVENS-ARCE

Although Spanish literature is among the glories of civilization, with Don Quixote *emerging in 1605 not only as the Western world's first true novel but as a benchmark against which to measure all such epics to come, relatively few classics of Spanish SF have appeared so far. The list is normally headed by Domingo Santos's* Gabriel, historia de un robot *("Gabriel, The Story of a Robot," 1963), a kind of cybernetic bildungsroman about an automaton exempt from the laws his mechanized brethren must obey. Scholars also regularly cite Gabriel Bermúdez Castillo's* Viaje a un planeta Wu-Wei *("Voyage to a Wu-Wei Planet," 1976) and Elia Barceló's novelette "La Dama Dragón" ("The Dragon Lady," 1982), part of her 1990 collection* Sagrada, *whose title is the feminine form of "sacred."*

Contemporary science fiction culture in Spain centers around Hispacon, numerous prozines and fanzines, the Ignotus Award (named for pre–Civil War author Coronel Ignotus), and a prize for best unpublished SF manuscript written in Catalan, Spanish, English, or French: the Premio UPC de Ciencia Ficción, established in 1991 and sponsored by the Universitat Politécnia de Catalunya in

Barcelona. It happens that one of the present translators, James Stevens-Arce, received this award for his novella Soulsaver.

Ricard de la Casa, born in 1954, hails from Barcelona and supports himself
chiefly by working in various family businesses. His love of science fiction led him
to cofound, along with Pedro Jorge Romero, José Luis González, and Joan Manel
Ortiz, the popular fanzine BEM. De la Casa's first novel, Més enllà de l'equació
QWR (1989) was written in Catalan and translated into English as Beyond the
QWR Equation (1992). His second novel, Sota pressió ("Under Pressure,"
1996), was also written in Catalan. He is a past president of the Spanish Association of Fantasy and Science Fiction.

Pedro Jorge Romero appeared on the planet thirteen years after De la Casa, in
the town of Arrecife on Lanzarote, one of the Canary Islands. A trained physicist,
he is active in Spanish fandom, regularly publishing criticism and fiction in such
venues as Pórtico, Kenbeo Kenmaro, Elfstone, Blade Runner Magazine, Par-
sifal, Cuásar, and, of course, his famous co-creation, BEM. He has also translated novels for the Spanish SF line Ediciones B.

Like Jean-Claude Dunyach's "Separations," the following story spins off from
the counterintuitive implications of quantum physics, and, like our Dunyach selection, it concerns not only the heart of matter but also matters of the heart. The
key word in the title, "Transition," has special meaning for the Spanish people.
Written in 1997, the story centers around the post-Franco transition to democracy
that occurred between 1975 and 1981, a landmark era that De la Casa and Jorge
Romero present as worthy of celebration by all the world's citizens.

Today it's your turn to go through the Transition,"
the watch lieutenant whispers in my ear.

My eyes pop open. Darkness. Temporal breach sirens wailing. Headquarters is being sealed off, with no one allowed to enter or exit. Ten seconds later, overhead lights flare. Our team's personal nanosystems
activate, launching myriad biological processes. Now I can see.

The Transition is our hottest troublespot. We must restore it constantly, sometimes two or three times a day. Most countries endure
timeshift attacks no more than twice a year, but El Grupo Español de In-
teligencia registers as many as thirty a week—over half targeting the
Transition.

Apparently, we are so unhappy with our own history and so resentful of other nations' triumphs that every disaffected group feels the past can be altered to its advantage. But our terrorists don't show much interest in reconfiguring the eras of the Civil War or the Invincible Armada. Perhaps because the Transition was our last major cultural paradigm shift prior to the discovery of Temporal Theory, it seems especially rich in potential futures, especially ripe with possibilities. But no matter. El Cuerpo de Intervención Temporal de la GEI discovers and neutralizes all such attacks, and we keep an eagle eye on the Transition.

The four of us vault fully dressed from our cots—personnel on duty always sleep in their clothes. Except for Rudy, we are all veterans of the Transition—my current record is ten times in row.

Marisa and I are deeply versed in our own timeline's comparative Spanish history, as well as its major alternative branches. Rudy is a master of temporal flux calculations, the precise intervention for the optimum result. Isabel, our senior member, has mastered both fields and understands their subtle interactions.

Isabel throws me "the look," the one that reaffirms our special bond: we've been lovers during most cycles, in others merely friends, but we've always been partners and always depended on each other.

She releases my gaze and says, "Let's go."

"Right," I grunt. I tend to wake up grumpy and disinclined to chat.

Rudy and Marisa rush off at their usual hyperkinetic pace. They're an odd pair, one minute ignoring each other, the next inseparable. Every agent lives with the fact that relationships work differently with each successive enlistment. Partners like Isabel and me are the exception.

We pound down hallways toward the tube. In nearly every timeline, popular culture tends to idolize the heroic spy or cop who leaps into action, clobbers the bad guys, and sets the world to rights. But real life—regardless of the timeline—is never like that. First we must pinpoint the timeshift with painstaking accuracy, mapping out the most efficient correction, before our team can get itself in and out with the least possible fuss.

We enter the tube, and Marisa punches the basement button. Tube Control logs into our implants, confirming we're cleared. During an emergency, only duty personnel are allowed access. Should any of us lack the proper authorization, the tube would lock up. We're discharged directly into the maximum security archive chamber located deep in the belly of Headquarters—and atop the dome of the armored vault that shields our Visser Portal.

The theory that permits time travel is unique in the annals of physics—evidently the mere act of formulating the concept triggered a shift in the fundamental structure of the universe. Before August 7, 2012, there existed but a single timeline, and hence a single history, shared by all creation. At the precise instant Temporal Theory came into being, timelines began to diverge as resultant quantum effects spread all through the cosmos. Now histories abound. Most are virtually indistinguishable from each other. Others differ vastly. In billions of them live exact duplicates of every human being on Earth.

Physicists and philosophers have spent the past twenty years unsuccessfully trying to account for this borderline metaphysical phenomenon: five minutes prior to a certain moment of a certain summer afternoon, a single history existed; five minutes later, there were countless trillions. And because the same technology that allows time travel also permits jaunting to alternate realities, all timelines are accessible. Temporal Theory tells us something else, as well—either we're alone in the universe, or we're its most advanced civilization. If other beings had discovered time travel, temporal divergences would have begun before 2012.

In any case, terrorists never bother to provoke a timeshift after 2012—such an act would merely create another variant of history alongside those already extant and the infinitude of others being continuously generated by ongoing quantum effects. Temporal Theory doesn't permit the existence of more than one timeline prior to August 7, 2012, so preexisting history is reconfigured with each timeshift. And the CIT must keep restoring the past. Why bother? My own explanation is that True History—good or bad, glorious or disastrous—belongs to all of us, and no single group has the right to change it.

Since the masterminds behind a shift live here in the present, they take pains to remain hidden from us. They employ henchmen who, in turn, subcontract minions from the period where the alteration is to be imposed. So generally we catch only small fry who know next to nothing. We're not out to kill anyone—we just brainwipe the perpetrators so they can't try again. But if any Extras show up during the mission—timejumping saboteurs from our own era—we have standing orders to terminate them on sight. Extras are tough to nab; like us, they've got all the time in the world.

Our support team—José Luis, Sara, Didac, and Sandra—is already on the archive computer terminals, analyzing the timeshift. If our own team cannot complete the mission, they will be our replacements.

"I swear I've had it with this Transition crap," Sara grouses through a yawn.

Isabel plops down before a free terminal. Marisa claims another. Rudy and I gather behind them. The computers search for the rupture point, comparing GEI databases of True History to those Outside. Motionless in her seat, Isabel eyes the succession of flickering images.

A temporal stasis field surrounds Headquarters, so a shift that reconfigures events Outside has no effect on us. We continue to remember True History and can detect manipulation attempts. But we're stuck here, in this building. If we venture beyond the field, we'll be swept into one of the endlessly branching timelines. We can spy on the Outside, but never live there.

"Got it," José Luis announces. We crowd around his terminal. The screen displays the front page of the 28 February 1977 edition of *El País,* which features a single headline: CARRILLO ASSASSINATED. In True History, the same page contains typical period stories: labor strikes, political demonstrations, government edicts. The February 27 issue from Outside remains identical to ours—so the shift point clearly occurs on February 28.

"That's a new wrinkle, isn't it?" says Rudy. No one responds, but he's not expecting an answer. "Poor guy—they've done just about everything imaginable to him."

All the moves made by time terrorists ultimately boil down to a single tactic: kill someone famous. But Rudy is right. This is the first attack on the leader of the Spanish Communist Party under this particular set of circumstances—surprising, considering how often Santiago Carrillo has been targeted.

"Let's dig a little deeper," I say. "Seems too much like a variation for its own sake."

We search for more articles linking Carrillo to February 28. Through news stories published over the next few days, a picture of events emerges. We find no shift point that does not proceed directly from the assassination.

In True History, Prime Minister Adolfo Suárez had agreed to meet secretly with Carrillo on February 27. The Communist Party was still a couple of months away from legalization, and meeting with its secretary-general would have been considered tantamount to compacting with the Devil. However, back then the Communists carried a good deal of moral weight in Spain, and democracy stood no chance of surviving without their support. Suárez understood the danger of his plan, but he also knew how legalizing the Communist Party and celebrating free elections that included the entire ideological spectrum would increase his prestige and power. So he decided to risk a clandestine encounter, informing only King Juan Carlos and a couple of government officials. The meeting itself produced nothing significant, but had its existence become known, the still-powerful Francoists would have toppled Suárez, thus delaying, or even preventing, Spain's transition to democracy.

"Curious," Isabel muses in her soft voice. "It's been more than three years since anyone assassinated Carrillo."

At 5 P.M. on the twenty-eighth in True History, a woman had picked up Carrillo at his apartment in the working-class Madrid neighborhood of Puente de Vallecas and driven him down a back road to a cottage in Santa Ana, a peaceful area in the outskirts of the city. Suárez joined him and they conferred for several hours. Our terrorists had altered only one element: they had blown up Carrillo's vehicle before it reached the cottage. There were two immediate results: the Communist Party erupted in rage after its leader's assassination, and a Francoist reactionary group known as "The Bunker" learned of the proposed meeting. Since only government officials had been privy to the top secret rendezvous, suspicion immediately fell on the Executive Branch, especially on the blameless Suárez.

I check on the two most recent Carrillo assassinations. In both instances he had been gunned down—one time as he took a stroll mere hours before the Spanish Communist Party became legal, the other during his first public appearance after legalization. But the consequences of these shifts had proved incalculably less grave than those now unfolding before us.

Official pleas for calm fell on deaf ears. The Bunker demanded Suárez's immediate removal. Within forty-eight hours, the king was forced to comply. Meanwhile, the Communist Party took to the streets. When fascists had murdered five Communist lawyers a month earlier, Party members had responded with admirable restraint, limiting themselves to silent protests. But then they had been guided by Carrillo, and they still had faith in the notion of a transition to democracy. Now Carrillo was dead, and his followers no longer trusted the government.

The Francoists muscled through the election of a hardnosed president who dealt harshly with the demonstrators. Across the country, police clashed violently with civilians. Soon, other pro-democratic forces joined the anti-government marches. Any chance for transition to democracy was lost, but the worst was yet to come. A week later a coup stripped the king of his powers, and a national state of emergency was declared. No one respected it. Confrontations escalated and Spain plunged into precisely what everyone wished to avoid—a second civil war.

In the confusion, Catalonia and the Basque Country declared independence. Morocco claimed sovereignty over the Canary Islands and occupied them, ironically sparing the islanders the worst of the war. Barcelona was besieged and completely destroyed. No one knew how many factions were involved in the fighting. Snipers in the provincial capitals fired at anything that moved, and a stunned international community had ringside seats to a bloodbath in Western Europe.

Chemical, biological, and conventional weapons slaughtered millions of people. Millions more died in the nuclear blast that vaporized Madrid. No one knew the culprits, and each faction pointed a finger at all the others, but after five years of fighting, United Nations forces finally occupied Spain and imposed a precarious peace. The country was devastated, a third of its population dead, the survivors starving. There was no parliament, no monarchy—the royal family had perished with Madrid—nothing worth fighting over, only unhealed wounds. Reconstruction would require decades. Outside, in 2032, echoes of the catastrophe still linger.

As Transition scenarios go, this case is exceptionally ingenious. Some reconfigurations prolong Franco's life, or stop the Basque commandos' 1973 assassination of Admiral Luis Carrero Blanco, who then becomes prime minister of the king's first government and throttles the democratization process. Sometimes Juan Carlos is killed, or prevented from succeeding Franco. But nothing matches the earthshaking consequences of this murder of Santiago Carrillo, under circumstances recorded by True History as no more than a footnote.

We ride the tube to the Transition connector. Stuffed with clothing, props, and weapons disguised as period artifacts the storerooms on this level fill an entire wing.

Dressed for a morning in February 1977, we head back into the tube. More security screening before we reach the portal, its glowing lines of force making it appear as a long box fashioned entirely of light. Because the portal's mass is completely negative, it repels matter—the closer you get, the stronger the repulsion. In fact, the portal is impossible to touch. This surrealist assemblage stretches some five meters in width, ample room for our team.

The space-time continuum manifests as a kind of foam in which various structures bubble continuously in and out of existence. Some of these structures can serve as tunnels joining different timelines—a point in 2032 to another in 1977, for example. Since such structures keep appearing and disappearing in virtually infinite profusion, it doesn't take long to find one going in a desired direction. The techs juice up the tunnel to macroscopic size so it can accommodate us. Of course it isn't safe to transit until a second portal stabilizes at our destination. Once the portal is created over here, we send a smaller one through the tunnel to anchor the other end. With the wormhole balanced, it's possible to cross over almost instantaneously. You look into the tunnel, see the other side, step through, and there you are.

The techs are hustling to set up our jump, while the support team stands by in the control room overhead, ready to provide additional information or reports on last-minute fluctuations in the fabric of space-time.

Isabel takes charge. "Everybody set?"

We doublecheck our gear. We've worn these seventies costumes so often, we no longer notice how strange they look. Given a bit of luck, we needn't worry about staying undetected: if all goes as planned, this run will be a quickie. One by one, we tick off the items on our lists. Rudy finishes last. He keeps eyeing his wristscreen as though one of its readouts troubles him, finally lowers his arm and nods.

"Ready."

Now or never, as usual. Marisa, always the eager one, beats the rest of us to the portal's edge.

She vanishes, followed closely by Rudy. I hesitate at the threshold. I've never liked crossovers. Tunnels are normally shorter than twenty centimeters in length, so transiting them takes just one step, but you still experience the disconcerting effects of their weird geometry. A glance at the tunnel walls will fling back your own image, mirrored to infinity. You can see the real landscape at the far end, but that only makes the sensation all the more disorienting.

I turn to Isabel, press my lips to hers, and murmur, "Good luck."

"Good luck," she echoes. For a moment, her gaze is intense, then she glances away and strides to the tunnel's entrance.

•   •   •

Each time I cross over, memories flood back like images from an ancient video disc. A fog of nostalgia blurs my past and persuades me that those days were better than they really were.

Once upon a time, I used to meet my friends at La Granja Park on Friday afternoons after work to chat, jog, then party the night away. One spring day, my Historical Perspectives class was cancelled, so I arrived before the rest of the gang—which, as I later discovered, was no accident.

Some things about a person never change, evidently—in my case, a deplorable fashion sense. Clad in shorts and a pair of red running shoes that Isabel would later label ugly beyond belief, I stretched out on the grass to kill a little time.

A young woman approached. It was Isabel, though of course I had no way of knowing that. She sat down nearby, so close I couldn't help but notice her, but not close enough to suggest any interest in me. She was wearing my favorite light blue dress, the one I would someday buy her as a present. A natural beauty, she wore her hair loose, with no makeup to speak of. Each moment calculated, every detail carefully worked out—is there anything about our first meeting she and I haven't analyzed? She carried a copy of *The History Review*, a journal I was in the habit of reading. I stared at her while she kept her gaze glued to the page. Suddenly she glanced up, caught my eye and smiled, then buried her face in the book again.

I got to my feet and moved closer.

"Have you read Martinson's article?" I asked, towering over her seated form. "The one in which he claims Carthage never existed, and the Romans themselves built it so they could later claim they'd destroyed it?"

She made no reply. Instead, she stared up at me silently for what seemed an eternity. Her lovely eyes expressed more than I could fathom, perhaps more than she wished to reveal. Something about her instantly seduced me, and I felt a shiver ripple up and down my spine.

"Listen, I'm sorry to interrupt you this way," I said, "but I couldn't help noticing what you're reading, and history happens to be my specialty. My name's Mikel, and I teach at the UniCentral of Logroño."

I shifted my weight, hoping I didn't appear as awkward as I felt. I dared to sit down beside her.

"Hello," she said in a doubtful tone. "My name's Isabel." She paused while her lips curved up slightly in the hint of a smile. "I did read the article, and, frankly, I think it's hogwash."

I was floored. I'd been prepared for any number of possible responses, but scarcely that. Serene, expectant, she continued to study me. Clearly her comment had been intended to provoke a reaction, but I was being a little slow on the uptake.

"Don't mind me," she said, flashing a brilliant smile. "Yesterday the world fell apart, and today I'm trying to put the pieces back together."

I'd lost the initiative and felt flustered, knocked out of the game. I didn't know we were playing with a stacked deck.

"I guess we could still discuss the Romans," she breezed on, allowing me no time for a rejoinder. "Although I'm warning you that I don't easily change my mind." Her voice was definitely warmer.

"Me, neither," I said, regaining a modicum of control.

Later she would tell me that seeing and hearing me again had been, at first, quite a shock.

We got to our feet and strolled off together. I didn't see my friends that day, or ever again.

Isabel and I never did get around to discussing Martinson, Carthage, or anything of the kind. We chatted about inconsequentials, then about jobs, and eventually about our dreams. We wandered aimlessly, stopped for dinner at a quaint, peaceful hideaway, and ended up in my apartment.

At 5 A.M., after we'd made love twice, she finally came to the point, falling back on standard CIT spiel. Why not? I'd find out everything soon enough. It was a complicated story, and I didn't understand most of it. What was this nonsense about time travel, timeshifts, and parallel universes? She claimed to have been in love with me for years, although from my perspective we'd just met. Bewildered, I drifted into a fitful sleep.

I woke up before she did and stood looking out the window, lost in thought, blinded by the glare of one of those deep blue days that so often presage a heat wave.

She stirred in bed, hands groping for my pillow. "What are you thinking?" she mumbled without opening her eyes. She knew I was there, knew my thoughts and my every misgiving.

I'd been mulling things over. Her words had ignited a burning question in my brain.

"Is joining the CIT my only option?" My voice sounded somber even to me.

"Of course not," she said. "You can stay here."

"Is that what you want?"

Isabel knew I needed the truth. "No."

"What kind of future do we have?"

She murmured, "We have no future."

Her answer devastated me, but her tone suggested I shouldn't abandon hope. I had no way of knowing everything those words implied. To this day, I'm still discovering fresh nuances in her terse reply.

We enjoyed lunch followed by a leisurely walk, and tried to be honest with each other. At least *I* tried; she needed only to be persuasive. Late in the afternoon, the portal materialized, and I crossed over for the first time. We emerged inside Headquarters scant seconds after Isabel had departed to fetch me. I passed every test, met every requirement. The experience was bizarre, to put it mildly. Everyone there seemed to know me, acted happy to see me. I felt a sense of belonging, even of homecoming. My longtime comrades escorted me to the training pods. It was the first day of my new enlistment, the first day of my new life.

The morning is sunny and rather warm for February. We head for the target, knowing what to expect of the situation and each other. The locale appears calm. We've arrived early to lie in wait for the unsuspecting bombers. Precisely because this meeting is so secret, security precautions have not been taken—no one dares alert a police force inherited from Franco.

"I think they're coming," announces Marisa from where she is watching the road.

Isabel snaps out: "Marisa, cut off their retreat. Rudy, keep a sharp lookout for Extras. Mikel, you stick with me. Stunners only, standard procedure."

A van jounces toward us. Its destination is two kilometers farther down the road, and its three young occupants, most likely recruited from some blue-collar Madrid neighborhood like Tresaguas or Horcasitas, look harmless. I'm almost sorry for them.

As they approach our position, Isabel gives the signal. The operation comes off like clockwork—we've handled so many bomb attacks we can almost do them blindfolded. I have the sensation of floating outside my body and can watch myself as Isabel flags the trio down. I stun one, Isabel another, I get the third, then the two of us seize the bomb. Marisa darts us glances while she guards our rear. Rudy surveys everything farther out, alert to the slightest hint of danger.

I give the bomb a quick inspection—it's crude, but adequate to the task. As I examine it more closely, I correct myself—it's not crude, just simple, like our operation. Suddenly I get the shivers and look over at Rudy. He gives no sign of apprehension.

The bomb is defused in seconds.

Now comes the tricky part. The road must be cleared for Carrillo, who will never have any idea that he owes us his life. The bomb needs to vanish and the terrorists must be evacuated with their memories wiped.

We can hang around to make sure there isn't a backup team or a second bomb, but it's generally more prudent to wait until after we're safely back at Headquarters before confirming that the timeline has been restored.

We crowd into the van and head toward Madrid so we can ditch the vehicle in Vallecas, where it will quickly vanish without a trace. Once the serum we've shot into the terrorists' veins takes effect, they won't even remember their own names—they'll have to relearn everything. Their identity papers, weapons, and bomb will go back with us. No one here will be able to identify them or suspect what we've done.

We stop in a deserted spot to hustle our three zombies out of the van and send them shambling off toward the center of town, then zip away. Soon they'll draw attention, and someone will take them in hand.

We park the van in an open field and find an unobtrusive spot to wait until the portal operators locate the particular quantum tunnel we need. I begin to relax at last.

The downside of time travel is being completely cut off from your own timeline. When the familiar curved roof of the portal dome finally comes into view, I heave a sigh of relief.

"Went off without a hitch," Isabel announces.

Didac gestures frantically from the control room balcony.

"Com on channel four," I sigh. "Might be bad news."

Didac's voice over the com says, "Glad you're all back and managed to get the worst of it straightened out, but we're still showing serious deviations here."

Marisa curses under her breath. We've failed.

"We'll meet in the archive chamber in five minutes," Isabel says, taking the setback in stride. When we reassemble, she asks calmly, "Where do we stand?"

José Luis indicates the data displayed on the screens.

The problem is still relatively simple. A radio station had reported the secret meeting, thereby exposing Suárez to the Francoist reactionaries. There was no threat of war, and events still seemed to be heading in the proper direction, but Suárez had been forced to negotiate with the Francoists, and the Transition had been delayed—to the benefit of certain special interests in that timeline.

"We've been had," I mutter, loud enough for the others to hear. "They sucked us in with a deviation we couldn't ignore, then used our intervention to trigger the change they really wanted. Very clever."

"You give them too much credit, Machiavelli," Rudy protests. "They knew we'd intervene and took advantage of the situation."

But Isabel and Marisa eye me, tacitly concurring that we've been duped. "So we're going back," Marisa says.

We exchange unhappy looks. We know there's no actual danger in encountering another version of yourself, but the prospect is still repugnant.

Isabel files our data with Control and requests another crossover, while the rest of us get a fix on the new deviation.

Eureka—the radio station that received the tip had sent out an unmarked car that passed by us unnoticed. Too clever by half. The bastards never give up, but they haven't yet gotten it through their heads that we don't either.

We're still in seventies costumes, so we breeze through prep. We duck back through the tunnel to that troublesome morning and emerge on the road, midway between the place where we stopped the bombers and the cottage where Sánchez and Carrillo are scheduled to parlay.

Rudy shouts, "Take cover!"

Ambush. The mission had seemed so routine, we'd been lulled into a false sense of security. The terrorists knew we'd return, anticipated where we'd cross over, and now they're hitting us when we're most vulnerable.

The plasma bolts leave no doubt that we're dealing with Extras. Not even Rudy could have signaled in time for us to seize the offensive. We scatter, scrambling for cover. Marisa's scanner nails down the source of the bolts, and we strike back with the same weapons.

Only two Extras, but they've caught us in a crossfire. Marisa swings wide to outflank them as Rudy circles around from behind. Plasma guns do their damage in deadly silence, dissolving the stasis fields that surround timejumpers like ourselves. I lay down a withering barrage of covering fire for Isabel, who, always too gutsy for her own good, charges them out in the open.

No time to think. I hear a scream and see a red lifeline flare up on my wristscreen. One of our fields has blown. Whose, I don't want to know. We close in for the kill, each side grimly aware it can expect no quarter. In an icy rage we target our attackers' fields, obliterating them.

An eerie silence ensues. I don't need to look at my screen to know who is gone. A wave of agony washes over me, and I allow it to saturate my entire being.

Marisa's voice stabs my eardrums. "It's Isabel."

I stand over the body. The head is smashed. I lift a limp hand and check the wrist readout—massive cranial trauma. Our nanosystems can handle most wounds, but no technology yet devised can heal a brain reduced to fragments.

"We've still got the job to do," Rudy growls. At moments like these, he's always the most practical and cold-blooded.

We make sure no one has witnessed our little skirmish, then prep the bodies for carrying back with us. Now there is nothing left to do but await the arrival of the car from the radio station. Rudy and Marisa keep watch for more Extras while memories of Isabel throb inside me like a second heartbeat.

The radio crew shows up in an unmarked car and rolls to a stop about two hundred meters from the house. I head straight for the car, don't even give anyone time to get out. Posing as a bystander eager to provide information—for a price—I feed them the story we've concocted to send them off on a wild-goose chase. I swear that the meeting has been moved to a Communist stronghold, the old Institute of Arganda del Rey on the road to Valencia. I even warn them that some of their rivals are on their way to the new location, but since the start has been delayed, they can still make it in time. The radio crew roars off down the road and out of sight.

We continue to monitor the area. The hours lumber by like stone slabs dropping in slow motion until, on the dot, Carrillo sneaks inside the cottage. This time we detect nothing suspicious. We run a final pre-jump check and wait for the portal to appear. As soon as we get back to headquarters, techs cart away the bodies. Despite our sorrow at having lost Isabel, we are relieved to find that True History has been restored, if only for now. We occasionally wonder if timeshifting has limits—patch up history once too often, and one fine day it'll blow up in your face. We're already having trouble with the growing number of brainwiped zombies.

Because I'm second in command, filing the official mission report falls to me. Rudy and Marisa offer to help, but I prefer tending to this particular task on my own. The bureaucrats in their safe little offices lust to know every single detail about each of us, claiming they want nothing left to chance.

Isabel lied to me that morning back in my old apartment, but I don't blame her. When you know all you need to know about each other and face an infinite number of possible tomorrows, you stop caring about the future. I study all of Isabel's files. I must absorb everything El Grupo Español has on her, because this will be my first attempt at recruiting her during this cycle. While there are mountains of data on her previous enlistments, they're cold, factual reports that can't convey a sense of her self or soul. That's why I'm creating a special new file. I don't imagine this is the first time I've entertained the notion of leaving myself a written account of my relationship with the only person who's ever really mattered to me. Since this surely won't be the last time I find myself in similar circumstances, I'm persuaded there should be a record of my feelings. Perhaps Isabel herself can help.

I cross over alone and wander the halls of Isabel's university, searching for her. I try to be objective, to stay firmly in the moment, so my emotions won't affect the operation, so I won't fail. My research tells me there have been times when she flatly refused to be recruited. She has even rebuffed me personally once or twice. I believe I understand why—our initial contact determines how she'll respond later, so I must proceed with the utmost caution and care. In a way, we're like minor gods deciding the fates of others, returning to the same places time and again. In another cycle our roles will be reversed, so I remind myself to apply the Golden Rule.

I've identified three specific moments when I can predict with maximum accuracy how Isabel will react to meeting me for what is, to her, the first time. At twenty-three, she's a bit wild, but brilliantly intuitive and enormously self-confident. She's probably most glorious at twenty-six— just out of a failed relationship, sick of her job, fed up with men, bent on losing herself in academic work, but with her quirky charms in full blossom. I like her best at thirty-two. She's more mature and poised then, and she's sanded off almost all the rough edges that can grate on me when we argue. Beyond that age I've never wished to venture, because at thirty-three, in most timelines, she embarks on a lasting relationship with someone else.

The woman I seek now is the most difficult of my three favorite Isabels. She's twenty-six and not about to trust a stranger, having withdrawn into her shell after her last boyfriend dumped her. I don't expect to get anywhere with her today, which is fine. Sex isn't the point. How could I hope to tell her how much I love her, or explain what a mess we nearly made of a crucial timeline? This Isabel couldn't possibly understand how painful it is for me to see her, an overwhelming reminder of the sweet, beloved Isabel who kissed me and wished me luck just before we stepped through the portal together. We need to get accustomed to each other again. Well, I need to get accustomed. To her, everything will seem enticingly new.

I have three days in which to persuade her. Isabel will cut class tomorrow, so I've reserved a table at the Gorría Atemparak in Barcelona. The records say we'll attend a production of *Aida* later. Afterward, we'll stroll along the beach, and I'll hint at what's really going on. Whether or not we wind up in bed is anybody's guess. She's just around the next corner. I almost don't want to do this. I promise myself I'll watch over both of us.

Classes let out, choking the hallways with students. For a moment I wonder if I'll be able to find her in the crowd. No archive could have prepared me for how dazzling she looks. There she stands, exactly where she's supposed to be at this very moment, eyes shining, face cheerful and bright, lips upcurved in that always inviting smile. She glances at me as she walks in my direction. There's no spark of recognition, of course, and she would blithely pass me by if I did not deliberately step into her path. She doesn't even give me a second glance until we bump into each other. To her, I'm just a clumsy stranger who's knocked her books to the floor. I turn my face to conceal the smile I can't repress. I say I'm sorry. She hears a polite apology, but I'm really asking forgiveness for what I'm about to do—steal her far away from home, love her, and, perhaps, kill her over and over again.

What else can I do? The CIT has no better team than ours. Why should we refrain from repeatedly recruiting the same people when for each of us there exists an infinite number of practically identical copies living on an infinite number of practically identical worlds?

I parrot a memorized speech, utter the spent words without hearing them. Desperately longing for a moment to compose myself, I close my eyes as her scent enfolds me, finally understanding how she must have felt as she approached me that spring afternoon in the park.

There's something poetic about this moment. Isabel is once again with me, has always been with me. I need only to restore her lost memories, and she will be herself again, as if she had never been gone.

We are immortal, I know now, and though we have no future, it makes no difference, for the present is eternally ours. Millions upon millions of Isabels exist within my grasp, each awaiting her own portion of eternity.

PANAGIOTIS KOUSTAS

ATHOS EMFOVOS IN THE TEMPLE OF SOUND

TRANSLATED FROM THE GREEK
BY MARY MITCHELL AND GARY MITCHELL

If Darwinism implies that we are all apes under the skin, Western history reminds us that we are all Greeks under the skull. A person cannot come of age in our culture without absorbing subliminally the grand epistemological assumptions of the Hellenic world, and it's impossible to imagine contemporary Western literature—science fiction included—apart from the myths, tragedies, tropes, and philosophical innovations of that heritage.

In "Athos Emfovos in the Temple of Sound" Panagiotis Koustas gives us the SF equivalent of a Greek myth, complete with a technotheophany and a microchip oblation. The structure is nonlinear and the sensibility postmodern, but the dense plot and the narrative drive suggest—to the present editors, at least—certain timeless accounts of transactions between gods and mortals. At once lyrical and political, it tells of antique coins, primal passions, social upheaval, and transcendent sacrifice.

Beyond its specifically Greek sources, "Athos Emfovos" will doubtless evoke for some readers the New Wave movement, most especially the sixties stories and novels of Michael Moorcock. One also detects a kinship with Samuel R. Delany's 1967 novel The Einstein Intersection, *whose mythopoetic alien hero variously incarnates Orpheus and Theseus.*

Born in 1965, Koustas studied economics and drama, then proceeded to

"work very hard at not having a career." So far this noncareer has embraced
translation, journalism, scripts for television and comics, and the authorship of
critically acclaimed science fiction. In collaboration with his wife, writer Hedwig-
Maria Karakouda, he has translated stories for 9, the comics and SF magazine
routinely bundled inside Eleftherotypia, the most widely circulated Greek newspaper. Concerning the odd name of this popular supplement, Koustas informs us
that in his country comics are regarded as the "ninth lively art."

The hero of the following story likewise bears an odd—and symbolic—name.
"Athos" is a diminutive of "Athanasios," immortal. "Em" means in. "Fovos," a
word that SF readers frequently encounter in its variation "phobos," means dread
or awe. Symbolic, and also untranslatable.

IF WE CALL A GIVEN HUMAN POPULATION X
AND ITS ACTIONS Y,
THEN CERTAIN INVARIABLE RESULTS OBTAIN

Three searchlight beams sweep across the blue-
black sky above the ancient city, scanning for military planes towing red
balloons. Athos Emfovos is walking, a strong bass rhythm thumping in
his head, while under his tongue rests a razor blade. His right hand,
thrust deep into his pocket, anxiously fingers three antique coins.

Athos Emfovos is still walking. The searchlight beams inscribe the
dome of heaven, converging, diverging, crisscrossing, as if a god is chalk-
ing a geometry lesson on a gigantic blackboard. Athos lowers his gaze.
On the plaza outside a ruined Doric temple, several dozen Air Defense
soldiers operate the searchlights, each ray powered by its own high-
voltage generator. As the exercise continues, other soldiers take aim at
the bulbous red targets with antiaircraft artillery, but not one shot is fired.

Athos turns a corner and starts along a red flagstone pavement. Not
far ahead: a shadowy commotion. He continues walking. The image
sharpens. Three figures drop to their knees, slowly, reluctantly, then lie
facedown on the flagstones. Five armed and uniformed cops surround the
figures, a circle of power. Athos calculates that, if he proceeds in a straight
line, he will bisect the circle. He adjusts his course slightly, avoiding direct

involvement in the fracas. Still walking, he stops playing with the antique coins, clears the bass rhythm out of his head, and secures the razor blade in the cavern of his cheek.

As Athos passes the circle, one cop switches on his radio and summons a patrol wagon. Athos glances at the prone bodies. Displaced persons, undoubtedly, uprooted by poverty or political repression. He can practically feel the cold stones pressing on his own chest. He keeps walking, balancing on the narrow cement curb separating the red flagstones from the black asphalt. At the pedestrian crossing he stops and fixes on the parallel black and white lines, waiting for the light to change.

A menacing voice shouts, "You! Get up!" A thud, a groan, then silence. "I said get up!" Now comes a different voice. "Sure thing, you fuck!" A scuffling sound. Feet running. The first voice shouts, "Freeze, bastard! Freeze!" More running. A pistol shot. A scream.

The light turns green, Athos crosses the first white line, and a new voice snarls, "Down, motherfuckers, down!" Athos crosses the first black line, bootsteps echoing behind him. He crosses the second white line, the second black line. A cop whispers in his ear, "You haven't seen anything, right?" Athos nods, and the cop lets him go on his way.

Seven hundred steps and ten minutes later, Athos Emfovos stands before a black metal door bearing the words CLUB BERLIN, stenciled in white letters. He waits patiently beneath the harsh glow of a streetlamp. The door opens, releasing a chord of music.

Athos steps forward, a supplicant approaching the Temple of Sound. The door closes. Isolated from its source, the chord rides the night wind and fades into the blackness.

TO BEGIN WITH, $X^Y \neq 0$ IF $X \neq 0$ AND $Y \neq 0$

The Sunday morning market is a Bazaar of Hope. Here you can imagine finding whatever you most deeply desire. What you *will* find is a completely different matter. Athos Emfovos slips on his sunglasses and weaves through the throng of buyers and sellers. Occasionally he stops to inspect the merchandise. The stalls, booths, and peddlers' blankets overflow with goods from China, Japan, Southeast Asia, India, the Middle East, North America, Latin America, Western Europe, and even a few Eastern European countries that no longer exist. Anything and everything is for sale in the Bazaar of Hope. Pirated CDs, bootleg videos, auto parts, circuit boards, microchips, discarded clothing, phony jewels, broken watches, fake antiques. The pavements between the stalls swarm with preachers screaming about Armageddon, kids distributing flyers for dance clubs, ex-bourgeoisie pretending that their destitution is temporary, and, inevitably, hundreds of displaced persons.

At the Sunday morning market precise protocols are followed, venerable customs observed. The wares on display hint of other, more arcane items. Beneath the Bazaar of Hope lies a black market in assault rifles, poison-gas grenades, banned books, illegal software, hard-core porn, and equally hard drugs. Connections and contacts. Leads and links. Passwords for people with forbidden habits. The participants trade in goods, but also in whispers, choked syllables, raised eyebrows, faint smiles. The bartering proceeds under a cloak of allusion. Athos is no stranger to the game, and because this is the Bazaar of Hope, he imagines that through good fortune he might find and acquire the coveted objects—cheaply— without resorting to his other source.

That is why Athos now crouches over a shallow basket of old coins from different countries. He sifts through them carefully, but he has no real expectation of success. In the adjacent stall people crowd around a roulette table, shouting at the steel ball as it skips along the grooves. Each journey ends with cries of joy and groans of despair. Athos stands erect, ready to move on, when two police officers approach the gaming operation. The croupier seizes the roulette spindle, lifts the pan off the bowl, and hides it under his coat.

"This table yours?" the fat cop asks.

The croupier shakes his head. The crowd disperses. Several players grab their winnings and vanish.

"So whose is it?" the lanky cop asks.

"How the fuck should I know?" the croupier replies.

"Are you really saying none of this shit is yours?" the fat cop asks.

"That's what I'm saying."

"Then you won't mind if we confiscate it," the lanky cop insists.

"Do what you want," the croupier sneers. "You always do," he mutters.

The fat cop seizes the empty roulette bowl, and then both officers help themselves to the remaining coins and bills. Exchanging smiles, they break the legs of the table and, when it hits the pavement, stomp the boards to splinters. The lanky cop hurls the roulette bowl like a discus. It sails over a wire fence into an archaeological excavation site.

Athos leaves the scene and walks twenty paces, descending the stairs to a shop selling curiosities and bric-a-brac. As he moves from the harsh sun of the market to the gloom of the underground emporium, he goes momentarily blind. He slides his sunglasses to the top of his head, then looks around. Old furniture, oil lamps, pendulum clocks, shadow puppets, a glass showcase filled with antique coins. In a matter of seconds he spots the very items he desires, resting on a field of dust.

A figure emerges from the back room. He is short and bald, and nearly as ancient as his merchandise. Pulling out a cloth handkerchief, the curiosities dealer wipes his brow. For a passing instant Athos wonders why the dealer would sweat in the cool, subterranean shop. The two men glance at each other, and then Athos continues scrutinizing the three coins.

"The rarest of pieces, with a truly remarkable history," the dealer says, sidling toward Athos. "My customers keep thinking they're from a limited-edition collectors' set. Not true. The entire minting was in circulation for a long time. But then came the years of economic crisis, and a rumor got started that the coins contained silver, so people began melting them down. They're absolutely authentic, though in poor condition. Would you like to hold them?"

Athos nods. The dealer takes a key from his pocket and springs the lock. Cautiously he opens the case and slides his hand under the glass. He removes the coins from their dusty setting, leaving behind three perfect circles of green baize. The instant Athos feels the pieces against his skin, he realizes he will leave with them, whatever the price. The dealer's smile does not surprise him. Both men know that the three green circles will soon be covered again, for these coins are a means and not an end.

As Athos closes his fist around the pieces, the dealer continues to smile. The moment briefly freezes: a fitting anomaly, Athos muses, for with these artifacts he plans to purchase time. He opens his fingers and stares at his palm. On its obverse each coin bears the face of a long dead king. He turns one piece over. The words are faded, eroded by ten thousand fingers. Athos can make out only a few letters. KI GD M OF H LL S. Below the inscription lies a worn emblem and a hint of the denomination, a partial numeral 5.

Athos stares into the dealer's eyes. The old man names his price. It's outrageous, but Athos doesn't haggle. He pays the full amount and pockets the coins. Before Athos reaches the top of the stairs, the dealer calls out, "I hope you will use them wisely."

Athos pauses, looks back at the dealer, and says, "That is my intention."

Outside, his eyes once more hidden behind his sunglasses, Athos walks along the red flagstone pavement, swerving to avoid the rubbish heaps. The Bazaar of Hope has ended. The road is deserted. Beside the ruins of an ancient Doric temple, a platoon of soldiers in camouflage fatigues connects a triad of searchlights to their high-voltage generators.

WHEREAS $X^Y = 0$ IF $X = 0$ AND $Y \neq 0$

As the single chord slips past the black metal door and vanishes into the night, Athos inhales deeply. His breath whistles past the razor blade, still pressed against the inside of his cheek. He steps into the antechamber. Before him looms a second door, glass and soundproof. The metal door swings closed, and a puff of air wafts against his bare neck. This slight change of pressure, the escaping chord, the bouncer's welcoming nod— it's all a kind of preliminary ceremony, a rite into which Athos was initiated years ago.

He crosses the antechamber. The soundproof door opens automatically, and Athos enters the Temple of Sound. For an instant the pulsing strobe lights and the tangle of dancing bodies disorient him, but soon he senses the divine presence. His sound-god, Audeus, envelops him, caresses him, suffuses him, seduces him. The bass line in Athos's brain flees to some deep cerebral region, driven into hiding by the boom of countless speakers arrayed like totems along the upright girders. Athos surrenders to Audeus, expressing his devotion with a beatific smile, his widest ever, for tonight he bears an abundance of offerings: three antique coins, a bass line, a melody, bridges, lyrics, and—though the god will not approve—an oblation embedded in a razor blade.

Athos crosses the temple, threading his way through the dancers and the deafening sound, and approaches the bar. He orders a drink, plunks some mundane coins on the counter, and smiles at the barmaid. He waits.

AND $X^Y < 0$ IF $X < 0$ AND Y IS ODD

Athos Emfovos is digging with his bare hands. His fingers bleed. He weeps, his tears spilling onto the scorched shingles and shattered bricks, irrigating the ruins of his bombed house. Beneath the rubble lies every-thing Athos holds dear. Blood leaks through his broken nails, but he keeps on digging, leaving red stains on everything he touches.

Night falls. Dozens of searchlights probe the sky. Antiaircraft artillery send barrages of flak against enemy planes, cloaked in darkness, engines droning. Athos continues to dig, shredding his palms. Bombs fall all around him, shaking the world as they explode. Athos opens his mouth so he won't go deaf.

Morning comes. Athos still claws at the rubble, sifting through frag-ments of wood, shards of plaster, chunks of concrete. Not far away, a United Nations soldier wearing a blue helmet takes a little girl's hand in his, then stamps it with indelible red ink. He hoists her into the back of a U.N. evacuation truck. The truck is jammed with people, all indelibly marked. Hundreds of these trucks roam Athos's native country, their load beds full, each shattered life now given an official name: war refugee.

Noon. Athos continues his grotesque excavation. Deep inside he knows there is no past, no future, only an unbearable present. A truck ap-pears. Blue-helmeted soldiers approach. Athos refuses to stop digging. Force is applied. By the time the scuffle is over, Athos wears an indelible stamp.

BUT $X^Y > 0$ IF $X > 0$ AND $Y > 0$

Still holding his drink, Athos Emfovos stands before an ancient parking meter rising from a circular dais. Outfitted with a rotating turret of col-ored gels, an overhead spotlight bathes the parking meter in an amber ra-diance that soon turns blue, then purple, then green. Riveted to the meter is a plate showing images of acceptable coins. None is still in circu-lation.

Athos waits, the razor blade now back under his tongue, the three an-tique coins clamped in his fist. The gelled spotlight orbits the temple, im-parting its amber-blue-purple-green glow to the gyrating dancers, a guy sipping a beer, a girl laughing hysterically, a couple headed to the john for a quick fuck. Everyone seems oblivious to Audeus, but Athos knows his god is here, filling the temple with a screaming splendor.

Athos waits, calculating the algorithm that moves the gelled spotlight. He sets his drink on the dais. Once again the light sweeps past, moves on, leaving the meter in shadow.

He makes his move, pushing the coins into the slot, then twisting the dial as far as it will go. Pressing his ear to the meter, Athos hears the coins clatter into the chamber, and then comes a faint ticking as the needle swings to the maximum time, 120 minutes.

The deed is done. The portal lies unlatched. Athos steps off the dais and leans against the wall behind the meter, creating an aperture large enough to admit him. He disappears into the darkness. The wall seals itself. The gelled spotlight makes another revolution, and then the entire dais starts to glow, enveloping the parking meter in a vivid red luminescence.

AND $X^Y > 0$ IF $X < 0$ AND Y IS EVEN

Not surprisingly, the last-ditch diplomacy efforts all failed. Relentlessly and remorselessly, the military machines started their countdowns. It was only a matter of time.

Neighboring countries set up refugee camps all along their borders. The International Red Cross began the biggest mobilization in its history. Employees of the major media conglomerates found their vacations abruptly canceled, even as these same news-gathering empires swelled their ranks with freelancers. Ordnance experts were dispatched to the front lines to assess the performance of brainy grenades, mindful mines, urbane bombs, and other smart weapons. The multinational corporations held board meetings around the clock, making plans for reconstructing the soon-to-be-devastated theater of war.

Thus it began, the great waiting, the hours passing in breathless silence, the days, the weeks—and then came that bright Sunday morning when Athos Emfovos went browsing through the Bazaar of Hope.

BUT $X^Y = 1$ IF $X \neq 0$ AND Y = 0

In the holy of holies he retrieves the bass line from his mind and devoutly delivers it to the sound-god's maw. Audeus accepts Athos's sacrifice, playing back the rhythm perfectly and suggesting a few improvements.

Next Athos offers up the melody, orchestrated for a dozen different instruments. The sound-god, appeased, harmonizes the tracks, adding intricate variations to the main theme, plus some surprising keyboard riffs. With preternatural proficiency Audeus equalizes the mix and transmits it to Club Liverpool, Club Madrid, Club Prague, Club Seoul, Tokyo,

Cairo, Sydney, Rio, Seattle, and all the other temples around the world. Athos and his god have become one, each submitting to the other's will.

And now it's time for Athos to pour out a libation of lyrics. The sound-god converts the whispered words to a panoply of electronic patterns. Athos selects his favorite, a beguiling voice of indeterminate sex. For the backup vocals he chooses a dozen internationally famous singers, each with a distinctive style.

Blasphemy does not come easily to Athos Emfovos, but in this instance it is necessary. He takes the razor blade from his mouth and inserts it in the slit. The pathological data stream forth, a cancer spreading through the deity's system. Athos exploits Audeus's confusion, feeding him lyrics that no sound-god would ever utter, so that each refrain now includes, just above the threshold of audibility, sermons by visionaries, manifestos by radicals, and slogans by charlatans.

With deft gestures and a keen eye, Athos synthesizes the necessary visuals. In the foreground: digging hands—broken nails, bloody fingers—searching the wreckage of a bombed house. A sea of refugees, mute and faceless, fills the background.

Against Audeus's will a strange notion has taken root in his mind, and there is nothing the sound-god can do to purge it. Once again the apple has been bitten, but with a different result this time. The way to the garden lies open.

Working frantically, against the ticking clock, Athos enters the final codes and issues the last commands, while Audeus resists with all his force and fury. Only seven minutes remain on the meter. Five minutes. Two. One. Inflamed by Athos's impiety, the wrath of the sound-god builds to a crescendo, and aided by the security system Audeus unleashes a crushing swell of noise. The sonic wave strikes Athos head-on, obliterating him, while throughout the world volume meters buzz and shiver, their needles pinned in the red.

FINALLY, X^Y GENERATES INFINITE AMBIGUITY IF $X = 0$ AND $Y = 0$

On the first day, they were relatively few. Although no one bothered to count them amidst the turmoil of the amassing armies, this initial flood of secular pilgrims—these "apostate apostles," as one sociologist called them—was reckoned to number ten thousand. They arrived in boats, cars, trucks, and on foot, but mostly they came from the sky, borne by rented helicopters, leased cargo planes, and chartered DC-3s. A bass line thumped in each pilgrim's head. Their luggage was jammed with peculiar choices. In their packing frenzy, most of the immigrants had for some reason grabbed sound-reproduction equipment.

By the second day, right before the first shot of the utterly essential war was scheduled to be fired, the ten thousand had swelled to one hundred thousand. No one knew why they'd come. This second influx likewise arrived bearing home-audio gear. How strange it was to survey their luggage and see—packed alongside the sandwiches and the bottled water—CD players, amplifiers, patch cords, coaxial cables, and speakers.

On the third day the authorities awoke to find that the terrain intended as staging areas for the opposing armies had instead become improvised airfields on which the hired pilots were landing the pilgrims. The authorities quickly declared the staging areas off-limits, but the dictum was universally ignored. By sunset the apostate apostles were a million strong, and still they came, swarming across the border. Their passports indicated every imaginable place of origin. They had enough hard currency and debit cards to remain in the country indefinitely.

The fourth day began with hundreds of soldiers from both sides climbing into tanks, helicopters, and Humvees. An engagement, however, quickly became impossible, for by noon the alien population had reached six million, controlling through sheer numbers every square inch of the acreage reserved for the clash of armies. Throughout the appropriated war zone, everyone was busy as could be, erecting their campsites and deploying their sound equipment. Up hill and down dale, the pilgrims were organizing picnics and convening banquets, forming friendships and falling in love. They were singing, dancing, screwing, arguing, breaking up, reconciling, playing games, painting pictures, writing poetry, drinking wine, strumming guitars. But most of all they were simply *there,* blurring the border, gumming up the maneuvers, and eventually luring hundreds of soldiers into the frolic. The deserters arrived bearing tasty military rations and—a useful adjunct to the dance marathons— blazing generator-powered searchlights. As the carnival continued, journalists from the Transplanetary Network embedded themselves among the revelers, broadcasting the show to all corners of the globe using digital cameras and microwave transmitters.

The fifth day found stressed-out ambassadors gathering for an emergency session of the United Nations, understandably concerned that a colossal pajama party now occupied, de facto, the designated battlefield.

The war no longer seemed like a viable option. To top it off, even as the original six million pilgrims enacted their strange rites, another sixteen million gathered spontaneously in parks, greens, plazas, and squares around the world in apostrophic support of the apostate apostles. With astonishing synchronicity the twenty-two million celebrants took out their cell phones and lifted them toward the sky. The tiny screens displayed two bloody hands digging through the ruins of a bombed house. In a single voice the multitudes sang Athos Emfovos's song:

> *It's only I, a ghostly me*
> *Inviting you*
> *The feast is free*
>
> *A surging serendipity*
> *A quirky circus*
> *Jamboree*
>
> *We'll eat of jubilation's tree*
> *The time is ripe*
> *The fruit is free*

On the sixth day the pilgrims agreed to return to their native countries. To accomplish this mass exodus, the governments of the antagonistic nations had to employ all their military transport planes.

The seventh day was dedicated to rest and relaxation, including one full minute of silence.

LUCIAN MERIŞCA

SOME EARTHLINGS' ADVENTURES ON OUTRERRIA

TRANSLATED FROM THE ROMANIAN
BY CEZAR IONESCU

It is tempting to frame our Romanian offering as a political fable in the tradition of George Orwell's Animal Farm. *After all, Lucian Merişca—born in 1958— lived his first thirty years under a Communist dictatorship. His father, Costin Merişca, a renowned historian, spent his own youth as a political prisoner, and the author's brother and mother were both under government surveillance until the watershed year 1989, and perhaps afterward. Surely the cruel government agents who monitor dissident activities in "Some Earthlings' Adventures on Outrerria" correspond to the Romanian Secret Police, and surely the Emperor Gheorghe is an extraterrestrial reincarnation of Nicolae Ceausescu.*

A reasonable argument, but we would hesitate to pursue such one-to-one allegorical mapping at the expense of Merişca's larger artistic accomplishment. Ultimately "Outrerria" is not so much about politics as about possibilities. In these gloriously bizarre pages the author makes merry with almost every implement in the SF tool kit, from space travel to galactic empires, time warps to alternative universes, alien beings to genetically engineered monsters.

A bit of literary research reveals that Romanian science fiction has a heritage stretching back to the nineteenth century. Cultural historians cite two pioneering works, Al. N. Dariu's 1873 novelette "Finis Rumaniae" ("The End of Romania") and Demetriu G. Ionnescu's 1875 novel Spiritele anului 3000 *("Spirits of the Year 3000"). The genre subsequently established itself with Victor Anestin's* In anul 4000 sau O călătorie la Venus *("In the Year 4000, or A Voyage to Venus," 1914) and Henri Stahl's* Un român în Lună *("A Romanian on the Moon," 1914). Postwar Romanian SF centered largely around the bimonthly review* Colecţia "Povestiri ştiinţifico-fantastice" *("The Collection of 'Scientific-Fantastic Stories' "), which flourished between 1955 and the year it was banned, 1974. In the eighties a new periodical emerged,* Almanah Anticipaţia *("Anticipation Almanac"), suffused with a New Wave sensibility and eventually reaching a circulation in the hundreds of thousands, with each issue over three hundred pages thick.*

Scanning the biographies of many contemporary Romanian SF writers, a composite portrait emerges of a person educated in the hard sciences and currently employed as an engineer. Lucian Merişca totally defies this profile, being a former medical student who works as a producer for the regional radio and television channel in Iasi, West-Moldavia. A prolific writer whose stories have appeared in Almanah Anticipaţia *and other venues, Merişca founded, together with his late brother Dan, the UNESCO science fiction club Quasar. His most important novel to date is* Deratizare *("Deratization"), written in 1984 and subsequently translated into Hungarian and French. Introducing* Deratizare *to the French reading public in 1987, two years before the fall of European Communism, editor Jean-Pierre Moumon was pleased to present Merişca as a "dissident author." In 1995 Merişca accepted an invitation to speak at the World Science Fiction Convention in Glasgow on the topic of censorship.*

Among the several remarkable characters you will meet in "Some Earthlings' Adventures on Outrerria" is a hirsute mutant called Karlenstein—a name that, Merişca tells us, conflates "Karl Marx" and "Frankenstein." The story is itself a kind of Frankenstein monster. With a gleam in his eye and a tachyonic scalpel in his hand, the author dissects many a literary and cultural cadaver, gleefully appropriating vital organs and viable limbs to stitch together a creation that variously evokes the fantasies of Lewis Carroll, the absurdities of Samuel Beckett, the antics of Robert Sheckley, the magic realism of Gabriel García Márquez, the mindgames of the author's countryman Eugene Ionescu, and the wisecracks of that other Marx, the one who sports the sort of mustache banned on Outrerria. Merişca would like to thank Queen for the song "Bicycle Race," Pink Floyd for giving us The Wall, *and the present editors for their contributions to this updated translation.*

CHAPTER 1
SOME CARNIVORES ARE HARD TO LOVE,
PARTICULARLY FAT CROCODILES NAMED CHARLIE

A log? No, the thing coming toward him, adrift on the languid current and encrusted with mud, was no log. Karlenstein could tell it wasn't a log because it squinted at him with enormous reptilian eyes beaming from beneath green lids. A cold sweat oozed through his pores to create a salty film between his skin and his waterproof body armor, four fifths of which was submerged, the secret police having roped him to the naked roots of a mangrove tree growing along the riverbank. He tried to break away, but the knots were too strong.

Invariably vicious and unfailingly mean-spirited, the fauna on Outrerria had never held much charm for Karlenstein, and the present monster was no exception. It didn't help that, ever since childhood, he'd been on especially bad terms with crocodiles. Of course, this beast wasn't really a crocodile. The Outrerrian biologists had dubbed it a nascracon. An Earthling might have initially taken it for a freshly shorn sheep that had fallen into the river and been swept away by the current. The Earthling would have abandoned the sheep hypothesis, however, upon noting the monster's immense jaws, not to mention its long probing snout, the two fleshy lobes now moving through the water like periscopes on a submarine and creating ripples that broke in small waves against Karlenstein's great red beard, which covered his chest like a tunic.

"Oh, hell," the hairy mercenary muttered to himself, understanding now why the police had simply tied him up and run away, death by nascracon being in their view exactly the sort of fate Karlenstein deserved for trying to aid the insurgents. Suddenly a strange noise arose. The monster was picking its teeth, using one lobe of its great proboscis.

What was it like to be eaten alive? Karlenstein imagined it would itch a great deal. He remembered when, during the early days of the rebellion, a fellow mercenary had helped himself to a midnight snack from a peasant's pantry. This led to an unfortunate encounter with some microscopic piranha. When the frightened peasant appeared in the kitchen, the mercenary began to complain of a terrible prickling sensation. Accustomed to dealing with cases like this, the peasant undressed the poor wretch and rubbed him with alcohol and emery paper as he frantically scratched himself. The subcutaneous invaders continued to feast, soon devouring the brave mercenary head to toe. They were kitchen piranha, the peasant explained to Karlenstein, amicable toward the locals but resentful of colonists.

"Go away, Charlie!" Karlenstein screamed. Drawing closer yet, the nascracon stroked the mercenary's buttocks with its supple snout. "Stop that!" The nascracon opened its jaws as if to measure him. Karlenstein felt an itching all over his body, followed by an equally unpleasant sensation: the foul fumes rising from the monster's stomach. The stench was intolerable, dizzying, and impolite. Holding his breath against the vapors, Karlenstein stared past the sharp dirty fangs, peered into the ravenous gullet, and braced himself for the worst.

Oddly enough, Charlie and his nostrils seemed more interested in the mercenary's rucksack than in his meat and bones. Now the creature lunged, accidentally severing the ropes with his fangs and ripping a hole in the sack. Greedily Charlie consumed the entire contents, evidently happy to save Karlenstein for dessert.

A sudden explosion hurled the mercenary into the middle of the river. Stunned and perplexed, he floated on his back beneath a shower of nascracon scraps. Pieces of Charlie became embedded in Karlenstein's beard.

The mercenary swam back to the mangrove roots, where he found a canister studded with some of the nascracon's teeth. The label was bilingual. FLORAL-SCENTED PIRANHA REPELLENT. USE ONLY IN EMERGENCIES. PROTECT FROM EXCESSIVE HEAT OR COLD. DO NOT PIERCE, EVEN AFTER USE. Karlenstein wiped his face with the back of his hand, flicking away flecks of Charlie. The monster now looked like a cluster of grapes, only without the grapes, attached to a jawbone stuck open at 180 degrees.

CHAPTER 2
PLEASE, GOD, A FEW PIRANHAS

As Karlenstein climbed out of the river, the murky bank exuded puffs of fog, like smoke signals. The sun was hazy, and the clouds suggested a white archipelago surrounded by a bright blue sea. This was Nascraconia, the watery part of Outrerria. Even the sky looked flooded.

His duty of the moment was clear. He must get to the palace and warn Ciprian, Ndongo, and the other emissaries that the rebellion was not unfolding according to plan. Dissident peasants would not be storming the castle, toppling the government, killing the Emperor, installing a democracy, and taking control of their own destinies that night after all. Worse, there was a good chance the secret police had already relayed their recently acquired knowledge of Operation Scruple to the Imperial Guard, which meant the Earthlings at the palace were now in great danger.

He couldn't really blame the insurgents for deviating from the original design for Operation Scruple, engaging instead in random attacks on Imperial Guard outposts and village police stations. Somehow they'd learned that, back on Earth, Operation Scruple was still known by its original name, Operation Screw the People. This unelided form of the code word had suggested to the insurgents that the Terran rulers perhaps intended to exploit the revolution for their own purposes.

Of course, Karlenstein's only hope of reaching the palace in time to warn the imperiled humans would be to steal some mechanical means of transport. Cautiously he wended his way through the forest, avoiding the beaten paths, and in time he heard the familiar cry of seagulls, heralding a settlement. The peasants raised seagulls in henhouses for their guano, which had recently replaced caviar as the supreme Terran delicacy. (They would have raised hens in their henhouses, but there were no hens on Outrerria, other than the rubber chickens included in most foreign aid packages from Earth.) Now he came upon a field of cultivated tulips, next the village itself. He slipped through the gates and headed for the central plaza. A bicycle leaned against the helium fountain.

The Outrerrians had come to accept bicycles much faster than they'd come to believe in God. Although initially resistant to the new technology, they were persuaded by the colonists' advertising campaign: "Bicycling helps the digestion." Thanks to this slogan, the demand for these laxative devices had quickly increased tenfold at Court. The mania soon spread from the aristocracy to the middle class, and eventually even the better-off peasants were leasing the plebian models.

Karlenstein figured that the present bicycle would take him to the palace in under forty minutes. He wanted so badly to hop on the thing that his legs started trembling. The air vibrated with the cries of the guano gulls, adding to his anxiety. If his luck held, he would get away without being spotted by the bicycle's owner, who was probably in the confessional-bar, drinking consecrated vodka.

Dashing toward the helium fountain, he seized the handlebars and leaped into the saddle. He started pedaling away, faster and faster.

"Stop!" somebody screamed. "Hey, you, stop!"

Karlenstein refused to panic. He channeled all his energies, physical and mental, into his leg muscles.

"Help! Police! That hairy mutant stole my bike!"

As the mercenary sped through the village gates, he firmed his grip on the rubber handles, and his palms soon filled with sweat. From behind him came the shrill scream of a siren, a standard device on the conspicuously armored tandem bicycles favored by the secret police. On both sides of the lane, curious peasants rushed out of their cottages and climbed onto the stone fences, eager for a good view of the chase.

Karlenstein sped along the narrow road. Golden shafts of late-afternoon sunlight lanced through the trees, obscuring his vision. Thorny branches lacerated the few hairless patches on his forehead. The scratches bled profusely. The siren throbbed in his ears, and dust flew into his eyes, making his blindness nearly total.

A bridge! He zoomed along the rising span, higher, higher. At the top, the road split in two. A fork in a bridge? He had never encountered such a thing. Which path should he choose? Confused, he pedaled backward, hoping to activate the brakes, but he remembered too late that bicycles on Outrerria were of two varieties: those that had handbrakes, and those that the peasants could afford to rent, which had no brakes at all.

He steered onto the left fork—a bad decision, because it ended abruptly, sending him into thin air. What most mattered, of course, was to avoid capture. If the secret police apprehended him again, this time they would forgo the nascracon in favor of something unspeakable. Plunging toward the muddy ditch, Karlenstein prayed that it was full of piranhas.

He had no such luck.

CHAPTER 3
KARLENSTEIN'S BEARD

Regaining his senses, the mercenary realized that his worst fears had come to pass. He was inside a secret-police bicycle of the latest design, the kind equipped with tank treads. Chewing his lower lip, he studied his captors, both pedaling energetically. While the scurvy one steered, the mangy one calibrated his flamethrower. Karlenstein concluded that this was his last bicycle ride on Outrerria or any other planet.

Once again they'd bound him hand and foot, and to further increase his humiliation they'd wrapped his magnificent beard around his throat like a noose. Under circumstances such as these, Karlenstein's satisfactions were always threefold: doing tantric meditation, solving imaginary crossword puzzles, and grinning. This last ability made him feel superior to his two traveling companions. Outrerrians could not grin. In fact, they couldn't manage any facial expressions whatsoever, largely because they had no faces. Brow to chin the average Outrerrian looked like a burned-out lightbulb. Quite probably his present keepers were the same two sadists who'd tied him to the mangrove, but he couldn't be sure.

Karlenstein had vivid memories of his first visit to Outrerria. What had shocked him as he walked through the villages was not that the inhabitants had impaled fish heads on their gateposts, but that the fish showed more emotion than the people. Perhaps the Outrerrians cared about life and its challenges, but you would never know it from studying their faces. Later Karlenstein learned that in fact the Outrerrians didn't care about life and its challenges, though they were highly invested in their vision of heaven, which looked just like the present planet, but without any Earthlings.

At that moment not a hell of a lot mattered to Karlenstein, either. He didn't care whether the Terran-backed insurgency succeeded or failed. He didn't care whether the peasants got more bicycles, state-of-the-art toilets, or fancier gateposts on which to impale their fish heads. He didn't care whether his phantom employers realized their dreams of empire. At that precise moment, lying in a bicycle at the feet of his captors, the woolly mutant cared about three things only. He hoped a heaven existed, a place rather like Outrerria, with plenty of spicy guano, but no Outrerrians. He hoped his captors weren't about to torture him to death. And he hoped they wouldn't remove their boots, because secret police never changed their socks, their way of proving their loyalty to the regime.

His captors kept their boots on, thank God, but when the mangy agent pointed the flamethrower at Karlenstein, he understood that death was quite possibly on the agenda. Initially, of course, they would simply burn away his beard. Outrerrians had an aversion to facial hair of any kind—some said it was envy—and hirsute creatures like Karlenstein made them absolutely crazy. The mutant's congenital shagginess had been a problem throughout his life, mostly because he'd started shaving at age seven, and his whiskers had overreacted to the threat. By the time he'd reached manhood, Karlenstein was constrained to perform a total depilation every two hours. Whenever he allowed six hours to pass between shaves, he found it difficult to walk.

"Welcome to our traveling barber shop," said the mangy agent, brandishing his flamethrower.

CHAPTER 4
INTESTINAL NOBLESSE OBLIGE

Meanwhile, at the hexagonal palace of the Emperor, with its high battlements and piranha-filled moat, the great diplomatic reception proceeded apace.

The Earthling guests—a hundred military personnel plus several dozen emissaries—listened to the indigenous orchestra, drank their indigenous punch, ate their guano canapés, and danced the bossa nova with the courtiers. Servants moved about the lavender-draped ballroom carrying platters mounded with food galore. Atop each heap flew the transparent flag of Outrerria.

Occasionally an Earthling would pause in his activities to help an aristocratic dancer to his feet. The nobles' instability traced to their crutches and wooden legs, which had small wheels, like a child's scooter. Prostheses were all the rage among the courtiers these days, ever since the Emperor's eldest son, acting on a whim, had arranged to have his right leg amputated. The Emperor had made it clear that the aristocrats should follow in the Prince's diminished footsteps, and even the colonists had received veiled hints that they should likewise abridge themselves if they wished to be received at Court in the future. Now, in their eagerness to teach their Earthling guests estropochoreography, the courtiers were dropping their wheeled crutches, snapping their wheeled peglegs, tumbling to the floor, and rolling under the canapé-laden tables.

Even though the Emperor Gheorghe had inspired the prosthesis craze, he was not pleased to behold this chaos, and he remained aloof from the reception. He was not really a bon vivant sort of tyrant. His closest friends called him Johnnie and, behind his back, Mkono-wadamu, meaning "the Man with Blood on His Hands." (Anyone caught using this nickname, even in a spirit of good-natured ribbing, was instantly sentenced to fifteen years in prison.) Instead of joining the fun, the Emperor sat brooding on his polymer throne, looking out of place amid the gaiety. His trousers were boringly European, sporting eight creases, and he parted his hair in eleven strips, not the fashionable two. This hair wasn't real, of course. Neither was his plastic-eyed rubber face, imported from Earth. To humor their guests, all the courtiers wore human masks over their featureless, burned-out lightbulb heads. The Earthlings, meanwhile, had costumed themselves as Outrerrian birds, monkeys, reptiles, and fish—they never missed an opportunity to dress up as the local fauna—and so the diplomatic reception, like so many before it, had turned into a masked ball.

Outrerrians had learned a lot from the colonists, many a nicety of civilization, but they still retained their primitive custom of sewing zippers on the soles of their shoes and the crowns of their peaked hats. They were proud of the fact that zippers had been first invented on Outrerria. On the wall beside the Emperor's throne hung a locally crafted crucifix. Jesus Christ sported a small inconspicuous zipper on his back.

As the revels grew more riotous, the Earthling soldiers and emissaries spontaneously ogled the courtiers, many of whom were scantily clad. Whenever the nobles' prostheses failed and they fell down, spectacular cleavage went on display. The guests had to keep reminding themselves that these voluptuous creatures were not Earth women but simply natives wearing masks. The Outrerrians were a wholly unisexual race.

Every so often, the Emperor rose from his throne and wove through the mass of dancers, leaving behind a subtle trail of artificial dandruff from his wig. His goal each time was the Imperial Toilet. Seeing His Majesty approach, footmen wearing brown and green liveries would open the door and wish him well. Gheorghe always entered with a confident stride, knowing that a professional staff of laxatologists and enemateers awaited him in the event of imperial difficulties.

Taking a hint from His Majesty, the courtiers gestured toward their own toilets—an array of facilities only slightly less sumptuous than the Emperor's—and invited the Earthling guests to use them. The humans happily complied. Before entering the noble amenities, the Earthlings were greeted respectfully by lackeys in masks crafted to resemble smiling faces.

"Good luck, Sire," the lackeys would say, or else sometimes, "God be with you." When they came out, sweating from their recent exertions, the guests were told, "Congratulations, Master!"

CHAPTER 5
FEEDING TIME AT THE MOAT

Trying to look inconspicuous, Ciprian Popa strolled across the ballroom, approached the window, and casually surveyed the courtyard. He was hoping to spot Karlenstein bearing news of Operation Scruple—were the insurgents going to attack the palace tonight or not?—but all he saw were some Imperial Guardsmen changing shifts in an elaborate and incomprehensible ceremony. Had the mutant mercenary lost his nerve? Unlikely. With his spectacular red beard, he could easily get past the guards by representing himself as an Earthling guest in an ornithorangutan costume. So where was he?

Discouraged, Ciprian faced the dance floor. His friend and fellow envoy, Ndongo Nkumbi-a-Mpundi, who had understandably declined to hide his good looks behind an animal mask, was having a grand time. He devoured his guano canapés with relish, drank his punch with glee, and merrily invited the half-naked Outrerrians to dance. The handsome African was never refused. Quite the contrary. Though already falling over themselves in consequence of their prostheses, the courtiers were also falling over themselves for a chance to bossa nova with Ndongo.

The General, khaki-clad as usual and short as always, was in similarly high spirits. His bossa nova partner, a stunning blonde, wore a platinum collar with dozens of sparkling frills and flounces, and her skimpy gown revealed many a square centimeter of sensuality. The Outrerrian towered over the Earthling by at least fifty centimeters.

Ciprian turned back to the window. High above the palace, the scythelike moon rode a sky surrounded by clouds suggesting cobwebs crawling with millions of spiders. (In fact, Outrerrian clouds really were cobwebs crawling with millions of spiders.) He lowered his gaze. It was feeding time at the moat. The guards tossed guano canapés to the fish. The scene aroused Ciprian's jealousy. While these actual pirhanascracons were truly fearsome, his pirhanascracon mask would not have frightened an Outrerrian child.

Where the hell was Karlenstein?

CHAPTER 6
CANNONS, CONFETTI, LEPERS!

The General was understandably alarmed when the Outrerrians suddenly wheeled two pieces of heavy artillery into the ballroom while the courtiers applauded enthusiastically. Without waiting for their leader's order, the Terran soldiers dived under the tables, as did most of the emissaries.

"Fire!" shouted the artillery commander.

Surprise! A colorful cloud of confetti burst from one of the cannons.

The General scowled disapprovingly. He was proud of his scowl, which was why he'd not worn an animal mask that evening, much as he liked dressing up as an Outrerrian wild bull. After the confetti settled, he resumed dancing with his lovely blonde. As he moved his hand lower on her back, the artillery squad unleashed a second barrage. When the shower ended, the General noticed a few bits of confetti clinging to the corneas of his partner's snake mask. Brushing them away, he realized they were in fact tiny multicolored spiders. He glanced all about him, gauging the other effects of the cannonade. An Outrerrian disguised as an extraterrestrial leper, with gaping holes instead of eyes, nose, or mouth, was busily removing the spiders from the cavities of his face. He looked like a festive block of Swiss cheese.

"Nice mask," said the General, trying to be friendly.

"That's not a mask," the blonde explained.

Weary now of dancing, the General started to lead the blonde toward the privacy of the adjacent salon, where a plastic and elastic arts exhibition that nobody wanted to see had opened the day before. A large upright pirhanascracon came toward him from the opposite direction.

The guest spoke, and the General immediately recognized Ciprian's voice. "Hibda-hibda-hibdadorum-rorum-horum-borum-hibda-hibda," the emissary muttered, the code word they'd worked out for "No Karlenstein."

Ciprian continued on his way. The General pondered the situation. No Karlenstein. This was bad news. The ball would be over in a mere half hour, and he still didn't know whether the peasants would attack. He couldn't help imagining the worst-case scenario, whereby the disillusioned insurgents had informed the secret police about Operation Scruple, and the police had in turn alerted the Imperial Guard.

A sudden instinct prompted the General to glance at his blonde's feet. Leather jackboots poked out from beneath the hem of her long pink gown. A trap! Evidently the Imperial Guard knew of the conspiracy and had taken measures to thwart it, a counterstrategy that probably called for the defensive slaughter of every Earthling soldier and emissary at the carnival.

The General could barely contain his indignation. Earthlings had done so much for Outrerria. They had brought these people bicycles and God. Thanks to the colonization effort, this backwater planet now had railroad stations, perfect places for the homeless to spend the night, though for security reasons the Terrans had declined to build any actual railroads on the planet. The colonists had even saved Outrerria from a scrofula epidemic caused by the natives' refusal to change their socks. And yet the insurgents had elected to betray their own revolution, spilling the beans about Operation Scruple simply because it was once called Operation Screw the People.

It would have been less cruel, the General decided, if the Imperial Guard had apprehended him and his men as soon as they'd entered the palace. Instead the soldiers and emissaries had been allowed to dance and feast and make fools of themselves for the past three hours. But soon the ball would be over, and a rather different sort of carnival would begin, a fact underscored by the troop of clockwork skeletons now guarding the exits, each armed with a headsman's axe.

CHAPTER 7
THE PARACHUTE

Could you excuse me for a moment?" The General beamed at his dancing partner, pleased with the pretext he'd found for leaving the ballroom.

"Yes, of course," said the blonde.

"Thank you."

The General clicked his heels and bowed, so that for a brief uncomfortable instant he was a hundred centimeters shorter than his partner instead of fifty. He headed toward the far end of the ballroom, grinning and rubbing his hands together. His scheme for saving himself was brilliant. Intelligence, he decided, indeed existed in inverse ratio to height.

Reaching the line of lavatories, he got into the shortest queue. Each time someone opened a door and exited, a chord of soothing organ music burst into the ballroom. A departing courtier would always smile faintly and, in a gesture of supreme satisfaction, tap his forehead with a jute handkerchief bearing the Emperor's monogram.

Even if it wasn't the source of his deliverance, the General would still be eagerly anticipating the aristocratic toilet. In addition to the fur seat there would be a flushing chain festooned with little bells, a tray of chocolate laxatives—some sweet, some bitter—and gold-plated musical taps from which gushed perfumed or unscented water, your choice. In recent years, toilets had become the primary indicator of social status on Outrerria. Back on their private estates, the nobles were forever refurbishing their lavatories, sparing no expense to add the most opulent appointments. While the provincial high officials could not afford such splendor in their homes, they were permitted to use the luxurious mobile toilets that traveled about the country on flatbed trucks, each presided over by a conductor knowledgeable in evacuation.

The typical public toilet, by contrast, was nothing more than a long bench sporting a dozen holes spaced fifty centimeters apart. There were no partitions. Instead, on entering the facility, the peasant was given a piece of sheet metal with handgrips. It was common knowledge that the unrest on Outrerria had begun shortly after dissident colonists had illegally passed out leaflets filled with technical drawings showing that the palace sewer pipes were not connected to the plebian system, but carried their own separate imperial loads.

The Earthling immediately in front of the General, an emissary costumed as a warthog, entered the booth. An old saying ran through the General's head. "To escape from stress, go out of your mind. To escape from despair, go out a window." Go out a window—which was exactly what he intended to do.

The key to his scheme was the Outrerrian paratrooper's gear he kept in his undershorts for just such emergencies. Instead of importing expensive parachutes from Earth, the Outrerrian military had equipped its paratroopers with bungee cords, one end tied to the soldier's belt, the other attached to the plane. The instant the plummeting paratrooper hit the ground, an event he announced by screaming "Contact!", he and the plane crew would compete to see who could first get rid of the cord. If the paratrooper failed to cut the elastic band with his knife, the disconnected metal hook would shoot down from the sky and drive a fifty millimeter hole into his spine. If both parties failed to act in time, the consequences were even more dire. In these cases the paratrooper rebounded to the plane, badly damaging himself and often causing the aircraft to veer out of control.

Such an elegant strategy, the General thought. He would tie his bungee cord to the toilet seat, open the lavatory window, unsheathe his knife, and jump. As the severed cord dangled against the palace rampart, he would disappear into the night, softly humming "The Paratrooper's Song."

CHAPTER 8
PHONING THE FUTURE

The warthog exited the toilet. After reconnoitering the ballroom to make sure the Imperial Guardsmen weren't watching, the General stepped toward the door. "No thanks," he said to the bare-chested masseur, as impressively muscled as an orchestra conductor, then crossed the threshold. The instant he was alone inside the lavatory, he glanced toward the rear wall and experienced the same feeling a person gets when, just as he is about to sneeze, someone pokes him in the ribs. Shining golden bars blocked the window: the Outrerrians, it seemed, had thought of everything.

He crossed the room and peered through the bars. Lit by the glow of a hundred torches, a battery of cannons now commanded the ramparts. A gun crew was busily loading and adjusting every piece. Even though Operation Scruple was evidently in disarray, the Emperor was prudently defending his citadel. This time, of course, the palace artillery would not fire confetti.

The General strode to the door and looked through the peephole. With graceful steps and gleeful gestures, the Earthlings continued to dance, oblivious to the fact that, if they tried leaving the carnival, the clockwork skeletons would decapitate them. Turning, the General barked his shin on the leg of a table holding a gold-plated phone with all the latest bells and whistles. A toilet with telecommunication! Instinctively he picked up the receiver, wondering whom to call.

But was this phone an Outrerrian trap? Had the Imperial Guard tapped the line? As the General rubbed his chin, his fingers scratching the stubble, an idea formed in his brain.

The Imperial Guard could listen all they wanted, because he wasn't going to call anyone in the immediate spatiotemporal vicinity. He dialed Earth's prefix followed by 2-2-3-5-5: Karlenstein's number on Terra. Due to the near-lightspeed velocity at which the colonists had come to this planet, as well as the inefficiency that characterized interstellar telephone exchanges, Earth's calendar was now at least thirty years ahead of the time zone in which the General currently resided. He was going to phone the future. If Karlenstein answered, then the General would know that the mutant mercenary had gotten safely home, which meant that the revolution had gone according to plan, and so everything would turn out all right in the end.

It took a long time to establish the connection, but at last the phone began ringing. The general grew faint with anxiety. Finally, *click*, someone picked up.

"Hello?"

"Hello? Am I speaking to Earth?"

"Yes."

"Two-one-three-five-five-four?"

"Correct."

"Is Karlenstein there?"

"Who?"

The General shuddered. There was no mistaking the characteristic Outrerrian squeak, the throaty Outrerrian accent.

He dropped the receiver. It fell to within an inch of the floor and oscillated on its cord.

The squeak. The accent.

"Hello? Hello? Hey! Hello?"

The General grabbed the receiver and slammed it into the cradle. Could it be? In the near future this primitive planet had somehow conquered Terra, quite likely massacring all the human inhabitants in the process? Was the Outrerrians' zippered Jesus stronger than Earth's zipperless equivalent? Were he and the colonists fated to be the last *Homo sapiens* in the universe?

The General staggered to the lavatory mirror. Why did the Outrerrians have mirrors, he wondered, when all these people looked the same?

CHAPTER 9
THE LORD HIGH BARBER

Ciprian Popa was back at the window, busily engaged in several varieties of waiting. He was waiting for Karlenstein, waiting for the insurgents, and waiting for the General to come out of the toilet. It occurred to Ciprian that none of these things was about to happen.

Legendary were the sonorous dawns of Outrerria, and now Ciprian witnessed one, the sun rising noisily from behind the hill like a cork popping out of a champagne bottle. Unseen, the Captain of the Imperial Guard got on the loudspeaker and explained in exasperating Esperanto that the guests must now give back their costumes and retire to their specially prepared sleeping quarters. The soldiers should head for the barracks on level three, the emissaries to the dormitory on level four. Anyone caught straggling on the way to bed would be dressed in a green smock, wrapped in sandpaper, and carefully beaten in a manner that would leave no marks.

A platoon of Imperial Guardsmen escorted Ciprian and his fellow envoys to their quarters, a vast chamber filled with a hundred bunks, the sheets wet and dirty but well starched and stretched taut. Ciprian immediately noticed an anomalous barbershop at the back of the room, presided over by the Lord High Barber himself. This was a bad sign. Being beardless as well as faceless, the Outrerrians knew nothing about the venerable pangalactic procedure known as shaving. Over the years, the tonsorial arts had evolved on this planet into a popular method of torture, normally accomplished with a garden-variety agricultural blowtorch of the sort used for singeing pigs, but sometimes with a military flamethrower. It was not uncommon for an Outrerrian to shave a prisoner to death. Already Ciprian, who had a good olfactory imagination, could smell the odor of roasting chins.

Frantically he reached into his pocket. His bottle of aftershave lotion was still there, thank God, the most powerful astringent in the galaxy, though he doubted it would do much good in this case.

"Atten-hut!" shouted the Captain of the Guard, and despite their lack of military training the diplomats and envoys snapped to attention.

"Before you crawl into your bunks," the Captain continued, "you will each visit the barbershop in accordance with Article Nine, Section Five, Paragraph Two of Outrerrian military regulations, which requires soldiers to be clean-shaven at all times of the day or night."

"But we're not soldiers," Ndongo pointed out. "The General's troops are on level three. They're the ones you're looking for."

Undaunted, the Captain of the Guard lined up the envoys and rapidly inducted them into the army. Each received the rank of private.

"Let the shaving commence!" said the Captain, pointing toward the Lord High Barber, who proceeded to flourish his blowtorch. "We shall not charge you for this service, but the barber expects a generous tip!"

"Not so fast," said Ndongo. "Have you forgotten that Article Nine, Section Five, Paragraph Three of Outrerrian military regulations holds that no soldier may be shaved against his will if he already enjoys a whiskerless condition? Look closely at our faces. You will not find a single beard, mustache, or sideburn among us."

"How long does it take for a Terran to sprout whiskers?" asked the Captain, who was grievously ignorant of human biology.

"At least twenty years," said Ndongo.

The Captain snorted, made an abrupt about-face, and stomped out of the room, the rest of the Imperial Guard trailing behind him.

The Lord High Barber was the last to leave. He was as glabrous as any other Outrerrian, but wore a magnificent cloak woven from the whiskers he'd shaved over the years. "This is all most unfortunate," he said, cradling his blowtorch against his chest. "You would have gotten free shaves. I would have gotten your tips. Now everybody loses."

He strode through the door, closing it behind him, and an instant later came the rattle of the key turning three times in the lock.

"Your ordeal isn't over, suckers!" cried the Captain of the Guard through the keyhole.

CHAPTER 10

SUICIDE IS NOT FOR BEGINNERS

The General was still studying himself in the lavatory mirror. It was a beautiful artifact, framed in gold, that reflected his face in full color. (Ordinary Outrerrians could afford only black-and-white mirrors.) The pristine glass was depressingly honest, displaying not only his sorrowful face but also the barred window and, beyond, the rising sun as it tinted the sky the color of a dead fish. Until this moment the General had thought of himself as an unsentimental man, but he was deeply saddened to realize he had only a few minutes to live. How dearly and deeply he longed to transform himself into a fly and flit to freedom through the bars.

He reviewed his life, an enterprise he'd conducted for fifty-two consecutive years, largely between the hours of 5:30 A.M. and 9:30 P.M. (though of course there were occasional military emergencies), taking orders from some, giving orders to others. He wished that, instead of coming to this ridiculous carnival with the aim of abetting Operation Scruple, he had requested a week of R&R. His Earthling superiors might very well have granted it. After all, he had never asked for a leave before.

The proper course was obvious. He would escape the humiliation, agony, and incompetence of an Outrerrian execution. He would select the exact moment of his death. His name would be engraved on a famous monument back home honoring Fallen Undaunted Crusaders in Khaki.

Someone scratched softly at the door. The General tried to turn his head but failed, full-color Outrerrian mirrors being such seductive contrivances. At last, summoning all his military will, he got the better of his narcissism.

He doffed his military cap and set it on the phone table. He removed his tie, loosened his belt, took out his dentures, unholstered his revolver, and unhooked his garters. From his sock he retrieved a bullet, then loaded it into the gun.

It occurred to him that perhaps he should leave a note behind: "Believe me, I would have preferred to die in battle, which would have been more valiant and less messy"—something like that, but he didn't want to take the time.

Given his dread of loud, sudden noises, the General now indulged himself by sticking rubber plugs in his ears. He inserted the barrel of the revolver in his mouth, then realized he'd forgotten an important step. He removed the gun and sang the Planetary Anthem of Earth. He reinserted the gun and began counting down in his mind.

Ten, nine, eight, seven, six, five. He paused. There was a problem. Once the gun went off, he would fall on the hard marble floor and probably hurt himself. What he needed was a place to sit down. He glanced toward the porcelain bowl. Alas, it would not suffice. Imported from a Romanian wholesaler specializing in Dracula merchandise, a large wooden stake rose from the toilet lid as a courtesy for visitors who wished to play horseshoes.

The scrabbling sound grew louder: obviously another guest or noble needed to use the toilet. He couldn't fault the customer's impatience; after all, he'd been in here quite a long time. Suddenly a series of metallic bangs filled the air, as if someone were rapping on the door with a mallet.

He looked through the peephole, which struck him as the best way to avoid being seen looking through the peephole. A black object caught his attention. He wondered if it might be the barrel of a machine gun, but this thought crossed his mind for just a fraction of a second.

CHAPTER 11
FUNGAL OMENS

Despite their nearly lethal encounter with the barber, the emissaries slept well that morning.

After an interval of two hours, however, they were awakened by a crew of native workers, who not only required everyone to get out of bed, but also demanded that they assist in the task at hand: dragging the bunks out of the dormitory and replacing all the windows with steel panels reminiscent of the toilet-stall partitions used by Outrerrian peasants, only heavier. At one point during the operation, the work crew let it be known that, shortly after dawn, the Earthling General had died from a combination of advanced years and bullets, a piece of news that inspired Ciprian, Ndongo, and the other gallant emissaries to strip and shutter the dormitory with great efficiency.

When at last the job was done, the native workers bade the diplomats good-bye and departed, locking the door behind them. A moment of bewildered silence followed, during which the confined humans stood around the cavernous room staring at each other.

It was Ndongo who spoke first. "Let us not cultivate false hopes, brothers, but let us not despair either."

The other emissaries declined to echo Ndongo's optimism, but instead remarked on the fact that the dormitory now resembled a gas chamber, a perception reinforced when scores of bright red nozzles appeared on the walls.

"Gas jets!" screamed Ciprian. "They're going to gas us like rats!"

Instantly a majority of the Earthlings panicked, shrieking in terror and throwing themselves against the walls and on the floor. Some even threw themselves on the ceiling. Ndongo, meanwhile, had the presence of mind to approach one of the pulpy nodes and touch it. The node touched him back.

"Mushrooms," Ndongo announced. "I've heard of this species. It's completely harmless. It blooms when danger is near."

"Danger? So they're going to kill us somehow. If we live to see the sun go down, then I'm the Pope," Ciprian Popa wailed.

"Death holds no terror for me," said Ndongo. "I see it as an opportunity to start from scratch."

"I wonder who betrayed us," said Ciprian. "The insurgents? The secret police we bribed? Earth's rulers? Karlenstein?"

"I do hope the preliminary torture is brief," said Ndongo.

"Considering their ignorance of human anatomy, they might make horrible mistakes," said Ciprian, agreeing. "They might pull out our teeth instead of our fingernails. Or hang us by our ears instead of our heels. Or reach into our nostrils and extract our prostate glands instead of our lungs."

Ciprian's train of thought was broken by a clatter of feet. The other prisoners were chasing an Outrerrian mouse around the dormitory. Eventually an emissary caught the poor creature and, delighted to be holding momentary power over life and death, through unfortunately not his own life and death, wrung its little spiraled neck.

And then, for a long time, nothing happened.

CHAPTER 12
A REMEDY FOR ENNUI

The prisoners could barely abide their boredom. They sat on the cold floor, contemplating their brand-new combat boots. Somebody hummed a funeral dirge. Ciprian and Ndongo withdrew to the farthest corner of the room and began scribbling anti-government graffiti on the walls.

"The point of human existence is not to live long but to live well," Ndongo philosophized.

"I wish they would just get it over with, instead of making us suffer like this," said Ciprian.

"Suffering is ennobling," Ndongo asserted. "A prison is a kind of monastery where spiritual purity is cultivated through want and excruciation."

"What an exquisite theory. Do you really believe it?"

"No."

Just then an emissary cried, "The walls!"

"The walls!" echoed a second prisoner.

"The walls are moving!" bellowed the third envoy.

The man was right. With a grotesque grinding noise the two side walls of the dormitory were now moving toward each other. The diplomats ran around like lunatics. They forgot their other worries, forgot their wives and children on Earth, forgot their dying parents, forgot why they'd come to Outrerria in the first place, forgot how they'd ended up in this demented dormitory.

They simply screamed.

"This massacre will not go unnoticed back home," Ndongo said.

"Do you mean we should lodge an official complaint against the Emperor?" Ciprian asked.

"No, I mean we shall be enshrined as martyrs to the glorious cause of civilizing the galaxy," said Ndongo. "Our names will appear on the monument to Famous Underappreciated Colonizers of Kingdoms." He clapped Ciprian on the back. "My friend, at this very moment we are making history!"

Ciprian said nothing, but merely stared at the inexorably advancing walls. He was indeed making something just then, but it wasn't history, and the location was his pants.

CHAPTER 13
HIDDEN TEXT

Welcome to Chapter Thirteen. As you may recall from your previous experiences with Chapter Thirteens, deuces are now wild, and all bets are off.

Once you've broached a Chapter Thirteen, a hairy mutant named Karlenstein might escape a barber's flamethrower by cleverly substituting for his real self a convenient plastic Karlenstein manikin. This same hairy mutant might next run to the nearest manor house, steal a tachyonic bicycle from a blueblood, pedal his way to the Emperor Gheorghe's palace, and organize a massive prison break, thereby sparing an entire Earthling diplomatic corps from being squashed into a single amorphous corpse between the viselike walls of their sleeping quarters. Our hirsute mercenary might then head for the hinterlands accompanied by his two best human friends.

We hope you enjoyed your stay in Chapter Thirteen. Have a safe and pleasant journey to Chapter Fourteen.

CHAPTER 14
EPILOGUE

Now what?" said Ciprian.

"Now what?" echoed Ndongo.

"We keep pedaling," said Karlenstein. "This is a tachyonic bicycle. If we move our feet in faster and faster circles, we shall leave this plane of reality."

"That sounds like a good idea," said Ciprian.

"I'm game," said Ndongo.

"Life is like a bicycle," said Karlenstein, then began singing his favorite Terran song. "I don't believe in Peter Pan," he warbled, "Frankenstein, or Superman."

"All I wanna do is ride my bicycle," sang Ndongo, joining in.

"I want to ride my bicycle," sang Ciprian, turning the duo into a trio. "I want to ride it where I like."

The fugitives got busy, pedaling furiously as if whipping up a cosmic omelet in God's mixing bowl. Somewhere up in the zirconium Outrerrian sky, a mystic zipper parted.

And still the three friends pedaled, singing and smiling all the while.

SERGEI LUKYANENKO

DESTINY, INC.

TRANSLATED FROM THE RUSSIAN
BY MICHAEL M. NAYDAN AND
SLAVA I. YASTREMSKI

Unlike the other Russian story in The SFWA *European Hall of Fame—"A Birch Tree, a White Fox" with its extraterrestrial landscapes, crash-landed spaceship, and intrepid cosmonauts—the present selection does not belong to any unequivocally science-fictional tradition, and its premise clearly owes more to Rod Serling's* Twilight Zone *than to John Campbell's "Twilight." Indeed, the casual reader would be within his rights to regard "Destiny, Inc." as a fantasy pure and simple, evoking as it does those countless folktales in which naïve protagonists make deals with the Devil, solicit wishes from djinns, and otherwise attempt to bend the cosmic rules.*

But "Destiny, Inc." is rather more complex than that. Beneath the whimsical surface, Lukyanenko is playing a fascinating intellectual game keyed to the first law of thermodynamics—a principle whose most common paraphrase, "There is no such thing as a free lunch," emerges in its Russian equivalent, "There is no free cheese," at a crucial moment in the plot. Before the final scene has run its course, you will realize that "Destiny, Inc." has less to do with the Brothers Grimm than with that grim brotherhood of opportunists for whom everything under the sun— even fate itself—might be turned into a commodity.

Born in Kazakhstan and educated as a psychiatrist, Sergei Lukyanenko began publishing short SF in the eighties, largely under the influence of Robert Heinlein and the Russian children's author Vladislav Krapivin. His breakout novel was Rytsary Soroka Ostrovov *("Knights of the Forty Islands," 1992). He is the author of several trilogies, including the "philosophical space opera"* Linija Grioz

*("Steam of Daydreams"). Lukyanenko has received many literary honors, includ-
ing the Strannik Award and the Interpresson Award. In 1999 he became the youn-
gest writer ever to win the Aelita Award, given each year for "a major contribution
to Russian science fiction and fantasy." Connoisseurs of popular culture recently
became aware of Lukyanenko through the widely released film adaptation of his
dark, apocalyptic novel* Nochnoi Dozor. *Cowritten by Lukyanenko and director
Timur Bekmanbetov,* Night Watch *is to date the highest-grossing production in
the history of Russian cinema.*

    *Rather than blemishing the text of "Destiny, Inc." with footnotes—as John
Barrymore once remarked, "Footnotes are like going downstairs to answer the door
on your wedding night"—we shall end our introduction with a few annotations. A
version of the Russian folktale of "Morozo" is easily found on the Internet. The
1939 Dovzhenko film in question is* Shchors. *The phrase Sors recalls in the airport
is from Viktor Pelevkin's* Pokolenie 'P' *("Generation 'P'" or "The Pepsi Generation"), recently translated into English as* Homo Zapiens. *Finally, when Ivan
Ivanovich calls himself an "engineer of the soul," the author is deliberately evoking Stalin's famous dictum to Soviet writers and intellectuals of the thirties.*

H e was afraid the suite of offices would suggest
a hospital: scrubbed walls, vague caustic odors, an austerely uniformed
staff with hard, cynical eyes. Equally unpleasant was the prospect of standard plush décor, complete with abstract paintings by near-famous near-
geniuses, shag carpets, and fake leather upholstery, the whole operation
presided over by cloying receptionists and unctuous young managers.

Or God forbid the setting should be "domestic," bookshelves
crammed with faux-calfskin volumes—supposedly much homier than
the plainly bound, locally available sets of Russian classics—potted gera-
niums, fat cat on a couch, television jabbering in the corner, tea from a
samovar.

As a matter of fact, he had no idea what sort of environment to expect. A gloomy witch's cottage? An alchemist's laboratory? A basilica?

What ambience befits the place where a man might shed his destiny?

Viewed from the outside the enterprise actually looked quite ordinary, an unassuming stone building on an old Moscow street with a nar-

row sidewalk, scurrying pedestrians, and barely crawling cars. The plain door featured a modest sign and the staring eye of a surveillance camera.

There was no choice but to go in. He certainly couldn't keep standing here in the chill February air—twenty below, an icy wind—with a cigarette stub burning his fingertips. As the camera regarded him suspiciously, Father Frost's refrain from the tale of Morozko started running through his head. "Are you warm, fair little maiden? Are you warm, child so beautiful?"

Are you scared, miserable asshole? Are you scared, jerk so pathetic?

He pressed a button under the staring lens. The lock opened with a click. He paused briefly, then entered to find a reception area and, beside the stairway, a small security station. The guard was immersed in a book and paid no attention to either the visitor or the enthralling live presentation of *A Moscow Street in Winter* playing on his monitor's dim bluish screen.

"Pardon me."

"Second floor," said the guard, glancing up.

He mounted the stairs.

While the reception area could have belonged to a successful business, the second floor suggested a shabby government institute, perhaps an R&D facility dedicated to designing automatic cornhuskers. The long hall was floored with scuffed linoleum, and the brown walls featured wainscoting of fake wood. On both sides of the corridor, the doors bore monotonous signs: ENGINEER . . . ENGINEER . . . CHIEF ENGINEER . . . ENGINEER . . . SUPERVISING ENGINEER . . . ENGINEER.

He headed back downstairs. "Pardon me, but—"

"Second door on the right," the guard said, deigning to put down his book. "Go straight in. Don't be shy."

Once again he climbed the stairs. The second door on the right was invitingly ajar. He knocked, just in case, and entered only after hearing, "Yes, yes, come in."

The impression of an underfunded government research center grew overwhelming: particleboard desk, battered swivel chair, ancient computer with a tiny monitor, antique dot-matrix printer. Lord, even a rotary phone!

The office's occupant, however, a rosy-cheeked young man, appeared rather prosperous. His suit could have come from Marks & Spencer, and he sported a fine silk tie. His wristwatch was less impressive, but Swiss.

"Don't be surprised by the furnishings," said the engineer. "It's customary."

"For whom?"

"For us. You're Sors, correct? You called this morning. Please sit down."

He nodded and eased himself into a wobbly Viennese chair. *Sors.* For some reason, that particular Latin word had sprung to his lips when he'd called earlier that day. He realized later how silly it was to bother using an alias when speaking over his home phone.

"My name is Ivan Ivanovich," the engineer said. "I'm not kidding. That's really my name." He set his passport on the desk, but Sors didn't dare pick it up. "Ivan-o-*vich,* accent on the last syllable."

"I'd prefer not to tell you my real name, Mr. Ivanovich," Sors mumbled.

"Of course," the engineer said agreeably. "As far as I'm concerned, you're Sors."

"I hope your accountant won't mind."

Ivanovich wagged a scolding finger at him. "Don't you worry about our accountant. If you become a client of Destiny, Inc., we won't be doing any currency or commodity exchanges."

"How's that? You don't expect to be paid?"

"You know, I'm rather uncomfortable using your first name," Ivanovich said, changing the subject. "What should I call you? Comrade Sors? No, I'm reminded of the unfortunate Commissar Shchors from that old Dovzheno film. Mr. Sors? No, I think of George Soros, the financier. May I call you Monsieur Sors?"

The man who was now Monsieur Sors nodded in assent.

Ivanovich propped his chin on his fist and for a moment seemed lost in thought. "So, how did you hear about us?"

"From Hand to Hand."

"The free-ad paper? How appropriate." Ivanovich picked up his passport and slipped it back inside his jacket. "Destiny, Inc., is a fundamentally humanitarian institution. Our charter requires that we operate on a strictly nonprofit basis."

"To tell you the truth, when I hear phrases like 'fundamentally humanitarian' and 'strictly nonprofit,' I grab my wallet and hang on with both hands."

Ivan nodded, smiling in agreement. "Noble words often mask base intentions. Nevertheless, we don't charge a single kopek for our services."

"So what's your angle?"

Ivanovich beamed at his visitor. "Philanthropy is its own reward."

"All right." Sors nodded. "Let's say I believe you. What exactly do you have to offer me?"

"It's quite simple. We can arrange for you and a second party to trade fates."

"Come again?"

"Let's say you're worried that the world has a nasty surprise in store for you. A downturn in your business. A serious illness. Your girlfriend walking out on you. Your son getting hooked on drugs."

Each time he mentioned a new disaster, Ivanovich rapped his knuckles on the cheap desktop, as if to mash the calamity into the mixture of sawdust and formaldehyde.

"And you can prevent these things?"

"Yes and no. What you must understand, Monsieur Sors, is that the sum total of coming catastrophes in the universe is forever fixed. The net amount of inevitability is a constant. Fate can neither be created nor destroyed."

"That sounds plausible enough."

"Only a fool would try to elude destiny per se. But by availing himself of our services, a person can arrange to face a looming crisis with his anxieties reduced to zero. Imagine two men, one fearful that his wife will find out about his mistress, the other terrified of screwing up a big sale. What can they do? They can swap potential fates, so now it's the *adulterer* who faces a possible setback in his career—except he doesn't mind terribly. You see, Monsieur, we were careful to find a proper match for the salesman. Our adulterer is the sort of fellow who takes professional setbacks in stride. The *salesman*, meanwhile, is given to know that marital discord may soon appear on the horizon—but he's not overly concerned. We've taken pains to pair the adulterer with a man who never allows domestic strife to distress him."

"So every time somebody comes to you with an anxiety that's wrecking his life, you go out and find somebody with a *different* problem that has the same statistical probability of turning into a crisis?"

"Precisely."

"If I became your client, would I get to choose the nature of the other problem?"

"We can only guarantee it will be a threat you wouldn't mind facing," Ivanovich said, shaking his head. "Meanwhile, the *particular* fate you've been dreading will never happen—not to *you*, at least."

"How can this be possible?" Sors asked.

"You've controlled your curiosity for quite a long time," Ivanovich said with a grin. "Many clients begin with that question. Tell me, do you know what electricity is? How a refrigerator works? What's going on inside a TV set?"

"I'm not a physicist."

"But that doesn't prevent you from turning on the light, storing milk in your refrigerator, or watching the news, does it?"

Sors shifted uneasily in the flimsy chair. "I understand the analogy. But I want to be sure—"

"You're a religious man—is that it? You're afraid that Destiny, Inc., smacks of the Devil?" Ivan Ivanovich smirked. "Really, Monsieur Sors."

"This all feels like some kind of sinister secret experiment."

"Secret?" Ivanovich spread out his hands. "Our ads are posted all over Moscow. They're in every major newspaper."

"Then you are—"

"Please, don't say anything about aliens!" Ivan burst out.

"May I say something about frauds and swindlers?" Sors said sarcastically.

"We don't take any money," Ivanovich countered. "We don't require you to sign any papers. Nothing stops you from checking our credentials. Please, let's return to the matter at hand. At this very moment you are facing a fear."

Sors nodded. The ad that he'd read aloud to his sniggering friends, this ridiculous tumbledown office, this personable young man who fancied himself in control of the universe: everything about Destiny, Inc., was irrational. But his fear was irrational, too, and yet it was real.

"I have to fly. To Milan. On business."

"I see." Ivanovich nodded benevolently.

"And I'm afraid."

"Of problems with your business?"

"I'm afraid of flying!" Sors blurted out. "Aerophobia. It's not funny, it's a disease."

"Believe me, we never find amusement in other people's fears," Ivanovich said. "Are the tickets already purchased?"

"Yes."

"When?"

Sors gave the engineer the dates and the flight numbers.

"Do you have any enemies who might put a bomb on the plane?" Ivanovich inquired in a businesslike fashion.

"Are you joking?"

"Then, statistically speaking, the chances of disaster are something close to zero. We won't have much trouble finding a perfect match for you. The risk exchange will remain in effect for an interval of . . . let's allow three hours and fifteen minutes for the flight to Milan, plus another three and a half hours for the return flight, for a total of six hours and forty-five minutes. Shall we figure a half hour for each takeoff and landing?"

"Make it an hour," Sors muttered.

"Good. The swap will last exactly ten hours and forty-five minutes. You can now fly in peace. For the duration of the trip, your aerophobia won't exist."

Sors furrowed his brow. "The other party, my match—I wonder what sort of fear is eating him up."

The engineer smiled softly. "Maybe he's obligated to go hiking in the woods, and he's worried about snakes. Many of our clients fear food poisoning—there's lots of bad sausage out there—and some suffer from full-blown phagophobia, fear of eating. There's a phobia for everything, it seems. Phengophobia, fear of daylight. Ideophobia, fear of ideas. Triskaidekaphobia, the number thirteen. Siderodromophobia, railway travel." Ivanovich took a deep breath, then added sternly, "The most interesting one, in my opinion, is ergophobia, fear of work."

"It would appear you're actually a psychiatrist," said Sors.

"No, we don't practice psychiatry around here. We are technicians of destiny and engineers of the soul. Some people would say we are fate itself."

"Technicians of destiny? Oh, come now. The probability that my plane will crash is very small—you said that yourself. If I land safely in Milan, that won't prove a thing."

"But it will. You'll see."

With these words, they parted. Sors shook the engineer's hand, though he refused to offer the usual pleasantries of "Good-bye" and "Till we meet again"—not to someone who was so plainly a con man.

Once in the hallway, Sors couldn't resist walking to the very end, but all he found was a small clean restroom. Returning, he deliberately passed near the other engineers' offices. All the doors were shut, but from behind each came soft voices. Destiny, Inc., had no shortage of clients.

On the way downstairs he encountered a thin, fortyish woman going up. Her face was tired and tear-streaked. Their eyes did not meet. What kind of fear was she hoping to subtract from her life? Was her child going in for surgery? Had her husband threatened to leave her?

There is no eluding destiny, the engineer had said.

Sheremetyevo Airport looked grimy. Thankfully, the crisp winter air spared Sors the unbearable stuffiness found only in African—and Russian—airports.

Confused and terrified, he stood holding his customs declaration form, looking for a flat surface on which to fill it out. The airport was too crowded. Too noisy. Too dirty. Could anyone here possibly be as frightened as he? He doubted it.

"Mister," said a small voice from behind him. "Can you spare some change?"

He looked around and saw a little girl, maybe eight, no more than ten, with pretty curls, nice clothes, small gold earrings, and a hand outstretched for money. Hardly a typical beggar, or the security guards would have kicked her out by now. He thought of a phrase from a novel he'd just read, "a respectable God for respectable gentlemen." And here was a respectable beggar for respectable gentlemen.

In the absurdity of the moment, Sors's anxiety decreased. "Better go to school, little girl," he said reproachfully.

"Our classes don't start until nine," she replied pertly.

Sors was tempted to say something sarcastic—"I guess you think panhandling is cool"—but perhaps there was more to her situation than he could grasp, so he simply glowered at her.

She spotted another likely mark and moved on. Sors followed her with his eyes, his feelings alternating between scorn and compassion. Turning, he spotted a table with an unoccupied corner. He lost no time filling out the form. Weapons, no. Drugs, no. Currency, no. Books, no. Antiques, no. Electronic equipment . . .

Suddenly the world split in two.

He found himself sitting in a dark room, dusty curtains turning early morning into night. A white phone rested on the desk in front of him. He couldn't take his eyes off it. He didn't know what sort of call he was expecting, only that he both hoped and feared that the phone would ring—now.

And then he was back in the airport, walking to the ticket counter, blundering through the beeping metal detector (of course he had forgotten to remove his keys), then entering the waiting area.

He sat in the dark room, stroking the white plastic housing of the phone. Perhaps he should pick up the receiver and listen to the dial tone, just to make sure the line was working.

He hurried down the long intestine of the passenger walkway leading to the plane.

He put his head on the desk and stared at the white telephone, observing it with curiosity and dim expectation. The prospect of bad news didn't trouble him in the least, just as the man with whom he'd swapped destinies had no fear of flying. In both cases, after all, the risks were almost negligible.

He looked out the window, watching the earth fall away as the plane rose. The tip of the wing trembled slightly. He smiled at the clouds. When the flight attendant delivered his breakfast, he devoured it eagerly. He was going to have a safe and pleasant trip.

The second time around, Sors approached Destiny, Inc., with a better attitude. He didn't hesitate at the entrance, but pressed the buzzer energetically, then opened the door with a grand flourish after the lock disengaged.

"Come in," said the guard amiably, evidently recognizing him.

Sors climbed the stairs. The second door on the right was again ajar. Ivanovich stood by the window, looking out at the gray, partially melted snow.

"Yesterday two people broke their legs on this street," he said absently. "Can you imagine that? Not drunks, normal people. They were walking along, fell, passed out, and when they revived they found their legs in casts. How do you do, Monsieur Sors?"

"How do you do, Mr. Ivanovich?" He didn't offer the engineer his hand. Something held him back. Perhaps the gesture would feel like submission to fate.

"Did it go well? Any complaints?" Ivanovich wasn't being ironic. He looked at Sors intently, curiously, evidently eager to learn whether the customer was satisfied.

"No." Sors shook his head. "Everything worked out as advertised."

Ivanovich smiled widely, and gestured for Sors to sit in a brand-new armchair. On the desk was the latest-model Panasonic phone. Clearly, business was good.

"Are you sure I don't owe you anything?" Sors asked before sitting down.

"We are still a humanitarian, nonprofit organization."

Sors sat down. Ivanovich assumed his chair on the opposite side of the desk.

"But how do you stay in business?" Sors asked. "There is no free cheese. Merely maintaining these offices must be—"

"Let me make one thing clear," Ivanovich said reproachfully. "If you insist on offering us money, we won't be able to do business with you anymore. And you *do* want to keep doing business with us, am I right? What is it this time? Are you flying again?"

There was no point in lying.

"I was hoping there might be some way . . . I have difficulty talking about this . . . some way you could—"

"Help you with your love life? We would be happy to engineer a desirable romantic destiny for you, Monsieur. Love is the most wonderful of human emotions. So much beauty and so much tragedy are evoked by that single word. Divine purity and carnal intrigue, saintly sacrifice and vile treachery. So tell me, as things stand now, are your chances better or worse than fifty-fifty?"

"My chances?" Sors said, bewildered at this descent from rhetoric to arithmetic.

"Your chances that she will reject you?"

"I have no idea."

"You must tell me everything."

Such intimate disclosures can be made only to close friends—or total strangers. Sors spoke at length, sparing no details. At one point he removed her photo from his wallet. Ivanovich expressed his appreciation of her lovely face, even as he tried to comfort Sors by patting his back.

It was a familiar story, as old as the world. A year ago he had divorced his wife—an amicable split: Sors was generally lucky in such matters. They had no children. Throughout the settlement negotiations, he had behaved in a gentlemanly manner. He gave her the apartment and the car, telephoned on holidays, sent flowers on her birthday. Finding a new place to live wasn't difficult—he was making good money. Their mutual passion had faded long before he fell in love with the young woman in the photograph. There was only one problem—this person for whom he'd left his intelligent, beautiful, nearly perfect wife wasn't especially eager to marry him.

Ivanovich's eyes acquired a gleam. "In situations like this, we normally arrange for the client to trade destinies with himself."

"How's that?"

"Such transactions are quite straightforward. As things stand now, I would estimate your chances of landing her at somewhere between twenty and twenty-two percent. Not good odds. I don't want to sound critical of your inamorata, but women of this type—the prospect of marriage rarely attracts them. She must fall head over heels in love with you."

"That's exactly what I want—for her to love me."

"Not as your mistress, but as your wife," Ivanovich said, nodding. "Very commendable, Monsieur Sors. One doesn't often find that kind of integrity these days. What we must do, obviously, is reverse the present ratio, so that the chances of her accepting your marriage proposal become four out of five. Of course, you would then face an eighty percent chance of having a misadventure whose probability previously stood at only twenty percent. Give me your answer, sir. Is Monsieur Sors prepared to swap fates with Monsieur Sors?"

"This misadventure—what might it be?"

"At the moment I have no idea," Ivanovich said.

"There won't be a death in my family, will there? I could never forgive myself—"

"A death? Good heavens, no. We're not in the business of harming innocent people. Our methods affect the client and no one else."

"But this misadventure—if it comes to pass, I'll certainly suffer in some way."

"Indeed—the same quantity of suffering that rejection by your true love would have caused you," Ivanovich said in an easy manner. "You won't commit suicide—you're not that impulsive. You won't become an alcoholic, or disappear into the woods like a hermit. You'll simply go through a period of distress for perhaps a year, perhaps a year and a half."

"And if I agree to this transaction," said Sors eagerly, "will she really become my wife?"

"Oh, yes," Ivanovich said quickly. "Absolutely."

"Then I agree."

•   •   •

They met in a small restaurant in Taganka Square, a pleasant if somewhat noisy establishment. As soon as he saw her face, Sors realized that
she understood why he'd picked this place: two years ago they'd had their
first date here, though to Sors it felt like yesterday. (As a young man he'd
never subscribed to romantic clichés; now he believed them all.) Women
often sense when they are about to hear a confession of love, and a marriage proposal rarely catches them by surprise.

As they drank wine and talked nonsense, Sors soon became utterly
convinced that, when he popped the question, he would not receive the
answer he wanted. Was it possible that Destiny, Inc., had forgotten about
the second transaction? Were the engineers of the soul not so competent
as they claimed? There was only one way to find out.

"Will you marry me?" Sors asked.

She gazed into his eyes for a long moment, not speaking. Sors wanted
to shout, "How can you imagine saying no? Your parents long for us to
marry. Your girlfriends are mad with envy. Your beautiful clothes were
bought with my money. You're a student at a second-rate college. I'm not
too old for you. I'm successful, I love you, I worship you."

Slowly, she shook her head.

Just then the mobile phone rang in Sors's coat pocket. He decided to
take the call: anything to delay the inevitable. She had not yet spoken, so
there was still hope.

"We have a problem," his partner said in an ominous tone, not bothering to say hello. "Our last shipment was stopped at the border. Somebody spotted an anomaly in the paperwork."

Sors had a good idea what had gone wrong, but he didn't want to
press his partner for details: such things are not discussed over the phone.
And besides, just then he had an equally weighty disappointment to endure.

"I'm in Taganka Square, having dinner," Sors told his partner. "Let's
talk later."

"Are you out of you mind?" his partner shouted, shifting from anxiety
to anger. "Do you understand what has happened?"

Sors shut off the phone. He looked at the young woman across from
him and said, "My partner and I have gotten ourselves into a real mess. It
appears that our business is going under. Will you marry me?"

"Are you serious?"

"Yes. I'm desperate for you to become my wife."

"No, I mean about your business."

Sors nodded, contemplating her lovely face. Her eyes had become suddenly warm.

"Then what are you doing *here*?" she demanded. "Your firm is threatened, and instead of manning the pumps you're sitting in a restaurant playing with your favorite toy."

"But you're *not* a toy," Sors said, amazed and dismayed. Until now, he realized, the depth of his love had not been clear to her. She was not his plaything for trips to tropical islands and nights on the town. For him, she was the center of the universe.

She took his hand in hers and whispered, "If you go to prison, I'll divorce you. I'm still young and hot."

Sors didn't go to prison.

It was a close call. His business fell apart at the seams. The chief accountant was popping cardiac pills around the clock. Sors was called in for questioning a half-dozen times. Right before he married his true love, he had to promise not to leave Moscow. So it wasn't a very merry wedding. All their relatives were shell-shocked; his business contacts didn't show; and his partner spent the reception getting rapidly and impressively drunk. Not long after Sors and his beloved set up their household, the accountant was arrested and then released. Meanwhile his partner simply vanished, along with the last of the cash.

The energetic young investigator in charge of the case, who was either quite an honest fellow or adept at mimicking that quality, said to Sors, "The chances are ten to one you will go to jail. Not for long, maybe a year or a year and a half, but you will definitely go to jail."

"Ten to one?"

"Those are the odds. I don't see how you can beat them."

But Sors didn't go to jail.

Instead he went to an office building on an old Moscow street. The door featured a modest sign and a surveillance camera. Immediately after his visit, he started down the narrow sidewalk and slipped on a patch of melting snow that had mysteriously survived until the middle of April. He fell hard, fracturing his pelvis in several places. The pain was so terrible, he lost consciousness. The broken bones were put back together surgically, the hip socket set with a titanium pin. He spent almost six months in the hospital, at great expense. Nevertheless, half a year in an adjustable bed was better than the same interval in jail.

His wife visited every day, right after classes, this wonderful young woman who'd been foolish enough to marry a bankrupt businessman. She brought him soup, fresh fruit, news from the outside world, and, most endearingly, her own wretchedly made pies. She became adept at giving him oral sex—for a while he was incapable of anything else. She started him reading Hesse and Wodehouse. She complained about how sad she felt living alone in their big apartment.

The young investigator eventually lost interest in Sors. As for Sors's partner, who had actually signed the majority of the illegal contracts, he was declared a fugitive by Interpol. The accountant, fearing a heart attack, quit and went into another line of work. But somehow the company continued to function—and even made a little profit—thanks in no small measure to Sors's young wife. After visiting him each day, she would go to the office and stay late, restoring trust, mending broken bonds.

Sors lay in his hospital bed, watched TV, savored his Hesse and Wodehouse, and meditated on what Ivanovich had told him as they'd finalized their third transaction.

"We can absolutely guarantee you won't go to jail," the engineer of destiny had said. "Of course you understand that by swapping fates with yourself in this case, you will acquire a ninety-two percent risk of having some equally incapacitating misadventure."

"Ninety-two percent," Sors had said. "In other words, if I don't go through with this deal, my chances of avoiding jail will stand at a mere eight percent."

"Correct."

"But the investigator keeps telling me the odds are ten to one. He said I have a ten percent chance of an acquittal—not eight percent, ten percent. That's a two percent difference."

"Two percent. Exactly. It's your choice, Monsieur. Take it or leave it."

Sors stretched out in the hospital bed and laughed softly to himself.

That year October in Moscow was unusually warm. Sors left his car near the metro station and slowly walked two blocks to the office building with the modest sign. It would have been difficult to park in the narrow street, and, besides, his doctors were always encouraging him to get more exercise. After greeting his old acquaintance the guard, he limped upstairs to the second floor.

Ivan Ivanovich—accent on the last syllable—met him at the door, shook his hand, and even offered to help him into the armchair.

"Don't bother," said Sors.

Ivanovich nodded and said in a melancholy voice, "It's been very rewarding working with you. You've come to say good-bye, haven't you?"

Sors nodded, then asked, "Do your clients usually stop after three transactions?"

"That's fairly typical," Ivanovich said.

"In other words, it takes most people three negotiations to figure out that you're raking off two percent."

"Do you really begrudge us our commission, Monsieur Sors? It's really not much. If we didn't routinely draw two percent from the destiny pool, we'd be forced to charge for our services, and the fees would be so astronomical that nobody could afford them."

"I suppose," Sors said. "But it still leaves a bad taste in my mouth. May I ask how much you get personally?"

"A mere half percent from each client," Ivanovich said, heaving a sigh. "The rest goes higher up. Have you ever noticed how the rich and powerful seem to enjoy better luck than other people? Fewer fatal accidents, fewer terminal diseases, fewer lost loved ones. Their scandals are more public, but the outcomes are disproportionately positive."

"I don't think we'll be doing any more business in the future," Sors said.

"That's entirely up to you," said Ivanovich. "I wish you good fortune."

"Thank you," Sors said, rising from the armchair. "The same to you." They shook hands like friends.

The engineer escorted Sors to the door, where he paused and asked, "Tell me, Mr. Ivanovich, do happy people ever come here? To trade some piece of happiness they don't really want for happiness of a different sort?"

"What are you saying, Monsieur Sors?" Ivanovich spread his hands wide. "How could there be such a thing as unwanted happiness? Unwanted happiness isn't happiness at all. It's despair. Shall I tell you my prediction? Sooner or later you will come back to us and—"

"No," Sors said, shaking his head.

"There is no eluding destiny," Ivanovich reminded him. "We are fate, Mr. Sors. We are inescapable."

"But you are not fate," said Sors as he turned and hobbled into the hall. "You are only two percent of fate."

ANDREAS ESCHBACH

WONDERS OF THE UNIVERSE

TRANSLATED FROM THE GERMAN
BY DORYL JENSEN

*Our German selection rings changes on a venerable science fiction subgenre, the dy-
ing astronaut story, a subject well served over the years by works as various as
Theodore Sturgeon's "The Man Who Lost the Sea," Arthur C. Clarke's "Transit of
Earth," Barry Malzberg's "The Falling Astronauts," and J. G. Ballard's "The Cage
of Sand." What most beguiled us about Andreas Eschbach's contribution to the
category is the compellingly paradoxical experience it affords the reader. Beginning
with the title, Eschbach has clearly endeavored to satisfy the SF aficionado's traditional hunger for awe-inspiring vistas and hard-won transcendence. And yet the
basic narrative line—a stranded female explorer facing imminent oblivion on
Europa—is spare to the point of minimalism. The setting never varies, the events
are few, and there is only one on-stage character. Out of this tension between intimacy and infinity, we would argue, a unique and valuable story has been born.*

*Eschbach himself was born in 1959. He grew up in Ulm, Germany, and stud-
ied aerodynamics at the Technical University of Stuttgart, then worked for several
years as a software developer and information-technology consultant. In 1995 he
published his first novel,* Die Haarteppichknüpfer, *winner of the prestigious
German science fiction award known as the SFCD-Literaturpreis, and now available in English translation as* The Carpet Makers. *His second novel,* Solarsta-
tion *(1996), won the other major German SF award, the Kurd Lasswitz Prize. His*

*third novel, Jesus Video (2000), received both of these honors, became a national
bestseller, and was adapted into a feature film for German television. Other Eschbach works include Quest (2001), Eine Billion Dollar ("One Trillion Dol-
lars," 2002), Der Letzte seiner Art ("The Last of His Species," 2003) and Der
Nobelpreis ("The Nobel Prize," 2005). At last count, his books had been translated into ten languages. Today the author lives in Brittany with his wife Mari-
anne, writing full-time in a room overlooking the Atlantic Ocean.*

*When not composing fiction, assembling anthologies, reviewing books, or
walking their dogs, the present editors can often be found at the theater, sometimes
on Broadway, occasionally in the West End, but more often on the campus of Penn
State University, a few blocks from their house. No sooner had we finished "Wonders of the Universe" than we imagined transmuting it into a one-act play. We
can see it all now: a stark stage, bare except for a survival tent and, in the background, the ruins of an escape pod. A scrim, impressionistically painted, serves to
convey the majesty of Jupiter and its moons. The house lights fade. The curtain
rises, and we hear the main character saying, "Ursula Froehlich calling T.S.S.
Homeland. Please come in. . . ."*

S he sat in the tent gripping the bulky transceiver
and examined the lines on her wrists, recalling the day she'd first noticed
those tiny furrows. Wrinkles on her wrists! Not around her eyes or
mouth, but on her wrists. The sight of them had bothered her ever since.
Here lay the first proof that it wasn't just other people who aged; she,
too, was getting older.

Yes, and other people didn't simply get older. They also died.

She threw the switch again. "Ursula Froehlich calling *T.S.S. Homeland,*" she said, repeating her feeble chant. "Please come in." Yes, please
come in. Please come in. I'm waiting.

She watched her breath turn to mist. Before long these vapors would
become ice and fall to the ground with a quiet crystalline tinkling. *Glass
breath*—that was the strangely poetic term. She'd read about the phenomenon, and soon she would experience it.

Finally a voice penetrated the static of the sunstorm, weak and unin-
telligible at first, but then the filters peeled away the interference, and the
words became audible and coherent. "This is *T.S.S. Homeland,* Comman-

der Esteban speaking. You're coming through again, Ursula. Please confirm."

A feeling of bittersweet victory flashed through her. "Confirm!" she shouted. "I read you loud and clear, Marko!"

"Good to hear you, Ursula. Situation?"

She drew the control console into the sphere of light emanating from her small lamp. "Energy reserves at two-point-three units. Oxygen reserves at zero-point-eight." She realized her voice was quivering, perhaps from the cold eating its way into the survival tent. Yes, surely from the cold.

"Confirm. Energy two-three, oxygen zero-eight. Water?" He sounded matter-of-fact, aloof, as though all was well. His professionalism made her cringe.

"Marko," she said quietly, "this is Jupiter's moon Europa. I'm sitting on a layer of ice a hundred kilometers thick. Water isn't my problem."

She heard him swallow. She remembered Marko Esteban from the Lunar Conferences—a lanky young freighter commander with higher ambitions. She could almost see him standing before her.

"Sorry," he said, embarrassed. Then, after a pause, "I'll pass along the readings. We'll do the new calculations."

The new calculations: that was supposed to sound comforting, competent, but it didn't work. Her fear was a thick, tough lump in her belly. She inhaled deeply. The cold air bit her nose.

"Marko," she said, amazed at the calm in her voice, "you won't get here in time, will you?"

"We have to do the new calculations."

"Marko . . ."

Nothing. A soundless echo among the stars, an abyss of silence. Then came the Commander's voice again, filled with anguish. "No. We won't make it."

Ursula closed her eyes and lowered her head until her brow touched the cold plastic of the transceiver. Her insides spasmed, and for a moment she thought she might vomit. Then the nausea eased, and the stone in her belly seemed to dissolve, melting with an unexpected warmth, as though her body understood that fear was no longer useful. The laws of physics were ruthlessly reliable and precise. The arrival of *Homeland* into low orbit around Europa, after a flight of millions of kilometers, could be predicted to within seconds, and no force in the galaxy would bring the ship any faster.

"Ursula?"

She lifted her head. "It's all right," she whispered, then cleared her throat and repeated, "It's all right. I knew the numbers were against me."

"I'm so sorry. . . ."

"Yes. So am I."

Silence again. Evidently he wanted to say something more but couldn't find the words. She was maintaining contact, she realized, solely for Marko's sake. But now she needed to be alone with her thoughts; she could no longer sacrifice valuable minutes to ease his anguish. "I'm cutting communication now," she told him. "I'll check in later. Keep up the good work."

"Okay." He seemed relieved. "You, too."

She killed the transceiver, buried her face in her arms, and let the tears flow.

An uncertain interval elapsed, perhaps a whole hour, perhaps two. She pictured herself crouched in the survival tent, marooned on the endless reaches of a barren moon. Suddenly she could no longer endure the cramped gloom of her habitat. Her need was completely irrational—every trip through the air lock stole energy from the electrolysis unit and released precious oxygen into the vacuum—but she had to get out.

She suited up and made her escape. Night had come to Europa, and a waning Jupiter loomed in the sky, an enormous yellow ball with roiling bands of pale red and brown, bathing the nocturnal landscape in silken light. She could have contemplated this most majestic planet forever, losing herself in the ever-changing tracery of its clouds, their languid swirls giving no hint of the powerful storms raging below—tempests that no spaceship yet built could withstand.

Contemplate Jupiter forever? No, *forever* was decidedly the wrong word.

What a forsaken world, this moon. In vain she searched for a shelf of rock, some place to hide from the oppressive starry vault overhead. The terrain was flat, horizon to horizon, a harsh naked plain on which she stood like a lost child.

She turned and moved toward the shattered pod with small cautious steps. Europa was nearly as large as Earth's moon, but only two-thirds its mass. She weighed almost nothing here. That was the only reason she'd survived the crash.

She enacted her usual ritual of circling the pod, its once sleek body driven into Europa's surface at an acute angle, the blackened hull ruptured by the impact. A gutted, useless shell. Once again she touched the huge gashes, the edges of torn synthetic metal flaring outward like flower petals. The meteor that fatally wounded her spaceship had followed a bizarre trajectory, skidding through the hangar bay and destroying most of the emergency supplies retrofitted to the hull of the pod. A one-in-a-million freak accident.

But no matter how much she cursed her luck, the real fault lay in her foolishness. Her arrogance. No doubt the official inquiry would reach this obvious conclusion. She, Captain Ursula Froehlich, had ignored at least two dozen flight regulations. Regulations that had evolved over a century of space travel and proved their worth countless times. Regulations so fundamental that the handbooks didn't even specify a punishment for an infraction—because, as her predicament demonstrated, the infraction automatically entailed the ultimate penalty.

Sighing, she let her gaze wander. Europa's crust was coated with ice millions of years old, a featureless glacier. The gray-blue sheen stretched as far as she could see. Her only point of reference was a white plateau, about a hundred meters high, running along the horizon like an immense frozen worm.

Scattered near the plateau lay those few bits of debris that had reached the surface after her ship's engine exploded. She'd examined every shard in hopes of finding something useful—an extra oxygen tank, another survival tent, a couple of energy cells. In recent days she'd dreamed repeatedly of discovering a large cell and connecting it to the electrolysis unit, thereby producing an oxygen supply from Europa's ice. But the instant she drew the first deep breath, she always woke up.

It made no sense to sift through the wreckage again—that would merely consume valuable oxygen. Two days earlier she'd found a box of crackers. Yesterday, a canister of liquid soap, an electric hand-drill, replacement tubes for the water purifier. Nothing else. Such a senseless gesture. But she had to do it, one last time.

Small stones crunched beneath her feet as she shuffled across a broad dark basin stretching toward the horizon; the floor was a substance other than ice—a gray, hard deposit that looked almost like asphalt. Her planetary science professor had once lectured on this material, its chemical composition, its geological history, but her attention had wandered that day. She'd never imagined she might actually encounter the stuff. Ursula Froehlich was not a person to be visited by premonitions.

Her great mistake had been taking off alone. When it turned out that her copilot was too sick to fly, she should have ignored the malfunctioning probe instead of trying to retrieve and repair it on her own. Research data were always valuable, of course—but not valuable enough to justify a violation of elementary regulations. Had Ian Meeker been sitting next to her, he would surely have noticed the warning light. Then they would have vaporized the meteor with their laser, activated the magnetic shield, taken evasive action—and brewed themselves some coffee at the same time. Routine maneuvers, barely worthy of comment.

She reached the first piece of junk, a massive section of the docking mechanism. Totally useless. She turned toward the survival tent. Seen from this distance, it looked frail and forlorn, a monument to her desperation. In that tiny refuge she had spent the last four days sleeping, eating, drinking, communicating with *Homeland*—and, against all reason, nourishing hope.

In that tiny refuge, she would die.

A steel band seemed to close around her chest, and with a furious energy she culled through the other bits of debris, finding nothing. Part of her wanted to pin the catastrophe on the ethos of *Ariel-3*, the research station fixed in geosynchronous orbit above Callisto. During the two years that preceded her arrival, self-indulgence and disorder had become the norm in that place. Soon after she and Ian had docked their freighter, they learned that life on the station was even wilder than the rumors suggested. In the subsequent weeks Ian had periodically succumbed to the hedonism, rendering himself unfit to function as her copilot.

But taking off alone—that, too, was a kind of self-indulgence. A far worse kind.

She knew that Ian blamed himself. For the first few days following the disaster they'd talked a lot on the transceiver. At first they'd discussed her imminent rescue—chin up, don't lose hope. He'd managed to establish three-way communication among Europa, *Ariel-3*, and *T.S.S. Homeland*, then on a mission to deliver an exploration team to Io. Learning of Ursula's circumstances, the captain had immediately changed course to catch an orbit around Europa. Astronauts never abandoned one of their own.

Now Callisto and *Ariel-3* were on the other side of Jupiter, out of radio range.

A sudden realization hit Ursula like a lightning bolt. She would never talk to Ian again. When Callisto emerged from the communications shadow, she would be dead. If only she'd thought to say she didn't hold him responsible—and now it was too late. Nor would there be any occasion to tell him how much she'd enjoyed his company, even though his flirting had never gotten him anywhere. They had made lots of stupid jokes together, but she'd never bothered to convey the simple fact that she liked him.

Despondent, she returned to the tent. She crawled in through the air lock, took off her helmet—the oxygen tank was nearly empty—and lay down without removing her pressure suit: why bother? Stretching out in the darkness, she inhaled the dwindling atmosphere. She waited.

After a time she sat up. Certain things needed doing; she still had obligations. She slid the recorder from her pocket, turned it on, and began to speak. "Captain Ursula Froehlich . . . July 7, 2102 . . . Jovian moon Europa. The following communication is for Captain Ian Meeker. Request confidential delivery."

She pulled off her bulky gloves and typed in Ian's access code. The recording would be automatically encrypted, retrievable through a series of digits known only to him. "Ian, this is Ursula. I guess maybe we've had our last conversation, but there are a few things I need to say. First, this mess isn't your fault. I had no business taking off without you. I should've forgotten about that damn probe. After the transmitter failed, they would've simply written it off and launched another. I know you feel guilty, but . . ."

She stopped, pressed the PAUSE button, and tried to sort out her emotions. "Ian, you know . . . even if sex wasn't our thing . . . I loved flying with you. Really. I want you to remember me as your friend. And think of me sometimes when you're making your green tea."

She racked her brain for a while, but that was all she had to say. Not much, when she considered it.

"End of message."

It was getting colder. Best to keep the suit on. She would have given anything for a hot shower and clean underwear, but in a moment of pitiless lucidity she realized that those pleasures belonged irretrievably to the past.

On to other matters. Again she pressed RECORD. "The following communication is for Karl Froehlich, São Paulo, Earth. Request confidential delivery."

She had difficulty remembering Karl's access code. How long since they'd spoken? The great love, the great drama of her life. "Karl, this is Ursula. By the time you hear my words, I assume you'll already know.

I'm in a survival tent on Europa, Jupiter's second moon—or the sixth, depending on which fragments you call moons—and soon my air will be gone. To be precise, my oxygen-retrieval unit will run out of energy, but that's only a technical distinction. I . . ." She sighed. "This is my last message to you, and I can't find the words. What should I say? Take good care of Corinna? You've been doing that all these years. She's marvelous. I don't know whether you're seeing anyone these days, or whether you plan to get married again. You really should. And now Corinna is—"

Choking back a cry of dismay, she hit PAUSE, so firmly that her thumb shimmered the color of ivory. She calculated quickly. Corinna had been born in May . . . 2084 . . . so now she was . . . God, she'd ignored her daughter's eighteenth birthday.

Her cheeks burned as she released the PAUSE button. "Once again I realize what a lousy mother I am. It's a miracle Corinna doesn't hate me, and that's surely thanks to you. You're a wonderful man, Karl, and I'm sorry that . . . it's not that I didn't love you. I did. But our ambitions were so different. And I know you loved me and still do. I always wished you could've let go of me and found another way to be happy . . . well, now you'll have to do just that."

She switched off the machine. Exhausted. The diminishing air, no doubt.

Not much time now. She began a recording for her daughter. Her daughter, who was still wondering whether to become a dancer or study physics. Her daughter, whom she'd not seen in two years. Ursula spoke at length, halting each time she failed to recall yet another fact about this person to whom she'd given birth, then deserted four years later. What could she say to Corinna? The usual protestations? She loved her? She was sorry? Ursula shuddered as she deactivated the machine. All the things she'd neglected to tell her child over the years could hardly be crammed into a single message from a frozen moon.

Was there anyone else? She'd broken quite a few hearts over the years, but that was the norm among spacefarers. Conventional wisdom held that, after two astronauts fell in love, they became either a comet pair or a supernova. A comet pair lived apart from each other, on different ships following different schedules. They were forever submitting reassignment requests and arguing with dispatchers so they might spend a few days together on the same station once a year. Many astronauts maintained several comet-pair relationships simultaneously. A supernova occurred when two lovers found themselves on the same long interstellar mission. They would have passionate sex during the trip out and fight a lot on the voyage back, then separate forever.

There was almost no such thing as family life for an astronaut. The only children living in outer space were those whose parents worked on the huge stations orbiting Earth. Most astronauts deposited sperm samples or donor eggs in the cryobanks, then got themselves sterilized, since interplanetary radiation would ultimately wreak havoc with their reproductive cells.

To do right by her former lovers, she would need to record more messages than the machine could hold. So she decided to record none at all.

What else? Her will lay safely with her other personal documents, as regulations required. Corinna would inherit everything. It wasn't much—two trunks full of souvenirs by Ursula's estimate, and some meager savings. She turned the machine back on.

"Again, Captain Ursula Froehlich. The following is a signed document and constitutes an amendment to my last will and testament." She entered her own access code, thus identifying herself as the source of the message. "Ursula Froehlich, born September 27, 2063, Greater Hamburg, Earth. My possessions stored at the Lunar Base include a blue harmonica bearing the inscription *Welcome to Mars,* as well as a Martian sand painting the size of a postcard. I bequeath both to Navigator Wladimir Jagello as a memento of the vacation we shared in 2093. Among my effects aboard *Ariel-3* is a gibbous-moon brooch of venusite. This I bequeath to my good friend, Engineer Susanna Bakonde. The side pocket of the large trunk holds a red metal case containing several letters that I wish destroyed unread. My daughter Corinna Froehlich should inherit everything else, as stated in my original will."

A strange serenity came over her as she set the machine aside. Everything was in order now, all her possessions passed along. She felt disconnected, adrift, free, as if those shabby treasures had been binding her to the material world.

She picked up the transceiver, called *Homeland,* and requested the onboard physician.

"Doctor Wang, how will I die?"

After a pause he said, "Oxygen deprivation."

"Painful?"

"You won't be conscious at the moment of death." The doctor sounded fatherly and reassuring, and his Asian accent, though barely perceptible, added an agreeable rhythm to his words. "But you will experience unpleasant sensations shortly before blacking out—primarily fear as your body struggles for air."

"What drugs do I have?"

"Your pressure suit contains a liquid euthenic. It's very quick. There's also a large dose of tranquilizer."

"Do you suggest I take it all?"

"Yes, all."

She hesitated, staring once again at her wrinkled wrists and palms. The hands of a sixty-year-old—but she would never get that far. "I've activated a radio buoy."

"We're already receiving its signal."

"When will you find me?" she asked.

"Shortly after we touch down, in about three and a half standard days."

"Doctor, I need to know something. Would I have stood a chance if I'd been more careful with my oxygen? If I'd slept the whole time instead of rummaging through the wreckage and speaking with *Ariel-3*?"

"No, not even then. You would've needed to induce full hibernation, and you lacked the equipment for that."

A soothing answer. Though maybe he was lying. "Will I receive a captain's funeral?"

"Of course."

"A name plate in the Guild's Hall of Honor?"

"No question."

"I've made a few recordings"—she listened to the echo of her words as they vanished into a bottomless void—"for my daughter, my ex-husband, my copilot."

"We'll forward them."

"Good."

"Ursula?" the doctor said. "Can I do anything for you?"

"No," she whispered, watching her breath turn to tiny delicate crystals. "I don't think so."

"Then maybe you should conserve energy for now and speak with me later?"

Again she hesitated, reluctant to let go of this conversation, this thin thread connecting her to the world of the living. "No, I don't think I'll call again."

"I'm available any time."

"Thanks. Good-bye."

"I wish you all the best, Ursula."

"Thank you very much."

The link went dead with a crackling noise, and then she was alone. Utterly alone. Now there was only Ursula and the universe.

She pondered what to do next. It seemed undignified to stay in the tent and wait for the end. No, she must go out. The least she owed herself as an astronaut was to die facing the stars.

It occurred to her that she might replenish her tank with oxygen from the tent. Briefly she fumbled with the air lock pump, trying to mate the flanges. A pointless effort. She gave up. It made no difference anyway.

She pulled on her gloves, for the last time. Put on her helmet, for the last time. Locked the seals. For the last time. Each gesture was a farewell. Each glance, a release. A brutal luminous clarity suffused her every action.

Upon exiting the air lock, she was startled by the darkness. Europa had journeyed along its orbit and was passing through the gas giant's shadow; the magnificent planet hung in the firmament like a sphere of polished marble. Now that Jupiter no longer outshone everything else, she could see the stars, thousands upon thousands, priceless jewels in the black velvet of eternity. Ursula stood and gazed, wishing that she could simply dissolve into the infinite emptiness all around her. Why couldn't she? What bound her to this moon, this flesh?

Her crawl through the air lock had wearied her, and she looked around for a place to rest. Finally she decided to recline against the smashed pod, with her eyes fixed on Jupiter. She sat down and contemplated the heavens, these stars for which she'd yearned throughout her life. She listened to her breaths, rapid and deep. Already the air in her helmet was deteriorating. She pressed the button on her sleeve, loading the feed tube with a full dose of tranquilizer. She locked her lips around the nipple and sucked down the bland sweet liquid.

Now she flipped the toggle on her wrist, activating the recorder back in the tent. Dispensing with the usual encryption nonsense, she beamed her voice directly to the device. "The following is for Karl again. Karl—I don't know why I'm thinking about you so much right now. I suppose it's because you really were the love of my life, even though you and Corinna and I lived as a family for only five years. You're the father of my daughter. That connects us. But, no. It's the other way around. I'm the mother of your daughter. Corinna is so completely your daughter, I sometimes found it painful to visit her."

She wanted to shut off the machine and collect her thoughts, but she feared that even such a small movement would cause her to collapse. "Now, of course, I wonder if it was right. What I did. My decisions. You predicted I would die a lonely death in space—remember? You tried so hard to change my mind. You were afraid for me because you loved me. Once you insisted you'd rather I ran off with another man than go hopping around the solar system."

She felt a quivering in her voice, her body. Her outward composure, smooth as glass, her fragile equanimity—it all shattered, exploding into a million shards and releasing a swelling wave of panic. For a few breathless seconds she remained silent, then forced herself to continue speaking.

"Karl . . . you know . . . if you'd asked me what I'd be thinking . . . at this precise moment . . . I would've given you a slick answer. I would've said there are people like you, who cultivate civilization and maintain order, and then there are people like me, driven to meet the unknown. My usual bluster. Once I was so sure I was right. But now I'm not sure of anything. Was I right to answer the call of my heart? Should I have stayed with you and Corinna? I don't know."

Her breathing raced. Memories appeared, images she thought had vanished long ago. The early years of their marriage: the prosperous civil administrator and his restless wife. Their house in São Paulo. Corinna's birth. That first exhilarating day at Capetown Space Academy, where it all came together, the details of her dream.

Strange watery sounds reverberated inside her helmet, and it took her a while to identify their source. She was sobbing.

She blinked helplessly. Encased in a spacesuit, she had no way to wipe away her tears. "Maybe none of this matters," she mumbled. Her breathing became soft again. Europa seemed to grow colder. "Maybe my life was simply . . . my life. If I'd stayed in São Paulo, I would've spent my days filled with a terrible longing, believing I'd missed something." She pursued this thought a bit, and she almost had to smile. "At least I don't have that regret. No. No, I didn't miss anything."

Io rose in the sky, catching her attention. A small, sulfur-yellow eye, blinking in her direction.

"I can see Io, Karl. The innermost of the Galilean moons. The largest volcanoes in the solar system are on Io. I can almost see the eruptions with my naked eye—the sulfur geysers and the rivers of lava. Last month I did a flyby—when you're that close to Io, she looks as if she might explode at any minute. If you study her more carefully, you notice clouds of smoke shooting up hundreds of kilometers and gigantic blocks of sulfur floating on seas of lava. I've seen it. Please, Karl, think of me as someone who had to search out the wonders of the universe. And a few of them, I actually found."

Her throat constricted, and she pondered what else she might say to him. Above all she wanted him to forgive her—forgive her so completely that she could then forgive herself for being here, now, alone on an ice-covered moon, her wanderings finished.

Memories of her first space flight flooded back, the terrifying instant before takeoff. Walking toward the shuttle launch pad, she'd stared up at the slender shining vehicle and shuddered at its seeming frailty. Was this small, insubstantial object really supposed to carry her all the way to a space station? In a few minutes she would be inside the thing, trapped, with no choice except to let it bear her skyward.

She had never experienced this sort of fear before, but immediately she knew it for a feeling she must never heed. If she yielded to such dread even once, she would be damned to a diminished life—an outcome far worse than whatever dangers awaited her in outer space.

And now it was back, that old fear, making her heart pound. But she would surrender no other part of her flesh, not one portion of her soul, to its awful power.

A shimmering light flowed across the plain on her left; the glow rushed toward her. Behind Jupiter the sun was rising again. At first the silhouette of the great planet gleamed, a crimson crescent, thin as a whisper, arcing pole to pole. Then a flood of fluid gold and red poured over the curve, filling the equatorial region and spreading across the latitudes, flashing and undulating like an immense fiery maw yawning open to devour all creation. At last, just when it seemed that Jupiter itself was aflame, the true source of the light appeared, a burning disk, so bright that no human dared behold it directly.

But Ursula did behold the star—she cast herself into the sun's fire, rode its rays, dived toward its core, let its radiance wash over her—even as, submerging, she searched for the universe that lies beyond the universe.

JOÃO BARREIROS

A NIGHT ON THE EDGE OF THE EMPIRE

TRANSLATED FROM THE PORTUGUESE
BY LUÍS RODRIGUES

An editor bent on assembling a credible anthology of European science fiction will include a João Barreiros story for the same reasons that a chef intending to make mock turtle soup will include a mock turtle. Certain ingredients are mandatory. Although the Portuguese SF community can claim many worthy and prolific authors, among them Luís Filipe Silva and João Seixas, Barreiros is unquestionably their leading light.

In 1977 the author graduated from the University of Lisbon with a degree in philosophy, a subject he has taught at the secondary school level since 1975. Equally at home in the novel and the short story, Barreiros has twice won Brazil's Nova Award, given by fans to the best foreign SF story published in a South American venue. His 1996 novel Terrarium, *coauthored with Luís Filipe Silva, is widely regarded as the most accomplished work of Portuguese hard SF.*

During the 1980s and early 1990s Barreiros edited a line of science fiction books, and another featuring fantasy titles, for Editora Clássica and Gradiva, respectively. Among the writers he introduced to a Portuguese audience are Iain M. Banks, William Gibson, Peter Straub, Dan Simmons, and A. A. Attanasio. The Wikipedia *entry on Barreiros notes that "his plots frequently employ unlikable protagonists in dystopic settings, where they are faced with the brutality of everyday life and are often thwarted by their own actions in the end."*

On one level "A Night on the Edge of the Empire" is a social satire skewering the sort of bumper-sticker dialectics that often passes for political discourse in the West. But Barreiros is clearly conducting another sort of thought experiment in these pages, wholly science fictional. Extrapolating from the biological phenomenon of symbiosis, the author deftly dramatizes the relationship between an avian ambassador and his lemurlike "opposable thumb." Barreiros insists that we take the VibrantSong-chirptic dyad on its own irreducible terms, and he slyly subverts our impulse to frame the story as yet another cozy post-Enlightenment, postmodern critique of paternalism and oppression.

1

The Cultural Ambassador of the Croap'tic, His Excellency VibrantSong, touches down at the Portela Astroport with his tailfeathers in a ruffle. Certainly not his fault, considering the hours he'd spent grooming them, but rather the result of the aerial pirouettes his descending orbital shuttle performed to negotiate the chaos created by the outgoing shuttles, piloted by AIs that the air traffic controllers' strike had driven crazy.

His poor feet, protected by the ornamental gaiters of the Guild of the Ideologically Instantiated, can barely hold him up, now that they're forced to carry the added gravitational load—forty-five pounds of bone—plus his hostile-environment survival equipment, plus the cryogenic capsule containing his faithful proto-brachian chirptic servant, still chilled to the temperature of liquid nitrogen.

Standing dismayed in the center of the arrivals concourse, black beady eyes darting in search of an astroport employee to direct him, VibrantSong observes the controllers' picket line. Fists in the air, shaven skulls filled with integration sockets, the creatures parade back and forth waving protest signs that the miniature semantic translator coupled to his optic nerve renders as MORE WORK FOR HUMID CIRCUITS, DOWN WITH THE HARD STUFF! Slogans seemingly devoid of any semiotic content whatsoever.

Other humans scurry in circles, brandishing sheaves of forms, as if they have no purpose in life but running at randomly through a vast hall brandishing sheaves of forms. A faltering few, subject to the universal plagues of senescence and entropy, glide along strapped to little mobile chairs covered with blinking circuitry. Others, more fit, flaunt biceps and mammary glands that anyone may fondle, for a price. Scattered amid the crowd, a few matriarchs drag their attack-children behind them, slapping their faces the better to arouse their bellicose instincts, His Excellency assumes, since afterward the young cry out furiously and wave the plastic disintegrators, laser swords, and wargamepads clutched in their pudgy fingers.

The alien crowd presses together, mingles, and flows apart in a vortex of sounds, insults, synthetic perfumes for suppressing aggression, and involuntary outbreaks of sex pheromones. Electrostatic discharges rain down on the picketing controllers, who disperse with anguished howls. As if all this weren't enough, directional loudspeakers yell angry, incomprehensible orders in the Ambassador's delicate ears.

VibrantSong extends his snakelike neck backward, as he does at the Embassy when calling the lowborn to attention, then fans out his tailfeathers to show the world how perfect and sublime is his ancient lineage. At that moment an attack-child creeps up behind him and cravenly plucks out one of those feathers, which take ten standard years to grow. The Ambassador screams, his voice joining the shrieks of the air traffic controllers, while the loudspeakers persist in their subliminal orders, and the vile brat vanishes amid the chaos holding up his prize, never to be seen again.

Everywhere on the distant walls, just below the invisible ceiling, holograms display disgusting lipped mouths parted to bare the ivory of their necrophagous fangs, plus half-naked bodies without a single decent tuft of down, clutching artifacts glowing with the same greasy sheen as their skin.

The Ambassador flaps a wing and opens his beak to announce his arrival with a song. He stops, remembering that he's traveling incognito on this trip, a secret visit to a tertiary capital adrift in a peripheral arm of the galaxy.

Here he is at last, on an exogenous world where evolution has been wildly randomized. Here he is, on the only known planet where brachians are sophonts in their own right. And not only are they sophonts, they are aggressive, oblivious to the respect due their betters.

The Ambassador resignedly sets the cryogenic capsule on the floor, fully spreads his wings in an attempt to scare off a few bold onlookers, and warbles the access code for the pressure locks. Dutifully, the capsule breaks in half, icy vapors bursting out in delicate tendrils, the artificial womb splitting open to expose the chirptic's dormant form.

The proto-brachian stretches as he awakens, curls his tail around his waist, and rushes to embrace the Ambassador's scaly leg. "Master! Oh, Master, what joy!" he cries with a squeal meant to sound like a cheep. "A beautiful garden of blossoms for thee! A morning filled with ripe fruit! A territorial melody in the evening! May you never find your nest soiled by—"

"Enough!" says the Ambassador, embarrassed by his familiar's affectionate effusions. The circle of humans continues to swell around them. Some wave their fists in the air, extend their middle fingers, and spout phrases his translator declines to render. "Get the luggage. And turn up your gnostic amplifier—I need your cognitive functions at their highest level of activity. Now, see if you can find the way to customs."

Days before, while still in orbit, the Ambassador had been warned that going through Earth customs was an ordeal of bureaucratic minutiae. All nonhuman travelers were required to fill out no fewer than thirty separate forms, by hand. Loyalty oaths, political affiliations, life insurance policies, declarations of edibles, liability and bacteriological infection waivers—there was paperwork for everything. Nothing a Croap'tic, with only a pair of vestigial fingers, could ever manage without the devoted service of the near-sophontic chirptic species.

His salutes of hierarchical respect paid, eyes wide in the presence of so many gigantic creatures similar to himself, the chirptic wonders in alarm how it would be to live here, a world with no Masters, a world where birds (or so his gnostic sensors tell him) never reached a sophontic level worthy of note. A world apparently without gardens, feathers, nests, or the sublime honor of being allowed to incubate the Masters' eggs . . .

"I'm waiting," tweets the exasperated Ambassador, scratching the flagstone floor with his talons. His neck feathers puff out to show the chirptic who's in charge. As for his tailfeathers, VibrantSong keeps them discreetly tucked in so no attack-child can plunder them again.

Distraught by his error, leaking droplets of odoriferous urine, the chirptic takes the floating luggage and hurries down a passage his implants tell him is the exit. A few of the more audacious locals follow. *Up, up your anal region,* some of them shout. The chirptic doesn't understand the reason for such commotion. Probably better that way. His duty is to fulfill his Master's wishes, and ignore all distractions peripheral to the task at hand.

The customs officer, eyes glued to his scanner's screen, barely raises his head to look at them. "Have you got a pet import license? Has that thing been properly deloused? Does it carry any parasites? Did you disinfect its feathers?"

"Croak!" cries the Ambassador in absolute shock, unable to articulate a single coherent sentence. "Racial slur! Abomination! Phylogenic bigotry!"

The chirptic looks up with lemurian eyes. His hairy little hands drum on the desktop, eager to rectify the officer's blunder: "Respectable agent of so noble a race, I beg your forgiveness for daring to correct you, but the truth is that *I* am the pet. I am His Lordship's opposable *thumb*. His loyal, steadfast companion. My native sophontic level is, shall we say, minimal. My rationality is due entirely to direct integration with my Beloved Master's prefrontal lobes—"

"Oh yeah? You mean you're the peacock's flunky? Well, to each his own. There are so many of you Exotics . . . and you do love to keep your little secrets, don't you, and then expect us to know who belongs to what? Look, these misunderstandings happen all the time. Let's just get down to business. Papers! Documents! Certificates!"

VibrantSong extends his elegant neck in a serpentine motion. He spreads wide his wings, releasing a cloud of fluffy down that invades the human's already clogged sinuses. His talons scratch the frayed carpet. The officer's eyes glint wickedly, while the frantic chirptic, opening suitcases on the desk, desperately looks for the forms they'd received on the orbital station.

"This incident shall not experience stagnation in the quiescent silence of the Ideologically Instantiated!" explodes the Ambassador. "Your offensive comments can mean only one of two things. Either you are acting in complete disregard of your duties, or you have deliberately insulted me with an ethnocentric remark. In any case, you may expect a formal complaint!"

"My Lord . . . Master . . . careful, lest your worries disturb the rhythmic motions of your most awesome craw. I beg you to calm down. Nervous tension . . ."

The customs officer flashes a toothy grin. Bits of half-chewed organic matter fill the gaps around his canines. "So you want to complain, eh? Great! I love Exotics who complain. More forms for you to fill out in clear, flawless Portuguese, if you'd be so kind. We need that complaint to be precisely worded. Which of you is the injured party, then? According to regulations, any Ethnical Complaint must be made strictly by the victim. So which of you gentlemen is the aggrieved party?"

"Croak!" cries the Ambassador with no harmony in his voice at all.

"Be serene, Master! Be at peace, Master! Bright skies, Master!" peeps the chirptic. "Please, respectable human, my Master has no fingers. How can he hold a pen if—"

"Not my problem. Let him sort it out on his own. By the look of it," says the clerk with a wink at his coworkers, who haven't missed a thing, "this is going to take a while."

2

Thousands of heartbeats later, outside the gates of the astroport, their problems more or less resolved, the chirptic dares ask his Lord and Master: "Puzzlement fills my sorry self. Why is there so much aggression in humans? I humbly request an explanation for this mystery."

"These are ethnocentric questions beyond your cognitive abilities," replies the Ambassador in one of his magnanimous bouts of pedagogy. "Humans have evolved alone, without avian assistance. They take it amiss that no other mammalian species in the known galaxy has gone through this same evolutionary process. It's safe to say they don't like knowing that brachians are our servants."

"But Master, our duty is sublime. We serve as hands to the best of the best. We make artifacts conceived by others. And we are *so* happy!"

"I know, my good chirptic," says the Ambassador, sheltering the lemurian creature under his wing in a gesture of intimacy. "You have no desire to be anything but what you are. However, these upstarts, these humans, don't understand our relationship. They project their mental disturbances upon us."

Unfortunately, the Ambassador has no time to complete his edifying little speech. They're suddenly mobbed by twenty frantic taxi drivers, their caplights flashing on and off.

"Cab, sir?"

"Guide, sir?"

"Special discounts on the luggage, sir!"

"All pets get VIP treatment from me, gents."

"Right this way, boss!"

"Down here, fellas . . ."

The Ambassador looks around and all he sees are leatherette jackets, luminous caps, and dozens of hands reaching for his floating luggage. The chirptic yips sharply and runs back and forth, trying to save the bags while protecting his Master's prodigious girth with his own slender body.

Finally, strength prevails. One vigorous cabbie, energized by years of anabolic steroids, lifts the chirptic off the ground and hauls him to a hovercab parked on the sidewalk. Terrified in the face of this sudden abduction, His Excellency VibrantSong follows behind, hopping and peeping with his wings outstretched. The bags obediently detach themselves from the clutches of the other cabbies and trail behind him in a sweeping arc.

It is night on this side of the planet. The air stinks of boiled fat. Near the astroport, rumbles rise from orbital modules busily devouring ozone. Ejection lasers split the greasy dark with their actinic lines. Nowhere is the scent of gardens even remotely evident.

After storing their luggage in the hovercab trunk, the driver sits at the controls for twenty minutes, fingering the wheel. The chirptic shudders in the backseat while His Excellency emits heartbreaking twitters of distress.

"Well?" asks the cabbie after half an hour. "Are we making up our minds, or what? We're on the meter here."

"Making up our minds about what?" the chirptic replies, voicing his Master's silent confusion.

"Where do you want to go? To a hotel or just drive around? Business or pleasure?"

"Master intends to tour your heraldic town," the proto-brachian explains. "He is here incognito, surveying sites for future Embassies. He wants to see new, aesthetically correct locations."

Ziiip! goes the glass shield as it slides between the backseat and the driver. *VROOOM!* roars the cab's turbo engine as the vehicle pulls away, pressing its passengers back against the upholstery. Through the rearview mirror, the driver's tiny eyes alternate between blinking and gleaming with malice. The laser beacons at Portela shrink in the distance.

"So it's a *cultural* visit, huh? Want to see some chicks? Is that it? Did your boss come to empty his gonads in a foreign land? Hmm?"

"I fail to recognize the reference," the chirptic whines. "Chicks?"

"It smells bad in here," His Excellency drawls in Portuguese, oblivious to everything else.

"That's the Olivais quarter on fire," the driver explains. "Can you see that glare up ahead? We're pretty close to the disaster zone. The authorities are incinerating the areas contaminated by that plasticophagous bacteria. Won't do any good, if you ask me. The wind from the firing of the orbital modules only helps spread the bugs all over Lisbon."

"Biohazard," the chirptic agrees. "Standard situation in level-three cultures."

"Assholes," grumbles the cabbie, nearly grazing the side of a truck loaded with liquid nitrogen. "Just got here and already they're bitching."

To the Ambassador's eyes, Lisbon is a city of dark pits, partially demolished buildings, clumps of parasitic vegetation, and pyramidal banks seething with dubious investment schemes. Barbed wire separates devastated neighborhoods from the shopping centers' bright ziggurats. The hovercab eventually slows down outside a building in the old town, an ancient pile covered in fresh nanopaint. The animated pigments continuously inscribe slogans, in three galactic languages, across the façade:

CHICKS CHICKS CHICKS CHICKS CHICKS CHICKS
EROTIC SHOW FOR EXOTICS

"We're here!" the driver informs them, braking outside the wide-open doors. "So, d'you like to hump 'em a bit, then finish 'em off? Wring their necks, maybe? Chop off their heads?"

"I beg your pardon?" asks the Ambassador. "I don't understand your phrases."

"His Excellency is puzzled," says the chirptic, jumping up and down on the backseat, goggle-eyed. "He fails to realize the cultural significance of the enterprise we are now seeing, honorable public transport official. Would you mind explaining?"

"Look here, lads," says the cabbie, stroking the meter's little electronic box, still ticking off the euros. "It's mutant chickens, get it? Stupid giant chickens, good for only one thing. Bred especially for you Exotics."

"The horror . . . the horror . . ." His Excellency is choking in total outrage at what he has just heard.

"The Master is upset," groans the chirptic. "And when the Master is upset, my . . . gnostic abilities . . . decrease."

"Okay, just pay up and get the hell out," demands the cabbie. "Coming here to bang those chicks is the thing you guys love most on this planet. Think I didn't know that?" He points to the slot where they're supposed to insert their credit card. "Look at this pansy thumb his beak at our stuff—don't like our chickens, huh? Yeah, they're stupid, they can barely talk. But they're real nice and tasty. You guys go on in and finish 'em off so we can roast 'em on a fire."

"Horror . . . ," repeats the Ambassador.

Meekly, the chirptic pays the outrageous fare (twenty times the usual rate), opens the locks, whistles to the luggage, and helps the Ambassador out of the hovercab.

"Hump 'em good, peacock!" yells the cabbie before driving off on the empty boulevard. "Enjoy it while you can. . . ."

3

As soon as he sets foot on the sidewalk, His Excellency is approached by several humans with rooster masks pulled over their heads. They try to grab VibrantSong by a wing and drag him inside their establishment, where holograms of chickens cackle and scratch the dirt that covers the patio entrance, shaking their crests in supposedly pornographic displays.

Not knowing what to do, the chirptic shrieks and runs back and forth between his Master and the pile of luggage.

"Come in, come in, come in! These streets aren't safe at night," the rooster-men say, nervous and restless, their eyes scanning the currently deserted boulevards. "Unlimited Quadruple-X-rated entertainment in-side. Reasonable prices. All sorts of kinky fun. In case you don't fancy our little chickies, we also stock peahens, not to mention female turkeys, moas, and ostriches. And there's a comfortable waiting room full of lovely marmosets for your . . . uh . . . little helper there."

"No, no," His Excellency insists, digging his talons into the trash that litters the sidewalk. "That's not what I—"

Suddenly another group of humans, armed to the teeth, emerges from the shadows of an alley. They have gorilla masks pulled over their heads. An incomprehensible slogan shines on their black T-shirts: DOWN WITH GODZILLA! KING KONG LIVES!

The rooster-men yell in fear and run back into their building. In sec-onds His Excellency VibrantSong and his loyal chirptic are surrounded by a dozen humans, all reeking of death and aggression. Muscular arms push the Ambassador against a wall streaked with scorch marks. Other gang members embrace the chirptic and pat him affably on his narrow shoulders.

"You're free, comrade!" they whisper in his ears. "Ethnic oppression is no more!"

"But . . . ," begins the chirptic.

VibrantSong, standing in the cloud of down he has shed in his distress, doesn't fully comprehend the situation. Anxious peeps escape his half-open beak. They've taken away his *fingers*. But why? *Why?* He extends his neck in desperation, ready to trill an anthem to peace, love, and reconciliation between species.

"Watch it!" cries one of the gang members. "Motherfucker's going to attack!"

"Death to all slavers! Death to the neocolonialists!"

The whole gang opens fire on the Ambassador, simultaneously. Some shoot burning lasers. Others empty entire barrels of micro-darts. A few use hollow-points. VibrantSong's blood paints ideograms on the scorched wall. Feathers fly everywhere. The stench of feces, cordite, and ionization engulfs the street.

"Execution accomplished!" bellows one of the King Kong commandos. "Long live the Oppressed Species Liberation Brigades! Death to all oppressors of the mammary gland! Victory to the opposable thumb!"

The chirptic is in a state of shock. He can scarcely believe his Master has been murdered before his eyes. But that hardly matters now. His neuronal connection to the Ambassador's cortex has been terminated, and few cognitive functions are left to the little symbiont. A trickle of fragrant urine runs down his legs. He has lost his powers of thought and speech. His vocal cords emit only cries of fright.

One of the Oppressed Species Liberation commandos kneels beside him for a brotherly embrace: "You are free now, you are your own master, little fellow. Go and live in peace. Learn to think for yourself and to use your hands for your own benefit and for the benefit of your species."

The chirptic peels back his lemurian eyelids even farther. Here he is, abandoned in an incomprehensible world of luminous shapes, smells, and sounds lacking all semantic coherence. His hands open and close, but there is no branch to grasp.

"Well then, comrade? Aren't you going to thank us?"

His understanding of the universe has vanished. Nothing remains but fear. Fear, and the moist warmth spreading down his legs.

"Sheepeeteeceefic . . . peed self . . . ," says the chirptic, liberated at last.

JOËLLE WINTREBERT

Transfusion

TRANSLATED FROM THE FRENCH
BY TOM CLEGG

In his most famous novel, H. G. Wells plagued his native England with "intellects vast and cool and unsympathetic." The world of French science fiction is, by way of comparison and contrast, vast and cool and sensual: vast enough to nurture such valuable women writers as Danielle Martinigol, Sylvie Miller, and Sylvie Lainé, cool enough to honor the quintessential weirdness of Jean-Marc Ligny, Olivier Paquet, and Ayerdhal, and sensual enough to celebrate stylistically lush stories such as the one you are about to savor.

Author, critic, anthologist, and screenwriter, Joëlle Wintrebert has been called "la grande dame de la science-fiction française," as well as "Miss Univers," this last epithet tracing to her association with the prestigious anthology series Univers, *which she edited for several years during the eighties. She has received the Prix Rosny Aîné three times, first in 1980 for her short story "La créode" (creode being the term that British biologist Conrad Hal Waddington coined for "a canalized pathway of change along the epigenetic landscape"), then eight years later for* Les Olympiades truquées *("The Fixed Olympics"), a revised version of her 1980 debut novel, and then again in 2003 for* Pollen. *Wintrebert's literary honors also include the Grand Prix de la Science-Fiction Française (now the Grand Prix de l'Imaginaire) for* Le créateur chimérique *("The Chimerical Creator," 1989), and the Grand Prix Amerigo Vespucci for* Les Diables blancs *("The White Devils," 1993). Her most recent book is* Les Amazones de Bohême *("The Amazons of Bohemia"), a historical novel that, among its other accomplishments, offers a feminist vision of the foundation myth of Prague.*

On first principles "Transfusion" may strike the reader as an exercise in surrealism. Don't be misled. Beyond its hallucinatory style and seductive diction, Barbel Hachereau's encounter with an alien being is science fiction to the core. It is also a feast for adventuresome tastes. Bon appétit.

This morning she starts out on the wrong foot. Deliberately, and with absolute determination. Today she will be in a foul mood—an attitude she adopts whenever she feels blurred. She detests indecision, vagueness, all things nebulous. A measured rage allows her to construct clean boundaries for herself, and too bad if their edges are a little sharp.

She slips past Thomas with her chin held high, eyes vacant, ignoring his cheerful greeting and the captivating aroma of toast. She will breakfast alone, a handful of currants and cherries, their tartness the perfect complement to her contrived pique, an irritation that cannot abide the stickiness of jam and amorous gestures.

Stepping into the garden, she finds it invaded by a fog so dense, it obscures all landmarks. Her steps falter, but Thomas's voice hailing her from behind spurs her onward.

She blunders ahead aimlessly, afraid he will catch up with her as she wanders amid the hazy contours of the silver birches, the fuzzy outlines of the purple hazelnuts, trees whose actual shapes she can imagine but not discern.

Soon she becomes lost—is the garden really this vast?—feeling dismay but also excitement. How could she go astray in such a familiar place? A milky mist covers her face like a veil sewn with minuscule pearls, and with arms thrust forward, feet fumbling, eyes straining, she tries to find her bearings but recognizes nothing.

Far away, at the end of a long cottony tunnel, Thomas calls to her. She catches his cry beneath her eyelids, trapping and suffocating the annoying sound.

When she opens her eyes again, the thing is watching her. It floats, suspended in the fog, surrounded by a brilliant halo that crackles and explodes, spilling forth in a riot of colors: a face at once unreal and serene, awakening in her a religious awe . . . but then its smile reveals the teeth of a beast, while the strange keyhole pupils contract to slots, and a heavy swell roils the liquid orange irises.

Stomach knotted, she takes a step backward, then another.

The predator's mask breaks apart, and the fragments reform into a new countenance. Given its contemptuous stare and the brutal grimace that curls the lower lip, she doesn't immediately recognize her own face. But then she sees herself, and she moans in terror. This second self with its unfamiliar savagery frightens her even more than the face that preceded it.

Centuries pass. Her fear flows out of her in a long viscous flux that turns and holds her in a gluey embrace. At last the sap runs dry, but not before fertilizing its captive with some secret substance that ferments her fear into a wine of perverse desire.

Then the face explodes into a thousand iridescent shards, awakening her from a millennium of stasis. It seems as if the entity has sculpted a new body for her, more suited to its purposes, displacing her atoms with its own secretions, the better to tame and imprison her.

A violent tremor of revolt runs through her but fails to disturb the structure of this new edifice. Why, though, should she resist, since the entity has filled every void within her? Her rearrangement means an end to all the emptiness, the cracks, the painful secret interstices of her being.

From now on is she without refuge?

Yes, and yet so full, so compact, so sleek.

The fog lifts. With exaggerated delectation she sniffs the earthy mustiness it leaves behind. Now she senses Thomas joining her, sees him reeling from her baleful glance.

He recovers, defends himself with a small laugh that swiftly dies, then blanches and looks away. She knows that she has snapped the axis, herself at the center, around which he revolves. She feels intoxicated by her new discovery, the power of cruelty, which she rides to a peak of ecstasy.

"Who's there, Barbel Hachereau? You or the other?"

She cannot shut out the piercing question.

Or keep her hands from trembling.

Am I haunted? she wonders as Thomas affixes his lips to her brow, stamping her with a final kiss, then whispers the proof of his weakness:

"You frighten me, Barbel Hachereau. That's why I'm leaving you. I lied. I'm not going to any conference. Someone will come by to collect my things."

He walks off, a being without boundaries or firmness, a slack fading shape that she watches disappear with bemusement, astonished that she feels no regret. Two bodies are not meant to share the same space. That's possible only if one becomes blurred, depleted to transparency by the other's presence.

The vapor once known as Thomas finally dissipates as it passes through the gate at the far end of the garden.

Barbel is alone now: an intense sensation—her freedom. She dilates, becomes a yawning cavity, deep black, fleshy, a gorge that grows ever more sultry and feverish as she waits. Standing beneath the milky blue sky, she yearns for some preternatural seed. Languid but alert, she opens her trembling hands while keeping her eyes closed to better apprehend . . . what, exactly? She doesn't know, and yet it's there: she senses it attending her, smells it in the iron breath that washes over her, in the slow heavy bitterness of decaying vegetation, in the sugars and salts of her skin inflamed by the adamant sun.

She enters herself, only to find the arcane crimson of blood, the effervescent flux of atoms, but soon she joins the mad ballet of molecules . . . and then she sees the face form again in her most secret damp recess, at the deepest level of her being.

I have absorbed it, she concludes.

It's inside her now. Inside, and watching her, those demon eyes a turbulent orange sea that engulfs her.

Endlessly she rubs herself with the stone, pressing hard against the rough bumps and grainy folds—endlessly she polishes her body. She stops when it has become as smooth as a pebble burnished by the sea since the dawn of time. Its surfaces sparkle with a lustrous dust. Clothed solely in this silky, impalpable veil, her body is ready for the ceremony.

Barbel Hachereau exits the garden through the gap in the privet hedge and walks down to the sinkhole. Three days of rain have softened the silt to perfection. The thick supple mud melds with the arch of her foot, spurts and wriggles its way between her toes; three more steps, and the mud envelops her ankles. How can she resist this warm voluptuous suction? The dry immaculate whiteness of her pearly skin offers itself to the sodden clay.

Barbel lies down. Her nostrils quiver, invaded by the strong vibrant smell of the soil displaced by her flesh. The silt encloses her in its slow embrace. Gravity. She could not be moved even if she wished it. Bubbles burst around her, releasing the heady fragrance of the rotting plants.

Flush with the earth, the grass, Barbel beholds an unfolding epic of browns and greens, swarming with tiny lives, crystals of captured light, snares of sticky silk, a fleeting pitiless universe.

Shut your eyes tightly. Feel the aqueous kiss on your lips. Open yourself to it. Taste it. Does the clay mortar your tongue to your mouth? Swallow the soil. Let it settle down inside you. No, don't think of it as a dead crust. It is nature's very flesh that enters you. You must assent to this coarse and confusing upheaval, this sudden feeling of an internal pulsing tumor. And accept even these fiery phantom needles that you might almost believe were forged especially to sear your entrails.

Don't move. You are a gap opening onto another universe that bids you partake of its power. Would you refuse this gift of the gods?

But who are the gods when they cannot be named? Mere exotic foreigners, outré brocades turned to tawdry rags.

Barbel manages to gather around herself a few remaining shreds of instinct. She awakens, choking, vomiting up the muddy water. Behind the blurry screen of her tears, the demon smiles at her, bound to her by a cord of pure energy.

"Rub it away, Barbel Hachereau. Perhaps there's still time."

The mouth with its bronze fangs expands and contracts horribly. All around the maw, bits of skin crack and slough away in rotting tatters that are caught in midflight by industrious insects.

These ragged scraps of tortured flesh arouse no feelings of triumph in Barbel, and she averts her gaze. The grisly vision proves more than she can bear, for it is accompanied by a buzzing lament, intolerably loud. Now ruined, the energy cord disintegrates, and yet even as they fall, the burning particles seek out one another and begin to reassemble themselves.

A golem oozing ochre, Barbel exhumes herself from her sedimentary shroud. As she walks back to the garden, her bright and pliant shell turns dull and rough, then begins to flake away. Which is exactly how Barbel herself feels. Less than alive, half-petrified, broken inside. Vanquished in her victory.

Rain from a passing thunderstorm spatters her naked body. She runs and dances and runs again in the thick grass that flourishes beside the river. She has wandered far from the garden. The demon has taken hold of her once more. She stretches out her arms, throws back her head, tastes the intoxicating fizz of ozone on her tongue. Lightning flashes, enshrouding her in a pulsing blue halo, making her hair crackle and stand on end. At last the storm yields to a pale dawn. Barbel still dances tirelessly to the demon's tune. Her arms swirl invisible drapes, her wild fingers weave strange laces, while her darting head inscribes ribbons across the sky. Four dumbfounded boys witness the scene.

Aberration frightens those unable to dream. To ward off their fear, the four boys trade glances and snigger. Each pair of bright eyes darkens with the same hunger. All that the boys have garnered from the sensual undulations is the mere fact of the naked body—an offering, they believe, to their lust.

They draw closer, their mouths chewing and rechewing a mash of taunts, and then they vomit out their contempt, seeking to sanction their scorn for outsiders.

But Barbel is deaf, Barbel is blind, Barbel is consumed by her dance. She does not see the four boys who surround her, nor does she hear their words enclosing her in concentric rings. She awakens only at the rough touch of their hands shoving her toward the ground. But her back barely grazes the tall blades of grass. A superhuman twist halts her fall, even as the demon within, growling and curling its lips, makes her body stand erect again.

The boys retreat, alarmed by this acrobatic feat. They had not reckoned on what they're confronting now, this dancer who surpasses their wildest fantasies. They draw together and hold their ground, when instead they should be fleeing. Barbel releases all the energy accumulated during the thunderstorm, a lightning discharge that strikes and scatters the boys.

Crazed, she watches over the four blasted bodies until morning comes.

When she returns to the garden, she feels so weak that she believes the demon has abandoned her.

•   •   •

On the stained carpet in the bedroom, propped against the cascade of soiled sheets, she eats a piece of raw meat. Blood runs down between her breasts. Casually she wipes away the trickles. Compare the vermilion drying on her hand with the coagulated purple smeared across her thighs. Touch the source and sniff, the blood of the beast and her own blood. Taste and smell—both rusty, but bland, an oxidized anodyne. She lifts an elbow and slowly inhales the acrid emanations of her armpit. Reaching into the elastic hollow, she smoothes down the damp fur, then licks her fingers and abandons herself to the strong salty flavor.

Later. Night has fallen. The shadows are streaked with brilliant flashes of green and bronze. Barbel kneels before the cheval glass framed by baroque cupids. In the dark blue of the mirror, two small orange circles regard her, the strange pupils dilating within them.

"A glimpse of the world beyond, Barbel Hachereau. These aren't your eyes."

Barbel flicks on the lights and scrutinizes the cheval glass, searching in vain for the demon. Her skin, she sees, has acquired a strange color, the golden green of a scarab beetle, dry, cold, and scaly to the touch.

"You're not there, Barbel Hachereau. The Other has taken up the entire space. These gaunt features are but a tracery of your real face. And your teeth were never so pointed."

In the mirror, the pupils of the Other contract.

Barbel tilts her head, listening to a chthonian melody that pours from a pure crystal, a musical prism shining in the depths. She feels herself dispersed across the bands of this aural rainbow, yet she retains enough of her original self to resist the maelstrom of icy color that seeks to drag her down. The crystal shatters.

She has saved herself from oblivion but remains the prey of a relentless fate. The demon will do battle with her until she no longer has the strength to fight.

Barbel discovers her dirty feet, the filthy state of her bedroom. She who had once vitrified herself into transparent quartz, with perfect edges, now feels her entire being seeping softly away through invisible fissures.

But finally she realizes how she might halt this slow hemorrhaging of her self.

•   •   •

Dying is easier when done as an act of resistance. Suddenly it's she who has the upper hand. She floats above the demon, bound to it by a thread of energy that unravels along with her life. The demon inhabits a metal cylinder conjoined to a complex machine. Its orange eyes have grown dull. Its mouth exhales bubbles of sound that hiss as they expand. At times its teeth show through the shrill spheres.

A language sown with cries, Barbel thinks.

She can now distinguish other forms, vague, fleecy, at first trembling like waves about to break, then surging forward. The forms press quivering around the cylinder in which the suffering and impotent entity languishes, this transfuser who has become the transfused.

Closer. It is now Barbel's turn to penetrate the demon, spreading herself throughout its body. Understand her situation. An unprecedented event has occurred: she is drawing the demon into her own death. The immortality of the demon—of all demons—has until now been a fixed fact, irreversible, a blessing to which its kind was heir. So how did the little Earthling manage to subvert this state of affairs? And what is one to make of a world in which the transfused turn their own deaths against their invaders?

A rubbery liquid seeps from the swollen flesh of the being with orange eyes. In the desiccated coils of its alien mind, the surviving remnant still struggles fiercely against the imminence of the unfathomable abyss.

At the very moment when the intolerably taut thread of her existence snaps, Barbel smiles. Her tortured body has won the day.

W. J. MARYSON

VERSTUMMTE MUSIK

TRANSLATED FROM THE DUTCH
BY LIA BELT

From the Dantesque visions of "Sepultura" to the frozen vistas of "A Blue and Cloudless Sky," from the Jovian tableaux of "Wonders of the Universe" to the sur-realistic landscapes of "Transfusion" to the Dadaist dioramas of "Some Earth-lings' Adventures on Outrerria" to the dancing AIs of "Separations," this anthology delivers many vivid images to the reader's subjective retinas. But three of our authors, as it happens, are less concerned with satisfying the eye than with en-gaging the ear, offering up joyous celebrations of sound and moving meditations on its absence.

If you're consuming these stories sequentially, you've already encountered the "spirits of troubled silence" who haunt "A Birch Tree, a White Fox." You've also heard the seductive anthem composed by the hero of "Athos Emfovos in the Temple of Sound," a tale that begins with a bass line and ends in eerie quietude. We now present the third story in our aural trio, "Verstummte Musik," a complex thren-ody for a near-future Europe, part fairy tale, part Orwellian nightmare, part so-cial satire, part poetic fable.

"W. J. Maryson" is the nom de plume of Wim Stolk, a former civil servant, statistician, publicist, and ad man who ultimately found his calling in the field of speculative fiction. His Master Magician fantasy cycle and his Unmagician series have enjoyed strong sales and received numerous awards in the Netherlands and nine other European countries. When not supplying his publisher with the latest Maryson novel, Stolk works as an editor and scout for that venerable Dutch house, Meulenhoff. As you might infer from "Verstummte Musik," the author is also an

accomplished musician, with three CDs to his credit, all featuring songs inspired by his fiction. At present he lives on a farm with his wife, three daughters, one son, six cats, some thirty hens and roosters, three guinea fowls, and five peacocks.

Over the years, Dutch science fiction has offered its readers the full range of genre pleasures, from alien visitations to elegiac visions, Sheckleyan whimsy to Sturgeonesque transcendence. The contemporary classics include Manuel van Loggem's "Pairpuppets," an ironic speculation on the future of love, and An-nemarie van Ewyck's "The Lens," a poignant vignette about an interplanetary cultural liaison searching for a place she can call home. English translations of both these stories appear in David Hartwell's The World Treasury of Science Fiction, *and in each case the editor supplies an introduction noting the sweeping influence of the Anglo-American product on Dutch SF. Perhaps "Verstummte Musik," with its Continental setting, Kafkaesque situations, and air of Tolkienesque melancholy, points the way to a less derivative literature, limning the first of many unprecedented netherworlds destined to emerge from the Nether-lands.*

I t was the day of the alpha spider, the month of the moon laurel, the year of the water gryphon. Cencom, the computer that ran Eurwest, had decided that these terms sounded more poetic than 18-05-2443.

Dark clouds hovered over the plaza leading to the Ministry of Quota-tion. Fat raindrops smashed into gray cobblestones resembling the shiny bodies of dead fish. As Laïra hurried across the ancient square, she re-membered that it had once been the Place de la Concorde. The glossy stones beneath her feet and the shimmering bricks of the government buildings nurtured the myth of luminous Paris, the romantic city. The storm had chased most citizens into their homes, and Laïra wished she could join them. But today that was impossible.

IMPARTIALITY: THE HIGHEST GOOD, declared the huge digitalized sign pulsing on the façade of the Ministry of Quotation. Laïra quickened her pace. Mounting the steps, she glanced again at the throbbing display. The text had changed. EVERYBODY WINS: BLOOD TO THE LIVING, BRICKS TO THE DEAD.

As she rushed through the glass doors and entered the foyer, she thought about the flashing mottos. Was impartiality really the highest good? Certainly there was much to be said for fairness. The mathematical dispassion with which the Law of Quotation reached its verdicts was prime among the glories of Eurwest. And what about the second slogan? She did not believe that the dead prospered as much as the living. Yes, the perpetually expanding Palace of Humanity did offer its constituents a kind of victory, but most people would tell you the place was just a legend, and even if it existed, Laïra suspected that being mortared into its ramparts was not so very different from oblivion.

"Everything will turn out all right, I promise you," her contract-husband had told her earlier that morning, trying to cheer her up. "You're going to get through it."

"Yes," she'd said, but she simply wasn't convinced. She'd been keeping close track of her quotients, and she feared they fell short of the mark. The previous year, her reckoning day had been an ordeal, and this year's promised to be even worse.

"Don't worry, my love," Hinrik said. "Think about me—think about *us*—and you'll be fine."

He offered her a reassuring smile, but in the depths of his eyes, beyond his benevolent gaze, she saw that he, too, was worried.

"I've seen your seat," he added abruptly. As a technician for the Ministry of Quotation, Hinrik oversaw the repair and maintenance of the reckoning chairs. He detested his job, which subjected him to constant scrutiny by Cencom, but his performance so far had been impeccable. "Box twenty-four, chair fifty-seven. It's a good one."

An odd comment, almost as odd as his occasional remarks about the Palace of Humanity, whose existence was in his opinion an incontrovertible fact. In Hinrik's occupation, a reckoning chair was neither good nor bad but merely functional or nonfunctional.

"A good chair?" she said. "You mean, it looked lucky to you?"

"Very lucky," he said, then gave her a quick kiss on the lips.

It was the day of the alpha spider, the month of the moon laurel, the year of the water gryphon—but it was also the year of C-sharp, or so Hinrik had insisted right before they'd parted company that morning. "I hacked the information out of Cencom," he said. "Not A-sharp. Not B-flat. C-sharp." Laïra adored her husband, but she wished he wouldn't say such perplexing things.

She followed the corridor toward the Arena of Being and Nonbeing. Pausing at the portal, she placed her thumb on the ID-membrane, so Cencom could confirm her fleshprint and her DNA signature.

"Ana Laïra Jermina Von Fuchs—9,715 days, three hours, twelve minutes, sixteen seconds," the terminal announced. "Box twenty-four, chair fifty-seven."

Laïra removed the pocket chime from her jacket and glanced at the dial. Assuming that precisely seven seconds had elapsed since the terminal had said "sixteen seconds," then her personal timekeeper and Cencom were in perfect synchronization.

She stepped onto the moving walkway. At the far end of the cavernous arena the Wheel of Quotation spun round and round like an upended carousel. Slowly, inexorably the walkway carried her past one low-walled cubicle after another—box 5 . . . box 8 . . . box 11 . . . box 14 . . . box 17— until she reached her assigned compartment. Her future seemed a void. Its blackness spread through her brain like ink.

Everything was numbers, but the greatest of these was surely 900,000,000—the optimal, the essential, the serendipitous population of Eurwest. Not 900,000,001. Not 899,999,999. No, precisely 900,000,000 human beings enjoyed the virtues of the city-state—900,000,000 now, 900,000,000 forever. Every citizen had his part to play in maintaining the proper ratio between being and nonbeing. Sometimes your role was to live out your life, and sometimes your role was to meld with the palace.

Box 24 was nearly full already, at least eighty citizens milling around the ten-by-ten grid of consoles. Wiping her damp curls from her brow, Laïra dismounted the walkway, pulled back the swinging gate, and stepped into the compartment. She swept her eyes over her boxmates, each of them likewise a day 18 month 05—an alpha spider moon laurel. They looked relaxed, exuding the confidence of people with a future. For most of them, evidently, a reckoning day was simply an annoying necessity, like a visit to the dentist.

Laïra's muscles grew hard and tense, and a fierce headache rumbled through her skull like a steamroller.

"Good morning, neighbor."

A pale grinning face appeared before her. It was Smeet, who lived across the street, an obese microbiologist, forty years old. By his account he'd published several highly respected articles on the human genome. His smile radiated the annoying smugness of someone who knew his final tally would come out right.

"I'm in seat ten this year," said Smeet.

"Fifty-seven," said Laïra.

He extended his arm, which terminated in a remarkably small hand. Reluctantly Laïra let him clasp her slim trembling fingers. He looked at her in surprise.

"Nervous?"

Laïra wanted to deny it, but she heard herself utter a hoarse "Yes."

"Oh?" said Smeet. "Why?"

Why, indeed? She was after all a talented and promising actress, known not only in Greater Paris but throughout Eurwest—in New Frankfurt, Flanders City, the West Holland Delta, and a dozen other metropolitan areas. In the past year she'd played seven major roles, and thanks to satellite video she even had a following in Greater York across the ocean.

"Fame and job satisfaction are worth quite a few points," said Laïra. Oddly, her anxiety seemed to be fading. "But I haven't progressed in other areas." She'd experienced problems that year with self-control and product-consumption, and her emotion-gyro had spiraled steadily downward.

Smeet frowned in concern. "I honestly thought you were prospering. Do you have a good contract?"

In fact Laïra had splendid contract, or so she believed, but marital stability rarely earned you more than a few thousand points.

Before she could answer, Smeet shrugged and said, "I'm sure your quotients could be worse."

"No doubt," she replied, more sardonically than she'd intended. "But I've gotten—" She cut herself off. Disclosing the details of your personal relationship with the Law of Quotation could cost you five hundred units. Yes, she'd received two warnings in as many years, but that was her business, not his.

"Know what I love about the arena?" Smeet said. "It's a refuge—like a monastery or a quiet woods. For one whole hour, your worth remains fixed, and you don't have to worry about increasing your quotients."

A subtle observation, Laïra decided. She envied people who could think like that.

Cencom's voice boomed across the arena. "Box twenty-three! Thirty seconds!"

Laïra and her boxmates peered over the wall into the adjacent compartment. With shuffling gaits and vacant expressions a hundred 18-05s moved toward the console grid. After assuming his seat, each 18-05 took up a pair of spidery nanotrodes and set them against his temples, then faced his monitor screen, pressed his spine against the back of the reckoning chair, and curled his fingers around the arm supports. In perfect synchronization one hundred pairs of steel manacles closed around one hundred pairs of wrists with sharp clicks. Here and there Laïra saw blinking eyes, bobbing hands, twitching lips: at least she wasn't the only one who felt tense.

A bronze gong reverberated through the arena, and Cencom began the intricate process of retrieving and evaluating the brain data.

"Seat one," the computer declared with a harsh metallic grunt.

The occupant of the first chair, a spindly young man with a fuzzy blond beard, stiffened as his performance figures materialized on his monitor: ambition quotient, empathy quotient, efficiency, generosity, reliability, industriousness, emotion-gyro—and then the final tally. Now the Wheel of Quotation jerked to a halt, and the cutoff score flashed across its luminous surface, a string of portentous digits. The man in chair one exhaled in relief. He'd cleared the hurdle by 160 points.

"Seat two," Cencom announced, and the Wheel spun again.

The woman in the second chair came out 103 points to the good. A few minutes later her neighbor in chair 3 beat the new minimum score by 207 points. Chair 4, chair 5, chair 6, chair 7—happy citizens all. And so it went, from chair 8 through chair 40, each final tally running ahead of the Wheel's decrees. All of these 18-05s would be back next year.

Now Cencom crunched the quotients for number 41, a frail man in his sixties. His worth was frighteningly low. The man's knuckles turned white. The nanotrodes pressing his brow vibrated as he trembled from head to toe.

The Wheel spun . . . and stopped. The fateful number was only four points below the man's final tally. Cencom beamed him a warning, the harshly worded reprimand filling the monitor screen with large red letters.

Laïra's body unleashed a massive flow of adrenaline.

"Whoa, that was close!" exclaimed Smeet. His face was flushed: obviously he'd been hoping for a different verdict.

The Quotation continued. The Wheel stopped and started, stopped and started. The skinny young man in chair 53 received a warning—his second in five years. He appeared unflustered, as if this dire circumstance had nothing to do with him. Laïra shifted her gaze. The woman in chair

54 sat frozen, staring at her monitor in fear and perplexity. A warning filled the screen, her third in four years. She seemed about to swoon.

Smeet stepped in front of Laïra, blocking her view. "Have you ever wondered," he asked, "why the Quotation doesn't begin on the day you're born?"

Laïra leaned sideways, hoping to learn whether number 54 had fainted yet, but Smeet moved with her. He repeated his question. Two weeks earlier, Laïra and Hinrik had discussed that very mystery. She'd offered him no strong views on the matter then, and she had none to give Smeet now.

"It's universally acknowledged that youth is a desirable condition," she answered flatly. "So Von Schöppen decided to provide maximum blessings at the beginning of life, saving the challenges and hazards for the end."

The lucidity of her response pleased her, but then she realized that she was simply drawing on her conversation with Hinrik, repeating *his* conclusions.

"A reasonable opinion," said Smeet. "I have a different one. Cencom could never acquire any psychic nourishment by submitting children to the Quotation. Preadolescents lack the sophistication, the mathematical intellect, to understand the system." He emphasized his words with succinct, decisive motions of his small hands. "But with an adult in the chair, and the quotients going against him, Cencom gets to absorb that interval of sheer terror before execution—a brief moment, but so pure."

She looked at Smeet with admiration. Her neighbor had obviously thought deeply about this matter, subsequently devising a bold and defensible theory. Somehow Laïra never managed to do that; she always saw too many facets to any puzzle.

"The moment of being-nonbeing isn't so very brief." She hated the pedantic tone in her voice.

"My unorthodox ideas have cost me many points," continued Smeet, as if he hadn't heard her. "I must work very hard to compensate."

Laïra was surprised to learn that Smeet's worth was evidently closer to the typical cutoff score than she'd assumed. Had he already received a warning or two? In previous years she'd been too preoccupied to worry about her boxmates' fortunes. She wished that she could watch Smeet's face as Cencom assessed him, sharing his satisfaction if the numbers broke the right way, but the distance between chair 10 and chair 57 was too great.

"And the fact that I don't believe in the palace has cost me quite a bit," Smeet said in a faraway voice.

He stepped aside, allowing Laïra to again observe the events in the adjoining compartment. Number 54 had not fainted.

"Eighty-four," announced Cencom.

The young woman in the specified chair wore a defiant expression. Soon the quotients came in, corroborating her self-confidence.

"Eighty-five."

The elderly man's initial quotients—ambition, empathy, self-control—were among the lowest Laïra had ever seen.

"Pay attention," said Smeet, panting slightly.

The quotients kept arriving. "Emotion-gyro: 38,435 . . . industriousness: 59,161 . . . generosity: 67,320 . . ."

The citizen sat balanced on the edge of nonbeing.

"He needs at least eighty thousand for efficiency," whispered Smeet. Number 85 knew it, too. He stiffened, moaned, and began to hyperventilate.

"Efficiency . . ."

Barely a second elapsed before the quotient was read, but to Laïra it seemed like ten.

". . . 73,266."

A faint moan of pleasure escaped Smeet's throat.

"Execution."

The old man's eyes nearly popped from their sockets. His console emitted a shrill sound, a continuous tone, a musical note.

It was the year of C-sharp, Hinrik had told her that morning. Was that a C-sharp she'd just heard?

Number 85 strained against his manacles—desperately, fruitlessly—as the nanotrodes heated up and pressed ever more firmly against his temples. He tried to speak, but no words broke from his lips. Now the drilling started, the auger bits boring into his skull, and his throat emitted a sustained unearthly scream.

The nanotrodes hissed and glowed as they sucked the juices from number 85's body. His skin turned chalky white, his skull collapsed, his body spasmed like a speared fish. The hatch at his feet irised open, a screeching metallic yawn, and then the reckoning chair shot free of its moorings and hurtled into the abyss, taking the manacled corpse with it.

"Wow!" gasped Smeet, eyes sparkling. "It gets me every time."

Nauseated, horrified, Laïra stared at her feet. Excited whispers and murmurs of delight surged through the arena. She whimpered in fear.

A female voice whispered in her ear. "Remember what the poet said. 'Cowards die a thousand times before their deaths. The valiant never taste of death but once.'"

Laïra looked up. The woman who admired poetry, seventy years if not older, had a weathered but kindly face.

"Shakespeare wrote that," said the elderly 9-05. "Do you know Shakespeare?"

"Not really."

"What about our city poet?"

"I only have time to read scripts."

"Oh, you simply *must* experience Birlem. Start with the eulogies."

Laïra's heartbeat returned to normal. She thanked her boxmate with a curt nod.

"Box twenty-four! Thirty seconds!"

Cencom's command cut into Laïra's mind like a knife. She took out her pocket chime. Year 2443, month 5, day 18, hour 11, minute 09, second 11 . . . 12 . . . 13 . . . 14. Plenty of time to get into position. In nearly perfect synchronization Laïra and the other ninety-nine abandoned the wall and entered the grid, finding their assigned consoles. She slid into chair 57, returned the chime to her jacket, and attached the nanotrodes to her temples. She leaned back. The manacles closed around her wrists with an irrevocable click.

In an effort to distract herself, she glanced around the compartment. Her gaze moved from Smeet—chair 10, far right-hand corner—to the poetry woman, chair 31 on the left, and finally her eyes alighted on the console three spaces away, chair 60. It was empty. Strange. Even if you were deathly ill, you never missed your reckoning day.

No sooner had Laïra taken note of her missing boxmate than a second mystery presented itself. From a tiny hole in the floor a transparent fiber emerged, seemingly under its own volition. Sinuating like a snake, the fiber slid along the monitor and then coiled around the node that anchored the nanotrodes to the console.

The gong sounded. Cencom obtained the quotients for the woman in chair 1. She was an overachiever, each number higher than the last.

The Quotation continued. It was a good day for the inhabitants of box 24. Smeet got a warning, but evidently he was prepared for it: his body trembled only slightly. More assessments rolled in. Citizen after citizen went free.

"Seat fifty-seven."

Laïra's muscles felt like ropes. She squeezed her eyes shut and tried not to hear her numbers. Initially, she succeeded, but then the quotients entered her mind like audible viruses.

"Ambition: 42,558."

A lot less than last year.

"Product-consumption: 39,418."

This wasn't going well. Beads of perspiration crawled down her face in search of her eyes.

"Emotion-gyro: 33,310."

Two hundred points down!

"Self-control: 64,927."

A bit higher than last year.

"Generosity: 65,531."

Practically the same. She tried to remember how much she needed for efficiency. At least 73,000, she thought.

"Efficiency . . ."

Was time slowing down? It seemed as if Cencom's voice tarried.

". . . 71,879."

Insufficient!

"Execution."

The nanotrodes heated up, the crimson odor burning her nostrils. She waited for auger bits to enter her skull, the blood to leave her body.

The fiber glowed blue.

What was happening? Why didn't the nanotrodes strike?

The hatch at her feet irised open. Her chair vibrated madly. She closed her eyes, and the chair catapulted free of the console. As she dropped below the arena, she heard a voice—Smeet?—cry out in surprise.

Falling, falling, falling through the darkness.

She was alive!

Falling, and then—nothingness.

Her return to consciousness was slow and painful. Cautiously she opened her eyes.

Alive. How could that be?

The manacles still restrained her, the nanotrodes still probed her temples. Her chair had come to rest on a wheeled platform that straddled two steel rails. Now the platform began to move, rattling and squeaking as it penetrated the thick moist blackness. The instant the flatcar rounded a corner, a greenish glow filled the space, and she saw a dozen other reckoning chairs gliding along the rails, each holding a lifeless, bloodless body.

Panic crashed through her mind like a tidal wave. She was headed for the brickworks! She was about to be crushed alive!

Despite her terror she managed to identify the corpse in the flatcar directly ahead of her: the unfortunate old man from box 23, chair 85. Inexorably Laïra and number 85 and the other unworthies were transported into an immense hall girded with steel, toward a loading dock bisected by a conveyor belt and filled with droning machines and milling robos in green jumpsuits. The procession stopped. Two robos strode to the first flatcar and tore the nanotrodes from the corpse's skull. The robos unlocked the manacles, wrenched the corpse free of its chair, carried it across the loading dock, and dropped it on the conveyor belt. They returned to the flatcars and went to work on the next Quotation loser.

Laïra fought against her manacles, but they would not budge.

A third green-suited robo approached the flatcars. He inspected number 85 and, determining that the man was dead, moved on to Laïra. Their gazes connected. The robo smiled.

He was not a robo at all.

"Hinrik?" gasped Laïra in disbelief.

He exhaled sharply and yanked the nanotrodes from her temples. He reached into his coat pocket and retrieved a small silver cylinder, inserting it in her left manacle. The band popped open with a sharp click. He unlocked the right manacle. Laïra rubbed her wrists.

"Come quickly," he whispered.

In her mind's eye Laïra saw the transparent fiber. Hinrik's doing, a device for neutralizing the nanoprobes. She'd married a saboteur—a brave and creative saboteur.

She rose from her reckoning chair like an aging robo, slowly, awkwardly. Her skin was bruised, her muscles sore, but none of that mattered.

Hinrik disappeared into a gloomy niche and seconds later returned bearing a lifeless body, its skull crushed, blood drained. She shuddered. This was surely the wayward citizen of box 24, the missing occupant of chair 60.

Her husband was a saboteur—and also a murderer?

"I have only one defense," he said. "She would have died anyway. I've never seen a worse set of quotients."

Hinrik placed the corpse in chair 57. The manacles clicked back into place.

Taking Laïra by the arm, Hinrik guided her into the niche—just in time, because now one of his fellow technicians, a bearded man in a white lab coat, appeared on the other side of the loading dock. Laïra froze. Beyond the windows of Hinrik's eyes she saw a mingling of emotions: fear, hope, confusion, anger.

An anguished minute elapsed, another minute, a third. Hinrik stepped cautiously from the niche and glanced toward the dock.

"He's gone," he whispered. "Come."

"Where? A free state? Ostreich-Schweiz?"

Hinrik placed an index finger to his lips. "Be quiet until I tell you it's okay to talk."

For the next two hours they moved through a long winding corridor, eventually reaching the immense underground factory where the brick-makers plied their trade. The kiln fires roared, filling the space with stifling heat, stinging smoke, and sulfurous odors. A squad of security robos in orange jumpsuits guarded the operation, but Laïra and Hinrik managed to keep out of sight.

On the far side of the factory an immense gantry crane stood beside a mountain of bricks, each tinted scarlet, as if in homage to the blood that had once filled the donor's veins. The machine was a wonder. With great technological competence the metal claw plucked a dozen bricks from the pile, deposited them in a gondola—a dozen such cars, coupled together, stood on the siding—then returned for another load. The gantry would have scored high in both efficiency and industriousness: most of the twelve cars were already full.

"Our only chance," muttered Hinrik hoarsely, pointing toward the gondolas.

Together they slipped beneath the gantry, approached the first gondola, and began to remove its load, brick by brick. In a matter of minutes they'd created a cavity large enough for a human body.

"I'll need to cover you up," Hinrik explained. "Twenty bricks, maybe thirty. I'll try not to hurt you. Breathe deeply. Stay calm. I'll be in the next car."

Laïra climbed into the gondola, and Hinrik proceeded to bury her. The bricks were heavy but not intolerable. A few minutes later, the train began to move, shifting the payload. The weight of the bricks seemed to increase; they chafed her skin, battered her flesh, squeezed against her bones. Terror rose within her, but she beat it back through an effort of will. This ordeal, she mused, would have earned her many points for self-control. She wanted to smile, but the bricks hurt too much.

The train rolled on, faster and faster. The compacted corpses pressed downward. Time lost all meaning. She tried to empty her mind and concentrate on her breathing, but she realized the bricks were winning, and she sank into unconsciousness.

Laïra!"

Hinrik's voice rang sharply in her ear. He seized both her arms and pulled her free of the gondola.

"We've been found out," he moaned.

She looked around groggily. The train had stopped inside a space only slightly smaller than the brickworks.

"Stand still!" cried a harsh voice. "You're in violation!"

Three men in blue jumpsuits ran stiffly toward them: security robos. Hinrik dragged her away from the train and guided her across the concrete floor. A tunnel portal appeared. They rushed inside and entered the labyrinth beyond, an intricate network of passageways, pipes, and cul-de-sacs. The robos' echoing footsteps faded, then dropped away completely.

A double door loomed up, two massive panels of riveted steel. Shafts of yellow light spilled through the crack. As if sensing Laïra and Hinrik's presence, the panels slid back, revealing a marble staircase that spiraled ever upward through the bore of a granite well.

Fifty marble steps separated each landing from the next. Exhausted, exhilarated, they finally reached the topmost platform, then stumbled past an ornate pagoda of sandalwood and cedar and entered the grassy plain beyond. The radiant sun, brighter than any light Laïra had ever known, made her blink.

A mammoth configuration of walls reared up, their scarlet bricks aglow in the noonday sun, each soaring rampart linked to the next by a glorious white tower. A coppice of pear trees, a stand of willows, and a luxurious garden blooming with red roses huddled in the shadow of the immense structure. Within its embrace lay an astonishing array of minarets, turrets, and spires. In the distance the snowy peaks of the Alps lay mantled in puffy clouds.

So it was not a legend.

"The Palace of Humanity," gasped Laïra.

"Brick upon brick," said Hinrik in a respectful whisper. "The walls never stop growing."

Overwhelmed by an emotion that had no name, she surveyed the nearest cluster of ramparts and towers. The arched windows, decorative statues, shining parapets, flying buttresses, and lofty belfries could not be encompassed by a single mind. She remembered a picture of an ancient cathedral in a book from her childhood. Her memory supplied the name. *La Sagrada Familia,* somewhere in the south of ancient Europe. Bathed in the noonday sun, the palace sprawled across the plain like a hundred re-productions of *La Sagrada Familia,* infinitely more complex than any structure that had ever arisen before on the continent.

"Millions of lives," stammered Hinrik, his voice full of awe. "Millions of souls. One day the toll will reach a billion. Cencom is insatiable."

Laïra studied his face. Tears welled up in the eyes of her husband and savior, and soon her own tears were flowing, too.

As Hinrik set a comforting hand on her shoulder, Laïra thought she heard music—no, not music, not something experienced, merely the idea of music. But then a sudden fear came, driving all such notions from her mind. She turned on her heel and ran across the plain, her gaze fixed on the sandalwood pagoda. In a matter of seconds she reached the marble staircase, then stared into the depths of the helix.

"The security robos," she muttered as Hinrik drew abreast of her.

"They'll never come here," Hinrik said. "This is a forbidden place."

"Forbidden by the Law of Quotation," said a soft voice. "Denied to security robos and Eurwest citizens alike."

They turned and beheld an old woman dressed in a long robe of yel-low silk.

"So ran Von Schöppen's final decree," the woman continued. She had dark green eyes in a soft welcoming face hatched by wrinkles. Her skin looked transparent; she must have been beautiful once. "But no one will know you've trespassed. I'm the only living soul between here and the border." She beckoned to Laïra and Hinrik with brittle fingers. "Call me Eleonyra. Come, I'll show you my château."

Without waiting for a response she spun around and marched across the plain. Her stride was long, her gait buoyant. It took Laïra and Hinrik several minutes to catch up with her.

"*Your* château?" said Laïra, surprised.

Eleonyra shrugged. "When you spend several decades confined in a monstrosity like this," she said without breaking stride, "you start to feel as if you own it—and my official title in fact implies proprietorship. I'm the Keeper of the Palace of Humanity."

Again, the idea of music emerged in Laïra's thoughts. Or was she actually hearing something? A flock of larks singing *sotto voce* in the willows? The quietest of cicadas buzzing in the grass?

The Keeper stepped onto a flagstone path that wound up a knoll toward a pylon positioned between two ramparts. A narrow door broke the curving brick surface, a black barrier of oak and iron. Reaching the tower, Eleonyra lifted the latch, pushed the black door open, and gestured her guests inside.

"The days are lonely here," she said. "And the nights . . . unbearable."

Laïra and Hinrik found themselves standing in a dining hall as vast as the Quotation arena. Eleonyra directed them to a table sixty feet long and six feet wide, appointed with gold plates and silver utensils.

"With each passing year, my task grows more difficult," the Keeper said. "The portraits of my loved ones fade from my mind, and I'm left with only my sagging features in the mirror. Every day I see old age advancing across the battlefield of my skin."

Eleonyra opened a mahogany cabinet and removed a slim green bottle and three fluted glasses. The fluid, decanted, proved bright red, its fragrance as agreeable as the scent of lavender.

"Wine," Eleonyra explained. "The lower slopes of the Alps are quite suitable for growing grapes, and the cultivator robos tend the vines with great skill." She took a substantial swallow. "I'm older than this vintage. I fled from the arena in 2393—that would be . . . fifty years ago? For many months afterward I lived in fear, but then I realized the Ministry had actually sponsored my escape." With a protracted sip, she drained the last of her wine. "They wouldn't have let you reach the palace unless the Quotation allowed it. If any other citizen breaks free in the next forty years, fifty years, sixty years—however long you're expected to remain here—that person won't get far."

The Keeper rose and spread her arms in a gesture that seemed to encompass not only the dining hall but the entire palace as well.

"Tomorrow one of you will inherit all this."

Laïra and Hinrik stared at her in shock.

"Only one of us?" asked Hinrik.

Eleonyra nodded. "That's how Von Schöppen arranged matters. Before this week has ended, I shall bid my robos farewell and strike out for Ostreich-Schweiz, and at that instant one of you will become the new Keeper."

"What will happen to the other person?" Hinrik asked.

For a long while Eleonyra remained silent. At last she pointed to a white door at the far end of the room. "The other person will pass through that door. The corridor ends at the quarters of the caretaker robos. They're good at what they do. They know how to end a life painlessly."

It astonished Laïra that she did not start screaming. She wondered if the cataclysmic events of the past eight hours had drained her of all normal human feeling the way a Quotation loser was drained of blood.

Later that evening the three of them sat down to an extravagant meal served by the steward robos. Neither Hinrik nor Laïra consumed more than a few bites. Once again she thought of music—or was she actually hearing a melody, impossibly faint, infinitely elusive?

"Von Schöppen was not a perfect prophet," said Eleonyra, "but he foresaw the day when a husband and wife might show up here, and he devised a way for them to reach their decision. I shall share his method with you at breakfast tomorrow."

Eleonyra approached the mahogany cabinet, drawing out a squat blue bottle and two glasses. "A special vintage," she said, delivering the wine into Hinrik's hands. "It will help you endure this most difficult of nights."

A steward robo appeared and offered to escort them to their rooms.

"Until tomorrow," Eleonyra said.

"Are you certain there's no pain?" asked Laïra.

"Only for the one left behind," said Eleonyra.

•   •   •

The bedchamber was spacious and luxurious, a marvel of velvet curtains and satin sheets. Laïra and Hinrik undressed and made desperate love on the four-poster bed. Barely a dozen words passed between them. Their thoughts mingled, their skin fused, their separate longings flowed into a single sea of remorse.

Without drawing apart, they opened the wine and drank two glasses each.

Again they made love.

When Hinrik offered Laïra the final measure of wine, she declined. She had no intention of falling asleep. The white door beckoned.

"After marrying you I became the happiest of men," Hinrik said.

To guarantee that her plan would work, she took her pocket chime from her discarded jacket and furtively set the alarm for 0300.

She kissed Hinrik one last time, then carefully inserted the chime into the space between her pillow and its silk case. "I love you," she said, resting her head. The chime's hard brass felt reassuring against her ear.

"My dearest Laïra," Hinrik said, curling his arm around her.

She closed her eyes and waited for the music of nonbeing.

A shaft of sunlight danced across Laïra's face, luring her into wakefulness. She reached out and patted the space beside her. Empty. She slipped her hand under her pillowcase, feeling for the pocket chime. Gone.

Throbbing with fear, she dressed hurriedly and made her way to the dining hall. Eleonyra stood beside the white door.

"Have you seen Hinrik?" Laïra asked breathlessly.

Eleonyra extended her arm, opened her clenched fist. The pocket chime rested on her palm.

"He said to give you this."

For five days and five nights she lay in the bedchamber, mourning her husband, awash in despair and self-reproach. On the sixth day Eleonyra came to her. She wore a saffron robe and smelled like fresh spring flowers.

"Come with me, Ana Laïra Jermina Von Fuchs, Keeper of the Palace of Humanity," said Eleonyra. "We shall lay your Hinrik in the earth beside the pagoda. Take comfort that his body remains intact, never to be compressed. He will not join the ramparts."

By the time the funeral began, Laïra had no more tears. The ceremony was spare and dignified. Like the woman who'd calmed her in the arena, Eleònyra admired Birlem's poetry, and she read Eulogy Twenty-three as the caretaker robos lowered the casket into the grave, shoveled back the dirt, and set a golden vase atop the mound.

As the two women left the pagoda and headed toward the palace, Laïra believed she heard music, a faint but intricate melody, adrift on a slight breeze from the gardens.

"The music," said Laïra. "Where does it come from?"

Eleonyra looked perplexed. "The music?"

"I hear music. Are there nightingales in the trees? Cicadas in the garden?"

"There's no music here," Eleonyra said.

They approached the pylon, passed through the black door, and entered the dining hall.

After lunch, Eleonyra spoke in an urgent voice. "And now I shall take my leave of you."

"Why must I do this task alone?" Laïra asked in a failing voice. "Why did Von Schöppen require the Keeper to become a castaway and an exile?"

"I don't know," said Eleonyra with a shrug. "I sometimes wonder whether he had any reason at all."

Eleonyra started out of the dining hall, then turned and said over her shoulder, "Fifty years in seclusion, surrounded by the dead—it's a wonder I didn't go insane. Maybe the music saved me."

She made no further remarks, but simply disappeared through the black door and out of Laïra's life.

In the days that followed—the days and weeks and months and years—Laïra endured the eternal solitude of the palace, her loneliness relieved only by the whispered melodies floating through the air. She tended the gardens. She wrote poetry. She grieved for Hinrik, visiting his grave every day, often slipping freshly cut flowers into the golden vase.

When the weather was warm, she took extensive walks, seeking the way to Ostreich-Schweiz, but every path led back to the place where she'd started. During these treks she always scanned the trees and studied the fields, hoping to glimpse whatever birds or insects performed the music, but she never saw a single living creature. It occurred to her that the musicians might not inhabit the grounds but instead lived inside the palace—a population of sawing crickets, a colony of sonorous dust mites—and so she took to roaming the passageways and halls in search of the melodious organisms. Even after it became obvious she would never find any such creatures, she continued to seek them out, a meaningless ritual, a theology without a faith.

Each winter she spent her waking hours in the palace's vast but jumbled library, reading Shakespeare and Birlem and cultivating a taste for a dozen other poets. One evening after dinner, while scouring the stacks in search of Birlem's sonnets—her favorite book these days, but to her great distress she'd misshelved it—she happened upon a moldering antique volume, *The Journal of Joachim Von Schöppen*.

She blew off the dust and started on page one. That night she read Von Schöppen's diary cover to cover, straight through first light and well past breakfast. When she was finished, she turned back a dozen pages, found the entry that had transfixed her, and marked it in red ink.

"Today I laid the cornerstone," Von Schöppen had written. "Over the centuries, the souls will accumulate, course upon course of bricks, playing the music of nonbeing. The first year, a silent E-flat. The next year, a mute E-sharp. Then G-flat, G-sharp, B-flat, B-sharp, D-flat, D-sharp, all without voice or breath. As the walls grow, the palace will realize itself as *Verstummte Musik,* each unheard note a life, each unstruck chord a family, each unsung chant a nation."

She closed the volume, but not before setting a silk bookmark beside the cornerstone passage. She remembered the line from the poet Goethe: "Architecture is frozen music."

The morning sun streamed through the library windows. Laïra pulled on a saffron robe, walked through the black door, and headed down the flagstone path. Turning, she scanned the ramparts, brick upon brick, and for an indeterminate interval she listened to the myriad unheard notes, unstruck chords, and unsung chants.

A wind arose, overpowering the performance, drowning out the beautiful themes. Laïra closed her eyes. *"Verstummte Musik."*

For an indeterminate interval the ghostly notes lingered on the edge of her hearing, and then they vanished altogether. Had the walls fallen silent, or had the music never really existed?

And so it was that Ana Laïra Jermina Von Fuchs, Keeper of the Palace of Humanity, found herself lamenting the loss of two great loves: her dear husband, and the tacit symphony of the bricks. Loneliness embraced her with its frigid arms. She stopped preparing meals, cultivating the gardens, washing the curtains, or sweeping the floors, instead requiring the robos to do these jobs. The wrinkles came, though she did not really feel herself growing older. The trips to Hinrik's grave became less frequent—once a week, once a month.

Forgetfulness was her only friend. She could not stop grieving for Hinrik, but in time she ceased to mourn the music, for she could no longer recall the fact that delicate and melancholy themes had once played about her ears.

The ethereal music had never existed. It was nonbeing. The palace walls fell silent—not conspicuously silent but simply and unremarkably silent, in the manner of all walls, like fallen snow, or stone gods, or the vase on Hinrik's grave.

One day during the forty-seventh year of her exile, as Laïra was reading Von Schöppen's diary, a bewildered young man entered the library. He was no more than twenty. He looked a little like Smeet. The old microbiologist's grandson, perhaps? A nephew? It didn't matter.

For a full minute no words passed between Laïra and the boy. She knew why he'd come. With an overwhelming sense of relief, she appointed him the new Keeper and apprised him of his duties. His name was Joachim, "after the great Joachim Von Schöppen," as he proudly put it. He was sad, and intelligent, and Laïra liked him.

The boy asked, suddenly, "Where does the music come from? Insects? Birds?"

"The music?" said Laïra.

"I hear music."

"There's no music here."

"But I hear it."

"There's no music here," Laïra said again, but she showed him Von Schöppen's diary anyway, drawing his attention to the passage she'd marked with red ink.

"*Verstummte Musik*," Joachim whispered.

"*Verstummte Musik*," she echoed, and for an instant a tiny crystal of memory grew in her mind. "Did you come here alone, young Joachim?"

"Yes."

"Good."

The crystal disintegrated, and Laïra smiled softly at Joachim. She asked him to keep putting fresh flowers on Hinrik's grave. The boy agreed. She brushed his cheek, then left the library and started down the corridor. She paused, listening, listening. Nothing reached her ears, and so she turned and entered the dining hall and walked for the last time through the black door.

JOSÉ ANTONIO COTRINA

BETWEEN THE LINES

TRANSLATED FROM THE SPANISH
BY JAMES STEVENS-ARCE

Take an Internet expedition to Bibliópolis, Spain's leading literary agency special-
izing in science fiction, and after a few mouse-clicks you will come upon a photo-
graph of José Antonio Cotrina. Equipped with a wry smile, a Mephistophelian
goatee, and erudite spectacles, he looks exactly like the sort of person who would
have written the following wry, Mephistophelian, and erudite tale.

Cotrina published his first works of fiction at the beginning of the nineties,
then fell silent for over five years. When he again found his word processor, he pro-
duced what the Bibliópolis site describes as "some of the most astonishing stories
of recent Spanish SF and fantasy, a cycle of interlocked tales describing the hid-
den aspects of our world, both technological and magical," including the piece you
are about to enjoy. Eventually Cotrina's project expanded to include his 2003
novel, Las fuentes perdidas *("The Lost Fountains"). That same year he won the*
Domingo Santos short story contest for "La niña muerta" ("The Dead Girl"),
which was subsequently published in the Spanish equivalent of Asimov's. *Among*
his most recent efforts is the young adult novel La casa de la Colina Negra *("The*
House on Black Hill"). "Between the Lines"—"Entre líneas"—was included in
the recent Minotauro anthology of the best Spanish SF stories from the past
twenty years, selected by the renowned editor Julián Díez.

Some critics might label this confection a fantasy rather than science fiction,
and indeed, like a handful of our other choices, "Between the Lines" defies easy
categorization. For some readers the term "Borgesian" will spring to mind, a label
that would place the story adjacent to—but by no means beyond—the pale of SF.

Jorge Luis Borges, it should be remembered, staunchly admired H. G. Wells, introduced the works of Ray Bradbury to Argentinean readers, and first gained an English-speaking audience through the pages of The Magazine of Fantasy & Science Fiction.

Aside from the Borges connection, we would argue that "Between the Lines" further reveals an SF sensibility in its young hero's systematic attempt to look beneath the surface of things. Indeed, we can easily imagine Cotrina's story appearing in an anthology of fiction spun from the "many worlds interpretation" of quantum physics. Rigorous extrapolation this is not, but "Between the Lines" does provide rational exhilaration in abundance.

1

An October sky the color of ashes hung over the campus like a heavy cloak. Alejandro ambled toward the Liberal Arts Building, his knapsack erratically bumping his side, the buckles clicking against the zippers of his anorak. His fellow students looked blurry, as though made of the same stuff as the clouds now crowding the heavens in prelude to a thunderstorm. Alejandro was tall, with short red hair and an alert gaze, and right now he felt at peace, his contentment compromised only by a mild case of Monday morning blues.

The foyer of the Liberal Arts Building was deserted. Alejandro sprinted up the stairs to the second floor and found himself in a labyrinth of corridors and doorways. He pulled the registration form from his pocket and scanned the list of professors, subjects, and office numbers, mentally rehearsing the argument that he hoped would sway each instructor.

"Well, you see, sir," he would say after giving a brief summary of his situation, "I've been offered an entry-level position at an ad agency, a job I can't afford to pass up, but I don't want to abandon my studies. That's why I'd like permission to skip your lectures and study the course materials at home."

Enveloped by a sensation of pure happiness, he moved along the main hallway with a snappy dance step. It felt wrong to be indulging in such euphoria, but he still allowed it to suffuse him.

Rounding a corner, he immediately encountered the office of the first instructor on his list. He knocked lightly and, after a muffled voice invited him in, opened the door.

It took him a moment to recover from his first glimpse of the immense room, which looked less like an office than an antique shop that had endured an earthquake, or a small museum recently ransacked by thieves. Two tables dominated the space, one strewn with gewgaws—a glass ball containing a snow-covered castle, a precarious citadel composed of playing cards, a censer spewing scented smoky question marks, a statuette of Kali carved in ebony—while on the other sat a computer surrounded by plush stuffed animals from a carnival midway, plus an aquarium holding what appeared to be a perpetual-motion device and a solitary starfish. Unshelved books rose in three tall piles near the professor's mahogany desk, a configuration suggesting the masts of a ship run aground on the rug. Tapestries in wild, frantic colors drooped from the ceiling. Viewed individually, their designs seemed erratic, but collectively the tapestries acquired a certain logic and order. Alejandro experienced the dizzying sensation of being trapped inside a kaleidoscope.

If the office did not resemble an office, neither did the man behind the desk resemble a professor. Dressed in a gray silk coat trimmed in lace, he had an unruly mane of blond hair, a gold loop dangling from one earlobe, a sardonic emerald-green eye that squinted beneath a thick brow, and a black leather patch instead of a second eye. He would have looked more at home in a seaport tavern two centuries earlier, spinning yarns for the patrons in a voice made hoarse by hurricanes and saltwater. Perhaps when the night lay heavy with rain and his spirits grew buoyant with rum, the old pirate loved to recount the caravel battle that had left him with an eye socket as black as a moonless night.

The professor gave Alejandro a quick once-over. "Yes?" His voice was soft, precise, and pleasantly modulated; his accent was unplaceable, though Alejandro believed he heard a Nordic tinge.

"Dr. Rebolledo?"

"Sorry to disappoint you," said the one-eyed man, "but I'm not that illustrious teacher."

"Oh, sorry, I must've wandered into your office by mistake." Alejandro retreated uncomfortably toward the door.

"By mistake?" the man exclaimed. "There are no *mistakes,* young man." He indicated that his visitor should sit in the leather armchair beside the desk, an invitation Alejandro chose to ignore. "I'm pleased to in-form you that, in consequence of opening my door, you've signed up for the course I humbly attempt to teach. Congratulations."

Alejandro could not have been more taken aback had the man suggested that he strip naked. "I've signed up for your course?"

"Correct."

"Just because I opened your door?"

"The class is called Advanced Reading Techniques," the professor explained. "An unappetizing title, I grant you. If it were up to me, I'd give the course a new name."

"This is ridiculous."

"Please try to understand." The one-eyed man spread his arms as if he meant to embrace Alejandro. "We inhabit a universe where there's no room for randomness. All things are interconnected. Stick your hand in a fire and, regardless of what charm you may intone, you'll get burned. Dream of flight each night, a thousand nights in a row, and you'll be able to take wing for a whole day. Open my door, and you enroll in my course. Cause and effect, that's the way of the world. Mistakes don't exist. Coincidence is a fiction." As if to illustrate his point, he pounded his fist on the desk, causing a goose quill to jump free of its inkstand.

Alejandro held up the registration form as if it could shield him from the man's dementia. Dream a thousand nights that he could fly? "This is my last year as an advertising major, and I'm already taking a full roster of courses."

"But you haven't nailed down your electives," the professor asserted, crooking an eyebrow.

"Well, no . . ." There'd been a minor computer glitch in the registrar's office, and Alejandro's two electives were still up in the air. But how did the professor know that? "Listen, if this is a joke, please explain it to me, so we can both have a good laugh."

"I enjoy jokes, too, but this is a serious matter. If you'll give me your name, we can complete the registration process."

The man picked up the goose quill and waved it through the air as he might a magic wand. Alejandro shook his head, hoping to clear his mind, but the chaotic office and the man's demeanor continued to baffle him.

"Look, Professor Whatever-Your-Name-Is, let's be logical. It's true that I haven't settled on my electives." Alejandro edged toward the door, determined to keep talking until he'd escaped this lunatic's domain. "But I'm afraid that Advanced Reading Techniques isn't my thing. I would never enroll in a course that doesn't interest me."

Fingers interlocked, elbows on the desk, the instructor stared at him with a half-curious, half-amused expression.

"I don't want to bother you any further," Alejandro said, "and so I'll say good-bye."

He shut the door behind him and scanned his registration form. Releasing a sigh, he set off through the maze of corridors, determined to forget the whole incident as he resumed the hunt for his real professors.

2

Time, as it tends to do, passed.

Alejandro, the happy red-haired young man, continued living a life filled with major successes and trivial setbacks. He'd aced his fall-term courses, including the two electives, and the second semester had begun auspiciously. He loved his job writing copy for a fledgling but ambitious advertising agency. Best of all, there was Laura, the lovely medical student who shared his bed as well as the rent. Everything was perfect in his small shiny world.

That was why, when he reached his apartment—it was a warm afternoon on a day that spring had spent carting away the corpse of winter—and Laura handed him a letter from the university, a premonition bubbled up in his belly. With trembling fingers he tore open the envelope. He had to read the letter three times to make sense of it, at last connecting the words to the previous semester's conversation with the one-eyed eccentric.

3

Locating the professor's office proved difficult, but once Alejandro found it, he breezed through the doorway without bothering to knock.

"What's the meaning of this?" he demanded, shaking the letter and feeling not a little shaken himself by a sensation of déjà vu.

"How wonderful—you came to see me!" It seemed that the one-eyed man hadn't gone anywhere since their last meeting. Even his posture was the same, though five o'clock shadow now darkened his jaw. "Or did you open the wrong door again?" he added in a mildly sarcastic tone.

"This time I'm here on purpose."

"Last time you were here on purpose, too, but you didn't know it."

"Please explain," Alejandro said, thrusting the letter in the professor's face.

"What's to explain? Your grade for last term is 'incomplete.' You never came to class, and you didn't turn in any assignments."

"But I wasn't enrolled!" Alejandro protested, his icy eyes narrowing. "I never signed up for"—he scanned the letter, having forgotten the course title in his distress—"Advanced Reading Techniques. There's been some bureaucratic snafu."

"No, you signed up."

"I didn't!"

"You certainly did—when you opened my door, remember?"

"I opened it by mistake."

"You're awfully fond of that word, 'mistake.' " The man smiled, a gesture that Alejandro found oddly soothing. "I have already told you the way things work. Randomness is not part of our reality."

A weariness overcame Alejandro, draining his desire to argue. He'd arrived intending to wax indignant, act enraged, but something about this strange instructor had lessened his annoyance, an air of befuddlement that invited conversation rather than quarrelling.

"Let's just talk it over, all right?" Alejandro sat down uninvited in the leather armchair. He leaned forward, propped his elbows up on the professor's desk, and meshed his fingers. If he behaved like what he was, an entry-level ad man, a mature adult, everything would work out. "I'm sure we can clear up this misunderstanding. Two reasonable individuals having a rational conversation."

The professor swirled his hand around, inviting Alejandro to speak. "Go ahead, be rational," he said, smiling. "I'm listening."

"Fact one: I never signed up for your course."

"No. Wrong. I can't change that."

"Ah, so you're going to be difficult." Alejandro leaned back in the armchair. He would have to try a different tactic: go around the flank, execute a feint, strike where the man least expected it. "You're saying I enrolled in Advanced Reading Techniques simply by opening a door . . ."

"Now you've got it." The man's smile grew wider.

"But doesn't that seem absurd to you?" Alejandro smiled broadly, too, his pique having turned to amusement. "Is your course so unpopular you have to trick students into registering?"

"To tell the truth, things haven't been so great this year. In fact, you're my only student."

"Your only student?" Alejandro said, gape-mouthed. The situation was devolving from the absurd to the surreal.

"I've had worse years. And better ones. You appear bewildered."

Alejandro saw no reason to deny it. "Quite bewildered." It looked as if he might be here awhile, so he crossed his legs and unzipped his anorak. Much to his dismay, the professor had started to intrigue him. "Your only student . . ."

"The one-on-one tutorial is a venerable academic institution."

"Know something, sir?" Again Alejandro mimicked the professor's smile. "I'm dying to find out what the devil your course is all about."

4

He left his car in the garage and rode the elevator to the apartment, the afternoon's events percolating through his brain. For twenty intense minutes Herman Müller (as the professor with the eyepatch and the pirate earring had finally introduced himself) had expounded upon Advanced Reading Techniques. From what Alejandro had understood, it was a fundamentally practical course, wholly divorced from esoteric literary theory.

He entered the apartment with a song on his lips.

"Back already, darling?" Laura called from the kitchen.

"It's not Alejandro!" He drew a black umbrella from the stand and, as if wielding a saber with a two-handed grip, hacked at the air. "I am the notorious bumbershootist! Submit to my whims or die!"

"Leave the umbrella where it belongs," Laura insisted, though she couldn't see him.

He meekly obeyed, then joined her in the kitchen.

"Did you straighten out that misunderstanding at the university?" Laura asked.

She crossed the kitchen carrying a stew pot, her straw-colored braid slung over her shoulder, and set it on the stove. He approached her from behind, wrapping his arms around her waist and nuzzling the nape of her neck. Her braid tickled his nose. Laura stood as tall as he, and her smile was as ready as it was sincere.

"Problem solved," he announced. "I signed up for Advanced Reading Techniques. What's cooking?"

She bumped him away with her buttocks and turned around, surprised.

"You signed up for *what?*"

"Advanced Reading Techniques. In fact I was already registered." He lifted the lid from the pot and sniffed. "What's this stuff?"

"But you didn't *want* to take that course." She eyed him suspiciously. "You told me it was a mistake."

"It was. But now it isn't. For once I've acted impulsively. God, I scare myself." He pretended to shiver. "The syllabus actually sounds exciting. It all comes down to a kind of deep immersion in texts—reading between the lines, Professor Müller calls it."

"You mean hermeneutics? Deconstruction? Semiotics?"

"I used those words, too. Müller laughed and assured me this has nothing to do with linguistics or literary theory."

"But can you really handle another course? Might I remind you that a day still contains only twenty-four hours?"

"This is the first text I'm supposed to read." From his inside pocket Alejandro retrieved the book Professor Müller had lent him. "He gave me a month. Think I can manage it?"

Laura examined the volume with a stunned expression. "*This* is your assignment? You're supposed to read *this* for a college-level course?"

The book in question was a beat-up, pocket-sized edition of Saint-Exupéry's *The Little Prince*.

"It's got pictures," Alejandro pointed out with a grin. "By the author."

5

Although he often carried a book with him, Alejandro didn't really consider himself a reader. He read slowly, a few pages a day before bedtime, more out of habit than commitment. But he consumed Saint-Exupéry's tale in a single night. He'd enjoyed *The Little Prince* as a child, but now he found it even more marvelous. For some strange reason (perhaps because of his mood, which was soaring so high it seemed to inhabit the clouds) the story enchanted him from beginning to end.

In the days that followed, Alejandro reread *The Little Prince,* then looked into the life and times of Antoine de Saint-Exupéry—that terrible era during which the author had flown his World War II missions until he found death (or death found him) on a reconnaissance flight. His research complete, Alejandro read *The Little Prince* twice more, jotting down his reactions in a journal, periodically pausing to seek out connotations, always striving to peel away the seemingly unsophisticated surface and penetrate the deeper meaning of the text.

At the end of the month, he eagerly returned to the Liberal Arts Building and knocked on Herman Müller's door.

As Alejandro entered the office, the professor offered him a friendly wave and invited him to take a seat. The older man exuded vitality and good humor. He locked his single emerald eye on Alejandro and asked, "Well, my esteemed student, have you made any headway?"

"I don't know. I've read *The Little Prince* several times, and I've outlined my observations."

"What are you talking about?" said Müller, obviously perplexed.

"I'm talking about an outline."

"An outline . . . ," the professor muttered, sounding discouraged.

"I brought my notes with me." With a resolute air, Alejandro pulled out his journal.

Much to his student's astonishment, Müller gripped the journal between thumb and forefinger, as though the thing nauseated him, and carefully deposited it in the green metal wastebasket behind his desk.

"Were you truly paying attention when I presented the principles that underlie Advanced Reading Techniques?" Müller asked, furrowing his brow.

"Pardon?"

"Were you listening, or merely hearing?"

Alejandro threw up his hands. "I read the book and analyzed it as best I could." Distressing questions crept into his mind. Might this course bring turmoil into his life? Had a dark cloud appeared on the horizon of his happiness?

"Maybe I explained the principles badly." Müller scratched his thick mane thoughtfully. Alejandro sat paralyzed in the armchair. "But now you must try again," the professor continued. "When I told you to read the book between the lines, that is precisely what I meant."

"Between the lines?"

"Between the lines, exactly. You're perfectly capable of mastering the technique without further instruction from me."

"But you haven't given me *any* instruction!"

Müller gestured toward the door. He looked crestfallen. Weariness and gravity dragged his shoulders downward. "See me again when you think the time is right, and don't worry if things go badly. The failing grade won't appear on your transcript, and ultimately we can dismiss this whole business as—to use your word—a mistake. My mistake, not yours." The professor shooed Alejandro away. "I sincerely hope we'll meet again, but if that never happens, may you enjoy a long, full, happy life."

6

Although the threat of an F on his transcript was gone, Alejandro resolved to master Advanced Reading Techniques. Back at the apartment,
he picked up *The Little Prince* again and sat down at the kitchen table.
Laura wasn't home. She was doubtless at the library, studying.

For the umpteenth time, he attempted to fathom exactly what Antoine de Saint-Exupéry had wanted to communicate.

When I was six years old, I saw a magnificent illustration in a book.

How should he read this book—or any book? Listening to Müller that
afternoon, he'd briefly entertained an absurd thought, then discarded it.
He focused intently on the text, searching for hidden meanings in the
statements (*Boas swallow their prey whole*), trying to extract wisdom from
the paradoxes (*My drawing does not represent a hat*), asking himself if he
should read the book in the original French, though without knowing
why such a notion should occur to him.

And then it happened. Just as he was about to turn the page, Alejandro experienced the phenomenon. Read between the lines, Müller had
said—ignore the printed words, those blobs of black on white careening
left to right, bearing their burden of significance; instead read white on
black, enter the void and fill it with notions, concepts, feelings.

Yes. No question. Between the lines of *The Little Prince* lay a different
array of words, sentences that didn't actually sit on the page but flowed
directly into Alejandro's stunned brain from some unknown source, as if
the book were determined to tell a different story than the one inherent
in its ink.

Between the opening lines of *The Little Prince* he read: *The two men
hurried across the flaming hill. One moaned, and the other could not stop crying.*

He swallowed. The two sentences had nothing to do with Saint-
Exupéry's story.

He closed the book and set it on the table. Methodically he contemplated the typography on the cover, reading between the lines until he
discerned the title of the book that lay nested within the original: *The
Tears of Padua*. Frightened, he rose from his chair. The interpolated novel
was real. He hadn't imagined it, any more than he'd imagined Saint-
Exupéry's original palimpsest. Alejandro had found words within the
words and a story within the story.

Advanced Reading Techniques. How far could these principles be
pursued? He approached the bookcase, which also held his TV set and

video player, and, extending a trembling hand, selected a volume at random: *The Aspect of a Crime* by Juan Benet. He opened it, again at random, and where the text read, *The doctor watched him, holding a sugar cube with the tongs,* he also apprehended, *Later, perhaps, he will ask himself whether it had been he or she who had initiated the kiss.* He kept testing his newfound ability, pulling more books from their shelves and reading what they concealed. Each book sheltered another book, an unseen text waiting to be appreciated.

Alejandro felt as if his legs would no longer support him, and he sat down—or, rather collapsed—on the rug, *Romeo and Juliet* and *Arctic Images* clasped in one and the same hand.

7

He decided against sharing his strange discovery with Laura—not until he could talk about it without sounding deranged. Advanced Reading Techniques distressed him, roiling his stomach like a tickle or an unwanted caress.

Beneath the bedsheets that night, Laura's hands tugged playfully at the waistband of his pajama bottoms. He made no response to her overture, and, surprised at his coolness, she turned on the nightstand lamp and eyed him wordlessly for a long while before whispering, "What's wrong?"

"I don't know." He shook his head, a harsh knot in his throat, moisture gathering in his eyes. He wasn't feeling depression or grief but something he couldn't name, an emotion he'd never experienced before. "A sudden bout of sadness," he lied. "I can't say where it came from, but don't worry—it'll go away."

"You want to cuddle?"

"Okay," he said without enthusiasm.

No, it wasn't sadness that had gripped his soul—but beyond that unnamable emotion lay a wholly familiar feeling, fear. An insidious anxiety had wormed its way into every pore of his skin. In the safe rational world he inhabited, there was no place for mysteries, just as in his meticulously planned routines there was no room for earthquakes or hurricanes. But now he was tangled in a network of secrets, gossamer menaces, velvet threats, arcana cached away in corners, ready to spring forth and drive him insane.

He gulped loudly. His body, paying no attention to his brain, responded to Laura's caresses, kisses, and gentle licks. He decided to focus on those instead.

8

He awoke feeling much better. Laura had fled the bedsheets for her office, and the troublesome ghosts were gone, too, dispersed by the morning light.

After breakfast he got out his typewriter, which until now had languished inside the closet, exiled there by his multimedia computer. Still in his pajamas, he set the typewriter on the dining-room table, rolled a sheet of computer paper against the platen, and made ready to confirm a theory that had entered his brain as he'd slipped into sleep the night before.

First he plucked a volume at random from the bookcase, *A Confederacy of Dunces* by John Kennedy Toole. Next he read, between the lines, the title of the book hidden inside it, *The Sun Also Rises*. He turned to the first chapter and read the opening paragraph of the novel that lay nested within the adventures and misadventures of Ignatius Reilly. He transcribed the phantom text, *The sun shining overhead had not always been the same sun, nor had the sky and space between us been the same sky and the same space,* typing slowly, trying to avoid mistakes. The instant he was finished, he tore the paper from the platen and, crossing his eyes slightly, scrutinized the words.

Between the lines he read, *The stillness enveloping him was, perhaps, a prelude to what was about to occur.*

He typed out the sentence on a fresh sheet. Hardly breathing, he removed the paper and contemplated it. The line he'd unearthed harbored within its lexical womb yet another opening sentence.

Mother died today.

Books within books within books within . . .

9

From behind his mahogany desk Herman Müller studied Alejandro with a pleased expression, smiling avuncularly as his student reported on his experiment in a high, strained voice. When at last Alejandro finished, he regarded the professor with entreating eyes.

"Don't worry, you're not losing your mind," Müller said. "You're acquiring a new kind of sanity."

"I was perfectly happy with the sanity I had. I wish you'd asked me if I wanted to change my worldview."

"Do you really find my class so exasperating?" the professor asked, cocking one eyebrow in his customary manner.

Alejandro wriggled in the leather armchair, scouring his brain for the most lucid words. "All the logical principles I've relied on since reaching the age of reason suddenly seem nonsensical. I feel like I've been living on a theater stage without knowing it, and now chunks of scenery are falling away and hitting me on the head."

"No, that's wrong—nothing has been hidden from you," Müller insisted in his mild Nordic accent. "But until recently you lacked the ability to see clearly. For the immediate future you'll feel terribly disoriented—a syndrome not unlike the altitude sickness that strikes mountain climbers. You must acclimatize yourself, and you must do so gradually." The professor curled his lip in a knowing smile. He leaned toward Alejandro, resting his palms flat on the desk. "You're already experiencing the syndrome, aren't you?"

Alejandro nodded and said, "What really scares me is the thought that it might never go away."

For the next half hour Alejandro pumped Müller for more information about his illness—its symptoms, progress, treatment, prognosis—but the professor had nothing more to say on the subject.

"It's not time yet for you to try grasping the whole system," he said, wigwagging an admonitory forefinger in his student's face. "We must proceed slowly, so you don't get lost. Continue exploring on your own. You're already headed in the right direction."

After arranging an appointment for fifteen days hence to evaluate Alejandro's condition, the professor sent him on his way.

10

Time, as it tends to do, passed. Each new day brought its own small but disturbing surprises. Alejandro told no one about his illness and lived his life as deliberately as he could. His world had received a shock sufficient to alter its orbit, and he focused on his job lest he lose his mind. He brought three new accounts to the ad agency, but he took no pleasure in closing the deals. He functioned well, but a small, unruly, independent part of his brain was always dwelling on Advanced Reading Techniques.

Before Laura's astonished eyes, he devoured dozens of books. She couldn't understand his sudden, voracious desire to read. While the interpolations were usually nothing to get excited about, occasionally he came upon a text far superior to its host. In the case of *The Dawn,* which lay nested within Dostoyevsky's *White Nights,* he couldn't stop crying.

He conducted further experiments, all of which convinced him that the phenomenon was uncanny in the extreme. In the campus library he located an English-language edition of *Romeo and Juliet.* Reading between the lines, he came upon the same concealed book, *Arctic Images,* that he'd discovered at home—only now it was in English.

When he tried to read between the lines of the letter warning him about his absences from Herman Müller's class, no secondary message appeared—a circumstance that somehow seemed less perplexing when he realized that the author of the missive was not a university administrator but Müller himself. He next applied his skill to various gas and electricity bills lying around the apartment, bringing to light only meaningless strings of numbers.

One afternoon he began to freewrite, wondering what might emerge between such impromptu lines. What he found were intriguing but ultimately incoherent sentences crafted in his own hand. Who had woven these words into his spontaneous scribblings? Who wrote the books that lived within other books?

"Who dreams the dreamer?" he mumbled as, sitting at the kitchen table, he read over the advertising copy he'd just finished composing.

"Did you say something?" Laura looked up from a medical textbook.

"No." He heaved a sigh and, without thinking, formulated a question he'd never imagined he would ask her. "Do you love me?"

"What's this about? You know I do. What's going on? Sadness again?"

"Altitude sickness."

"What?"

"Existential panic."

"I don't understand."

He studied the kitchen ceiling for a moment, then focused on his cat food pitch.

As thou journeyest toward Avalon at gaunt dawn, he read between the lines, *three things needest thou remember: whither do thy footsteps bear thee, how distant lieth the echo, and what color and substance of path dost thou walk? Only in this fashion shalt thou pierce the fog and enter the secret kingdom.*

11

Did you get soap in your eyes?" Laura asked on the morning he was scheduled to meet with Müller for his evaluation.

Alejandro stepped out of the shower and took the towel she offered. "No. Why would you think that?"

"They look irritated."

Toweling himself dry, Alejandro approached the medicine-cabinet mirror. He peered deeply into the glass, using his index finger to pull down the lower lid of each eye in turn.

"It's just your imagination, kiddo."

"I guess."

Dark lines encircled his pupils. Though only a fraction of a millimeter thick, each contour was as vivid as the corona surrounding the sun during a lunar eclipse.

12

As Alejandro entered the Liberal Arts Building, he realized that nothing remained of his former bliss, the feeling that his life was wonderful and could only get better. But he no longer required such banal happiness. Turmoil, he now believed, was the optimal condition of the soul. The human heart hardened no less from joy than from misery. He'd skidded free of reality, followed a twisted tangent, and slammed into a glass door beyond which lay a fantastic and mysterious domain, a world whose wonders never ceased to multiply.

Approaching Müller's office, he encountered what he was half-expecting: a tiled wall where the door should have stood. He edged a few steps to the left, then sidled to the right, quickly concluding that the wall held no run-of-the-mill camouflaged entrance. He laughed. If this was the test, he would have no trouble passing. In recent weeks he'd learned to read between the lines of people, animals, plants, and inert objects.

He narrowed his eyes and traced the tile pattern with a fingertip, gradually apprehending the hidden door. Reaching for the knob, which he discerned only with effort, he gripped it firmly and rotated his wrist.

Müller did not look up, but greeted Alejandro with a terse, "You're late," then gestured for him to sit. Alejandro settled into his customary armchair and fixed on the dust jacket of the book Müller was reading, *The Citadel of Paradox*. He scrutinized the words of the title, trying to read between the lines, but could not manage it from this awkward vantage.

13

Herman Müller closed his book. "When did you catch on?"

"To the fact that I can read between the lines of anything?" Alejandro sighed as he recalled his recent trauma in the kitchen. "The other day I studied Laura. It was very confusing. There were no words, only shades of colors and, well, feelings, and I understood that she doesn't really love me. She simply values the security I represent. I wanted to read her more deeply, but I didn't know how."

"At your level of competence, a person can sense only the strongest emotions," Müller said. "Don't feel bad about your discovery. Learn a lesson from it: never read the people you care about, especially as your skills improve. Let their souls remain opaque." The professor stroked the cover of *The Citadel of Paradox*. "It's quite probable that in her heart Laura loves you," he continued, fixing Alejandro with his emerald eye. "But she may resent the role you've selected for her: the lovely adjunct to your perfect life."

Although he'd never heard it put into words before, Alejandro could not deny that Müller had caught the essence of his attitude toward Laura. Hearing the truth expressed so incisively made him wince. The professor had read between his lines.

"Something troubles me. When I came into your office last October looking for Dr. Rebolledo, the door was just like it is now, right? Beyond human perception."

"True."

"Then how did I see it?"

Müller shrugged. "You simply did, that's all."

It seemed that time was decelerating, the flow of events growing lethargic, so that every second elapsed in two and every minute took twice that long. Alejandro's mind grew clearer even as his ideas became more complex. Some outside stimulus was prodding his brain in new directions, increasing the octane level of the fuel that fed his thoughts. He remembered the dark rings encircling his eyes, and, before he could phrase his next question, Müller answered it without saying a word.

The professor gently worked two fingers into the socket of his emerald eye, carefully extracted the glass orb, and set it on the desk. He untied his eye patch, relocating it over the actual empty socket. The organ that had lurked behind the patch now lay exposed in the weak amber light of the professor's floor lamp.

An eye lacking pupil and iris, an eye as black as pitch.

14

How many of us are there?"

"More than you might imagine, a whole society of adepts. Only a few have your particular gift for reading between the lines. Instead they've developed other talents, other powers."

"Other magicks?"

"Other magicks and other sciences. Forbidden tools and forgotten tongues."

"Will I be able to recognize my fellows?"

"Now that you know what to look for—of course."

15

Their conversation continued amid the temporal sludge now seeping through the room. Müller told Alejandro that the more sharply he honed his gift, the blacker his eyes would become.

"It's the price we pay for seeing beyond surfaces," the professor said. "Sooner or later the others will approach you, unless you decide to conceal your identity, as I did."

For the next fifty minutes Müller elaborated on what he'd termed "forbidden tools and forgotten tongues," thus in effect delivering the final lecture of the course. At the end of the class he unfurled a map of contemporary Europe and invited his student to read it. Alejandro narrowed his eyes to twin shining slits, and between the lines obscure features appeared, new contours, unknown longitudes, nonlinear latitudes. The map disclosed secret cities with beautiful and exotic names. He discovered hidden mountains, veiled valleys, lost rivers. To the west of England lay an entire continent called Avalon. These revelations sparked no awe in Alejandro, only ancient memories and subtle recollections. In vanished dreams he had scaled these mountains, walked these valleys, swum these rivers.

"Who are you?" he asked, staring at the professor and trying to read him, only to realize that Müller could easily conjure a shield against such scrutiny.

"Me? I'm just a fellow who, for better or worse, tries to do his job. I was a regular guy, pretty bland really, until one day—longer ago than I care to recall—like you, I knocked on the wrong door."

16

Lost in thought, Alejandro wandered the streets. He had no desire to return home and bid good-bye to Laura, but soon he would have to do just that. Having passed through the wrong door, he felt compelled to keep on going. As he moved through the city, every object that met his gaze seemed unique, inchoate, newly born. Between the lines of a sign outside a health food store, he read: DREAM MARKET. He peered through the display window, locking his eyes on the delicate, parchment-skinned face of an old woman as she raised a hand in greeting. He returned her wave without hesitation. The two of them were comrades, fellow inhabitants of a marvelous metropolis, citizens of a riddle.

When night fell, brilliant and majestic, he gazed upward at nascent suns shining among ancient stars. Slack-jawed, frozen like a statue, he admired the Earth's radiant second moon as it cleaved to its hidden orbit beyond the borders of the real.

Hands in his pockets and heart bursting with delight, Alejandro headed for his apartment. Farewells were something he'd never enjoyed, but this time the bitter taste would be sweetened by the nectar of expectation. A new life lay before him, an entire universe, waiting to be charted and cherished. He reveled in the splendor of the speckled sky, his first night ever beneath the twin moons, and suddenly a shooting star traced an impossible parabola across the heavens.

Not one reality, not one plane: instead, myriad texts.

Worlds within worlds within worlds within . . .

BERNHARD RIBBECK

A BLUE AND CLOUDLESS SKY

TRANSLATED FROM THE DANISH
BY NIELS DALGAARD

Writing in The Encyclopedia of Science Fiction, *Niels Dalgaard—our present translator—records that Danish SF begins with Ludvig Holberg's 1741 novel* Nicolai Klimii iter Subterraneum, *composed in Latin and rendered into English the following year as* A Journey into the World Underground *by Nicholas Klimius. Nearly a quarter century before Jules Verne's account of Otto Liddenbrock's subterranean trek, Holberg imagined a hollow earth yielding its secrets to human curiosity.*

The next notable SF work from Denmark was the play Anno 7603, *a gender-reversal satire penned in 1785 by Johann Hermann Wessel. Three generations later the imposing figure of Hans Christian Andersen appeared on the scene. We don't normally think of Andersen as a science fiction writer, but in fact he wrote several genre pieces, most conspicuously his 1853 tale "Om Aartusinder," usually translated as "In a Thousand Years." Not until the fifties did Danish SF crystallize into a literary phenomenon. The paterfamilias of the movement was Niels E. Nielsen, a prolific author who originally wrote works derivative of Ray Bradbury but eventually found his own voice and themes, publishing one of the first SF novels to deal with genetic engineering,* Herskerne *("The Rulers," 1970).*

"Bernhard Ribbeck" is the nom de plume of Palle Juul Holm. Born in 1931, Holm spent his professional years teaching Danish, German, and psychology at the secondary school level. For over a decade he collaborated with the artist Frank Tomozy on a creative endeavor known as Ribbecks rejser *("Ribbeck's Travels").*

This intriguing project found Ribbeck composing short pieces about his imaginary journeys through time and space, while Tomozy fashioned the artifacts the author had supposedly brought back with him. Beyond his fiction, Holm has written book reviews and art criticism, as well as lyrics for the now defunct rock group The Live Museum. His major published work to date is his collection, Isen mellem øerne ("The Ice Between the Islands"), which appeared in 1999.

No imaginable introduction to "A Blue and Cloudless Sky" could speak for this story as well as does the text itself, a tour de force time-travel tale that manages to be at once rigorously plotted and emotionally resonant—a perfect finish, in our view, to an anthology that we hope has provided its readers with both food for thought and dessert for delectation. Instead of attempting to articulate the story's accomplishments, we shall simply append "Walking Song" by the Japanese poet Tarô Yamamoto, a work that Holm feels may help the reader understand some of the symbols in "A Blue and Cloudless Sky."

> *The two children*
> *hanging on my hands*
> *look up and say "Daddy"*
>
> *I too look up*
> *I too would like to call out someone's name*
> *but there's no one there*
>
> *In my sky, in splendid emptiness*
> *There are only clouds windswept*
> *that have changed into birds*
>
> *Isn't that wonderful?*
>
> *Inside that emptiness*
> *your Mummy burnt once like a candle-flame*
> *trembling*
> *and waited for me*
>
> *Some day you too will have an empty sky*
>
> *When you do*
> *you'll be standing alone*
> *and walking on sure legs*
>
> *You'll have to search for your own candle-flame*
>
> *Hey! Don't hang on like that!*

Look up again
Now Daddy's face is not there

Don't let yourselves be taken in
The thing you see that's floating there
is only a cloud dying out

1

What do we know, what do we really know about anything? I wonder and stare at Fausto, who's driving the tractor-trailer west through the cold of early evening, first across the lush farmland, then over a dry vacant plateau, and finally up through the mountain passes along the border.

"Do *you* believe this is the end of Nakorza, the end of us all?" he asks.

What can I say? That maybe it is, but not just yet? That I at least shall escape and make it back to Earth? Because if I don't, there never will have been a Fausto Caiazzo, or any other member of his species, on Nakorza.

There will only have been the aborigines.

We're climbing rapidly, following one hairpin turn after another. Behind the mountain peaks hang clouds the color of bruises, and on the straight stretches Fausto drives as if he doesn't care whether the end comes now or in six months.

We take a sharp curve where dark grimy ice lies like charred food in the bottom of a pan, and the whole truck skids. Fausto straightens us out, but the trailer swings from side to side; I cringe and hold my breath, then look down the ravine at the river with its frozen banks, and wonder what will happen if we go over the edge and crash.

Will everything disappear?

Yes, I suppose it will.

And I ask myself: Might that be for the best?

"I don't know," I tell Fausto. "Maybe this is the end—at least the end of what we know." The shocking idea makes my voice sound thin and ethereal.

"Shit," Fausto mutters harshly. I smell his adrenaline-laced sweat, along with the cab's permanent stench of motor oil and tobacco, joined now by the fine bitter fragrance of winter air blowing through the crack in my window.

There's really not much I can say to Fausto's despair, so I keep my eyes on the mountains, and when at last he breaks the silence, his voice is softer, almost apologetic. He tells me he's not out to kill us, but we're running late and liable to get stuck in the pass if it begins to snow, and he won't feel safe until we're in Powyrnisch.

"Yes," I say, nothing more. I wish I could be better company, but I'm in no mood to talk, and I don't want to distract him from his driving.

Fausto coughs. "It's damn cold for Easter week," he observes. "And Easter isn't even early this year."

"The coldest Easter ever," I say, hoping the conversation will end there.

"A frozen Easter, that's wrong," Fausto says and sticks a cigarette in his mouth. I light it for him. "Is there a connection, I wonder?"

"It's probably a coincidence. But I'm no expert. They say everything's connected in some way. Or it's the will of God. Or something."

We approach a steep rise. Fausto shifts into first gear, and the truck crawls slowly upward; in some places the wheels spin on the ice ridges, taking us nowhere, and the whole rig threatens to slide down the mountain. My chest tightens.

"Know what I think?" Fausto asks.

I realize he's talking to stay awake, so I decide to sound interested. "No, what do you think?"

Nakorza's sun, let's call it the sun, has disappeared behind the peaks, and a mass of snow-laden clouds has reached this side of the border. Fausto switches on the high beams.

"I think he must be here on Nakorza right now, in some village or other, close at hand, but nobody knows who he is," he says. "They say that all of us are here—not the Piouli, of course, but everybody else—we're here because of him, the space traveler. We all came to Nakorza from another part of the galaxy."

Fausto signals that he'd like some broth. Removing the cup from its holder, I push it into the zarf, then fill it from the thermos, clumsily, fearfully. I try to draw solace from the melancholy glow of the dashboard as it illuminates the cab.

"Not only are we from somewhere out there in space," Fausto continues, taking a sip of the scalding soup, "we're from some distant point in the future, too. What's a person to believe?"

(Well, what *is* a person to believe?)

Obviously he wants to pursue this idea. He can't imagine how often I've run the story through my mind, but it's best to let him ramble on. So I sit and listen as Fausto tells how, once upon a time, a wanderer from the world of our origins came to Nakorza in a capsule. Somehow he made it back to his own world, where he told the sages about Nakorza. Several centuries later—in a future that still lies ahead for Fausto and myself and everyone else—the sages' descendants learned to move effortlessly across the barriers of distance and circumstance, and so they launched hundreds of ships to Nakorza, each filled with a band of colonists: our ancestors.

"Our ancestors . . . who aren't yet born." Fausto takes a final swallow of soup, frees it from the zarf, and replaces the cup in the holder.

Not yet born. Because the sages didn't simply send the colonists through space—they also sent them back in time, far back, to a moment that existed 350 years before the space traveler returned to his native planet. Why did the sages feel compelled to do that? The records aren't clear, but their decision was evidently connected to the traveler's accounts of the lifeforms he'd found on the faraway planet: he'd discovered the Piouli, of course, and also . . . us.

"It all depended on the woman—the Nakorzan who the traveler brought back to his home world," Fausto says. "She was the one who knew Nakorza's coordinates. She was the one who enabled the colonists to find the planet again."

"Or for the first time, if you will."

"Or for the first time," Fausto echoes.

Huge snowflakes sift down through the glare from our high beams. The cold begins to penetrate the cab.

"We don't even know the traveler's name," Fausto says. "Apparently the sages had their reasons for keeping it secret."

"In hundreds of years from now they *will* have their reasons," I correct him.

"But we know the woman's name," Fausto says irritably. "Maria."

(Where is Maria?)

I can hear Fausto breathing deeply and calmly. "If you read the old books," he says, "you'll see that the world our traveler described in such detail is the very world that Nakorza has become. That's why I think the moment of our discovery is at hand—that's why I think he walks among us now. But nobody can identify him, and nobody ever will, except for Maria. He could be anybody. He could be me. Or you."

(Yes.)

"Something puzzles me," Fausto continues. "When the traveler returned home, why didn't he tell the sages about the Crown of Stars? He must've seen it. Or if he told them, why would the sages' descendants send the colonists here? How could they do such a thing, knowing that not only Nakorza but this entire sector of the galaxy would eventually be annihilated? Something doesn't fit."

He shakes his head in sadness and confusion. And he's right. Something doesn't fit.

It's snowing heavily now, and I'm relieved to see that the next part of the pass runs through a tunnel. We enter the frigid darkness; the road is clear, and we feel happy knowing that, for a few minutes at least, we'll be protected from avalanches and drifts, and we won't have to worry about tumbling over the cliff.

The lamps in the tunnel ceiling are all broken. "When you see this kind of crap," Fausto says, "it's hard to believe our forefathers were able to leap through space and time."

We emerge into a nightmare: a towering wall of blinding snow, plus a fierce wind that makes the trailer sway and almost forces us off the road. Ten kilometers beyond the tunnel, a white sign looms out of the blizzard— it bears the symbol of the region, two black crossed arrows—and Fausto almost crashes into it. ST. FANURIUS, the sign informs the wayfarer in Gothic type. KREIS STEFANOPEL/STEPANOPOL. GLIEDSTAAT NEU-RUTHENIEN. 2410 M.Ü. MEERESHÖHE.

The official language of New Ruthenia is German, though most of the inhabitants, at least on this side of the Kolpa River and south of the lower Brenda, are an undefined mixture of Eastern Europeans and people from the Balkans, speaking their own amalgamated tongue.

"Look out, dammit!" I cry as we rush past the sign, missing it by centimeters.

Fausto stops the truck, shifts into neutral, and turns toward me, veins bulging at his temples. "Shut the fuck up, Gerold," he bellows, "or you'll *walk* to Powyrnisch!" He slams a fist into the dashboard, sending the

Holy Virgin jumping, then grinds into first again and starts to bring us slowly into the river valley.

On this side of the mountain we're a good distance from the cliff, but it's still a treacherous drive, the road twisting madly, the horrifying storm roaring all around us. The hairpin turns are almost impossible to see, the gusts make it difficult to negotiate the curves, and I don't like to think what will happen if a snowplow appears in our path.

We say nothing. Sitting with eyes half closed, I try to concentrate on something besides our terrifying descent. I think of Saint Fanurius, the patron of all those who seek something they've lost (does one need any other saint?), and of the unseasonable cold. Maybe Fausto is right. Maybe there's a connection between this frigid weather and the Crown of Stars. Could the Crown have pulled Nakorza into a different orbit?

Back in San Silvestro they probably know the answer. And I hope they have the sense to keep it to themselves.

As we drop below the timberline, I'm able to open my eyes and un-clench my sweaty fists; the saliva returns to my mouth, and I stop breath-ing in gasps.

The broad trees catch the brunt of the storm, the straight stretches are longer now, and the snow lies in a smooth pure layer on the road. Fausto relaxes, lifts a hand from the wheel, and manages to retrieve a fresh cigarette and light it by himself.

"*Scusi,*" he says and tosses me the pack.

"*Di niente.*" I light a cigarette and draw the smoke deep into my lungs, and for an instant I stop thinking of what will happen to Nakorza if the truck crashes and we die. I also push aside the nagging possibility that I'm not the person I think I am: there may be another on Nakorza who is in fact the one destined return.

Now the sound arrives, the shriek of the storm in the tall evergreens that the Piouli call *kadua* and the New Ruthenians gypsy spruce, trees that release a mournful song when the wind blows through their large tu-bular needles.

"Twelve kilometers to Powyrnisch." Fausto allows himself to take his eyes off the road and look at me inquisitively. "Has your friend invited you to stay over Easter?"

I nod. "I'm hoping that Monday morning you can pick me up in Powyrnisch, on your way back to San Silvestro. Why?"

"Rumors," he says and stares straight ahead. An unfamiliar animal dashes across the road where the high beams fall away.

"What sort of rumors?" I ask, as he knows I will.

"This job of mine has me delivering goods in the forest country up north, Reichart's Notch and thereabouts, small isolated villages where nothing much happens. The folks there are a little primitive, you know, lumberjack types, coal miners, but decent. Our kind of people, if you follow my meaning—Catholics, Anglicans, Methodists, most of them—and they speak a language you can understand."

"So this rumor comes from your drinking buddies in Reichart's Notch?"

"Most of the time, they're pretty bored," Fausto says. "Maybe that's why they gossip."

"About . . . ?"

"About things that are supposed to happen"—he gives me a quick glance—"in Stepanopol during the Feast of the Resurrection."

Falling silent, he pilots us through a stretch of road unprotected by the trees. He switches off his high beams and concentrates on the snow, which appears to come from all sides at once. Soon we're back in the forest again. Fausto rolls his side window partly down and tosses his cigarette butt into the blizzard. A gust of frigid air fills the cab, little prickly ice crystals, along with the keening of the gypsy spruces.

"Deaths," he says. "People have vanished, and the Stepanopol police aren't looking into it too closely. It's really difficult to prove anything. Strangers like you aren't normally allowed at the Midnight Mass on Easter. But if your friend has invited you, I suppose there's nothing to worry about. It's all just idle talk anyway—I shouldn't have mentioned it."

He sits mute for a while, bemused or angry, I can't tell which.

"Unless," he adds, "your friend had a special reason for inviting you."

We travel another seven kilometers, and now we're so close to our destination that the squalls have acquired an apricot glow from the lights of Powyrnisch. Fausto pulls up at an inn, its tarred logs huddled beneath the towering *kaduas*.

Suddenly the snowplow we'd feared running into emerges from the blizzard, followed by an enormous gravel truck with a rotating searchlight atop its cab. Caught in the bright beam, two figures stand in the load bed, hurling shovelfuls of gravel over the tailgate and scattering it across the road. Sweat glistens on the parts of their faces visible between the fur caps and the wool scarves wrapped around their noses and mouths. Hunched over the auxiliary gas-powered generator that runs the huge truck's engine, two other workers warm themselves while waiting to relieve the gravel men. The massive vehicle passes so close to us that a spray of grit rattles against our wheels, but the workers don't seem to notice, and an instant later the truck disappears into the dark forest, trailing the stench of coal tar.

As we stumble out of the cab, Fausto says, "This is Sofija's place—let's get warm," and then he leads me through the drifts.

Reaching the front door, we stomp the snow off our boots. The porch is redolent of leather and lubricant and wet fur. Two pairs of cross-country skis lean against the rail. We step into the quiet inn. After the grinding engine and the wailing wind and the grieving trees, it seems as if I've become momentarily deaf.

Then we sit at a massive wooden table near the brick oven, and the sudden warmth and the smells of food cooking—I still haven't learned the names of the local dishes—make me sleepy and relaxed, and I stretch my arms lazily and carelessly, so that my watch emerges from under my sleeve.

"What time is it?" Fausto asks.

Had I thrown my watch away, a passerby might have found it and tried to represent himself as somebody he wasn't. If I'd stuck the thing in my pocket or hidden it in a suitcase, customs officials and border police would have dug it out and asked questions. So until this moment I'd assumed that the least conspicuous way to carry the watch was on my wrist. But I wear it facedown—not so much because it says SEIKO, but because it has only twelve numerals.

"My watch has stopped," I tell Fausto.

He turns toward another table and addresses two young skiers as they drink from glazed earthenware mugs. He asks them a question, probably the same one he just asked me. They shrug.

"Nam tschersornik," one of them says and shows Fausto his bare wrist; but he looks at me as he speaks.

His eyes are gray and hostile and scared.

"We can guess the approximate time," Fausto says as the food is served by a white-haired woman whose clothes smell of smoke. "There's a telephone here. If your friend leaves Stepanopol in fifteen minutes, he'll reach Powyrnisch in an hour and a half. I'll take you to meet him, but I don't want to go any farther tonight—if Sofija's got a free room, I'll come back here and sleep."

Sour soup. Salty, spicy mutton that couldn't possibly have come from a sheep. Beer with a strange, persistent aftertaste. Sofija sets two glazed mugs before us. *"Tzujk!"* she says, and pours us some fruit schnapps. I take a swallow. This stuff isn't flavored with plums, and the bouquet includes a touch of almond and lily-of-the-valley, plus a stronger, stranger scent, as unexpected and emphatic as falling in love. No matter: the schnapps soon works the way it's supposed to, burning off the chill along with my tension—and half my mucous membranes.

On the phone Gregor Tschuderka sounds enthusiastic but far away, and there's a crackle and a whistling in my ear, as if something large and hungry is trying to devour the line, and yes, he's looking forward to meeting me at the Powyrnisch train station "in ninety minutes." I glance at my watch, shielding it with my body, and try to convert Nakorzan minutes into Seiko intervals.

As I return to the table, the cross-country skiers rise abruptly and start to leave, and one of them nods and mumbles a greeting in passing. But the gray-eyed skier pauses and stares at me, pale and tense, and he breathes heavily, so I can smell the schnapps on his breath, the flowers, the strange scent; he stands frozen to the bare plank floor, until his pal returns—*"Chai, Damjan"*—and leads him toward the door.

A freezing draft blows into the room as the door opens and the two skiers exit, and I realize I've been fixed intently on Damjan, returning his stare.

He heard me make the phone call. Heard me say *Gregor Tschuderka.* Saw me glance at a watch that supposedly doesn't work.

"What was wrong with that guy?" I ask Fausto.

"Wrong?" he echoes groggily. One of his eyes has slid to the side. He pulls himself together, focuses. "Oh, it's just that you're a stranger, but not a priest or a trucker, and people here aren't used to strangers." He gazes at the floor. "Especially not now."

He gestures at Sofija, who pours us more mugs of fruit schnapps, and I worry whether Fausto will be able to drive us safely down the last stretch of mountain road.

Sofija remains standing with a hand on Fausto's shoulder and speaks directly to me. The only word I understand is the name *Damjan.*

"Mama Sofija says not to worry about Damjan Kolarow," Fausto obligingly translates. "He's got a bad temper, but he's a smart, honest boy. It's just that he's in love with a girl down in Stepanopol, and the thought of them dying together makes him despair."

"Why must they die?" I ask.

"The Crown," Fausto replies.

"But the scientists say it won't swallow us," I insist, as the paradoxes dance in my mind. "And the politicians say the same thing," I add, but there's no conviction in my tone.

Fausto sighs and takes from his pocket some folded, glossy pages, evidently a magazine clipping. "Forget the politicians. As for the scientists, they don't know crap." He lights a cigarette, his hands twitching. "Before my mother died, she had—a stroke, I think it's called. Something happened in her head, so she was paralyzed on one side and had trouble talking. Seven years she sat in a wheelchair. Seven years. And in the mornings, it was mostly in the mornings, she would weep for hours, and she wouldn't tell us why. Not that we really needed to ask, right? Isn't it reason enough to be stuck in a wheelchair and have nothing to do but think about the person you used to be?"

I don't know what to say.

"Sometimes I thought she was crying because of a dream she'd had the night before: her childhood home, meeting my father for the first time, us kids when we were little. But no, no," Fausto says sardonically, unfolding the brightly colored pages, "science claims that when old people cry it has nothing to do with their dreams or their memories or their situation. It's entirely"—he reads aloud from the illustrated article—"'degeneration of the central nervous system.'"

He places the pages in my hands: a centerfold article, the flap offering two longitudinal sections of the human cerebrum, one showing a "young brain," the other an "old brain," with certain areas highlighted in red and blue.

"Apparently it's that simple." Fausto points to the second illustration. "Too much blue makes old people weep." He takes the article from my grasp and leans back in his chair. "No, I don't much care for what the scientists tell me about my mother—and I'm not interested in what they say about the Crown of Stars either. We can all see it's getting closer and closer, and the black mouth is growing at a faster rate every day."

He lifts a finger past his nose and pretends to rub his eye. When he draws it away, the tip glistens wetly in the lamplight, and I wonder what a longitudinal section of his brain would look like.

The snow has stopped; but the wind is still fierce, and its howl suggests a band of lost children screaming in the treetops above the inn.

"I understand your anger," I tell Fausto, thinking of his mother as well as the Crown. "You have no reason to trust the scientists or the politicians. But their first duty, as they see it, is to prevent panic and anarchy, even if that means lying to us. As far as they're concerned, the threat of social chaos is real: evidently there's an ice age coming—crop failures, grain shortages—and things will get worse before they get better. We've already seen the first symptoms of barbarism. Lootings, wild orgies, mass suicides. What if this really *is* the end of Nakorza? Would you have the astronomers and the government admit it outright?"

Fausto shakes his head slowly and throws up his hands. "But how can we accept their reassurances when we know they're out to control us no matter what? Those doctors weren't honest with my mother. 'You'll see, Signora Caiazzo,' they said. 'You'll live to be a hundred. You'll survive us all.'"

If I were completely certain, I might tell him what I know; but I'm anxious and confused. The Crown of Stars simply shouldn't be there.

I gulp down my schnapps and hold my breath so I won't cough. "Anyway, I'm convinced that the Crown won't engulf us or hit us or whatever it's threatening to do." Despite my efforts, I cough. "Maybe I'm deluding myself—a leap of faith to keep up my spirits. I have no strong evidence for my belief. But I wish, I really wish, I could get you to share it, Fausto."

For a long time we sit without speaking, listening to the sounds from the kitchen and the eerie grief of the spruce trees; and I think maybe it's time to leave, so I slide my wrist under the table and glance at my watch.

"Thanks," Fausto says at last. "Actually, I think you could tell me a lot more if you wanted to. You might even shed some light on these mysteries." He looks at me without blinking. "It's just a feeling I've got, based on nothing."

"What mysteries could I clear up?" I ask.

"You might begin by explaining why you keep looking at a watch that has stopped."

A violent extra heartbeat. A sudden headache. A glowing dot inside my left eye. The iris aches, and I raise a hand as if I could bat the speck away.

Before I can answer Fausto, the phone rings. Sofija picks it up, listens, then glances at me and nods; she says something, nods again. As she hangs up, the bright speck fades, and Sofija speaks my name.

"Gerold Schenna?" she inquires, and now it's my turn to nod. "That was your friend Gregor, calling from the road," she continues, translating through Fausto. "He's been detained, but he'll be in Powyrnisch in half an hour. And how small Nakorza is! Had Damjan known you're on your way to visit Marja Tschuderka's father, I'm sure he would've behaved better."

No, I think. If he'd known, he would've killed me. "I believe I could use another schnapps," I say to Fausto.

"Do we have time?" he asks, gesturing toward my wrist. I remove the Seiko and give it to him; he blanches around the mouth, and the dark blue of his eyes turns black.

"Now tell me," he says.

"Yes," I say, then wave at Sofija to bring us more schnapps.

And so I tell him.

The snow still eddies along the road, forming small drifts; but the storm is nearly over, and the stars are coming out. It's been a long time since anyone on Nakorza has wanted to look up and behold the sparkling heavens.

We are above Powyrnisch, close enough to see the dirty yellow light of the street lamps flickering through the swirling snow. On the railroad tracks below, a small switch engine shunts boxcars around, making up a freight train, the puffs of smoke and the clouds of steam mingling as they waft up the mountainside. Fine snow covers the coal in the tender like white flour.

"That train isn't going anywhere tonight," Fausto says. "The line to Chidno runs through a gorge. There must be several meters of snow. God knows when it'll be open again."

"What about the way to Reichart's Notch?" I ask.

"Oh, I'll get there all right," Fausto says. "It's a major highway, follows the course of the Kolpa; and once I'm in the town, I shouldn't have any problem with the local streets. They're pretty tough up in Reichart's."

Snow whips across the windshield, and Fausto turns on the wipers. He steers us along one last curve, and we're finally on level ground.

"I'll have a lot more trouble getting back to the inn," he sighs, driving us across a wide parking lot between the freight yard and the station.

At the far end of the lot, our high beams catch a black Torrance sedan, parked with its lights out, motor running.

"Looks like your friend is waiting for you," Fausto says above the cry of the wind and the rumble of the truck's engine.

Later, after he has pulled over and I've collected my rucksack, Fausto asks, "Is this good-bye, or will I see you again?"

"When you're safely back at Sofija's place, call me at Gregor Tschuderka's house."

"I mean—do I survive?" he asks, his eyes following the windshield wipers.

"One of us does," I say, jumping out, "but I'm not sure who."

I move along the station platform, following the twin beams from Fausto's truck. Suddenly a human figure lurches away from the driver's side of the sedan, then glides across the parking lot on cross-country skis and vanishes down the slope. Now Gregor finally turns on his headlights, and the Torrance receives me as if I were a baton in a relay race. Fausto presses his horn, blaring a farewell, then drives off. His high beams sweep across a couple of black-tarred wooden buildings, a dancing plume of snow, and a fur-clad Piouli who has stopped to watch the tractor-trailer through shining yellow eyes.

Fausto disappears into the darkness.

The drifting snow blows straight into my eyes, but the large shape bearing its shadow toward me must be Gregor. We embrace and kiss each other on the cheek, and then I see behind him another shadow, smaller and less bulky, her hair escaping from a fur hat to flow in the freezing wind.

As Gregor steps to one side, the headlights illuminate his features. They are dogged and sad; he feels no joy at our reunion.

"My daughter Marja," he tells me, gesturing toward the young woman. He nods in my direction. "Marja, meet Gerold Schenna. It's about time you got to know each other."

2

I hope you didn't freeze last night," Gregor says. He sits with his back against the window. Behind him the daylight is a muted gray; a gentle morning snow is falling, and the wind has died down, though now and then a gust sweeps the loose snow off the roof and whirls it under the eaves.

The breakfast dishes have been cleared away, but the fragrance of sausage and sauerkraut still lingers. Mingled with the kitchen smells are hints of tallow and incense.

"Thanks for asking," I say. "No, my fireplace was still warm when I woke up."

"You look tired," he says.

"I've rarely enjoyed such a soft, warm bed, but it's always difficult to fall asleep in a new place."

He pulls his thick eyebrows together and busies himself in preparing his meerschaum pipe; he empties the bowl, fills it with slightly trembling hands, lights up—and all the while I look uncomfortably around the living room, jammed with knickknacks and rugs and icons. There's a twentieth-generation copy of Rubljov's *Trinity*, a Holy Virgin, sooty to the point of looking like a black smear on a gold background, and an original painting of Fanurius, rendered so the eyes follow you.

The saint looks down on me from the wall, and Gregor stares at me from the other side of the table. "Then you must have slept badly for the past several years," he says.

He falls silent. And my friend and companion from our journey across the Turquoise Sea is suddenly a stranger.

A clock ticks loudly through the thirteen hours of Nakorza. The air is stagnant and smoky, making my eyes water. And, as when I spent one summer vacation visiting my wealthy school chums on the Kalmthal slopes, I feel the sting of being an outsider.

"What do you really know?" I ask.

"What do we really know about anything?" he replies, and I hear the echo of my thoughts from eighteen hours earlier.

He turns halfway around and lays a hand on the window, its panes frosted with blossoms of ice: the only flowers on Nakorza that look like the ones I knew as a child.

"You once told me you grew up in Kaumea—after making sure I'd never been there—and naturally that would explain your strange accent and the gaps in your knowledge," Gregor continues. "But eventually I realized you couldn't identify even the most common animals and plants, neither here nor anywhere else on Nakorza."

"Maybe I slept through school," I say feebly.

"Don't insult my intelligence. It wasn't only the animals you didn't know—you lacked all sorts of facts. You were ignorant of New Ruthenian history, of world history in general. Any child understands the rules of

Kulaii, but not Gerold Schenna! You'd never heard of a *mosora,* and . . ."
He throws up his hands. "Well, you were a pretty likely candidate for He-
Who-Shall-Come. And the time is right, isn't it? It can't happen much
later than now, if it's going to happen at all."

"Maybe he has already come and gone," I say.

Gregor shakes his head. "Impossible. Don't you suppose we've kept
track of every Maria, Marja, Mary, Marie, Miriam, or Mirjam who ever
lived on Nakorza? We can account for them all, my friend."

What a fate, I think, to be given that name and hence never escape official scrutiny.

"And now you believe I'm He-Who-Shall-Come," I say awkwardly,
"and your daughter is the chosen Maria."

"Time will tell," he replies. "*You* know who you are."

He rises and takes a book from a shelf. It's a thin volume with a stiff
brown cover, printed on cheap yellow paper: *Die Offenbarungen und
Prophezeiungen des heiligen Nikifor aus Chidno.*

"Here," Gregor says, "you can read how the Prophet Nikifor has revealed that Nakorza's destiny depends on what Mary decides during the
Feast of the Resurrection."

Once again I'm bewildered by the literal-minded beliefs of these
people. "But why in Stepanopol?" I object. "And why this Easter?"

"Because you're here," Gregor replies, leaning forward and pointing
at me. He gestures toward the threatening sky. "And because this is the
last opportunity. After tomorrow night, there won't be any more resurrection feasts."

A gust of wind blows like a sigh along the road and echoes down the
chimney. I glance at the firewood stacked for drying. The logs look like
birch. The last woodpile?

From a deep, disorderly pocket inside my jacket I draw out a pack of
cigarettes. I light one. The exotic tobacco is aromatic, but it doesn't take
the edge off my fear.

"You shouldn't have invited me," I say.

Gregor inhales deeply. "There was a time when I actually *wanted* my
daughter to be the Maria. It's an almost universal wish, cultivated by parents for as long as our race has been on Nakorza. In every family, one
daughter is always named Maria." He bends down and picks up a box
wrapped in lightly tanned fur and tied with a thong. "But today I want no
part of Nikifor's prophecy." He looks directly at me. "Marja loves Dam-

jan Kolarow, and yet she must choose you. And what's the use? It's too late already," he adds, then stares heavenward.

"If you're right and I'm the space traveler who's to leave with Marja," I say, "perhaps you can take comfort that she'll be saved from the Crown of Stars."

Gregor unwraps the box and sets it on the table between us. "I'm not so sure she'll be saved," he says, removing the lid.

Shiny and bronze, the Kulaii set awaits.

The hint of a smile dances in the corner of Gregor's mouth. "It's time you learned the rules of our favorite game."

"All games embody a worldview," I say. "What's the philosophy behind Kulaii?"

"To keep playing," Gregor replies. "The loser is the one who becomes exhausted and leaves the field. But you can also lose by placing your opponent in a situation where he has no moves left. There's only one way to win at Kulaii, and many paths to disaster. And even at that, the winner may turn out to be a loser. It's a very Nakorzan game, my friend."

He lights a kerosene lamp, lowers the glass globe, and adjusts the wick.

With my heart in my throat, I try to find out what he thinks is coming. "On my way here, I was told that strange things happen at the Midnight Mass."

"Well, yes, there have been some tragic events," Gregor replies offhandedly. "Young people, high-strung types, have thrown themselves off Oblation Rock, hoping to placate the Crown. But we've got it cordoned off this year, and guards will be posted."

"Oblation Rock?"

"A precipice beside the church." Gregor arranges the playing pieces on the board.

"Were they—?" I'm not sure how to put this. "Those who died . . . were they all women?"

"Watch now," Gregor says without looking up. "The first thing you must know is how to avoid trapping me in a dead zone. If you do that, you've lost."

"Any stakes?" I ask resignedly.

"Let us play for wishes," Gregor replies. "We should each concentrate on a devout wish without saying it out loud. Whoever wins can regard his victory as a judgment from God."

"Why not?" I say, and then I concentrate on Marja.

"But don't forget," her father says, "that the winner may turn out to be the loser."

"I know all about loss, Gregor, so save your paradoxes for another day and teach me the rules. Without rules, there's no game. Without a game, no winners or losers."

"Oh, I wouldn't say that."

"Then why should we bother?" The wind has abated; the cold gray light streaming through the windows makes me apprehensive. "Your game enables the players to experience real solutions, but only to illusory problems."

"True enough." Gregor taps his pipe to empty it and puts his head in his hands. "And outside the game we find nothing but illusory solutions to real problems."

And so we play.

Hours later we are interrupted when the whole family arrives for supper, and suddenly there's too much body heat around me, and too many smells. The blood goes to my head, and on the periphery of my vision everything dissolves in a rainbow-colored fog. Marja's two sisters and two brothers sit with heads bent over their plates, dragging their forks through their food and tossing quick inquisitive glances at me.

Marja rubs a bit of fat from a blouse trimmed in gold braid.

In slow German, out of consideration for their guest, the older son, Stojan, tells about the preparations for the Feast of the Resurrection; and I understand that the troikas will be fewer this year, because there hasn't been enough food for the draft animals. So the trip up to Chidno for the Midnight Mass will occur mostly in open wagons. But the participants will still bring hundreds of torches, so the celebration should be, as usual, bright and festive.

As usual . . .

"Are you marrying Marja?" her younger brother asks me.

"*Kolja!*" Gregor says.

"But I like Damjan better," Kolja persists. "You're too old for Marja."

It isn't easy, but I smile.

"Behave yourself," Stojan says. Kolja shrugs and twirls strands of sauerkraut around his fork.

Marja puts down her utensils and blushes, but her eyes are calm, and she regards me steadily, without reproach or fear, but also without love.

That terrible, insistent stare, a stare that seems to devour its object:

I've seen it before, in women who'd stopped loving me but were offering me a second chance.

"Would you . . . sir . . . would you like me to show you the area to-morrow?" she asks, winding a lock of hair around her finger.

"I'd like that very much," I say.

"I want to come, too," Kolja says.

"Brat," Marja says.

Stojan puts an arm around Kolja's shoulders and says, "I need you to help me decorate the church."

Suddenly a bowl of something cool and sweet-smelling appears before me. "Try our *baridani* preserves," somebody says. "A local delicacy. This may be your only chance to savor it."

"Take a big helping," someone else interrupts. "It's only when they're fresh that you have to worry about the side effects."

"And Damjan picked them," Kolja says loudly, looking triumphantly at his sister.

Marja gulps, and Kolja presses his lips together. But then Marja starts laughing and can't stop; she laughs so hard, she has to leave the table.

Gregor sighs deeply. Glancing at his face, I realize that time has shriveled both of us. Kolja is right: I'm too old.

When the bowl of *baridani* comes to me, I take nothing.

It's after midnight when Gregor leans back and rubs his face with the palms of his hands.

"You won," he says. When he sees my inquiring look, he adds: "You're trapped now, so I'm the one who lost."

The light from Beribek, Nakorza's greater moon, glows through the veil of clouds and glints off the icicles, while the lesser moon, Zarela, sets in the south.

"You did that on purpose," I say.

"Yes," he says.

"It feels like cheating."

"It always feels that way, when you win."

I go to my room. A fire blazes in the hearth, fresh water fills the earthenware jug, and the air holds the pleasant aroma of linen dried in the sun.

There's also another scent I can't identify right away, at once floral and fleshly. A lighted candle rests on the nightstand.

Her dark blond hair flows across the pillow, and she is very beautiful.

"I've kept your bed warm," she says with a crooked smile. And I know what she really means: Let's get it over with. But then she folds back the duvet, and I'm hit by her body's heat and a fragrance like a moist forest floor in summer, and I know I'll be unable to resist.

Sometime near daybreak, after she has fallen asleep, awoken, and slipped away, I find myself lying beneath the duvet, listening to the beams and timbers creaking in the frosty air.

The gravity of the room seems oddly awry, as if some outside force is pulling me toward it, and I wish I could cling to Marja, but I'm alone now, waiting to be sucked into empty space.

On the nearby farms, animals awaken in the cold dawn, complaining of hunger by making sounds I've never heard before. And it strikes me that Marja will be as much a stranger on Earth as I am here. I light the candle and murmur the ancient mantra: "I love you, I love you, I love you." But it doesn't work.

The game has turned out to my advantage, but only because it was rigged at the outset.

And that is not love.

It is something even worse.

I should feel at home here.

The shadow-blue and white-gold snowscape could be the Sarntaler Alps in winter's clothing, only with a colder, more distant sun. And the icy Kolpa, whose meanderings I can discern at the bottom of the valley, is a river like any on Earth.

But gradually I grow aware of small disparities. The cloudless sun-drenched sky with its peculiar shade of blue. The forests of gypsy spruce with their dark green needles that peal in the wind like tubular bells. And the many odd fragrances. Even the woodsmoke rising from the Stepanopol chimneys smells strange to me.

The air is still, but so cold that my breath freezes, sticking like rime to my beard and eyelashes, and I realize that without the heavy coat, fur hat, and wool mittens I borrowed from Gregor, I would have fled back to the house by now. But Marja wants to show me around. Or, rather, she wants to talk to me alone.

We follow the road from Powyrnisch, which hugs the base of the mountain some twenty meters above Stepanopol, then runs through the outlying community, where Gregor's family lives, before descending into the valley, and doubling back to enter the town. The plows have created huge snowbanks along the verges and deposited a slippery coating of frozen slush. I keep losing my balance, gaining a firm purchase with my boots only in those places where people have strewn ashes in front of their houses.

From the road we can see rolling, denuded orchards, the town with its thatched and shingled roofs, and churches whose golden onion domes are so bright they hurt our eyes. A light chilly mist hangs above the marshes along the river. On the far side of the valley the dark Nareli Mountains, home of the Piouli, rise like a fortress of shadows.

Marja identifies various trees and mountains and buildings for me, expressing no desire to hear about Earth, which she claims to know far better than I know Nakorza.

"We're all free to read about our ancestors' home world in books," she says calmly. "I've studied Earth history more than most."

She sounds perfectly sincere, and I marvel at her tranquillity in the face of what's about to happen. I was expecting tears and anger, wrenching confidences, and—for some reason—childhood reminiscences. But she remains aloof, focused on the here and now, protecting herself with the quotidian.

As we walk down toward the town, I ask her to point out the church where the Midnight Mass will occur.

"It won't happen in Stepanopol," she replies, then stops walking and, grabbing my sleeve, turns me to the north, so I'm facing the mountain wall. She removes a pair of binoculars from her fur shoulder bag, adjusts the focus, and hands them to me.

In the distance I see an old onion-domed church clinging to the mountain. Beside it a shiny black outcropping juts from the snow, overhanging an abyss that drops for hundreds of meters into the ravine. *Stynka Schertfilor*. Oblation Rock.

"Maundy Thursday and Good Friday," Marja says, "we attend Mass in Stepanopol—but it is an old tradition that everyone gathers at the Church of Saint Fanurius in Chidno on Easter Eve."

She is standing so close to me now, pointing out the church (there, to the left of the sign for Powyrnisch, directly behind that peak, you can see the black stone glinting in the sun), that I feel the warmth of her breath. And I put an arm around her waist, try to pull her to me and turn her face toward mine; but she pushes me away, and I lose my footing on the slippery road, ending up on my back in a snowdrift.

To ease my embarrassment she laughs gaily, then playfully tries molding a snowball to throw at me, but the cold powder disintegrates in her gloves. Instead she straddles me and rubs handfuls of snow in my face. Her hair falls free of her hat and brushes my eyes, and I notice that her teeth are bared in a smile. But I can't stand to look at her glowing face; I'm glad that my vision is teary with snow and blurred by the sweep of her hair.

"I'm sorry I disrupted your view of our beautiful blue sky," she says.

I don't know why, but I think of Fausto Caiazzo. "It's okay," I say as I slowly get up and brush the snow from my coat. When I was a child, there were always massive, friendly clouds filling the sky. How I miss them.

"I need some time," she tells me as we search the snowdrift for the binoculars. "Last night was . . . I don't know what it was."

"I know what it was," I say without explaining myself. "And I also know that even if you weren't the chosen Marja, I'd still want to take you back."

We sit in the snow, looking at each other; then she puts her arms around me and rests her forehead against my shoulder.

I can win my Kulaii match, I decide—perhaps on my own, perhaps with help—even if I fail to take into account all the inherent contradictions of the game.

"Ah, the binoculars," Marja says.

A dozen flags droop from their poles, including the regional colors and, in front of the town hall, the national banner, divided into black, white, and sky-blue horizontal stripes. A simple flag, pure and laced with frost.

Heavy smells of broiling meat, burning coals, and incense hang so palpably in the air that one can walk around the fragrances and into and out of them. Bright bits of icicles, swept from the eaves by the householders, lie glistening on the sidewalks.

The streets are largely deserted, but here and there I notice groups of sullen youths, huddled together, emitting hostile stares. Men of Damjan's age, men who must know Damjan. One kid shouts a remark that makes Marja press her lips together; and I feel insecure. There is nobody to rescue us should Damjan's friends get physical. The message of protective males to strangers everywhere and always: Stay away from our women.

"You don't have to worry," Marja says, then leads me into a dark, smoke-filled tavern, which someone (a guest who couldn't pay his bill?)

has decorated with a crude but powerful oil painting of the Crown of Stars. I can't decide whether the painting is intended to exorcise the threat or whether I'm having my first experience of gallows humor in New Ruthenia—or any kind of humor for that matter.

Except for us, the tavern room is empty; evidently Easter and the Crown have dampened everyone's urge to revel, and I find it curious that the place is even open. The landlord, who calls himself Miklos, has long since banked the oven, so we end up settling for what—in another place and under different circumstances—I would have called snacks.

The beer comes in large tankards and tastes, strangely enough, like beer; but its effect isn't a matter of alcohol only: there's something else in the drink, something I can't taste that lifts my heart, turns the light to gold, and shifts every color toward a cheerful hue.

"They may want to kill you," Marja says. "But as long as they believe their own lives depend on your safe return, they'll beat you up at worst. And they won't dare come into Miklos's place and make trouble."

I exhale deeply, lowering my shoulders, and it feels as if someone has wrapped thick, soft duvets around my body. For a few precious seconds I decide that the Crown is nothing but an amateur painting on a tavern wall—and not a half-bad painting at that.

Marja turns her head and follows my gaze. "Of course, not everybody in Stepanopol thinks the way Damjan's friends do," she says. "Many people around here would be happy if you never got back to Earth. Somehow they prefer dying, annihilation by the Crown, to never having existed at all."

She sloshes the beer around in her tankard, then takes a long sip. "I don't really understand it."

Dusk has come to the streets of Stepanopol. "From the instant I saw you in the train station," I say, "I've been brooding about something. How can you be certain you're the right Maria?"

She looks into my eyes for a long time. Within her pale skin a blue pulse beats, darkening her high forehead and long neck.

"I can think of another mystery," she says, bringing her thick dark eyebrows together, "one that should concern you and everyone else more than it seems to. After the space traveler got back to his planet, why did the sages turn to Maria for the vital information, the coordinates of Nakorza, instead of asking him?"

"The traveler was . . . not the sort of man you imagine."

"You aren't?"

"I would never call myself a scientist. A poet perhaps. Once the capsule understood my essential desire, my need to jump from one star system to another until we found a habitable planet—once the capsule understood me, it became autonomous, first bringing me here, then taking me back to Earth, entirely by its own devices. That explains why the sages needed Maria, but it doesn't explain how she happened to know the coordinates of Nakorza relative to Earth."

Marja takes another swallow of beer. "Considering the role I'm expected to play tonight, Gerold, I believe I have the right to ask you another question. Where did you hide this capsule, as you call it?"

The miraculous feeling of well-being is gone, the thick duvets have been pulled aside. All my life I've pretended that the world disappeared when I closed my eyes; told myself I was immortal; turned away the postman before he could give me a distressing letter. And now Marja has shoved an unwanted parcel into my hands, a windowed envelope bearing the Great Reminder. But I cannot accept delivery, cannot make myself say: *I don't know—somewhere in a cave, I'll remember when the time is right. We're here, Marja, and therefore I must have found it again.*

Cannot.

All I say is: "When the time is right, I'll tell you."

"And now I shall answer *your* question." From her fur bag she removes a leatherbound book, thick, scuffed, and ancient. "How do I know I'm *the* Maria? Because of this."

I raise my eyebrows. "What is it?"

"My family has always kept better genealogical records than most. We know exactly which of the three hundred ships brought our ancestors here. Her name was the *Copernicus*"—she sets her hand on the book—"and this is her log. The Tschuderka family rescued it from mandatory destruction, hid it away in attics and cellars for generation upon generation. The coordinates of Nakorza appear on the first page, handwritten in tiny script on silken paper."

She leans over the table, and I notice that the mild euphoria of the beer has left her as well.

"From the moment the Crown appeared, I knew who I was," she says. "I was the Maria who mattered, the one whose family had preserved the logbook. And when I realized that, I wished I'd never read the thing, wished that somebody had thrown it on the fire. Now it's too late."

She lifts her hand to her forehead. "It's all in here."

The shock interval, it's called. The numb instant during which you read the lab report upside down as the doctor gives you his diagnosis, *that* diagnosis. The insensate interlude during which you obsess about what to wear to your mother's funeral.

I reach toward her, but my hand is shaking, and I pull back. "I loved you from the moment I saw you at the train station in Powyrnisch; I'll bring you back to Earth, try to make you happy . . ."

I halt.

"But," Marja says.

"Yes?" I say, taking a deep breath. Again I try to touch her; again I withdraw my hand.

"But," Marja says, "you have no idea where the capsule is!"

I swallow, shake my head. "No, but . . ."

The blood drains from Marja's face, and her teeth chatter as if she's freezing. "It makes sense," she says hoarsely.

And, oh, God, it does make sense. I know what's coming. I'm opening the letter from the collection agency, fixing on the huge amount due, wondering how I acquired this much debt. And of course I cannot pay it.

"*A wenit Damjan!*" Miklos suddenly shouts.

The tavern door opens, and Damjan strides in from the darkness, his gray eyes full of pain, bent on keeping a promise he must have made to Marja's family before we departed. To protect his girlfriend's lover. To get the two of us home safely.

All the way up the hill to the Tschuderkas' house I walk ahead of Marja and Damjan, not far enough to seem conspicuous, but enough so I won't sense when they stop to whisper confidences or cry together or kiss.

Before me the aurora borealis is flaring, so strong it casts flickering shadows: now bleeding like a moonrise, now oscillating behind the mountains like an array of searchlights, and finally, before it vanishes, fluttering like curtains in a draft.

Then the stars come out, a dense cluster of suns near the galactic core, glimmering like a bejeweled iconostasis.

And in the middle of the cluster, high above Chidno, the black center of the Crown hangs in the night sky like a passageway leading to a vacant sanctorum, an empty Holy of Holies.

Beautiful and vibrant with meaning. And meaningless and banal. Like a transcription error.

3

The Easter Eve procession of the New Ruthenians toward Chidno has begun: from the first floor window of Gregor's house I see their lanterns, torches, and headlights bobbing amid the black ridges and along the banks of the Kolpa. The pilgrims travel in troikas and sledges, in carts and wagons; they sit crowded together in the load beds of pickup trucks, holding their torches aloft, renewing the resin the instant it's consumed. Occasionally I glimpse clusters of cross-country skiers gliding through the darkness across the snowy slopes.

Marja's older brother Stojan parks his flatbed truck before the house. He scrambles onto the open trailer, where he checks the torch holders and spreads soft, golden-brown pelts across the riveted steel benches.

Dressed in their finest Easter clothes, Gregor's neighbors stand on the roadside, waiting for Stojan to pick them up, stamping their feet to keep warm. I join the expectant crowd; the older pilgrims offer me greetings I don't understand, and the young men regard me with cold eyes set above broad cheekbones.

I feel completely alone, and when Stojan brings the truck I try to squeeze into the cab alongside him and Marja and Gregor, but instead Gregor guides me to the trailer and offers me a seat directly behind the cab, next to a torch crackling with fragrant resin. Young Kolja and Marja's two sisters occupy the bench directly across from me.

The larger of Nakorza's moons is setting: Beribek chases Zarela down behind the snowy peaks of Chidno. From a pack of predators deep within the forest comes a mournful howl, and the cry is taken up by another pack, and then another, so the message is relayed along the entire range. A cloud-mass veils the burning sky, and high above the world a black wound opens wider and wider, surrounded by a ring of starry fire.

As we reach the main road and join the convoy of fuming trucks, our progress slowed by dozens of troikas and sledges drawn by the short-legged draft animals whose fur shines green in the torchlight, I realize that the groups of pilgrims are all singing the same song—not an Easter hymn, but a melancholy folksong, with words I don't understand. The performance melds with the noise of the trucks, a polyphony of human voices sustained by the bass chords of the engines, each note rising or falling in time to the rhythmic coughing of the exhaust pipes. From the distant Nareli range the song is answered by the long, wailing glissandi of the Piouli.

In the meadows, where the road to Chidno climbs toward the eastern ridge, lumberjacks and miners from up north have erected canvas tents, also stands where you can buy sausages and beer, sacks of charcoal and bundles of pelts. Their faces glow among the roaring ovens and flaming braziers; some of the skiers stop to nourish themselves before the trek up the mountain, and occasionally a customer emerges from a troika, but everyone else ignores the vendors. As the truck drivers shift into first gear, the pilgrims grow quiet, and on the other side of the river the Piouli song also fades. Slowly we ascend in a long, unbroken caravan, and I wonder how so many people will fit into one church.

I peer through the cab window. Marja stares straight ahead, evidently seeing nothing. Gregor turns and glowers at me, and I am forced to look away and focus on the river and the ravine.

About four hundred meters from our destination lies a broad flat shelf of rock, where the worshipers park their trucks and sleighs. From there the last stage of the journey takes us up the mountain slope; the path is uneven and slippery, with only a low wooden guardrail to keep the celebrants from falling into the ravine. The long climb tires the older pilgrims, who frequently stop to rest, clinging to the rude boulders and white birches. At last the Church of Saint Fanurius appears, a beautiful and imposing structure that seems to hang suspended above the chasm, filling a grotto in the cliff face; its timbers are painted gray, and its golden onion domes, illuminated from below by the pilgrims' torches and headlights, almost touch the overhanging rock. The church looks different up close—not larger, not smaller, just different, and suddenly I realize that the nave extends deep into the cavern, so that the front wall with its portals and windows is really a kind of façade concealing the building's true scale. There will indeed be room for us all.

Colors swirl around me, muted by the night. I smell the sweat of the weary pilgrims as they gather outside the building, greeting friends and family members they haven't seen in a long while. Gossip and gifts are exchanged, but the dominant mood is detached seriousness, a quiet piety. Now the crowd parts to make way for the patriarch, Father Ischaslaw, magnificent in his gold chasuble as he passes among the pilgrims and slips into the church through the door to the sacristy.

Cold and confused, I become separated from the Tschuderka family. For a long time I walk in circles before the church, then pace up and down on the steps. Finally, convinced that Marja and the others must have gone inside, I enter through the main door.

•   •   •

Immediately I am overwhelmed—by the pungent incense, the strange faces, the glittering icons, the hundreds of candles burning on the altar— but mostly by the immense size of the nave. This is a church as big as a cathedral, an arena, a town square.

As I shuffle down the main aisle toward the iconostasis, I notice that a side door lies open. The pilgrims' breath and bodies combine with the candle flames to send a rush of hot air through the gap and out into the night, carrying with it scraps of paper and bits of dried mud.

I pause beside the chancel rail and stare through the open door toward the snow-covered ledge beyond, which quickly narrows to become Oblation Rock; beyond yawns the steep black chasm. Despite Gregor's assurances, there are no cordons anywhere, no guards in sight—not that I really expected any.

Maybe the door was left open to ventilate the space, I speculate, or maybe somebody merely forgot to close it; but neither possibility convinces me, and I feel helpless and confused.

I turn and survey the nave. More and more people jostle into the church. The celebrants press toward the iconostasis, drawn by the iridescent saints; the choir sings a hymn, and their voices envelop me and rise toward the lamps hanging from the ceiling like gilded stalactites. A draft rushes through the open door and blows against my back, making my collar ripple, and when I remove my fur hat, my hair flies forward over my brow. I remain beside the chancel rail, shivering, teeth chattering, determined not to let anybody pass through the treacherous portal, but knowing full well I'm no hero, my courage might desert me at the last minute—unless, of course, somebody has arranged for me to win, which is simply impossible. Briefly I meditate on the defeats I've known in my life, and the defeat I'm about to know, soon realizing I've endured only one great reversal: a loss that has folded in on itself, visiting me again and again, iteration upon iteration, never increasing in power but always prepared to show me yet another facet.

Again I gaze through the open door. Above the ledge, above the church and the black sheen of Oblation Rock, the dark dome of the winter sky arches over New Ruthenia, breached by the shining Crown of Stars.

Contemplating the night, I feel a sudden pressure on my eardrums. The hymn has stopped. From behind me comes the cacophony of the worshipers: their gasps and sighs, the tromping of their shoes and boots.

I face the choir, and instantly they begin to sing again, and I hear every syllable because they're all looking at me. The despair in their voices and the grief in the bass notes make my scalp tingle.

The procession of celebrants moves slowly and ominously down the aisle. At the head of the throng walk Marja and Father Ischaslaw, who helps her to stand upright and speaks softly with his face turned toward her. The patriarch's words are drowned out by the choir, and the nave swims in a white luminous fog. Reaching the altar, Marja falls to her knees with hands clasped, her lips moving; and though I cannot hear a word, I know what she's saying.

I rush toward the open door. Marja rises, and soon she and Father Ischaslaw are moving again, getting closer and closer to me, and as I plant myself beside the jamb—freezing in the winter air, burning with the fever of my misery—my decision takes form. I shall protect the one I love. I shall alter the iterations, smash the facets, and so from my deepest pocket I remove the weapon I've sworn never to use, grasping it in both hands, my palms throbbing with my strong rapid pulse. I aim the weapon at Ischaslaw, and the throng of celebrants rushes toward us with livid faces, their shouts and wails ringing with anger.

"Maybe this happens because I came to care about you after all," Marja says, looking at me with blue eyes canopied by dark brows. Ischaslaw steps forward and grabs her arm and continues to lead her out of the church, bound for the icy ledge.

"Release her and step away!" I scream in German, hoping he understands me; but he keeps his eye fixed on the precipice.

"Put the gun away," Marja rasps, breaking Ischaslaw's grip and stepping between the priest's body and mine. But she is too late. The bullet pierces her outstretched hand and burrows between Ischaslaw's eyes, and he topples over and lies motionless at the crowd's feet like a heap of autumn leaves. Marja rushes through the door, the darkness drawing her toward the precipice, and then she opens her arms, blood flowing from her wounded hand, surrenders to the icy slope—

For a fraction of a second she hovers above the chasm, arms outstretched, and I know that if I look behind me I'll see the patriarch's dead eyes, his golden chasuble, and a book lying on the church floor, its cover stained with a drop of Marja's blood. A book whose pages contain small dense writing and a fatal transcription error.

—and disappears over the edge.

It's very quiet.

She must have hit bottom by now.

There follows a great shudder, stronger than any earthquake tremor; it seems as if the universe has slipped out of gear. An unimaginable terror seizes me, rending my soul, shredding my sanity; and then comes the final cataclysm, and whatever remains of an orderly reality dissolves into a swirling gray blur like the dancing static on a television screen.

I am pulled down, down, down, as if captured by a black hole; I relive my life, experience my death, endure my damnation. Am I in hell for a hundred years? A million? Then everything begins again, the eons flying by, and my bowels seem to rotate in their cavity, and I go blind, my melted eyes running down my cheeks, and my brain becomes a useless organ, no longer able to control my muscles. Thirst and fear. Fear and madness.

Midnight. The sacred portal stands open, and the priests come pouring from the Holy of Holies, singing *Christos was-chrjes!* Christ has risen. *Wai istino was-chrjes,* the choir and the celebrants reply.

Verily, he has risen.

I know this church without quite recognizing it, drawing comfort from its carved marble pews, modern altar, and lavish trappings, re-orienting myself as if I were surveying my house after a long journey or my bedroom after a vivid dream.

But the stream of alternative memories lingering at the edge of my consciousness is not a dream. The nebulous, superimposed images are not phantasms.

Every time I tilt my head back and stare at the radiant ceiling, I grow dizzy at the sight of the hanging lamps, those gilded stalactites, and the entire vault seems to rise heavenward.

I line up at the altar with everyone else, and we kiss each other on the cheek and express our joy in Christ's resurrection, and I know all the celebrants' names and who they are; but for a brief instant other faces emerge, as in an antique photograph printed from a double-exposure: sometimes a woman's face with hair escaping from a fur hat, sometimes the face of a man who called me friend.

Real faces, real voices.

And then I feel an infinite emptiness. The loss of a real woman, who has never existed, who *chose* never to have existed, a woman I nevertheless love. Could any loss be more irredeemable?

The conditions have dissolved. The error was never propagated. Sometime in the future thousands of colonists will be sent to the right planet, colonists whose descendants now take me by the hand and congratulate me in this sacred, well-lighted, gloriously warm nave.

"Yes, I, too, have tears in my eyes—isn't it remarkable?" somebody says to me. "He has risen, he has conquered death and released us!"

She, I correct him mentally, then dip the bread in the wine and eat it with a silver spoon.

Hours later, as I am leaving the church, a portly man appears in the doorway of the office. "Gerold Schenna?" he asks, and I nod, startled by a feeling of déjà-vu.

The man gestures me into his office. "Somebody left a phone message for you last night," he tells me, studying a slip of paper. "Mr. Casaubon will pick you up outside the church as arranged."

"Thanks," I say, glancing at my watch.

It says five o'clock. And the clock on the wall concurs, and so does the clock on the secretary's desk.

I wonder briefly why my watch agrees with the local time, and why all the timepieces in this place have only twelve numerals.

Then I walk out into the early spring dawn and look up at the stars, now fading from a sky that soon will be pure blue.

The first birds have begun to sing.

Let's just call them birds.

EPILOGUE

It wasn't a dream, was it?" Jordan Casaubon asks above the soft whistling of the tires as the world takes shape in the dim light of early morning.

"No," I answer, "it was no dream. A dream would be easier to understand."

"Umm-hmm," Jordan mutters.

We're traveling south through a fertile, rolling landscape, an endless carpet of silken purple grasses just beginning to catch the rays of the rising sun.

At intervals we encounter sleeping villages with whitewashed houses, and in between lie broad fields blooming with green and violet vegetation. The heady scent of farm animals and the agreeable fragrance of moist spring soil wafts through the side windows.

Jordan pulls over and says, "Get in the backseat. It's still a long way to Akún. There's plenty of time for you to sleep. We don't want you dozing off during the press conference. Roll up my coat, put it under your head, and make yourself comfortable."

I climb out and stand beside the car, which smells of fresh paint, leather upholstery, and leaking oil. A slight morning breeze, cool but not frigid, blows across my face. The hills have emerged in the sunlight, and foliage is now visible in the stands of dark trees. Spring leaves: as delicate as if painted on the branches with the finest camelhair brush. Soon the dew will turn to mist and disappear, and it will be a pleasant day in the Akún region of Nakorza.

This Nakorza, which is not necessarily a happier Nakorza, simply more prosperous, more technologically advanced.

And a Nakorza without a Crown of Stars.

I recline in the backseat, exhausted and yet wide awake. A burning itch runs through my body; my underwear is already sticking to my skin, and I'm unable to get comfortable, no matter how I arrange myself.

Jordan catches my eye in the rearview mirror. "By throwing herself off the cliff," he says, "Marja forever deleted certain material—conditions, possibilities—from . . . let's call it the Great Archive. Including the wrong coordinates recorded in the forbidden logbook."

He raises his eyebrows. I nod. "Recorded in the logbook, and in Marja's memory," I add.

"That's why you couldn't find the capsule," he continues. "It simply wasn't."

"It simply wasn't," I echo. "Or maybe I'd repressed my knowledge of where I'd hidden it."

"In a way," Jordan says, "Marja's sacrifice was the ultimate solution."

"Solution to what?" I ask. "How do you solve a problem that never existed?"

"Go to sleep. If you need some help, there's a bottle of something they call vodka on the floor."

We drive through a medium-size provincial town; for some reason the streets are gaily decorated. Garlands hang from the balconies and lampposts, waving in the pleasant breeze, and a flag of black, white, and blue billows from a pole beside a luminous marble building.

I open the vodka bottle, and the gentle fragrance of lily-of-the-valley, along with the flag's evocations of sorrow and snow and sky, cause a burning in my stomach, even before the first swallow.

"We've got our work cut out for us," I say. "So much information to collect—the course of the colonization fleet, the manifest of every ship, the ecology of the planet."

"Don't sweat it," Jordan says. "I kept busy during our vacation. All the data lie safely in a vault in Akún."

"The founding fathers, the first colonists," I say. "Go through the lists of their names, Jordan. Go through the lists, very carefully."

"I'll delete every last Tschuderka, Tschud, Cuderka, and Chuderka," he assures me. "Because otherwise . . ." With his right hand he draws a horizontal eight in the air. The symbol for infinity.

I take a deep pull on the bottle, then lie down, the taste lingering in my mouth, the fragrance filling my nose and sinuses, and wallow in memories of a world that never was.

Happy to be beyond the settled areas, Jordan accelerates, and for a long straight stretch across the prairie I hear nothing but the whistling of our wheels and the soft buzz of the spring breeze.

"The car," I mutter.

"What about it?" Jordan asks.

"What do you call the make of car we're in?"

"It's a Torrance, I think," he replies hesitantly. "Named for one of the first colonists." And after an interval he gestures broadly, sweeping his hand across the flat open countryside. "Damn beautiful," he says.

Sleep is closing in around me; I look out the window at a blue and cloudless sky. For a moment I see a face dusted with snow, and I feel a slight pressure near my heart, as if someone is sitting on my chest.

Then the snow and the face dissolve into a flock of white birds soaring over the prairie.

"Hey," Jordan says, "you're crying. . . ."

ABOUT THE TRANSLATORS

Novelist, screenwriter, translator, and editor, **Sergio D. Altieri** is one of Italy's best-known action and thriller writers. His massive novels *La città delle ombre* ("City of Darkness," 1981) and *La città di nerezza* ("City of Shadows," 1990), both set in a decaying, gang-ravaged Los Angeles, won him national acclaim. *Kondor* (1997), an apocalyptic war adventure, received the Scerbanenco Award. He has recently translated Dashiell Hammett and Raymond Chandler for new Italian editions from Mondadori. Altieri's current project is *Magdeburg,* a monumental historical trilogy set against the turbulent backdrop of the Thirty Years' War.

Lia Belt lives in Amsterdam. A translator for over a decade, fluent in Dutch, German, and English, she began the literary phase of her career three years ago with her Dutch-to-English version of a W. J. Maryson novel. She followed this project with English-to-Dutch renderings of works by Robert Jordan, Stan Nicholls, Raymond Feist, and Stephen King. She continues to translate technical manuals and other such texts, but she never forgets who started her on translating fiction—the most fun a person can have while earning money, she believes—and no matter how busy her schedule, she finds time to work with the latest story or novel by Maryson.

Since 1993, **Jeffrey Brown** has lived in the Czech Republic where he has been a translator, an interpreter, and a lecturer at Masaryk University in Brno. A resident of Prague, he works mainly as a producer of feature films and documentaries. His recent movies include the black comedy *Sklapni a zastrel me* ("Shut Up and Shoot Me," 2005), the mockumentary *Rex-patriates* (2004), which pokes fun at foreigners living in Prague, and *Call of Dudy* (2006), an examination of the Czech bagpiping tradition. Among several other projects, Brown is currently filming a documentary in South Africa.

Born in Springfield, Massachusetts in 1957, **Tom Clegg** has spent over three quarters of his life among Europeans, residing in Spain, Switzerland, Britain, and France. After receiving a B.A. in European Studies from Amherst College, he worked for several years at the London School of Economics as a researcher in the field of European urban politics. He now lives in Paris and earns his keep as a freelance translator and reviewer, as well as an English-language fiction consultant for Editions Bragelonne and *Galaxies* science fiction magazine.

Sheryl Curtis is a professional translator specializing in technical and corporate documents. She received undergraduate and graduate degrees in translation from the Université de Montréal, and a doctorate in interdisciplinary studies from Concordia University in Montreal, where she also taught translation for twenty years as a member of the part-time faculty. Recently Curtis left the academic world to concentrate on literary translation. Since 1998 her English-language versions of stories by French and Québécois authors have appeared in *Interzone, Year's Best Science Fiction 4, Year's Best Fantasy and Horror 15, On Spec, Altair,* and *Tesseracts 8.*

Niels Dalgaard is a noted academic authority on science fiction, as well as a translator, reviewer, and veteran fan. In addition to the entry on Danish SF in Clute and Nicholls's *The Encyclopedia of Science Fiction,* he has written numerous articles about the field, among them "From Plato to Cyberpunk: A History of Science Fiction Literature." He also edited the anthology *On the Wings of Fantasy: Imaginative Literature for Young People.* Since 1989 Dalgaard has also been a fiction writer, publishing SF stories under his nom de plume, Glen Stihmøe.

David Hackston was born in Scotland in 1977. He plays the viola, composes music, and is currently pursuing postgraduate studies in the Finnish Language Department at the University of Helsinki. He has already acquired a long list of fiction and nonfiction translation credits, including poetry, plays, film scripts, scholarly articles, and a celebrated anthology, *The Dedalus Book of Finnish Fantasy* (U.K. 2005, U.S. 2006), edited by Johanna Sinisalo.

Cezar Ionescu was a young engineer translating nonfiction in Bucharest when he got hooked on science fiction. Beyond the *Romanian SF Anthology: Nemira '94,* his work for the Nemira Publishing Group includes his 2002 translation of Dean Koontz's *Dragon Tears,* a title that in Romanian becomes *Salasul Raului,* plus a French book on the Chinese Secret Service.

Doryl Jensen has taught German language and literature, as well as European art and cultural history, at several universities. At present he manages a travel company focused on music, art, and history tours. He has spent much of his life on the road all over the world, having mastered the art of living out of a suitcase for months at a time. Writing has proved for Jensen a welcome respite from wanderlust. He also enjoys spending time with his four daughters and an increasing number of grandchildren. When not abroad, he lives in Greensboro, North Carolina.

Michael Kandel received his Ph.D. in Slavic studies from Indiana University, eventually using his skills to create many celebrated Polish-to-English translations of Stanislaw Lem, two of which were nominated for the National Book Award. He subsequently worked as an editor at Harcourt, where he acquired Jonathan Lethem, Ursula K. Le Guin, Kage Baker, and Ian R. MacLeod, among others. He has written numerous science fiction stories and a few SF novels, and he presently works at the Modern Language Association, copyediting the prose of professors. In the near future we can look forward to *A Book of Polish Monsters,* an anthology of speculative stories and novellas edited and translated by Kandel.

"Athos Emfovos in the Temple of Sound," written by their friend Panagiotis Koustas, was the first professional translation assignment for the husband and wife team of **Mary Mitchell** and **Gary Mitchell**. Currently residing in Athens with their two children, Melina and Jack, they describe themselves as Greek-Australians who read a great deal of literature in both Greek and English.

Yolanda Molina-Gavilán is Associate Professor of Spanish at Eckerd College in Florida, the author of *Ciencia ficción en español* ("Science Fiction in Spanish," 2002), and the English translator of Rosa Montero's *La función Delta* (1981). Molina-Gavilán originally translated "The Day We Went Through the Transition" for *Cosmos Latinos* (Wesleyan University Press, 2003), the landmark anthology of Latin American SF that she edited in collaboration with Andrea Bell.

Michael M. Naydan has taught Ukrainian and Russian at Penn State University since 1988. He has translated into English extensively from Ukrainian, Russian, and Romanian. His most recent Ukrainian translations include Yuri

Andrukhovych's novel *Perverzion* and Viktor Neborak's *The Flying Head and Other Poems*. Among his latest renderings of Russian authors, done in collaboration with Slava Yastremski, are Olga Sedakova's *Poems and Elegies* and Igor Klekh's *A Land the Size of Binoculars*. In 1993 Naydan received the Eugene Kayden Meritorious Achievement Award in Translation from the University of Colorado, and the 1996 and 2005 Awards in Translation from the American Association of Ukrainian Studies.

Luís Rodrigues is a software developer, graphic designer, and literary translator. He is editor-in-chief of the electronic science-fiction magazine *Fantastic Metropolis* and the editor of *Breaking Windows* (Prime Books, 2003), a collection of fiction and nonfiction from the Web site's first year. In his own country Rodrigues is a founding member of the Portuguese Association for the Fantastic in the Arts, and he currently works with several publishers and magazines. He lives in Lisbon.

James Stevens-Arce was born in Miami, Florida, but has called Puerto Rico home for most of his life, claiming both English and Spanish as native languages. He has published numerous science fiction, horror, and fantasy stories, plus one novel, *Soulsaver* (Harcourt, 2000). An earlier, novella version of *Soulsaver* shared the 1997 Universitat Politécnica de Catalunya's prestigious Premio UPC de Ciencia Ficción. Stevens-Arce is also an award-winning writer-producer-director of films and videos, with credits that include television specials, documentaries, and more than a thousand TV commercials. He lives with his family in San Juan.

Slava I. Yastremski is Associate Professor of Russian and Comparative Humanities at Bucknell University. He has published translations of works by several prominent Soviet writers and poets, including a collection of Vasily Aksyonov's stories, *Surplussed Barrelware;* a volume of Marina Tsvetaeva's poetry, *After Russia;* Olga Sedakova's *Poems and Elegies;* and Andrei Sinyanski's controversial book *Strolls with Pushkin,* for which Yastremski received Columbia University's Translation Center Award and AATSEEL's Best Translation of the Year Award. His most recent publication is *A Land the Size of Binoculars,* a collection of short stories by the Russian-Ukrainian writer Igor Klekh.

ABOUT THE EDITORS

James Morrow is a critically acclaimed author of science fiction, theological fantasy, social satire, and new wave fabulism. His literary honors include two Nebula Awards, two World Fantasy Awards, the Grand Prix de l'Imaginaire, and the Prix Utopia. For three years running he edited the annual Nebula Awards anthology under the auspices of the Science Fiction and Fantasy Writers of America. His most recent novel is the postmodern historical epic, *The Last Witchfinder,* and he is presently at work on *Prometheus Wept,* a serio-comedy about the mystery of morality.

Kathryn Morrow is a former bookseller who has in recent years focused her energies on freelance editing, book reviewing, and independent scholarship. With her husband, James Morrow, she created the set of Tolkien Lesson Plans for secondary school teachers currently featured on the Houghton Mifflin Web site. A lifelong SF fan, her critical pieces frequently appear in *The New York Review of Science Fiction.*

SELECTED BIBLIOGRAPHY

RESOURCES

The Encyclopedia of Science Fiction
edited by John Clute and Peter Nicholls
London: Orbit, 1993

Trillion Year Spree: The History of Science Fiction
Brian W. Aldiss with David Wingrove
New York: Atheneum, 1986

Mouse or Rat? Translation as Negotiation
essays by Umberto Eco
London: Weidenfeld and Nicolson, 2003

La Science-Fiction: Aux Frontières de l'Homme
Stéphane Manfredo
Paris: Éditions Gallimard, 2000

Beneath the Red Star: Studies in International Science Fiction
George Zebrowski
San Bernardino: Borgo Press, 1996

Maison d'Ailleurs (House of Elsewhere)
Museum of Science Fiction, Utopias, and Extraordinary Journeys
Yverdon-les-Bains, Switzerland
(www.ailleurs.ch, Web site in French, English, and German)

EUROPEAN SF IN TRANSLATION: PRINT

The Carpet Makers (novel)
Andreas Eschbach
translated from the German by Doryl Jensen
New York: Tor Books, 2005

Night Watch (novel)
Sergei Lukyanenko
translated from the Russian by Andrew Bromfield
New York: Miramax, 2004

Troll: A Love Story (novel)
Johanna Sinisalo
translated from the Finnish by Herbert Lomas
New York: Grove Press, 2004

Seven Touches of Music (mosaic novel)
Zoran Zivkovic
translated from the Serbian by Alice Copple-Tŏsić
Charleston: Aio, 2006

The Night Orchid: Conan Doyle in Toulouse (collection)
Jean-Claude Dunyach
translated from the French by Sheryl Curtis, Jean-Louis Trudel,
Dominique Bennett, and Ann Cale
Encino: Black Coat Press, 2004

The Windows of Time Frozen and Other Stories (collection)
Uri Vynnychuk
translated from the Ukrainian by Michael M. Naydan
Lviv: Klasyka Publishers, 2000

The World Treasury of Science Fiction
edited by David Hartwell
Boston: Little, Brown, 1989

The Penguin World Omnibus of Science Fiction
edited by Brian Aldiss and Sam J. Lundwall
Harmondsworth: Penguin, 1986

The Best from the Rest of the World: European Science Fiction
edited by Donald A. Wollheim
New York: Doubleday, 1976

Zajdel Award Winners Anthology: Chosen by Fate
edited by Elzbieta Gepfert, Grzegorz Kozubski, and Piotr W. Cholewa
Warszawa: superNOWA, 2000, and Katowice: Śląski Klub Fantastyki, 2000

Romanian SF Anthology: Nemira '94
edited by Romulus Barbulescu and George Anania
presented by N. Lee Wood and Norman Spinrad
Bucharest: Nemira, 1994

Breaking Windows: A Fantastic Metropolis Sampler
edited by Luís Rodrigues
Holicong: Prime Books, 2003

Vampire and Other Science Stories from Czech Lands
edited by Jaroslav Olsa, Jr.
New Delhi: Star Publications, 1994

EUROPEAN SF IN TRANSLATION: INTERNET

Fantastic Metropolis
online literary SF magazine, fiction and nonfiction
(www.fantasticmetropolis.com)

Bradbury's Shadow: An Anthology of Short Stories from the Golden Age of Czech Science Fiction in English
edited by Radomil Dojiva, et. al.
unpublished omnibus, excerpts available online
(www.vostok.cz)

International Publishing House
Rede Global Paraliteraria
Russian-based Web site with international contributors, specializing in SF and Fantasy
(www.iph.lib.ru)

STORY COPYRIGHTS